ORIGINAL SIN

P. D. James

ORIGINAL SIN

Alfred A. Knopf
New York   1995

THIS IS A BORZOI BOOK
PUBLISHED BY ALFRED A. KNOPF, INC.

Copyright © 1994 by P. D. James

Library of Congress Cataloging-in-Publication Data

James, P. D.
    Original sin / P. D. James.
        p.   cm.
ISBN 0-679-43889-0
1. Dalgliesh, Adam (Fictitious character)—Fiction.
2. Publishers and publishing—England—London—Fiction.
3. Police—England—London—Fiction.   4. London
(England)—Fiction.   I. Title.
PR6060.A467O75   1994
823'.914—dc20   94-26094
                                                         CIP

Manufactured in the United States of America
First American Edition

CONTENTS

This novel is set on the Thames and many of the scenes and places described will be familiar to lovers of London's river. The Peverell Press and all the characters exist only in the imagination of the author and bear no relation to places or people in real life.

Book One

FOREWORD TO MURDER

I

For a temporary shorthand-typist to be present at the discovery of a corpse on the first day of a new assignment, if not unique, is sufficiently rare to prevent its being regarded as an occupational hazard. Certainly Mandy Price, aged nineteen years two months, and the acknowledged star of Mrs. Crealey's Nonesuch Secretarial Agency, set out on the morning of Tuesday 14 September for her interview at the Peverell Press with no more apprehension than she usually felt at the start of a new job, an apprehension which was never acute and was rooted less in any anxiety whether she would satisfy the expectations of the prospective employer than in whether the employer would satisfy hers. She had learned of the job the previous Friday, when she called in at the agency at six o'clock to collect her pay after a boring two-week stint with a director who regarded a secretary as a status symbol but had no idea how to use her skills, and she was ready for something new and preferably exciting, although perhaps not as exciting as it was subsequently to prove.

Mrs. Crealey, for whom Mandy had worked for the past three years, conducted her agency from a couple of rooms above a newsagent and tobacconist's shop off the Whitechapel Road, a situation which, she was fond of pointing out to her girls and clients, was convenient both for the City and for the towering offices of Docklands. Neither had so far produced much in the way of business, but while other agencies foundered in the waves of recession Mrs. Crealey's small and under-provisioned ship was still, if precariously, afloat. Except for the help of one of her girls when no outside work was available, she ran the agency single-handed. The outer room was her office, in which she propitiated clients, interviewed new girls and assigned the next week's work. The inner was her personal sanctum, furnished with a divan bed on which she occasionally spent the night in defiance of the terms of the lease, a drinks cabinet and refrigerator, a cupboard which opened to reveal a minute kitchen, a large television set and two easy chairs set in front of a gas fire in which a lurid red light rotated behind artificial logs. She referred to her room as the "cosy," and Mandy was one of the few girls who were admitted to its privacies.

It was probably the cosy which kept Mandy faithful to the agency, although she would never have openly admitted to a need which would have seemed to her both childish and embarrassing. Her mother had left home when she was six and she herself had been hardly able to wait for her sixteenth birthday, when she could get away from a father whose idea of parenthood had gone little further than the provision of two meals a day which she was expected to cook, and her clothes. For the last year she had rented one room in a terraced house in Stratford East, where she lived in acrimonious camaraderie with three young friends, the main cause of dispute being Mandy's insistence that her Yamaha motor bike should be parked in the narrow hall. But it was the cosy in Whitechapel Road, the mingled smells of wine and takeaway Chinese food, the hiss of the gas fire, the two deep and battered armchairs in which she could curl up and sleep, which represented all Mandy had ever known of the comfort and security of a home.

Mrs. Crealey, sherry bottle in one hand and a scrap of jotting pad in the other, munched at her cigarette holder until she had manoeuvred it to the corner of her mouth, where, as usual, it hung in defiance of gravity, and squinted at her almost indecipherable handwriting through immense horn-rimmed spectacles.

"It's a new client, Mandy, the Peverell Press. I've looked them up in the publishers' directory. They're one of the oldest—perhaps the oldest—publishing firm in the country, founded in 1792. Their place is on the river. The Peverell Press, Innocent House, Innocent Walk, Wapping. You must have seen Innocent House if you've taken a boat trip to Greenwich. Looks like a bloody great Venetian palace. They do have a launch, apparently, to collect staff from Charing Cross Pier, but that'll be no help to you, living in Stratford. It's your side of the Thames, though, which will help with the journey; I suppose you'd better take a taxi. Mind you get them to pay before you leave."

"That's OK, I'll use the bike."

"Just as you like. They want you there on Tuesday at ten o'clock."

Mrs. Crealey was about to suggest that, with this prestigious new client, a certain formality of dress might be appropriate, but desisted. Mandy was amenable to some suggestions about work or behaviour but never about the eccentric and occasionally bizarre creations with which she expressed her essentially confident and ebullient personality.

She asked: "Why Tuesday? Don't they work Mondays?"

"Don't ask me. All I know is that the girl who rang said Tuesday. Perhaps Miss Etienne can't see you until then. She's one of the directors and she wants to interview you personally. Miss Claudia Etienne. I've written it all down."

Mandy said: "What's the big deal, then? Why have I got to be interviewed by the boss?"

"One of the bosses. They're particular who they get, I suppose. They asked for the best and I'm sending the best. Of course they may be looking for someone permanent, and want to try her out first. Don't let them persuade you to stay on, Mandy, will you?"

"Have I ever?"

Accepting a glass of sweet sherry and curling into one of the easy chairs, Mandy studied the paper. It was certainly odd to be interviewed by a prospective employer before beginning a new job, even when, as now, the client was new to the agency. The usual procedure was well understood by all parties. The harassed employer telephoned Mrs. Crealey for a temporary shorthand-typist, imploring her this time to send a girl who was literate and whose typing speed at least approximated to the standard claimed. Mrs. Crealey, promising miracles of punctuality, efficiency and conscientiousness, despatched whichever of her girls was free and could be cajoled into giving the job a try, hoping that this time the expectations of client and worker might actually coincide. Subsequent complaints were countered by Mrs. Crealey's invariably plaintive response: "I can't understand it. She's got the highest reports from other employers. I'm always being asked for Sharon."

The client, made to feel that the disaster was somehow his or her fault, replaced the receiver with a sigh, urged, encouraged, endured until the mutual agony was over and the permanent member of staff returned to a flattering welcome. Mrs. Crealey took her commission, more modest than was charged by most agencies, which probably accounted for her continued existence in business, and the transaction was over until the next epidemic of 'flu or the summer holidays provoked another triumph of hope over experience.

Mrs. Crealey said: "You can take Monday off, Mandy, on full pay of course. And better type out your qualifications and experience. Put 'Curriculum Vitae' at the top, that always looks impressive."

Mandy's curriculum vitae, and Mandy herself—despite her eccentric appearance—never failed to impress. For this she had to thank her English teacher, Mrs. Chilcroft. Mrs. Chilcroft, facing her class of recalcitrant eleven-year-olds, had said: "You are going to learn to write your own language simply, accurately and with some elegance, and to speak it so that you aren't disadvantaged the moment you open your mouths. If any of you has ambitions above marrying at sixteen and rearing children in a council flat you'll need language. If you've no ambitions beyond being supported by a man or the state you'll need it even more, if only to get the better of the local-authority Social Services department and the DSS. But learn it you will."

Mandy could never decide whether she hated or admired Mrs. Chilcroft, but under her inspired if unconventional teaching she had learned to speak English, to write, to spell and to use it confidently and with some grace. Most of the time this was an accomplishment she preferred to pretend she hadn't achieved. She thought, although she never articulated the heresy, that there was little point in being at home in Mrs. Chilcroft's world if she ceased to be accepted in her own. Her literacy was there to be used when necessary, a commercial and occasionally a social asset, to which Mandy added high shorthand-typing speeds and a facility with various types of word processor. Mandy knew herself to be highly employable, but remained faithful to Mrs. Crealey. Apart from the cosy there were obvious advantages in being regarded as indispensable; one could be sure of getting the pick of the jobs. Her male employers occasionally tried to persuade her to take a permanent post, some of them offering inducements which had little to do with annual increments, luncheon vouchers or generous pension contributions. Mandy remained with the Nonesuch Agency, her fidelity rooted in more than material considerations. She occasionally felt for her employer an almost adult compassion. Mrs. Crealey's troubles principally arose from her conviction of the perfidy of men combined with an inability to do without them. Apart from this uncomfortable dichotomy, her life was dominated by a fight to retain the few girls in her stable who were employable, and her war of attrition against her ex-husband, the tax inspector, her bank manager and her office landlord. In all these traumas Mandy was ally, confidante and sympathizer. Where Mrs. Crealey's love-life was concerned this was more from an easy goodwill than from any understanding, since to Mandy's nineteen-year-old mind the possibility that her employer could actually wish to have sex with the elderly—some of them must be at least fifty—and unprepossessing males who occasionally haunted the office, was too bizarre to warrant serious contemplation.

After a week of almost continuous rain Tuesday promised to be a fine day with gleams of fitful sunshine shafting through the low clusters of cloud. The ride from Stratford East wasn't long, but Mandy left plenty of time and it was only a quarter to ten when she turned off The Highway, down Garnet Street and along Wapping Wall, then right into Innocent Walk. Reducing speed to a walking pace, she bumped along a wide cobbled cul-de-sac bounded on the north by a ten-foot wall of grey brick and on the south by the three houses which comprised the Peverell Press.

At first sight she thought Innocent House disappointing. It was an imposing but unremarkable Georgian house with proportions which she knew rather than felt to be graceful, and it looked little different from the many others she had seen in London's squares or terraces. The front door was closed and she saw no sign of activity behind the four storeys of eight-paned windows, the two lowest ones each with an elegant wrought-iron balcony. On either side was a smaller, less ostentatious house, standing a little distanced and detached like a pair of deferential poor relations. She was now opposite the first of these, number 10, although she could see no sign of numbers 1 to 9, and saw that it was separated from the main building by Innocent Passage, barred from the road by a wrought-iron gate, and obviously used as a parking space for staff cars. But now the gate was open and Mandy saw three men bringing down large cardboard cartons by a hoist from an upper floor and loading them into a small van. One of the three, a swarthy under-sized man wearing a battered bush-ranger's hat, took it off and swept Mandy a low ironic bow. The other two glanced up from their work to regard her with obvious curiosity. Mandy, pushing up her visor, bestowed on all three of them a long discouraging stare.

The second of these smaller houses was separated from Innocent House by Innocent Lane. It was here, according to Mrs. Crealey's instructions, that she would find the entrance. She switched off the engine, dismounted and wheeled the bike over the cobbles, looking for the most unobtrusive place in which to park. It was then that she had her first glimpse of the river, a narrow glitter of shivering water under the lightening sky. Parking the Yamaha, she took off her crash-helmet, rummaged for her hat in the side pannier and put it on, and then, with the helmet under her arm, and carrying her tote bag, she walked towards the water as if physically drawn by the strong tug of the tide, the faint evocative sea smell.

She found herself on a wide forecourt of gleaming marble bounded by a low railing in delicate wrought iron with at each corner a glass globe supported by entwined dolphins in bronze. From a gap in the middle of the railing a flight of steps led down to the river. She could hear its rhythmic slap against the stone. She walked slowly towards it in a trance of wonder as if she had never seen it before. It shimmered before her, a wide expanse of heaving sun-speckled water which, as she watched, was flicked by the strengthening breeze into a million small waves like a restless inland sea, and then, as the breeze dropped, mysteriously subsided into shining smoothness. And, turning, she saw for the first time the towering wonder of Innocent House, four storeys of coloured marble and golden stone which, as the light changed, seemed subtly to alter colour, brightening, then shading to a deeper gold. The great curved arch of the main entrance was flanked by narrow arched windows and above it were two storeys with wide balconies of carved stone fronting a row of slender marble pillars rising to trefoiled arches. The high arched windows and marble columns extended to a final storey under the parapet of a low roof. She knew none of the architectural details but she had seen houses like this before, on a boisterous ill-conducted school trip to Venice when she was thirteen. The city had left little impression on her beyond the high summer reek of the canal, which had caused the children to hold their noses and scream in simulated disgust, the overcrowded picture galleries and palaces which she was told were remarkable but which looked as if they were about to crumble into the canals. She had seen Venice when she was too young and inadequately prepared. Now, for the first time in her life, looking up at the marvel of Innocent House, she felt a belated response to that earlier experience, a mixture of awe and joy which surprised and a little frightened her.

The trance was broken by a male voice: "Looking for someone?"

Turning, she saw a man looking at her through the railings, as if he had risen miraculously from the river. Walking over, she saw that he was standing in the bow of a launch moored to the left of the steps. He was wearing a yachting cap set well back on a mop of black curls and his eyes were bright slits in the weatherbeaten face.

She said: "I've come about a job. I was just looking at the river."

"Oh, she's always here, is the river. The entrance is down there." He cocked a thumb towards Innocent Lane.

"Yes, I know."

To demonstrate independence of action, Mandy glanced at her watch, then turned and spent another two minutes regarding Innocent House. With a final glance at the river she made her way down Innocent Lane.

The outer door bore a notice: PEVERELL PRESS—PLEASE ENTER. She pushed it open and passed through a glass vestibule and into the reception office. To the left was a curved desk and a switchboard manned by a grey-haired, gentle-faced man who greeted her with a smile before checking her name on a list. Mandy handed him her crash-helmet and he received it into his small age-speckled hands as carefully as if it were a bomb, and for a few moments seemed uncertain what to do with it, finally leaving it on the counter.

He announced her arrival by telephone, then said: "Miss Blackett will come to take you up to Miss Etienne. Perhaps you would like to take a seat."

Mandy sat and, ignoring the three daily newspapers, the literary magazines and the carefully arranged catalogues fanned out on a low table, looked about her. It must once have been an elegant room; the marble fireplace with an oil painting of the Grand Canal set in the panel above it, the delicate stuccoed ceiling and the carved cornice contrasted incongruously with the modern reception desk, the comfortable but utilitarian chairs, the large baize-covered noticeboard and the caged lift to the right of the fireplace. The walls, painted a dark rich green, bore a row of sepia portraits. Mandy supposed they were of previous Peverells and had just got to her feet to have a closer look when her escort appeared, a sturdy, rather plain woman who was presumably Miss Blackett. She greeted Mandy unsmilingly, cast a surprised and rather startled look at her hat and, without introducing herself, invited Mandy to follow her. Mandy was unworried by her lack of warmth. This was obviously the managing director's PA, anxious to demonstrate her status. Mandy had met her kind before.

The hall made her gasp with wonder. She saw a floor of patterned marble in coloured segments from which six slim pillars rose with intricately carved capitals to an amazing painted ceiling. Ignoring Miss Blackett's obvious impatience as she lingered on the bottom step of the staircase, Mandy unselfconsciously paused and slowly turned, eyes upwards, while above her the great coloured dome spun slowly with her; palaces, towers with their floating banners, churches, houses, bridges, the curving river plumed with the sails of high-masted ships and small cherubs with pouted lips blowing prosperous breezes in small bursts like steam from a kettle. Mandy had worked in a variety of offices, from glass towers furnished with chrome and leather and the latest electronic wonders to rooms as small as cupboards with one wooden table and an ancient typewriter, and had early learned that the office ambience was an unreliable guide to the firm's financial standing. But never before had she seen an office building like Innocent House.

They mounted the wide double staircase without speaking. Miss Etienne's office was on the first floor. It had obviously once been a library but the end had been partitioned to provide a small office. A serious-faced young woman, so thin she looked anorexic, was typing on a word processor and gave Mandy only a brief glance. Miss Blackett opened the interconnecting door and announced, "It's Mandy Price from the agency, Miss Claudia," then left.

The room seemed to Mandy very large after the ill-proportioned outer office and she walked across an expanse of parquet flooring towards a desk set to the right of the far window. A tall dark woman got up to receive her, shook hands and motioned her to the opposite chair.

She said: "You have your curriculum vitae?"

"Yes, Miss Etienne."

Never before had she been asked for a CV, but Mrs. Crealey had been right; obviously one was expected. Mandy reached down to her tasselled and garishly embroidered tote bag, a trophy from last summer's holiday in Crete, and handed over three carefully typed pages. Miss Etienne studied them and Mandy studied Miss Etienne.

She decided that she wasn't young, certainly over thirty. Her face was sharp-boned with a pale delicate skin, the eyes shallowly set with dark, almost black, irises under heavy lids. Above them the brows had been plucked to a high arch. The short hair, brushed to a sheen, was parted on the left side, the falling strands tucked behind her right ear. The hands which rested on the CV were ringless, the fingers very long and slender, the nails unpainted.

Without looking up, she asked: "Is your name Mandy or Amanda Price?"

"Mandy, Miss Etienne." In other circumstances Mandy would have pointed out that if her name were Amanda the CV would have said so.

"Have you had any previous experience of working in a publishing house?"

"Only about three times during the last two years. I've listed the names of the firms I've worked for on page three of my CV."

Miss Etienne read on, then looked up, the bright luminous eyes under the curved brows studying Mandy with more interest than she had previously shown.

She said: "You seem to have done very well at school, but you've had an extraordinary variety of jobs since. You haven't stuck to any of them for more than a few weeks."

In three years of temping Mandy had learned to recognize and circumvent most of the machinations of the male sex, but was less assured when it came to dealing with her own. Her instinct, sharp as a ferret's tooth, told her that Miss Etienne might need careful handling. She thought, That's what being a temp is, you silly old cow. Here today and gone tomorrow. What she said was: "That's why I like temporary work. I want to get as wide a variety of experience as possible before I settle down to a permanent job. Once I do, I'd like to stay on and try to make a success of it."

Mandy was being less than candid. She had no intention of taking a permanent job. Temporary work, with its freedom from contracts and conditions of service, its variety, the knowledge that she wasn't tied down, that even the worst job experience could end by the following Friday, suited her perfectly; her plans, however, lay elsewhere. Mandy was saving for the day when, with her friend Naomi, she could afford a small lock-up shop in the Portobello Road. There Naomi would fashion her jewellery and Mandy would design and make her hats, both of them rising rapidly to fame and fortune.

Miss Etienne looked again at the curriculum vitae. She said dryly: "If your ambition is to find a permanent job, then make a success of it, you are certainly unique in your generation."

She handed back the curriculum vitae with a quick impatient gesture, rose to her feet and said: "All right, we'll give you a typing test. Let's see if you're as good as you claim. There's a second word processor in Miss Blackett's office, on the ground floor. That's where you'll be working, so you may as well do the test there. Mr. Dauntsey, our poetry editor, has a tape he wants transcribed. It's in the little archives office." She got up and added, "We'll fetch it together. You may as well get some idea of the layout of the house."

Mandy said: "Poetry?" This could be tricky, typing from tape. From her experience it was difficult with modern verse to know where the lines began and ended.

"Not poetry. Mr. Dauntsey is examining and reporting on the archives, recommending which files should be retained, which destroyed. The Peverell Press has been publishing since 1792. There's some interesting material in the old files and it ought to be properly cata-logued."

Mandy followed Miss Etienne down the wide curved stairs, across the hall and into the reception room. Apparently they were to use the lift and it ran only from the ground floor. It was hardly, she thought, the best way to get an idea of the layout of the house, but the comment had been promising; it looked as if the job was hers if she wanted it. And from that first view of the Thames, Mandy knew that she did want it.

The lift was small, little more than five feet square, and as they groaned upwards she was sharply aware of the tall silent figure whose arm almost brushed her own. She kept her eyes fixed on the grid of the lift but she could smell Miss Etienne's scent, subtle and a little exotic but so faint that perhaps it wasn't scent at all but only an expensive soap. Everything about Miss Etienne seemed to Mandy expensive, the dull sheen of the shirt which could only be silk, the double gold chain and gold stud earrings, the cardigan casually slung around her shoulders which had the fine softness of cashmere. But the physical closeness of her companion and her own heightened senses, stimulated by the novelty and excitement of Innocent House, told her something more: that Miss Etienne wasn't at ease. It was she, Mandy, who should have been nervous. Instead she was aware that the air of the claustrophobic lift, jerking upwards with such maddening slowness, was quivering with tension.

They shuddered to a stop and Miss Etienne hauled back the double-grille gates. Mandy found herself in a narrow hall with a facing door and one on the left. The door ahead was open and she saw a large cluttered room filled from floor to ceiling with wooden shelves tightly packed with files and bundles of papers. The racks ran from the windows to the door with just enough room to walk between them. The air smelled of old paper, musty and stale. She followed Miss Etienne between the ends of the shelves and the wall and to another, smaller, door, this time closed.

Pausing, Miss Etienne said: "Mr. Dauntsey works on the files in here. We call it the little archives office. He said that he'd leave the tape on the table."

It seemed to Mandy that the explanation was unnecessary and rather odd, and that Miss Etienne hesitated for a second, hand on the knob, before turning it. Then, with a sharp gesture, almost as if she expected some obstruction, she pushed the door wide open.

The stink rolled out to meet them like an evil wraith, the familiar human smell of vomit, not strong but so unexpected that Mandy instinctively recoiled. Over Miss Etienne's shoulder her eyes took in at once a small room with an uncarpeted wooden floor, a square table to the right of the door and a single high window. Under the window was a narrow divan bed and on the bed sprawled a woman.

It had needed no smell to tell Mandy that she was looking at death. She didn't scream; she had never screamed from fear or shock; but a giant fist mailed in ice clutched and squeezed her heart and stomach and she began shivering as violently as a child lifted from an icy sea. Neither of them spoke but, with Mandy close behind Miss Etienne, they moved with quiet almost imperceptible steps closer to the bed.

She was lying on top of a tartan rug but had taken the single pillow from beneath it to rest her head as if needing this final comfort even in the last moments of consciousness. By the bed stood a chair holding an empty wine bottle, a stained tumbler and a large screw-top jar. Beneath it a pair of brown laced shoes had been neatly laid side by side. Perhaps, thought Mandy, she had taken them off because she hadn't wanted to soil the rug. But the rug was soiled and so was the pillow. There was a slime of vomit like the track of a giant snail gummed to the left cheek and stiffening the pillow. The woman's eyes were half-open, the irises turned upwards, her grey hair, worn in a fringe, was hardly disarranged. She was wearing a brown high-necked jumper and a tweed skirt from which two skinny legs, oddly twisted, stuck out like sticks. Her left arm was flung outwards, almost touching the chair, the right lay across her breast. The right hand had scrabbled at the thin wool of the jumper before death, drawing it up to reveal a few inches of white vest. Beside the empty pill bottle there was a square envelope addressed in strong black handwriting.

Mandy whispered as reverently as if she were in church: "Who is she?"

Miss Etienne's voice was calm. "Sonia Clements. One of our senior editors."

"Was I going to work for her?"

Mandy knew the question was irrelevant as soon as she asked it, but Miss Etienne replied: "For part of the time, yes, but not for long. She was leaving at the end of the month."

She picked up the envelope, seeming to weigh it in her hands. Mandy thought, She wants to open it but not in front of me. After a few seconds Miss Etienne said: "Addressed to the coroner. It's obvious enough what's happened here even without this. I'm sorry you've had this shock, Miss Price. It was inconsiderate of her. If people wish to kill themselves they should do so in their own homes."

Mandy thought of the small terrace in Stratford East, the shared kitchen and one bathroom, her own small back room in a house in which you'd be lucky to find enough privacy to swallow the pills, let alone die of them. She made herself gaze again at the woman's face. She felt a sudden urge to close the eyes and shut the slightly gaping mouth. So this was death, or rather this was death before the undertakers got their hands on you. Mandy had seen only one other dead person, her gran: neatly shrouded with a frill at her neck, packaged into her coffin like a doll in a gift box, curiously diminished and looking more peaceful than Gran ever had in life, the bright restless eyes closed, the over-busy hands folded in quietude at last. Suddenly grief came upon her in a torrent of pity, perhaps released by delayed shock or the sudden acute memory of the gran whom she had loved. At the first hot prick of tears she wasn't sure whether they were for Gran or for this stranger sprawled in such defenceless ungainliness. She seldom cried but when she did her tears were unstoppable. Terrified she would disgrace herself, she fought for control and, gazing round, her eyes lit on something familiar, unfrightening, something she could cope with, an assurance that there was an ordinary world continuing outside this death-cell. On the table was a small tape recorder.

Mandy went over to it and closed her hand round it as if it were an icon. She said, "Is this the tape? Is it a list? Do you want it tabulated?"

Miss Etienne regarded her for a moment in silence, then she said, "Yes, tabulate it. And two copies. You can use the word processor in Miss Blackett's office."

And in that moment Mandy knew that she had the job.

2

Fifteen minutes earlier Gerard Etienne, chairman and managing director of Peverell Press, was leaving the boardroom to return to his office on the ground floor. Suddenly he stopped, stepped back into the shadows, delicate-footed as a cat, and stood watching from behind the balustrade. Below him in the hall a girl was slowly pirouetting, her eyes upwards to the ceiling. She was wearing thigh-length black boots flared at the top, a short tight fawn skirt and a velvet jacket in a dull red. One thin and delicate arm was raised to hold on her head a remarkable hat. It seemed to be made of red felt and was wide-brimmed, turned up at the front and decorated with an extraordinary array of objects: flowers, feathers, strips of satin and lace, even small fragments of glass. As she turned it flashed and gleamed and glittered. She should, he thought, have looked ridiculous, the peaked childish face half-hidden by untidy swathes of dark hair, topped by such a grotesque confection. Instead she looked enchanting. He found himself smiling, almost laughing, and was suddenly seized with a madness he hadn't felt since he was twenty-one, the urge to rush down the wide staircase, sweep her into his arms and dance with her across the marble floor, out through the front door and to the rim of the glittering river. She had finished her slow turn and followed Miss Blackett across the hall. He stood for a moment savouring this upsurge of folly which, it seemed to him, had nothing to do with sex but the need to hold distilled a memory of youth, of early loves, of laughter, of freedom from responsibility, of sheer animal delight in the world of the senses. None of it had any part in his life now. He was still smiling as he waited until the hall was clear and then slowly descended to his office.

Ten minutes later the door opened and he recognized his sister's footsteps. Without looking up he said: "Who is the child in the hat?"

"The hat?" For a moment she seemed not to understand, then she said: "Oh, the hat. Mandy Price from the secretarial agency."

There was an odd note in her voice and he turned, giving her his full attention. He said, "Claudia, what's happened?"

"Sonia Clements is dead. Suicide."

"Where?"

"Here. In the little archives office. The girl and I found her. We were fetching one of Gabriel's tapes."

"That girl found her?" He paused and added, "Where is she now?"

"I've told you, in the little archives office. We didn't touch the body. Why should we?"

"I mean where is the child?"

"Next door with Blackie, working on the tape. Don't waste your pity. She wasn't alone and there isn't any blood. That generation is tough. She didn't blink an eye. All she worried about was getting the job."

"You're sure it was suicide?"

"Of course. She left this note. It's open but I haven't read it."

She handed over the envelope, then walked to the window and stood looking out. After a couple of seconds he slid out the flap and drew the paper carefully from the envelope, then read aloud. " 'I am sorry to cause a nuisance but this seemed the best room to use. Gabriel will probably be the one to find me and he's too familiar with death to be shocked. Now that I live alone I might not have been discovered at home until I began to stink and I find that one has the need to preserve some dignity, even in death. My affairs are in order, and I have written to my sister. I am under no obligation to give a reason for my act, but in case anyone is interested it is simply that I prefer annihilation to continued existence. It is a reasonable choice and one which we are all entitled to make.' "

He said: "Well that's clear enough, and in her own hand. How did she do it?"

"With drugs and drink. There isn't much mess, as I said."

"Have you phoned the police?"

"The police? I haven't had time yet. I came straight to you. And is it really necessary, Gerard? Suicide isn't a crime. Can't we just ring Dr. Frobisher?"

He said curtly, "I don't know whether it's necessary but it's certainly expedient. We don't want any doubts about this death."

"Doubts?" she said. "Doubts? Why should there be doubts?"

She had lowered her voice and now they were almost whispering. Almost imperceptibly they moved further from the partition towards the window.

He said: "Gossip, then, rumours, scandal. We can phone the police from here. There's no point in going through the switchboard. If they bring her down in the lift we can probably get her out of the building before the staff know what's happened. There's George of course. I suppose that the police had better come in by that door. George will have to be told to keep his mouth shut. Where is the agency girl now?"

"I've told you. Next door, in Blackie's room, doing her typing test."

"Or, more likely, describing to Blackie and anyone else who comes by how she was taken upstairs to get a tape and found a dead body."

"I've instructed them both to say nothing until we've told all the staff. Gerard, if you think you can keep this quiet even for a couple of hours, forget it. There'll be an inquest, publicity. And they'll have to bring her down by the stairs. You can't possibly fit a body bag on a stretcher in the lift. My God, though, this is all we needed! Coming on top of the other business, it's going to be great for staff morale."

There was a moment's silence in which neither moved towards the telephone. Then she looked at him and asked: "When you sacked her last Wednesday, how did she take it?"

"She didn't kill herself because I gave her the push. She was a rational woman, she knew she had to go. She must have known that from the day I took over here. I always made it clear that I thought we had one editor too many, that we could farm out the work to a freelance."

"But she's fifty-three. It wouldn't have been easy for her to get another job. And she's been here for twenty-four years."

"Part-time."

"Part-time but working almost full-time. This place was her life."

"Claudia, that's sentimental nonsense. She had an existence outside these walls. What the hell has that to do with it anyway? Either she was needed here or she wasn't."

"And is that how you broke it to her? No longer needed."

"I wasn't brutal, if that's what you're implying. I told her that I proposed to employ a freelance for some of the non-fiction editing and that her post was therefore superfluous. I said that although she didn't legally qualify for maximum redundancy pay we would come to some financial arrangement."

"Arrangement? What did she say?"

"She said that it wouldn't be necessary. She would make her own arrangements."

"And she has. Apparently with distalgesic and a bottle of Bulgarian cabernet. Well at least she's saved us money but, by God, I'd rather have paid out than be faced with this. I know I ought to feel pity for her. I suppose I shall when I've got over the shock. Just now it isn't easy."

"Claudia, it's pointless to reopen all those old arguments. It was necessary to sack her and I sacked her. That had nothing to do with her death. I did what had to be done in the interests of the firm and at the time you agreed. Neither you nor I can be blamed for her suicide and her death has nothing to do with the other mischief here either." He paused then said: "Unless of course she was the one responsible."

She didn't miss the sudden note of hope in his voice. So he was more worried than he would admit. She said bitterly: "That would be a neat way out of our troubles, wouldn't it? But how could she have been, Gerard? She was off sick, remember, when the Stilgoe proofs were tampered with and visiting an author in Brighton when we lost the illustrations for the Guy Fawkes book. No, she's in the clear."

"Of course. Yes, I'd forgotten. Look, I'll ring the police now while you go round the office and explain what's happened. That's less dramatic than getting everyone together for a general announcement. Tell them to stay in their rooms until the body has been removed."

She said slowly: "There is one thing. I think I was the last person to see her alive."

"Someone had to be."

"It was last night, just after seven. I was working late. I came out of the cloakroom on the first floor and saw her going up the stairs. She was carrying a bottle of wine and a glass."

"You didn't ask her what she was doing?"

"Of course I didn't. She wasn't a junior typist. For all I knew she was taking the wine to the archives room to do a spot of secret drinking. If so it was hardly my concern. I thought it odd that she was working so late, but that's all."

"Did she see you?"

"I don't think so. She didn't look round."

"And no one else was about?"

"Not at that hour. I was the last."

"Then say nothing about it. It isn't relevant. It doesn't help."

"I did have a feeling, though, that there was something strange about her. She did look—well—furtive. She was almost scurrying."

"That's hindsight. You didn't check on the building before you locked up?"

"I looked in her room. The light wasn't on. There was nothing there, no coat, no bag. I suppose she'd locked them in her cupboard. Obviously I thought she'd left and gone home."

"You can say that at the inquest, but no more. Don't mention seeing her earlier. It might only lead the coroner to ask why you didn't check the top of the building."

"Why should I?"

"Exactly."

"But, Gerard, if I'm asked when I saw her last . . ."

"Then lie. But for God's sake, Claudia, lie convincingly and stick with the lie." He moved over to the desk and lifted the receiver. "I suppose I'd better dial 999. It's odd, but this is the first time in my memory that we've ever had the police at Innocent House."

She turned from the window and looked full at him. "Let's hope that it's the last."

3

In the outer office Mandy and Miss Blackett sat each at her word processor, each typing, eyes fixed on the screen. Neither spoke. At first Mandy's fingers had refused to work, trembling uncertainly over the keys as if the letters had been inexplicably transposed and the whole keyboard had become a meaningless jumble of symbols. But she clasped her hands tightly in her lap for half a minute and by an effort of will brought the shaking under control, and when she actually began typing the familiar skill took over and all was well. From time to time she glanced quickly at Miss Blackett. The woman was obviously deeply shocked. The large face, with its marsupial cheeks and small, rather obstinate mouth, was so white that Mandy feared that at any moment she would slump forward over the keyboard in a faint.

It was over half an hour since Miss Etienne and her brother had left. Within ten minutes of closing the door Miss Etienne had put her head round it and had said: "I've asked Mrs. Demery to bring you some tea. It's been a shock for both of you."

The tea had come within minutes, carried in by a red-haired woman in a flowered apron who had put down the tray on top of a filing cabinet with the words: "I'm not supposed to talk so I won't. No harm in telling you, though, that the police have just arrived. That's quick work. No doubt they'll be wanting tea now." She had then disappeared, as if aware that there was more excitement to be had outside the room than in.

Miss Blackett's office was an ill-proportioned room, too narrow for its height, the discordancy emphasized by the splendid marble fireplace with its formal patterned frieze, the heavy mantelshelf supported by the heads of two sphinxes. The partition, wooden for the bottom three feet with paned glass above, cut across one of the narrow arched windows as well as bisecting a lozenge-shaped decoration on the ceiling. Mandy thought that, if the large room had had to be divided, it could have been done with more sensitivity to the architecture, not to mention Miss Blackett's convenience. This way it gave the impression that she was grudged even enough space in which to work.

Another but different oddity was the long snake in striped green velvet curled between the handles of the two top drawers of the steel filing cabinets. Its bright button eyes were crowned with a minute top hat and its forked tongue in red flannel hung from a soft open mouth lined with what looked like pink silk. Mandy had seen similar snakes before; her gran had had one. They were intended to be laid along the bottom of doors to exclude draughts, or wound round the handles to keep the door ajar. But it was a ridiculous object, a kind of kid's toy, and hardly one she had expected to see in Innocent House. She would have liked to have asked Miss Blackett about it but Miss Etienne had told them not to talk and Miss Blackett was obviously interpreting this as prohibiting all speech except about work.

The minutes passed silently. Mandy would shortly be at the end of her tape. Then Miss Blackett, looking up, said: "You can stop that now. I'll give you some dictation. Miss Etienne wanted me to test your shorthand."

She took one of the firm's catalogues from her desk drawer, handed Mandy a notebook, moved her chair beside her and began reading in a low voice, hardly moving her almost bloodless lips. Mandy's fingers automatically formed the familiar hieroglyphics but her mind took in few of the details of the forthcoming non-fiction list. From time to time Miss Blackett's voice faltered and Mandy knew that she too was listening to the sounds outside. After the initial sinister silence, they could now hear footsteps, half-imagined whispering, and then louder footfalls echoing on the marble and confident masculine voices.

Miss Blackett, her eyes on the door, said tonelessly: "Perhaps you'd read it back now?"

Mandy read back her shorthand faultlessly. Again there was a silence. Then the door opened and Miss Etienne came in. She said: "The police have arrived. They are just waiting for the police surgeon and then they'll be taking Miss Clements away. You'd better stay here until it's all clear." She looked at Miss Blackett. "Have you finished the test?"

"Yes, Miss Claudia."

Mandy handed up her typed lists. Miss Etienne glanced at them dismissively and said: "Right, the job is yours if you want it. Start tomorrow at nine-thirty."

4

Ten days after Sonia Clements' suicide and exactly three weeks before the first of the Innocent House murders, Adam Dalgliesh lunched with Conrad Ackroyd at the Cadaver Club. It was at Ackroyd's invitation, given by telephone with that conspiratorial and slightly portentous air with which all Conrad's invitations were invested. Even a duty dinner party given to pay off outstanding social obligations promised mystery, cabals, secrets to be imparted to the privileged few. The date suggested was not really convenient and Dalgliesh rearranged his diary with some reluctance while reflecting that one of the disadvantages of advancing age was an increasing disinclination for social engagements combined with an inability to summon the wit or energy to circumvent them. The friendship between them—he supposed the word was appropriate enough; they were certainly not mere acquaintances—was based on the use each occasionally made of the other. Since both acknowledged the fact, neither could see that it needed justification or excuse. Conrad, one of the most notorious and reliable gossips in London, had often been useful to him, notably in the Berowne case. On this occasion Dalgliesh would obviously be expected to confer the benefit, but the demand in whatever form it came would probably be more irritating than onerous, the food at the Cadaver was excellent and Ackroyd, although he could be facetious, was seldom dull.

Later he was to see all the horrors that followed as emanating from that perfectly ordinary luncheon, and would find himself thinking: If this were fiction and I were a novelist, that's where it would all begin.

The Cadaver Club is not among the most prestigious of London's private clubs but its coterie of members find it among the most convenient. Built in the 1800s, it was originally the house of a wealthy if not particularly successful barrister who, in 1892, bequeathed it, suitably endowed, to a private club formed some five years earlier which had regularly met in his drawing-room. The club was and remains exclusively masculine, the main qualification for membership being a professional interest in murder. Now, as then, it lists among the members a few retired senior police officers, practising and retired barristers, nearly all of the most distinguished professional and amateur criminologists, crime reporters and a few eminent crime-novelists, all male and there on sufferance since the club takes the view that, where murder is concerned, fiction cannot compete with real life. The club had recently been in danger of moving from the category of eccentric to the dangerous one of fashionable, a risk which the committee had promptly countered by blackballing the next six applicants for admission. The message was received. As one disgruntled applicant complained, to be blackballed by the Garrick is embarrassing, but to be blackballed by the Cadaver is ridiculous. The club kept itself small and, by its eccentric standards, select.

Crossing Tavistock Square, in the mellow September sunshine, Dalgliesh wondered how Ackroyd qualified as a member until he recalled the book his host had written five years earlier on three notorious murderers: Hawley Harvey Crippen, Norman Thorne and Patrick Mahon. Ackroyd had sent him a signed copy and Dalgliesh, dutifully reading it, had been surprised at the careful research and the even more careful writing. Ackroyd's thesis, not entirely original, had been that all three were innocent in the sense that none had intended to kill his victim, and Ackroyd had made a plausible, if not entirely convincing case, based on a detailed examination of the medical and forensic evidence. For Dalgliesh the main message of the book had been that men wishing to be acquitted of murder should avoid dismembering their victims, a practice for which British juries have long demonstrated their distaste.

They were to meet in the library for a sherry before luncheon and Ackroyd was already there, ensconced in one of the leather high-backed chairs. He got to his feet with surprising agility for one of his size and came towards Dalgliesh with small, rather prancing steps, looking not a day older than when they had first met.

He said: "It's good of you to make time, Adam. I realize how busy

you are now. Special adviser to the Commissioner, member of the
working party on regional crime squads and an occasional murder
investigation to keep your hand in. You mustn't let them overwork you,
dear boy. I'll ring for sherry. I thought of inviting you to my other club
but you know how it is. Lunching there is a useful way of reminding
people that you're still alive, but the members will come up and
congratulate you on the fact. We'll be downstairs in the Snug."

Ackroyd had married in late middle age, to the astonishment and
consternation of his friends, and lived in connubial self-sufficiency in
an agreeable Edwardian villa in St John's Wood, where he and Nelly
Ackroyd devoted themselves to their house and garden, their two
Siamese cats and Ackroyd's largely imaginary ailments. He owned,
edited and financed from a substantial private income *The Paternoster
Review*, that iconoclastic mixture of literary articles, reviews and gossip,
the last carefully researched, occasionally discreet, more often as malicious as it was accurate. Nelly, when not ministering to her husband's
hypochondria, was an enthusiastic collector of 1920s and 1930s girls'-
school stories. The marriage was a success, although Conrad's friends
still had to remind themselves to ask after Nelly's health before enquiring
about the cats.

The last time Dalgliesh had been in the library the visit had been
professional and he had been in search of information. But then the
case had been murder and he had been greeted by a different host.
Little seemed to have changed. The room faced south over the square
and this morning was warm with sunlight which, filtering through the
fine white curtains, made the thin fire almost unnecessary. Originally
the drawing-room, it now served both as sitting-room and library. The
walls were lined with mahogany cases which held what was probably
the most comprehensive private library of books on crime in London,
including all the volumes of the Notable British Trials and Famous
Trials series, books on medical jurisprudence, forensic pathology and
policing and the club's few first editions of Conan Doyle, Poe, Le Fanu
and Wilkie Collins, in a smaller case as if to demonstrate fiction's innate
inferiority to reality. The large mahogany showcase was still in place,
filled with articles collected or donated over the years: the prayer book
with the signature Constance Kent on the flyleaf; the flintlock duelling
pistol supposedly used by the Reverend James Hackman for the murder
of Margaret Wray, mistress of the Earl of Sandwich; a phial of white
powder, allegedly arsenic, found in the possession of Major Herbert
Armstrong. There was an addition since Dalgliesh's last visit. It lay
curled, sinister as a lethal snake, in pride of place beneath a label stating

that this was the rope with which Crippen had been hanged. Dalgliesh, turning to follow Ackroyd out of the library, mildly suggested that the public display of this distasteful object was barbaric, a protest which Ackroyd as mildly repudiated.

"A trifle morbid, perhaps, but 'barbaric' is going a little far. After all, this isn't the Athenaeum. It probably does some of the older members good to be reminded of the natural end of their previous professional activities. Would you still be a detective if we hadn't abolished hanging?"

"I don't know. Abolition doesn't help with that particular moral dilemma as far as I'm concerned, since personally I would prefer death to twenty years in prison."

"Not death by hanging?"

"No, not that."

Hanging, for him, as he suspected for most people, had always held a particular horror. Despite the reports of Royal Commissions on capital punishment which claimed for it humanity, speed and the certainty of instantaneous death, it remained for him one of the ugliest forms of judicial execution, encumbered with horrifying images as precisely lined as a pen drawing: mass victims in the wake of triumphant armies, the pathetic, half-demented victims of seventeenth-century justice, the muted drums of the quarterdecks of ships where the navy exacted its revenge and issued its warning, women convicted in the eighteenth century of infanticide, that ridiculous but sinister ritual of the small black square formally placed atop the judge's wig, the concealed but ordinary-looking door leading from the condemned cell to that last brief walk. It was good that they were all part of history. For a moment the Cadaver Club was a less agreeable place in which to lunch, its eccentricities more repugnant than amusing.

The Snug at the Cadaver Club is well named. It is a small basement room at the rear of the house with two windows and a French door opening onto a narrow paved courtyard bounded by a ten-foot ivied wall. The yard could comfortably accommodate three tables, but the members of the club are not addicted to dining outside, even in the occasional hot spell of an English summer, apparently regarding the habit as a foreign eccentricity incompatible with the proper appreciation of food or the privacy necessary to good talk. To dissuade any member who might be tempted to this indulgence, the courtyard is furnished with terracotta pots of various sizes planted with geraniums and ivy, and space further restricted by a huge stone copy of the Apollo Belvedere propped in the wall against the corner and rumoured to be the gift of an early member of the club whose wife had banished it from their suburban garden. The geraniums were still in full bloom and the bright pinks and reds glowed through the glass, enhancing the immediate impression of welcoming domesticity. The room had obviously once been the kitchen and one wall was still fitted with the original iron grate, its bars and ovens polished now to ebony. The blackened beam above was hung with iron cooking instruments and a row of copper pans, battered but gleaming. An oak dresser ran the whole length of the opposite wall, serving as a receptacle for the display of the gifts and bequests of members which were deemed unsuitable for, or unworthy of, the library cabinet.

Dalgliesh remembered that the club had an unwritten law that no offering from a member, however inappropriate or bizarre, should be rejected, and the dresser, like the whole room, bore witness to the idiosyncratic tastes and hobbies of the donors. Delicate Meissen plates were ranged in incongruous proximity to Victorian ribbon-decorated souvenirs bearing pictures of Brighton and Southend-on-Sea; a toby jug which looked like a fairground trophy stood between a Victorian Staffordshire flatback, obviously original, of Wesley preaching from a double-decker pulpit, and a fine Parian bust of the Duke of Wellington. An assortment of coronation mugs and early Staffordshire cups was suspended in precarious disorder from the hooks. Beside the door hung a painted glass picture of the burial of Princess Charlotte; above it a stuffed elk's head with an old Panama hat slung on its left horn gazed glassy-eyed with lugubrious disapproval at a large and lurid print of the Charge of the Light Brigade.

The present kitchen was somewhere close; Dalgliesh could hear small agreeable tinklings and from time to time the thud of the food lift descending from the first-floor dining-room. Only one of the four tables was set, the linen immaculate, and Dalgliesh and Ackroyd seated themselves beside the window.

The menu and wine list were already to the right of Ackroyd's place. Taking them up, he said: "The Plants have retired, but we've got the Jacksons now, and I'm not sure that Mrs. Jackson's cooking isn't even better. We were lucky to get them. She and her husband used to run a private nursing home but they got tired of the country and wanted to return to London. They don't need to work but I think the job suits them. They've kept on with the policy of having only one main dish a day at luncheon and dinner. Very wise. Today, white-bean-and-tuna-fish salad followed by rack of lamb with fresh vegetables and a green salad. Then lemon tart and cheese to follow. The vegetables will be fresh. We still get all the vegetables and eggs from young Plant's smallholding. Do you want to see the wine list? Have you a preference?"

"I'll leave that to you."

Ackroyd cogitated aloud while Dalgliesh, who loved wine but disliked talking about it, let his gaze range appreciatively over the muddle of a room, which despite, perhaps because of, its air of eccentric but organized chaos was surprisingly restful. The discordant objects, not carefully placed for effect, had through time achieved a rightness of place. After a lengthy discussion on the merits of the wine list in which Ackroyd apparently expected no contribution from his guest, he fixed on a chardonnay. Mrs. Jackson, appearing as if in response to some secret signal, brought with her the smell of hot rolls and an air of bustling confidence.

"Very nice to meet you, Commander. You've got the Snug to yourself this morning, Mr. Ackroyd. Mr. Jackson will be seeing to the wine."

After the first course had been served, Dalgliesh said: "Why is Mrs. Jackson dressed as a nurse?"

"Because she is one, I suppose. She used to be a matron. She's a midwife too, I believe, but we've no call for that here."

Not surprisingly, thought Dalgliesh, since the club didn't admit women. He said: "Isn't that goffered cap with streamers going a bit far?"

"Oh, do you think so? I suppose we've got used to it. I doubt if the members would feel at home if Mrs. Jackson stopped wearing it now."

Ackroyd wasted no time in coming to the purpose of the meeting. As soon as they were finally alone he said: "Lord Stilgoe had a word with me last week in Brooks'. He's my wife's uncle, incidentally. Do you know him?"

"No. I thought he was dead."

"I can't think how you got that idea." He prodded at his bean salad irritably and Dalgliesh remembered that he resented any suggestion that someone he knew personally could actually die, and certainly not without the prior knowledge of himself. "He isn't even as old as he looks, not eighty yet. He's remarkably spry for his age. Actually he's publishing his memoirs. The Peverell Press are bringing them out next spring. That's what he wanted to see me about. Something rather worrying has happened. At least his wife finds it worrying. She thinks he's had a direct threat of murder."

"And has he?"

"Well, he's received this."

He took some time in taking the small oblong of paper from his wallet and passing it over to Dalgliesh. The words had been accurately typed on a word processor and the message was unsigned.

"Do you really think it wise to publish with Peverell Press? Remember Marcus Seabright, Joan Petrie and now Sonia Clements. Two authors and your own editor dead in less than twelve months. Do you want to be number four?"

Dalgliesh said: "More mischievous than threatening, I should have thought, and the malice directed against the Press rather than Stilgoe. There's no doubt that Sonia Clements' death was suicide. She left a note for the coroner and wrote to her sister telling her that she intended to kill herself. I don't recall anything about the first two deaths."

"Oh, they're straightforward enough, I should have thought. Seabright was over eighty and had a bad heart. He died from an attack of gastroenteritis which brought on a heart attack. Anyway, he was no loss to Peverell Press. He hadn't produced a novel for ten years. Joan Petrie killed herself driving to her country cottage. Accidental death. Petrie had two passions, whisky and fast cars. The only surprise is that she killed herself before she killed someone else. Obviously the poison pen dragged up these two deaths as make-weights. But Dorothy Stilgoe is superstitious. She takes the view, why publish with Peverell when there are other publishers?"

"And who is actually in charge now?"

"Oh Gerard Etienne. Very much so. The last chairman and managing director, old Henry Peverell, died in early January and left his shares in the business in equal parts to his daughter, Frances, and to Gerard. His original partner, Jean-Philippe Etienne, had retired about a year previously, and not before time. His shares also went to Gerard. The two older men ran the firm as if it was their private hobby. Old Peverell always took the view that a gentleman inherited money, he didn't earn it. Jean-Philippe Etienne hadn't taken an active part in the firm for years. His moment of glory, of course, was in the last war, where he was a hero of the Resistance in Vichy France, but I don't think he's done anything memorable since. Gerard was waiting in the wings, the crown prince. And now he's well on stage and we're likely to see action if not melodrama."

"Does Gabriel Dauntsey still run the poetry list?"

"I'm surprised you need to ask, Adam. You mustn't let your passion for catching murderers put you out of touch with real life. Yes, he's still there. He hasn't written a poem himself for over twenty years. Dauntsey's an anthology poet. The best is so good that it keeps reappearing, but I imagine most readers think he's dead. He was a bomber pilot in the last war, so he must be well over seventy. It's time he retired. The poetry list at Peverell Press is about all he does nowadays. The other three partners are Gerard's sister, Claudia Etienne; James

de Witt, who's been with the firm since he left Oxford; and Frances
Peverell, the last of the Peverells. But it's Gerard who runs the firm."

"What is he planning, do you know?"

"Rumour has it that he wants to sell Innocent House and move to
Docklands. That won't please Frances Peverell. The Peverells have
always had an obsession about Innocent House. It belongs to the
partnership now, not to the family, but any Peverell thinks of it as the
family home. He's already made other changes, some staff sacked,
including Sonia Clements. He's right, of course. The firm has got to be
dragged into the twentieth century or go under, but he's certainly made
enemies. It's significant that they had no trouble at the Press until
Gerard took over. That coincidence hasn't escaped Stilgoe, although
his wife is still convinced that the malice is directed against her husband
personally, not the firm, and against his memoirs in particular."

"Will Peverell lose much if the book is withdrawn?"

"Not a great deal, I imagine. Of course they'll hype the memoirs as
if their disclosures could bring down the Government, discredit the
Opposition and end parliamentary democracy as we know it, but I
imagine that, like most political memoirs, they'll promise more than
they deliver. But I don't see how it can be withdrawn. The book is in
production, they won't let it go without a struggle, and Stilgoe won't
want to break the contract if it means publicly explaining why. What
Dorothy Stilgoe is asking is, was Sonia Clements' death really suicide
and did someone interfere with Petrie's Jag? I think she's satisfied
enough that old Seabright died from natural causes."

"So what am I expected to do?"

"There must have been inquests in the last two cases and presumably
the police carried out an investigation. Your people could take a look
at the papers, have a word with the officers concerned, that sort of
thing. Then, if Dorothy could be assured that a senior Metropolitan
detective has looked at all the evidence and is satisfied, she might give
her husband, and Peverell Press, some peace."

Dalgliesh said: "That might serve to satisfy her that Sonia Clements'
death was suicide. It will hardly content her if she's superstitious, and
I don't see what will. The essence of superstition is that it isn't amenable
to reason. She'll probably take the view that an unlucky publisher is as
bad as a murderous one. I suppose she isn't seriously suggesting that
someone at Peverell Press put an unidentifiable poison in Sonia Clements' wine?"

"No, I don't think she's going as far as that."

"Just as well or her husband will have his profits eaten up by a libel action. I'm surprised he didn't go straight to the Commissioner or to me direct."

"Are you? I'm not sure. It would have looked—well, shall we say a little timid, a trifle over-concerned. Besides, he doesn't know you, I do. I can understand why he spoke to me first. And of course, one can hardly see him calling in at the local nick, joining the queue of lost-dog owners, assaulted wives and aggrieved motorists and explaining his dilemma to the duty sergeant. Frankly I don't think he believed it would be taken seriously. His view is that, having regard to his wife's concern and that anonymous note, he's justified in asking the police to take a look at what is happening at the Peverell Press."

The lamb had arrived, pink and succulent and tender enough to be eaten with a spoon. In the few minutes of silence which Ackroyd thought a necessary tribute to a perfectly cooked meal, Dalgliesh recalled the first time he had seen Innocent House.

His father had taken him to London for his eighth-birthday treat; they were to spend two whole days sightseeing and stay overnight with a friend, who was a parish priest in Kensington, and his wife. He could remember lying in bed the night before, fitfully sleeping and almost sick with excitement, the cavernous immensity and clamour of the old Liverpool Street Station, his terror of losing his father, of being caught up and swept along with the great army of grey-faced marching people. In the two days in which his father had intended to combine pleasure with education—to his scholarly mind the two were indistinguishable—they had perhaps inevitably tried to do too much. The visit had been overwhelming for an eight-year-old, leaving a confused memory of churches and galleries, restaurants and unfamiliar food, of floodlit towers and the dancing reflection of light on the black creased surface of the water, of sleek, prancing horses and silver helmets, of the glamour and terror of history made manifest in brick and stone. But London had laid on him her spell, which no adult experience, no exploration of other great cities had been able to break.

It was on the second day that they had visited Westminster Abbey and later taken a river steamer from Charing Cross Pier to Greenwich and he had first seen Innocent House, glittering in the morning sun, seeming to rise like a golden mirage from the shimmering water. He had gazed at it in wonder. His father had explained that the name was derived from Innocent Walk, which ran behind the house, at the end of which had once stood an early-eighteenth-century magistrates' court. Defendants taken into custody after their first hearing were removed to the Fleet prison; the more fortunate walked down the cobbled lane to freedom. He had started to tell his son something of the house's architectural history, but his voice had been overpowered by the tour-guide's booming commentary, loud enough to be heard by every boat on the river.

"And here, coming up on our left, ladies and gentlemen, is one of the most interesting buildings on the Thames: Innocent House, built in 1830 for Sir Francis Peverell, a noted publisher of the day. Sir Francis had visited Venice and had been very impressed by the Ca' d'Oro, the Golden House on the Grand Canal. Those of you who have had holidays in Venice have probably seen it. So he hit on the idea of building his own golden house on the Thames. Pity he couldn't import Venetian weather." He paused briefly for the expected laughter. "Today it is the headquarters of a publishing firm, the Peverell Press, so it's still in the family. There's an interesting story about Innocent House. Apparently Sir Francis was so absorbed by it that he neglected his young wife, whose money had helped him to build it, and she threw herself from the top balcony and was instantly killed. The legend has it that you can still see the stain of her blood on the marble, which can't be cleaned away. It's said that Sir Francis went mad with remorse in his old age and used to go out alone at night trying to get rid of that tell-tale spot. It's his ghost that people claim to see, still scrubbing away at the stain. There are some watermen who don't like sailing too close to Innocent House after dark."

All eyes on deck had been docilely turned to the house but now, intrigued by this story of blood, the passengers moved to hang over the rail; voices murmured and heads craned as if the legendary stain might still be visible. Eight-year-old Adam's over-vivid imagination had pictured a white-clad woman, blonde hair flying, flinging herself from the balcony like some demented storybook heroine, had heard the final thud and seen the trickle of blood creeping and starting across the marble to drip into the Thames. For years afterwards the house had continued to fascinate him with a potent amalgam of beauty and terror.

The tour-guide had been inaccurate about one fact: it was possible that the suicide story had also been embellished or untrue. He knew now that Sir Francis had been enchanted, not by the Ca' d'Oro, which, despite the intricacies of its fine tracings and carvings, he had found, or so he had written to his architect, too asymmetrical for his taste, but by the Palace of Doge Francesco Foscari, and it was the Ca' Foscari which his architect had been instructed to build for him on this cold, tidal river. It should have looked incongruous, a folly, unmistakably Venetian and Venetian of the mid-fifteenth century. And yet it looked as if no other city, no other site would have been right for it. Dalgliesh still found it difficult to understand why it should be so successful, this unashamed borrowing from another age, another country, a softer, warmer air. The proportions had been changed and surely that alone should have rendered Sir Francis's dream an impracticable presumption, but the reduction in scale had been brilliantly carried out and the dignity of the original somehow maintained. There were six great central window arches instead of eight behind the finely carved balconies of the first and second floors, but the marble columns with their decorated pinnules were almost exact copies of the Venetian palace, and the central arcades here, as there, were balanced by tall single windows, giving the façade its unity and grace. The great curved door fronted a marble patio leading to a landing-stage and a flight of steps to the river. On either side of the house two brick Regency town houses with small balconies, presumably built to house coachmen or other servants, stood like humble sentries of the central magnificence. He had seen it from the river many times since that eighth-birthday celebration but had never been inside. He recalled having read that there was a fine Matthew Cotes Wyatt ceiling in the central hall and rather wished he could see it. It would be a pity if Innocent House fell into the hands of philistines.

He asked: "And what exactly has been going on at Peverell Press? What's worrying Lord Stilgoe apart from his poison-pen letter?"

"So you've heard the rumours. Difficult to tell. They're being rather cagey about it and I don't blame them. But one or two little incidents have become common knowledge. Not so little either. The most serious happened just before Easter, when they lost the illustrations for Gregory Maybrick's book on the Guy Fawkes conspiracy. Popular history, no doubt, but Maybrick knows his period. They expected to do rather well with it. He'd managed to lay his hands on some interesting contemporary plates, never before published, as well as other written records, and the whole lot were lost. They were on loan from the various owners and he'd more or less guaranteed their safety."

"Lost? Mislaid? Destroyed?"

"The story is that he delivered them by hand to James de Witt, who was editing the book. He's their senior editor and normally responsible for fiction but old Peverell, who edited their non-fiction, had died about three months earlier and I suppose they either hadn't had time to find a suitable replacement or wanted to save money. Like most houses they're laying off rather than taking on. The rumour is that they can't keep afloat much longer. Not surprising with that Venetian palace to maintain. Anyway, the illustrations were handed over to de Witt in his office and he locked them in his cupboard while Maybrick watched."

"Not in a safe?"

"My dear boy, we're talking about a publishing house, not Cartier's. Knowing Peverells, I'm only surprised that de Witt bothered to lock the cupboard."

"Was his the only key?"

"Really, Adam, you're not detecting now. Actually it was. He kept it in a battered old tobacco tin in his left-hand drawer."

Where else? thought Dalgliesh. He said: "Where any member of the staff or any unaccompanied visitor could lay hands on it."

"Well, someone obviously did. James didn't need to go to the cupboard for a couple of days. The illustrations were due to be delivered personally to the art department the following week. You know that Peverells have put out their artwork to an independent firm?"

"No, I didn't know."

"More economical, I suppose. It's the same firm that's been doing the jackets for the last five years. Rather well, actually. Peverells have never let their standards slip on book production and design. You can always tell a Peverell book just by handling it. Until now, of course. Gerard Etienne may change that too. Anyway, when de Witt looked for the envelope it had disappeared. Huge fuss, of course. Everyone questioned. Frantic searches. General panic. In the end they had to confess to Maybrick and the owners. You can imagine how they took the news."

"Did the stuff ever come to light?"

"Not until too late. There were doubts whether Maybrick would want to publish at all but the book was in the catalogue and it was decided to go ahead with alternative illustrations and some necessary changes to the text. A week after they'd finished printing, the envelope and its contents mysteriously reappeared. De Witt found it in his cupboard, exactly where he had placed it."

"Which suggests that the thief had some respect for scholarship and had never intended to destroy the papers."

"It suggests a number of possibilities, spite against Maybrick, spite against the Press, spite against de Witt or a somewhat warped sense of humour."

"Peverells didn't report the theft to the police?"

"No, Adam, they didn't place their confidence in our wonderful boys in blue. I don't want to be unkind but the police haven't an impressive clear-up rate when it comes to domestic burglary. The partners took the view that they stood just as good a chance of success and would cause less upset to staff if they undertook their own enquiry."

"By whom? Were any of them free of suspicion?"

"That, of course, is the difficulty. They weren't then and they aren't now. I imagine that Etienne adopted the Head Beak's strategy. You know, 'If the boy who's responsible will come to my study after prep in confidence and return the documents no more will be heard of the matter.' It never worked at school. I don't suppose it was more successful at Peverells. It was obviously an inside job, and it isn't as if they employ a large staff, only about twenty-five people in addition to the five partners. Most of them are old faithfuls of course, and the story is that the few who aren't have alibis."

"So it's still a mystery."

"And so is the second incident. The second serious incident—there have probably been minor mischiefs which they've kept quiet about. This one concerns Stilgoe, so it's just as well that so far they've managed to keep it from him and it hasn't become public property. The old boy really would have something to feed his paranoia. Apparently, when the page proofs had been read and a number of alterations agreed with Stilgoe, they were packaged and left overnight under the counter in the reception office, where they were due to be collected next morning. Someone opened the package and tampered with them, changed a number of the names, altered punctuation, deleted a couple of sentences. Fortunately the printer who received them was intelligent and thought some of the changes odd, so he telephoned to check. The partners have managed, God knows how, to keep this contretemps secret from most of the staff at Innocent House and, of course, from Stilgoe. It would have been extremely damaging to the firm if it had got out. I understand all parcels and papers are locked up overnight now and no doubt they've tightened security in other ways."

Dalgliesh wondered whether the perpetrator had from the first intended the alterations to be discovered. They seemed to have been made with very little attempt to deceive. It surely wouldn't have been difficult to alter the page proofs in a way which would seriously damage the book without arousing the suspicions of the printer. It was odd, too, that the poison pen hadn't mentioned the alterations to Stilgoe's proofs. Either he or she hadn't known, which would absolve the five partners, or the poison pen had wanted to frighten Stilgoe but not to provide evidence which would justify him in withdrawing the book. It was an interesting little mystery but not one on which he proposed to waste the time of a senior police officer.

Nothing more was said about the Peverell Press until they were taking their coffee in the library. Ackroyd leaned forward and asked a little anxiously, "Can I tell Lord Stilgoe that you'll try to reassure his wife?"

"I'm sorry, Conrad, but no. I'll get him a note to say that the police have no cause to suspect foul play in any of the cases which concern him. I doubt whether it will do much good if his wife is superstitious, but that is her misfortune and his problem."

"And the other trouble at Innocent House?"

"If Gerard Etienne believes that the law is being broken and wants the police to investigate he must get in touch with his local station."

"Just like anybody else?"

"Precisely."

"You wouldn't be prepared to go to Innocent House and have an informal word with him?"

"No, Conrad. Not even for a sight of the Wyatt ceiling."

5

On the afternoon of Sonia Clements' cremation Gabriel Dauntsey and Frances Peverell shared a taxi from the crematorium back to number 12 Innocent Walk. Frances was very silent on the journey, sitting a little apart from Dauntsey, gazing out of the window. She was hatless, the light-brown hair a shining helmet which curved to touch the collar of her grey coat. Her shoes, tights and handbag were black, and there was a black chiffon scarf knotted at her neck. They were, Dauntsey remembered, the same clothes she had worn at her father's cremation, a contemporary understated mourning, nicely holding the balance between ostentation and a decent respect. The combination of grey and black in its sombre simplicity made her look very young and emphasized what he most liked in her, a gentle old-fashioned formality which reminded him of the young women of his youth. She sat distanced and very still, but her hands were restless. He knew that the ring she wore on the third finger of her right hand had been her mother's engagement ring and he watched while she twisted it obsessively under the black suede of her glove. He wondered for a moment whether to reach out and silently take her hand, but resisted the impulse to a gesture which he told himself might only embarrass them both. He could hardly keep holding her hand all the way back to Innocent Walk.

They were fond of each other; he was, he knew, the one person at Innocent House in whom she felt she could occasionally confide; but neither was demonstrative. They lived a short staircase apart but visited

each other only by invitation, each anxious not to intrude or impose on
the other, or to initiate an intimacy which the other might find unwelcome or come to regret. As a result, liking each other, enjoying each
other's company, they saw less of each other than if they had lived miles
apart. When they were together they spoke chiefly of books, poetry,
plays they had seen, programmes on the television, seldom of people.
Frances was too fastidious to gossip and he was equally reluctant to get
drawn into controversy about the new regime. He had his job, his flat
on the bottom two floors of number 12 Innocent Walk. Neither might
be his much longer, but he was seventy-six, too old to fight. He knew
that her flat, above his, had an attraction for him which it was prudent
to resist. Sitting in the high-backed chair, with the curtains drawn against
the gentle half-imagined sighing of the river, stretching out his legs
before the open fire after one of their rare dinners together when she
had left him to make coffee, he would hear her quietly moving about
the kitchen and would feel a seductive peace and contentment stealing
over him which it would be only too easy to make a regular part of his
life.

Her sitting-room stretched the whole length of the house. Everything
in it was attractive: the elegant proportions of the original marble
fireplace, the oil of an eighteenth-century Peverell with his wife and
children above the mantelshelf, the small Queen Anne bureau, the
mahogany bookcases on each side of the fire, topped with a pediment
and with two fine Parian heads of a veiled bride, the Regency dining
table and six chairs, the subtle colours of the rugs glowing against the
gold of the polished floor. How simple, now, to establish an intimacy
which would open to him this gentle feminine comfort so different from
his own bleak and underfurnished rooms below. Sometimes, if she
telephoned with an invitation to dinner, he would invent a prior
engagement and take himself out to a local pub, filling the long hours
in the smoke and clatter, anxious not to return too early since his front
door, in Innocent Lane, lay directly under her kitchen windows.

This evening he felt that she might welcome his company but was
unwilling to ask for it. He wasn't sorry. The cremation had been
depressing enough without having to discuss its banalities; he had had
enough of death for one day. When the taxi drew up in Innocent Walk
and she said an almost hurried goodbye and unlocked her front door
without once looking back, he felt a sense of relief. But two hours later,
after he had finished his soup and the scrambled eggs and smoked
salmon which was his favourite evening meal and which he prepared,
as always, with care, keeping the gas low, drawing the mixture lovingly

from the sides of the pan, adding a final spoonful of cream, he pictured her eating her solitary supper and regretted his selfishness. This wasn't a good night for her to be alone. He telephoned and said: "I'm wondering, Frances, whether you would care for a game of chess."

He could tell from the joyous rise in her voice that the suggestion had come as a relief. "Yes, I would, Gabriel. Do please come up. Yes, I'd love a game."

Her dining table was still set when he arrived. She always ate with some formality even when alone, but he could see that the meal had been as simple as his own. The cheese board and the fruit bowl were on the table and she had obviously had soup but nothing else. He could see, too, that she had been crying.

She said, smiling, trying to make her voice cheerful: "I'm so glad you've come up. It gives me an excuse to open a bottle of wine. It's odd how much one dislikes drinking alone. I suppose it's all those early warnings about solitary drinking being the beginning of the slide into alcoholism."

She fetched a bottle of Château Margaux and he came forward to open it. They didn't speak again until they were settled, glasses in hand, before the fire, when, looking into the flames, she said: "He should have been there. Gerard should have been there."

"He doesn't like funerals."

"Oh Gabriel, who does? And it was awful, wasn't it? Daddy's cremation was bad enough but this was worse. That pathetic clergyman who did his best but who didn't know her and didn't know any of us, trying to sound sincere, praying to the God she didn't believe in, talking about eternal life when she didn't even have a life worth living here on earth."

He said gently: "We can't know that. We can't be the judge of another's happiness or unhappiness."

"She wanted to die. Isn't that evidence enough? At least Gerard came to Daddy's funeral. He more or less had to, though, didn't he? The crown prince saying farewell to the old king. It wouldn't have looked good if he'd stayed away. After all, there were important people there, writers, publishers, the press, people he wanted to impress. There was no one important at today's cremation, so he didn't have to bother. But he ought to have come. After all, he killed her."

Dauntsey said more firmly: "Frances, you mustn't say that. There's absolutely no evidence that anything Gerard did or said caused Sonia's death. You know what she wrote in the suicide note. If she had planned to kill herself because Gerard had sacked her I think she would have said so. The note was explicit. You must never say that outside this room. This kind of rumour can be deeply damaging. Promise me—it is important."

"All right, I promise. I haven't said it to anyone except you, but I'm not the only one at Innocent House who's thinking it, and some are saying it. Kneeling there in that awful chapel, I was trying to pray, for Daddy, for her, for all of us. But it was all so meaningless, so futile. All I could think about was Gerard, Gerard who ought to have been sitting there in the front row with us, Gerard who was my lover, Gerard who isn't my lover any more. It's so humiliating. I know now, of course, what it was all about. Gerard thought, 'Poor Frances, twenty-nine and still a virgin. I must do something about that. Give her the experience of her life, show her what she's missing.' His good deed for the day. His good deed for three months, rather. I suppose I lasted longer than most. And the ending was so sordid, so messy. Isn't it always? Gerard is very good at beginning a love-affair, but he doesn't know how to end it, not with any dignity. But then, nor do I. And I was deluded enough to think that I was different from his other women, that this time he was serious, in love, wanting commitment, marriage. I thought we would run Peverell Press together, live in Innocent House, bring up our children here, even change the name of the firm. I thought that would please him. Peverell and Etienne. Etienne and Peverell. I used to practise the alternatives, trying to decide which sounded better. I thought he wanted what I wanted—marriage, children, a proper home, a shared life. Is that so unreasonable? Oh God, Gabriel, I feel so stupid, so ashamed."

She had never before spoken so openly to him, never shown the depth of her anguish. It was almost as if she had been silently rehearsing the words, waiting for this moment of relief when, at last, she was with someone she could trust and in whom she could confide. But coming from Frances, who was always so sensitive, reticent and proud, this uncontrolled pouring forth of bitterness and self-disgust appalled him. Perhaps it was the funeral, the memory of that earlier cremation, which had released the pent-up hatred and humiliation. He wasn't sure that he could cope with it but knew that he must try. This fluency of pain demanded more than the soft pabulum of comfort: "He isn't worth it, forget him, the pain will pass with time." But that last was true, the pain did pass with time, whether it was the pain of betrayal or the pain of bereavement. Who knew that better than he? He thought: The tragedy of loss is not that we grieve, but that we cease to grieve, and then perhaps the dead are dead at last.

He said gently: "The things you want—children, marriage, home, sex—are reasonable desires, some would say very proper desires. Children are our only hope of immortality. They aren't things to be ashamed of. It is your misfortune, not your shame, that Etienne's desires and yours didn't coincide." He paused, then said, wondering if it were wise, whether she would find the words crudely insensitive: "James is in love with you."

"I suppose so. Poor James. He hasn't said so, but he doesn't need to, does he? Do you know, I think I could have loved James if it hadn't been for Gerard. And I don't even like Gerard. I never did, even when I wanted him most. That's what's so terrible about sex, it can exist without love, without liking, even without respect. Oh, I tried to fool myself. When he was insensitive or selfish or crude I made excuses. I reminded myself how brilliant he was, how handsome, how amusing, what a wonderful lover. He was all those things. He is all those things. I told myself that it was unreasonable to apply to Gerard the petty standards one applied to others. And I loved him. When you love, you don't judge. And now I hate him. I didn't know that I could hate, really hate, another person. It's different from hating a thing, a political creed, a philosophy, a social evil. It's so concentrated, so physical, it makes me feel ill. My hate is the last thing I think about at night and I wake up with it every morning. But it's wrong, a sin. It has to be wrong. I feel I'm living in mortal sin and I can't get absolution because I can't stop the hating."

Dauntsey said: "I don't think in those terms, sin, absolution. But hate is dangerous. It perverts justice."

"Oh justice! I've never expected much in the way of justice. And hate has made me so boring. I bore myself. I know I bore you, dear Gabriel, but you're the only one I can talk to and sometimes, like tonight, I feel I have to talk or I might go mad. And you're so wise, that's your reputation anyway."

He said dryly: "It's easy to get a reputation for wisdom. It's only necessary to live long, speak little and do less."

"But when you do speak you're worth listening to. Gabriel, tell me what I must do."

"To get rid of him?"

"To get rid of this pain."

"There are the usual expedients: drink, drugs, suicide. The first two lead to the third, it's just a slower, more expensive, more humiliating route. I don't advise it. Or you could murder him, but I don't advise that either. Do it in fantasy as ingeniously as you like, but not in reality. Not unless you want to rot for ten years in prison."

She said: "Could you stand that?"

"Not for ten years. I might manage three but not more. There are better ways of coping with pain than death, his death or yours. Tell yourself that pain is part of life, to feel pain is to be alive. I envy you. If I could feel such pain I might still be a poet. Value yourself. You're no less a human being because one selfish, arrogant, insensitive man doesn't find you lovable. Do you really need to value yourself by the standard of any man, let alone Gerard Etienne? Remind yourself that the only power he has over you is the power that you give him. Take that power away and you take away the hurt. Remember, Frances, you don't have to stay with the firm. And don't say that there has always been a Peverell at the Peverell Press."

"There has since 1792, even before we moved into Innocent House. Daddy wouldn't have wanted me to be the last."

"Someone has to be, someone will be. You owed your father a certain duty in life but it ceased with his death. We can't be in thrall to the dead."

As soon as the words were out of his mouth he regretted them, half expecting her to ask "What about you? Aren't you in thrall to the dead, your wife, your lost children?" He went on quickly: "What would you like to do if you had a free choice?"

"Work with children, I think. Perhaps train as a primary-school teacher. I've got my degree. I suppose it would only mean another year's training. And then I think I'd like to work in the country or in a small country town."

"Then do it. You do have a free choice. But don't go searching for happiness. Find the right job, the right place, the right life. The happiness will come if you're lucky. Most of us get our share of it. Some of us get more than our share, even if it's concentrated into a little space of time."

She said: "I'm surprised you don't quote Blake, that poem about 'joy and pain being woven fine, a clothing for the soul divine.' How does it go?

> *Man was made for Joy and Woe;*
> *And when this we rightly know*
> *Thro' the World we safely go.*

Only you don't believe in the soul divine, do you?"

"No, that would be the ultimate self-deception."

"But you do go safely through the world. And you understand about hate. I think I've always known that you hated Gerard."

He said: "No, you're wrong, Frances. I don't hate him. I feel nothing for him, nothing at all. And that makes me far more dangerous to him than you can ever be. Hadn't we better start a game?"

He took out the heavy chessboard from the corner cupboard and she moved the table between the armchairs then helped him to set out the pieces. Holding out his clenched fist for her to choose black or white, he said: "I think you ought to give me a pawn, the tribute of youth to age."

"Nonsense, you beat me last time. We play even."

She surprised herself. Once she would have given way. It was a small act of self-assertion and she saw him smile as with his stiffened fingers he began to set out the pieces.

6

Miss Blackett went home every night to Weaver's Cottage in West Marling in Kent, where, for the past nineteen years, she had lived with her older widowed cousin, Joan Willoughby. Their relationship was affectionate but had never been emotionally intense. Mrs. Willoughby had married a retired clergyman, and when he died, three years after the marriage, which Miss Blackett privately suspected was as long as either partner could have borne, it had seemed natural for his widow to invite her cousin to give up her unsatisfactory rented flat in Bayswater and move to the cottage. Early in these nineteen years of shared life a routine had established itself, evolving rather than planned, which satisfied them both. It was Joan who managed the house and was responsible for the garden, Blackie who, on Sundays, cooked the main meal of the day, which was always eaten promptly at one o'clock, a responsibility which excused her from Matins although not from Evensong. It was Blackie who, rising first, took early-morning tea to her cousin and made their nightly Ovaltine or cocoa at half past ten. They holidayed together, for the last two weeks in July, usually abroad, because neither of them had anyone with a stronger claim. They looked forward each June to the Wimbledon tennis championship and enjoyed the occasional weekend visit to a concert, a theatre or an art gallery. They told themselves, but did not say aloud, that they were lucky.

Weaver's Cottage stood on the northern outskirts of the village. Originally two substantial cottages, it had in the 1950s been converted into one dwelling by a family with definite ideas about what constituted rural domestic charm. The tiled roof had been replaced with reed thatch from which three dormer windows stared out like protruding eyes; the plain windows were now mullioned and a porch had been added, covered in summer by climbing roses and clematis. Mrs. Willoughby loved the cottage, and if the mullioned windows made the sitting-room rather darker than she would ideally have liked, and some of the oak beams were less authentic than others, these defects were never openly acknowledged. The cottage with its immaculate thatch and its garden had appeared on too many calendars, had been photographed by visitors too often for her to worry about small details of architectural integrity. The main part of the garden was in the front, and here Mrs. Willoughby spent most of her spare hours, tending, planting and watering what was generally admitted to be West Marling's most impressive front garden, designed as much for the pleasure of passers-by as for the occupants of the cottage.

"I aim for something of interest throughout the year," she would explain to people who paused to admire, and in this she certainly succeeded. But she was a true and imaginative gardener. Plants thrived under her care and she had an instinctive eye for the placing of colour and mass. The cottage might be less than authentic but the garden was unmistakably English. There was a small lawn with a mulberry tree which in spring was surrounded by crocuses, snowdrops and later the bright trumpets of daffodils and narcissi. In the summer the heavily planted beds leading to the porch were an intoxication of colour and scent, while the beech hedge, trimmed low so as not to obscure the view of the glories beyond, was a living symbol of the passing seasons, from the first tight, tentative buds to the crisp gold and reds of its autumn glory.

She always returned from the monthly PCC meeting bright-eyed and invigorated. Some people, Blackie reflected, would have found the fortnightly skirmishes with the vicar about his partiality for the new liturgy over the old and his other minor delinquencies dispiriting; Joan seemed to thrive on them. She settled herself, plump thighs parted, stretching the tweed of her skirt, feet firmly planted, before the pie-edged table and poured the two glasses of amontillado. A dry biscuit cracked between the strong white teeth, the cut glass, one of a set, with its delicate stem looked as if it would snap in her hand.

"It's inclusive language now, if you please. He wants 'Through the Night of Doubt and Sorrow' at next Sunday's Evensong, but we're supposed to sing 'Person Takes the Hand of Person, Marching Fearless

Through the Night.' I soon put a stop to that, supported by Mr. Higginson, thankfully. I can forgive that man the price of his bacon and the way he lets that mangy old cat of his sit in the window on the corn flakes when he acts with sense at the PCC, which, to do him justice, he usually does. Miss Matlock suggested 'Sister Takes the Hand of Sister.' "

"What's wrong with that?"

"Nothing, except it's not what the author wrote. Had a good day?"

"No. It hasn't been a good day."

But Mrs. Willoughby's mind was still with the PCC. "I'm not particularly fond of that hymn. Never have been. I can't think why Miss Matlock's so keen on it. Nostalgia, I suppose. Childhood memories. Not much doubt and sorrow about the congregation at St Margaret's. Too well fed. Too well-off. Still, there will be if the vicar tries to cut out the eight o'clock 1662 Holy Communion on Sundays. There'll be plenty of doubt and sorrow in the parish then."

"Has he suggested it?"

"Not in so many words, but he's keeping an eye on the size of the congregation. You and I must keep up our attendance and I'll see if I can stir up some of the villagers. All this trendiness is Susan, of course. The man would be perfectly amenable if he weren't egged on by his wife. She's talking of going off to be trained for the diaconate. Next thing they'll be ordaining her priest. They'd both do better in a large inner-city parish. They could have their banjos and guitars and I dare say the people would quite like it. What was your journey like?"

"Not bad. Better tonight than this morning. We were ten minutes late at Charing Cross, a bad beginning to a bad day. It was Sonia Clements' funeral. Mr. Gerard didn't go. Too busy, so he said. I suppose she wasn't important enough. Naturally that meant I felt I had to stay."

Joan said: "Well that was no hardship. Cremations are always depressing. You can get some satisfaction out of a well-conducted funeral, but not out of a cremation. Which reminds me that the vicar actually proposed using the Alternative Service Book when he buries old Merryweather next Tuesday. I soon put a stop to that. Mr. Merryweather was eighty-nine and you know how he hated change. He wouldn't think he'd had a proper Christian burial without the 1662 book."

When, on Tuesday, Blackie had returned home with the news of Sonia Clements' suicide, Joan had taken it with remarkable composure. Blackie told herself that she oughtn't to be surprised. Her cousin frequently confounded her by an unexpected response to news and events. Small domestic inconveniences would provoke outrage, a major tragedy was taken with stoic calm. And this tragedy, after all, couldn't be expected to touch her. She had never known, not even met, Sonia Clements.

Breaking the news, Blackie had said: "I haven't gossiped with the junior staff, of course, but I gather that the general feeling in the office is that she killed herself because Mr. Gerard sacked her. I don't suppose he did it tactfully either. Apparently she left a note but it didn't mention losing her job. People take the view, though, that she'd still be here if it wasn't for Mr. Gerard."

Joan's response had been robust. "But that's ridiculous. Grown women don't kill themselves because they've been sacked. If losing your job was a reason for suicide we'd be having to dig mass graves. It was very inconsiderate of her, very thoughtless. And if she had to kill herself she should have done it somewhere else. After all, it might have been you who'd gone to the little archives room and found her. That wouldn't have been at all pleasant."

Blackie had said: "It wasn't very pleasant for Mandy Price, the new temp, but I must say she took it very coolly. Some young girls would have had hysterics."

"No point in getting hysterics over a dead body. Dead bodies can't harm you. She'll be lucky if she sees nothing worse in life than that."

Blackie, sipping her sherry, looked across at her cousin from under lowered lids as if seeing her dispassionately for the first time. The solid, almost waistless body, the firm legs with the beginnings of varicose veins above surprisingly shapely ankles, the abundant hair, once a rich brown, still thick and only slightly grey, worn in a heavy bun (a fashion which hadn't changed since Blackie had first known her), the cheerful, weather-coarsened face. A sensible face, people might say. A sensible face for a sensible woman, one of Barbara Pym's excellent women but with none of the gentleness or reticence of a Barbara Pym heroine, applying a ruthless kindness to the problems of the village, from bereavements to recalcitrant choirboys, her life as regulated in its pleasures and duties as the liturgical year which gave it shape and focus. And so had Blackie's life once had shape and focus. It seemed to Blackie that she had no control over anything, her life, her job, her emotions, and that in dying Henry Peverell had taken with him an essential part of herself.

Suddenly she said: "Joan, I don't think I can go on at Peverells. Gerard Etienne is getting intolerable. I'm not even allowed to deal with his personal calls. He takes them on a private line in his office. Mr. Peverell used to leave our door ajar, propped open with that draught-excluder snake, Hissing Sid. Mr. Gerard keeps it shut and he's had a high cupboard moved against the glass partition to give himself more privacy. It's not very considerate. It cuts off even more of my light. And now I'm expected to house the new temp, Mandy Price, although all the work for her has to be routed through Emma Wainwright, Miss Claudia's PA. She ought to be sitting in with Emma. Now that Mr. Gerard has had the partition moved my office is cramped even for one. Mr. Peverell would never have agreed to a partition that cut the dining-room across the window and the stuccoed ceiling. He hated the partition and fought against it when the alterations were first made."

Her cousin said: "Can't his sister do something? Why not have a word with her?"

"I don't like to complain, particularly not to her. And what could she do? Mr. Gerard's the managing director and the chairman. He's ruining the firm and no one can stand up to him. I'm not even sure that they want to, except perhaps for Miss Frances, and he's not going to listen to her."

"Then leave. You don't have to work there."

"After twenty-seven years?"

"Long enough for any job, I'd have thought. Retire early. You joined their pension scheme when old Mr. Peverell set it up. I thought at the time that was very wise. I advised it, if you remember. You won't get a full pension of course, but there'll be something coming from that. Or you could take a nice little part-time job in Tonbridge. That wouldn't be difficult to find with your skills. But why work? We can manage. And there's plenty to do in the village. I've never let the PCC make use of you while you're at Peverells. As I told the vicar, my cousin is a personal secretary and spends all her day typing. It's unfair to expect her to do it in the evenings and weekends. I've made it my business to protect you. But it would be different once you were retired. Geoffrey Harding is complaining that acting as secretary to the PCC is getting too much for him. You could take that on for a start. And then there's the Literary and Historical Society. They can certainly do with some secretarial help."

The words, the life they so succinctly described, horrified Blackie. It was as if, in those few ordinary sentences, Joan had pronounced a life sentence. She realized for the first time how unimportant a part West Marling played in her life. She didn't dislike the village; the rows of rather dull cottages, the shaggy green beside a malodorous pond, the modern pub which tried unsuccessfully to look seventeenth-century with a gas-fired open hearth and black-painted beams, even the little church with its pretty broach-spire evoked no emotion as strong as dislike. This was where she lived, ate, slept. But for twenty-seven years the centre of her life had been elsewhere. She had been glad enough

to return by night to Weaver's Cottage, to its comfort and order, to her
cousin's undemanding companionship, to good meals elegantly served,
to the sweet-smelling wood fire in winter, the drink in the garden on
warm summer nights. She had liked the contrast between this rural
peace and the stimulus and challenges of the office, the raucous life of
the river. She had to live somewhere since she couldn't live with Henry
Peverell. But now she realized, in an overwhelming moment of revelation, that her life at West Marling would be insupportable without her
job.

She saw that life stretching before her in a series of bright disjointed
images projected on the mind's screen in a clicking, inexorable sequence;
hours, days, weeks, months, years of unfulfilled predictable monotony.
The small household chores which would give her the illusion of
usefulness, helping in the garden under Joan's supervision, acting as
secretary or typing for the PCC or the WI, shopping in Tonbridge on
Saturdays, Holy Communion and Evensong on Sundays, planning the
excursions which would provide the highlights to the month, not rich
enough to escape, with no excuse to justify escape, and nowhere to
escape to. And why should she wish to leave? It was a life her cousin
found satisfying and psychologically fulfilling, her place in the village
hierarchy secure, the cottage her acknowledged property, the garden
her continued interest and joy. Most people would think that she,
Blackie, was lucky to share it, lucky to live rent-free (they'd know that
in the village, that was the kind of fact they knew by instinct), a beautiful home, her cousin's companionship. She would be the less regarded
of the two, the less popular, the poor relation. Her job, imperfectly
understood in the village but magnified in importance by Joan, had
given her dignity. Work did bestow dignity, status, meaning. Wasn't
that why people dreaded unemployment, why some men found retirement so traumatic? And she couldn't find herself what Joan described
as "a nice little part-time job" in Tonbridge. She knew what that would
mean: working in an office with half-trained girls fresh from school or
secretarial college, sexually on-the-make, resented for her efficiency or
pitied for her all-too-obvious virginity. How could she lower herself to
a part-time job, she who had once been confidential personal assistant
to Henry Peverell?

Sitting immobile with a glass of half-drunk sherry before her and
staring into its amber glow as if mesmerized, her heart was in tumult,
her voice crying wordlessly, "Oh my darling, why did you leave me?
Why did you have to die?"

She had hardly ever seen him outside the office, had never been
invited to his flat at number 12, and had never invited him to Weaver's

Cottage or spoken to him of her private life. Yet for twenty-seven years he had been central to her existence. She had spent more of her waking hours with him than with any other human being. To her he was always Mr. Peverell, and he had called her Miss Blackett to others, Blackie to her face. She couldn't remember that her hands had ever touched his since that first meeting twenty-seven years ago, when, as a shy seventeen-year-old fresh from secretarial college, she had come to Innocent House for her interview and he had risen smiling from his desk to greet her. Her typing and shorthand skills had already been tested by the secretary who was leaving him to get married. Now, looking at the handsome scholarly face and into his incredibly blue eyes, she had known that this was the ultimate test. He had said little about the job—but then why should he? Miss Arkwright had already explained in intimidating detail what would be expected of her—but he had asked her about her journey and had said: "We have a launch which brings some of the staff to work. It can pick you up at Charing Cross Pier and bring you to work by the Thames—that is unless you're afraid of water."

And she had known that this was the test question, that she wouldn't get the job if she disliked the river. "No," she said, "I'm not afraid of water."

After that she had spoken little, almost incoherent with the thought of coming each day to this glittering palace. At the end of the interview he had said, "If you think you can be happy here, suppose we both give each other a month's trial."

At the end of the month he had said nothing, but she knew there was nothing he need say. She had been with him until the day he died.

She remembered the morning of his heart attack. Was it really only eight months ago? The door between their offices had been ajar, as it always was, as he liked it to be. The velvet snake with its intricately marked back, its red forked flannel tongue, had been curled at the foot. He had given one call, but in a voice so harsh and strangled that it was hardly recognizable as human, and she thought she was hearing some waterman shouting from the river. It had taken her a couple of seconds to realize that this disembodied, alien voice was calling her name. She had leapt from her chair, hearing it skid across the floor, and was at his desk, staring down at him. He was still in his chair, rigid, as if seized by rigor, not daring to move, grasping the arms with white knuckles, his eyes bulging beneath a forehead on which the sweat had started in glistening globules thick as pus. He gasped, "The pain, the pain! Get a doctor!"

Ignoring the telephone on his desk, she had fled to her own office as if only in that familiar place could she cope. She fumbled with the telephone book, then remembered that his doctor's name and number were in the small black reference book in her desk. She yanked open the drawer and plunged in her hand to find it, trying to remember the name, wanting desperately to return to that horror in the chair yet afraid of what she might find, knowing that she must get help and get it quickly. Then she remembered. Of course, the ambulance. She must call an ambulance. She punched at the telephone keys and heard a voice, calm, authoritative, and gave her message. The urgency, the terror in her voice must have convinced them. The ambulance would be on its way.

She recalled what happened afterwards, not in sequence but in a series of disconnected but vivid pictures. At the door of his office she had just time to glimpse Frances Peverell standing impotently at his side before Gerard Etienne came towards her and, firmly closing the door, said: "We don't want anyone else in here. He needs air."

It was to be the first of all the rejections that followed. She remembered the noises as the paramedics worked on him; his head turned from her as they bore him past covered in a red blanket; the sound of someone sobbing, someone who could have been herself; the emptiness of the office, empty, as it was in the morning when she arrived before him, or as it was at night when he left first, but now everlastingly, permanently empty of everything that had given it meaning. She had never seen him again. She had wanted to visit him in hospital and had asked Frances Peverell what time would be convenient, only to be told: "He's still in intensive care. Only family and the partners are allowed to visit. I'm sorry, Blackie."

The news had at first been reassuring. He was better, much better. They hoped he would soon be out of the intensive-care unit. And then, four days after the first, he had suffered a second, massive, heart attack and had died. At the cremation she had sat in the chapel three pews back, among other members of the staff. No one had consoled her; why should they? She wasn't one of the officially bereaved, not one of the family. When, outside the chapel, inspecting the wreaths of the mourners, unable to help herself, she had broken down, Claudia Etienne had looked briefly at her with a mixture of wonder and irritation, as if to say, "If his daughter and his friends can control themselves, why can't you?" The grief had been made to seem in bad taste, as presumptuous as was her wreath, ostentatious among the family's simple cut flowers. She had remembered overhearing Gerard Etienne's comment made to his sister. "God, Blackie's overdone it. That wreath wouldn't disgrace a New York Mafia funeral. What's she trying to do, making everyone think she was his mistress?"

And next day, at a small private ceremony, the five partners had
thrown his ashes into the Thames from the terrace of Innocent House.
She hadn't been asked to take part but Frances Peverell had come into
her office and said: "You might like to join us on the terrace, Blackie.
I think my father would have liked you to be there." She had stood
well back, careful not to be in their way. They had stood a little distanced
from each other, close to the edge of the terrace. The white ground
bones which were all that remained of Henry Peverell were in a tin
which looked to her curiously like a biscuit tin. They passed it from
hand to hand, took out a fistful of the grains and dropped or flung
them into the Thames. She remembered that it had been high tide with
a fresh breeze blowing. The river, ochre-brown, had slapped against
the jetty walls, sending out small droplets of spray. Frances Peverell's
hands had been damp; the fragments of bone had stuck to them and
afterwards she had wiped her hands surreptitiously against her skirt.
She had been perfectly calm as she had spoken by heart the words from
Cymbeline, beginning:

> *Fear no more the heat o' the sun,*
> *Nor the furious winter's rages;*
> *Thou thy worldly task hast done,*
> *Home art gone and ta'en thy wages.*

It seemed to Blackie that they had forgotten to decide on the order
of speaking and there was a short silence before James de Witt moved
closer to the edge of the terrace and spoke words from the Apocrypha.
"The souls of the righteous are in the hands of God, and there shall
no torment touch them." Afterwards he had let his portion of ashes
trickle from his hands as if counting every separate grain.

Gabriel Dauntsey had read a poem by Wilfred Owen which was unfamiliar to her, but afterwards she had looked it up and had wondered
a little at his choice.

> *I am the ghost of Shadwell Stair.*
> *Along the wharves by the water-house,*
> *And through the cavernous slaughter-house,*
> *I am the shadow that walks there.*
>
> *Yet I have flesh both firm and cool,*
> *And eyes tumultuous as the gems*

Of moons and lamps in the full Thames
When dusk sails wavering down the Pool.

Claudia Etienne had been the briefest, with just two lines:

The worst that can befall us, measured right,
Is a long slumber and a long goodnight.

She had spoken them loudly but rather fast with a fierce intensity which gave the impression that she disapproved of the whole charade. After her had come Jean-Philippe Etienne. He hadn't been seen at Innocent House since his retirement a year earlier and had been driven up from his remote house on the Essex coast by his chauffeur, arriving just before the ceremony was due to begin and leaving immediately afterwards without sharing the buffet lunch prepared in the boardroom. But his passage had been the longest and he had read it in a flat voice, holding on to one of the finials of the railings for support. De Witt had told her afterwards that it was from the *Meditations* of Marcus Aurelius but at the time only a brief passage impressed itself on Blackie's mind:

In a word all the things of the body are as a river, and the things of the soul as a dream and a vapour; and life is a warfare and a pilgrim's sojourn, and fame after death is only forgetfulness.

Gerard Etienne had been last. He had flung the ground bones from him as if shaking off all the past, and had spoken words from Ecclesiastes:

For to him that is joined to all the living there is hope: for a living dog is better than a dead lion.
For the living know that they shall die: but the dead know not any thing, neither have they any more a reward; for the memory of them is forgotten.
Also their love, and their hatred, and their envy, is now perished; neither have they any more a portion for ever in any thing that is done under the sun.

Afterwards they had turned away silently and gone up to the boardroom to their cold luncheon and wine. And at two o'clock precisely Gerard Etienne had walked without speaking through Blackie's room to the office beyond and had seated himself for the first time in Henry Peverell's chair. The lion was dead and the living dog had taken over.

7

After Sonia Clements' cremation James de Witt declined the invitation of Frances to join her and Gabriel in their taxi, saying instead that he felt in need of a walk and would take the tube from Golders Green Station. The walk from the crematorium was longer than he had expected, but he was glad to be alone. The rest of the Peverell Press staff had been driven home in the undertaker's cars and he couldn't decide which would have been worse, to contemplate Frances's taut unhappy face with no hope of comforting her or to be crushed in an over-full, ostentatious car with a gaggle of junior staff who had preferred a funeral to an afternoon's work and whose tongues, released after the spurious solemnity of the funeral, would have been inhibited by his presence. Even the temp, Mandy Price, had been there. But that was reasonable enough; after all, she had been present at the finding of the body.

The cremation had been a grim affair and for that he blamed himself. He always did blame himself, and sometimes reflected that to have so lively a sense of sin without the religion which could assuage it by absolution was an uncomfortable idiosyncrasy. Miss Clements' sister, the nun, had been at the funeral, appearing as if by magic at the last moment to take her seat at the back, and disappearing again with equal speed at the end, pausing only to shake hands with those of the Peverell Press staff who pressed forward to mutter their condolences. She had previously written to Claudia requesting the firm to make all the funeral arrangements and they should have done better. He should have taken more interest instead of leaving it all to Claudia, which in effect had meant leaving it to Claudia's secretary.

There should, he thought, be a service designed for those without a religion. Probably there was and they could have discovered it if they had taken the trouble. It might be an interesting, and possibly even lucrative, publishing venture, a book of alternative funeral rites for humanists, atheists and agnostics, a formal ceremony of remembrance, a celebration of the human spirit with no reference to its possible continuing existence. Striding to the station, his long coat flapping open, he amused himself selecting passages of prose and verse which might be included. De la Mare's "Look thy last on all things lovely," for a touch of nostalgic melancholy. Perhaps Oliver Gogarty's "Non Dolet," Keats' "Ode to Autumn" if the dead person were old and Shelley's "To a Skylark" if he were young. Wordsworth's "Lines Written Above Tintern Abbey" for the nature worshipper. There could be songs instead of hymns and the slow movement from Beethoven's *Emperor* Concerto would be an appropriate funeral march. And there was, of course, always the third chapter of Ecclesiastes:

> To every thing there is a season, and a time to every purpose under the heaven:
> A time to be born, and a time to die; a time to plant, and a time to pluck up that which is planted;
> A time to kill, and a time to heal; a time to break down, and a time to build up.

He could have concocted something suitable for Sonia, perhaps including extracts from a book she had commissioned and edited, a commemoration of twenty-four years of service to the firm which the living Sonia would have thought appropriate. It was odd, he thought, how important were these rites of passage, designed surely to comfort and minister to the needs of the living since they could never touch the dead.

He stopped to buy two cartons of semi-skimmed milk and a container of washing-up liquid at the supermarket at Notting Hill Gate before letting himself quietly into the house. It was apparent that Rupert had company, the sound of voices and of music came clearly down the stairs. He had hoped that Rupert would have been alone and wondered, as he so often did, that a man so ill could stand so much noise. But it was, after all, cheerful noise and Rupert stood it only for a limited period.

It was he, James, who coped afterwards with the inevitable reaction. Suddenly he felt that he couldn't face any of them. Instead he went into the kitchen and, without taking off his coat, made himself a mug of tea, then opened the back door and carried it out with him into the quietness and darkness of the garden and sat down on the wooden bench by the back door. It was a warm evening for late September and, sitting there as the darkness deepened, distanced from the racket and bright lights of Notting Hill Gate by no more than eighty yards, it seemed to him that this small garden held suspended in its quiet air all the remembered sweetness of summer and the loamy richness of autumn.

For ten years, ever since his godmother had left it to him, the house had been a source of unfailing pleasure and contentment. He hadn't expected to enjoy such a keen or self-indulgent satisfaction in ownership, having deceived himself since boyhood with the conviction that, except for his pictures, material possessions were unimportant to him. He knew now that one possession, and that the most solid and permanent, had become central to his life. He liked its unassuming Regency façade, the shuttered windows, the double drawing-room on the first floor looking out over the street at the front and with a conservatory built out at the back, giving a view of his own small garden and those of his neighbours. He liked the eighteenth-century furniture which his godmother had brought with her to the house when comparative poverty had driven her to this then humble street, not yet gentrified, still a little shabby. She had left him everything but her pictures, and here their tastes differed and he didn't repine. The drawing-room was fitted with bookshelves four feet high on every wall, and above them he had hung his own prints and water-colours. The house still retained an air of discriminating femininity but he had no wish to impose upon it a more masculine taste. He came back to it each evening, into the small but elegant hall with its faded wallpaper and its gently curved staircase, with a sense of entering a private, secure and wholly pleasing world. But that was before he took in Rupert.

Rupert Farlow had published his first novel with the Peverell Press fifteen years previously and James could still remember the mixture of excitement and awe with which he had read the manuscript, submitted not through an agent, but to the Press direct, badly typed on unsuitable paper and accompanied by no explanatory letter but merely with Rupert's name and address, as if he challenged the as yet unknown reader to recognize its quality. His second novel, two years later, had been less generously received, as second novels often are after a spectacular initial success, but James hadn't been disappointed. Here, confirmed, was a major talent. And then silence. Rupert was no longer seen in London and letters and telephone calls went unanswered. It was rumoured that he was in North Africa, California, India. And then, briefly, he had reappeared but he had brought no new work with him. There had never been another novel and now there never would be. It was Frances Peverell who mentioned to James that she had heard that Rupert was dying of AIDS and was in a West London hospice. She didn't visit but James did, and continued to visit. Rupert was in remission but the hospice staff were in difficulty about what to do with him. His flat was unsuitable, his landlord unsympathetic, he hated the camaraderie of the hospice. These things emerged without complaint. Rupert never complained except about the trivia of life. He seemed to regard his illness not as a cruel and unjust affliction but as an end ordained and inescapable, to be endured, not resented. Rupert was dying with courage and grace, but he was still the old Rupert, malicious or mischievous, tricky or temperamental, as you chose to describe him. Tentatively, afraid that the offer might be resented or misunderstood, James had suggested that Rupert should join him in Hillgate Village. The offer had been accepted and four months earlier Rupert had moved in.

Peace, the old order, the old security, had all vanished. Rupert found difficulty in managing stairs so James had installed a bed for him in the drawing-room and he spent most of the day there or in the conservatory when it was sunny. There was a lavatory and shower on the first floor and a room little bigger than a cupboard which James had made into a kitchen fitted with an electric kettle and a double burner where he could make coffee or toasted sandwiches. The first floor had become, in effect, a small self-contained flat which Rupert had taken over and on which he had imposed his untidy, iconoclastic, mischievous personality. Ironically the house had become less peaceful now that it was home to a dying man. There was a constant stream of callers: Rupert's present and old buddies; his reflexologist; the masseuse, who left behind her a smell of exotic oils; Father Michael, who came, so Rupert said, to hear his confession but whose ministrations seemed to be regarded by him with the same amused indulgence with which he accepted those concerned with his bodily needs. The friends were seldom there when James was home, except at weekends, although the evidence of their visits met him every evening: flowers, magazines, fruit, bottles of sweet-smelling oils. They gossiped, made coffee, were given drinks. Once he said to Rupert, "Does Father Michael enjoy his wine?"

"He certainly knows which bottles to bring up."

"That's all right then."

James didn't grudge Father Michael his claret as long as the man knew what he was drinking.

He had provided Rupert with a brass hand-bell, strident as a school bell, which he had found in the Portobello Market, so that Rupert could summon him from his bedroom above if he needed help in the night. He now slept badly, half expecting to hear that clamorous summons, imagining, half-awake, the rumble of death-carts in plague-ridden London, the wailing call, "Bring out your dead."

He could remember every word of that conversation two months ago, Rupert's watchful ironic eyes, his smiling face daring him to disbelieve.

"I'm just telling you the facts. Gerard Etienne knew that Eric had AIDS, and he made sure that we met each other. I'm not complaining, far from it. I had some choice in the matter. Gerard didn't actually tuck us up in bed together."

"It's a pity you didn't exercise it, the choice."

"But I did. I don't pretend that I gave it much thought. You never knew Eric, did you? He was beautiful. Very few people are. Attractive, handsome, sexy, good-looking, all the usual adjectives, but not beautiful. But Eric was. I've always found beauty irresistible."

"And that's all you required in a lover, physical beauty?"

Rupert had mimicked him, eyes and voice gently mocking.

"And that's all you required in a lover? My dear James, what sort of world do you live in, what sort of person are you? No, that wasn't all I required. Required. Past tense, I notice. It would have been a bit more sensitive to watch your grammar. No it wasn't all. I wanted someone who fancied me too and had certain skills in bed. I didn't ask Eric whether he preferred jazz to chamber music, or opera to ballet, or, more important, what wine he preferred. I'm talking about desire, I'm talking about love. Christ, it's like explaining Mozart to the tone-deaf. Look, let's leave it at this: Gerard Etienne deliberately threw us together. At the time he knew that Eric had AIDS. He might have hoped we'd become lovers, he might have intended us to become lovers, he might not have cared a damn either way. Perhaps he was amusing himself. I don't know what he had in mind. I don't much care. I know what I had in mind."

"And Eric, knowing he had an infectious disease, didn't tell you? What in God's name was he thinking of?"

"Well, not at first. He told me later. I'm not blaming him, and if I don't you can keep your moral judgements. And I don't know what he was thinking of. I don't pry into my friends' minds. Perhaps he wanted a companion for the last mile or so before he set off to explore that long silence." He had added: "Don't you forgive your friends?"

"Forgiveness is hardly a word to use between friends. But then, none of my friends has infected me with a fatal disease."

"But my dear James, you don't exactly give them the chance, do you?"

He had questioned Rupert with the detached persistence of a trained investigator, needing to force the truth out of him, desperate to know. "How can you be sure that Etienne knew Eric was ill?"

"James, don't cross-examine me. You sound like a prosecuting counsel. And you do love euphemisms, don't you? He knew because Eric told him. Etienne asked him when he could expect another book. The Peverell Press had done rather well with his first travel book. Etienne had got it cheap and probably hoped for the next one on the same terms. Eric told him there wouldn't be one. He hadn't the energy or the inclination. He had other plans for the rest of his life."

"And those included you."

"Eventually. It was two weeks after that conversation that Etienne arranged the river trip. Suspicious in itself, wouldn't you say? Not Etienne's kind of jolly at all. Chug chug down dear Old Father Thames to inspect the flood barrier, chug chug back again with smoked-salmon sandwiches and champagne. How did you manage to avoid it, by the way?"

"I was in France."

"So you were. Your second home. Odd that old Etienne has been so content to spend all these years away from his native land. Gerard and Claudia don't go there either, do they? You'd think they might occasionally like to see the place where Papa and his mates had such a jolly time popping away at Germans from behind the rocks. They never go and you can't keep away. What do you do there, check up on him?"

"Why should I do that?"

"It was only a remark, I meant nothing. Anyway, you'll never pin anything on old Etienne. He's been authenticated; there's no doubt there, the genuine hero."

"Go on about the river trip."

"Oh, it was the usual thing. Giggling typists, Miss Blackett a little tipsy, red puffy face, that awful virginal archness. She'd brought that draught-excluder snake with her. Hissing Sid they call it. Extraordinary woman. Absolutely no humour, I would have said, except about that snake. Some of the girls hung it over the side threatening to drown it, and one of them pretended to feed it champagne. In the end they wound it round Eric's neck and he wore it all the way home. But that was later. On the way up-river I took refuge in the bow. Eric was standing there alone, perfectly still, like a figurehead. He turned and looked at me." Rupert paused, and then said almost in a whisper: "He turned round and looked at me. James, what I've just told you, better forget."

"No, I shan't do that. Are you telling me the truth?"

"Of course, don't I always?"

"No, Rupert, not always."

Suddenly his reverie was broken. The kitchen door was flung open and Rupert's buddy thrust out his head. "I thought I heard the front door. We're just off. Rupert was asking if you were back. You usually go straight up."

"Yes," he said, "I usually go straight up."

"So what are you doing out here?"

He asked it with little curiosity, but James replied: "Musing on the third chapter of Ecclesiastes."

"I think Rupert wants you."

"I'm coming now," and he mounted, painfully as an old man, to the disorder, the warmth, the exotic overcrowded muddle that was now his sitting-room.

8

It was nine o'clock and on the top floor of a terraced house off Westbourne Grove Claudia Etienne lay in bed with her lover.

She said: "I wonder why one always feels randy after a funeral. The potent conjunction of death and sex, I suppose. Did you know that Victorian prostitutes used to service their clients in graveyards on the flat tops of the tombs?"

"Hard, cold and sinister. I hope they got piles. It wouldn't turn me on. I'd keep thinking of the rotting body underneath and all those bloated worms creeping in and out of the orifices. Darling, what extraordinary facts you do know. Being with you is an education."

"Yes," she said. "I know it is." She was wondering whether he, like her, had more than historical facts in mind. "Being with you," he had said, not "loving you."

He turned towards her, propping his head on his hand. "Was the funeral ghastly?"

"It managed to be tedious and grim at the same time, canned music, a coffin which looked as if it had been recycled, a liturgy revised to offend no one, including God, and a parson who did his best to give the impression that we were engaged in something that had meaning."

He said: "When my turn comes I'd like to be burnt on a funeral pyre by the sea like Keats."

"Shelley."

"That poet, whoever he was. A hot windy night, no coffin, lots of booze and all one's mates swimming naked, then dancing round the fire, all being happily warmed by me. And the ashes could be washed away by the next tide. Do you think if I left instructions in my will someone would arrange it?"

"I shouldn't rely on it. You'll probably end up at Golders Green like the rest of us."

His bedroom was small and the floor space almost entirely occupied by a five-foot-wide Victorian bed in ornamental brass, the high bedposts crowned with knobs. From these Declan had suspended a Victorian patchwork quilt, in part badly tattered. It hung above them as they made love, lit by the bedside lamp, a rich patterned canopy of gleaming silk and satin. Some shreds of the silk hung down and she had an impulse now to pick at them. The scraps were, she saw, lined with old letters, the black spider-marks of the long-dead hand plainly visible. A family's history, a family's troubles and triumphs pressed down upon them.

His kingdom, and it seemed to her a kingdom, lay beneath them. The shop, the whole property, was owned by Mr. Simon—she had never learned his forename—and he rented the top two floors to Declan at a ridiculous sum and paid him with equal frugality for managing the shop. He himself was always there in his black skull-cap to greet favoured customers, sitting at a Dickensian desk just inside the door, but otherwise he took little part in buying and selling, although he controlled the flow of cash. The front of the house was arranged under his personal supervision, the pick of the furniture, pictures and artefacts displayed to advantage. It was the back of the ground floor which Declan had made his domain. It was a long conservatory of strengthened glass with at each end two palm-trees, the slender trunks of iron, and the fronds, which trembled as the hand brushed against them, sheets of tin painted a bright green. This touch of Mediterranean sun contrasted with the conservatory's faintly ecclesiastical air. Some of the original lower panes of glass had been replaced by oddly shaped pieces of stained glass from demolished churches: a jigsaw of yellow-haired angels and haloed saints, lugubrious apostles, fragments of a nativity scene or of the last supper, domestic vignettes of hands pouring wine into pitchers or lifting loaves of bread. Placed in happy disorder on a variety of tables, piled up on chairs, were the objects acquired by Declan and it was here that his personal customers rummaged, exclaimed, admired and made their discoveries.

And there were discoveries to be made. Declan, as Claudia admitted, had an eye. He loved beauty, variety, oddity. He was extraordinarily knowledgeable in fields of which she knew little. She was as amazed by the things he knew as by the things he didn't know. Occasionally his findings would be promoted to the front of the shop, when he would immediately lose interest in them, but his love for all his acquisitions was fickle. "You do see, Claudia darling, how I had to have it? You do see how I couldn't not buy?" He would stroke, admire, research, gloat over every acquisition, give it pride of place. But three months later it would have mysteriously disappeared, to be replaced by the new enthusiasm. There was no attempt at display; objects were jumbled together, the worthless and the good. A Staffordshire commemorative figure of Garibaldi on a Horse, a cracked Bloor Derby sauce tureen, coins and medals, stuffed birds under domed glass, sentimental Victorian water-colours, bronze busts of Disraeli and Gladstone, a heavy Victorian commode, a pair of art-deco gilt wood chairs, a stuffed bear, a heavily encrusted German air-force officer's cap.

She had said, examining the latter: "What are you selling this as, property of the late Field Marshal Hermann Goering?"

She knew nothing about his past. Once he had said in a broad and unconvincing Irish accent, "Sure, aren't I just a poor Tipperary boy, my ma dead and my pa off God knows where," but she didn't believe it. There was no hint to background or family in his light, carefully cultivated voice. When they were married—if they were married—she supposed that he would tell her something about himself, and if not she would probably ask. At present an instinct warned her that it was unwise and kept her silent. It was difficult to imagine him with an orthodox past life, parents and siblings, school, a first job. It sometimes seemed to her that he was an exotic changeling who had spontaneously materialized in that crowded back room, reaching out acquisitive fingers to the objects of past centuries, but himself having no reality except in the present moment.

They had met six months earlier, sitting in adjacent seats in the tube on a day when there had been a major breakdown on the Central Line. During the seemingly interminable wait before they were instructed to leave the train and make their way along the track, he had glanced at her copy of the *Independent* and, when their eyes had met, had smiled apologetically and said: "I'm sorry, it's rude I know, but I'm slightly claustrophobic. I always find it easier to cope with these delays when I have something to read. Usually I have."

She had replied, "I've finished with it. Do have it. Anyway I've got a book in my briefcase."

So they had sat together, both reading, neither speaking, but she had been very aware of him. She told herself that this was a result of tension and of a touch of fear. When the instructions to leave the train had at last come there was no panic, but it had been a disagreeable experience and for some very frightening. One or two comedians had reacted to the tension with attempts at crude humour and loud laughter, but most had endured in silence. There had been an elderly woman sitting close to them in obvious distress and they had half carried her between them, helping her along the track. She told them that she had a heart condition and was asthmatic and was afraid that the dust in the tunnel might cause an attack.

When they reached the station and had left her in the care of one of the nurses on duty, he had turned to Claudia and said: "I think we deserve a drink. I need one anyway. Shall we find a pub?"

She had told herself that there was nothing like a common peril followed by a shared benevolence to promote intimacy and knew that it would be wiser now to say goodbye and be on her way. Instead she had agreed. By the time they finally parted she knew where it would end. But she had taken her time. She had never begun a love-affair without the private assurance that she was in control, more loved than loving, more likely to cause pain than to be hurt herself. She couldn't be sure of that now.

About a month after they had become lovers he had said: "Why don't we get married?"

The suggestion—she hardly regarded it as a proposal—was so surprising that for a moment she was silent. He went on: "Don't you think it would be a good idea?"

She found that she was treating the suggestion seriously without knowing whether to him it was just one more of the ideas he occasionally put forward without expecting her to believe them, and apparently not much caring whether she did or not.

She said slowly: "If you're serious then the answer is that it would be a very bad idea."

"All right, let's get engaged. I like the idea of a permanent engagement."

"That's an illogicality."

"Why? Old Simon would like it. I could say 'I'm expecting my fiancée.' He'd be less shocked when you stay the night."

"He's never shown the slightest sign of being shocked. I doubt whether he would care if we fornicated in the front room provided we didn't frighten the customers or damage the stock."

But he did occasionally speak of her to old Simon as "my fiancée," and she felt she could hardly deny the description without making both of them seem foolish or giving the whole thing an importance which it didn't merit. He didn't again mention marriage but she was disconcerted to realize that, with part of her mind, the idea was beginning to take hold.

When she had arrived that evening from the crematorium she had greeted Mr. Simon, then gone straight into the back room. Declan had been peering at a miniature. She enjoyed watching him with the object with which, however transitory the affection, he was momentarily enthused. It was a picture of an eighteenth-century lady, her décolleté bodice and frilled chemisette painted with great delicacy, the face under the high powdered wig perhaps too sweetly pretty.

He had said: "Paid for, I imagine, by a wealthy lover. She looks more like a tart than a wife, doesn't she? I think it could be by Richard Corey. If so, it's a find. You do see, darling, how I had to have it?"

"Where did you get it?"

"A woman who had advertised some drawings she thought were originals. They weren't. This is."

"How much did you pay?"

"Three fifty. She would have taken less. She was pretty desperate. I like to spread a little happiness by paying slightly more than is expected."

"And it's worth about three times as much, I suppose."

"About that. Lovely, isn't it? The thing itself I mean. There's a strand of her hair curled in the back. I don't think this should go into the front room, it could be nicked in a second. Old Simon's eyes aren't what they were."

She said: "He's looking pretty ill to me. Shouldn't you encourage him to see a doctor?"

"No point, I've tried. He hates doctors. He's terrified they'll send him into hospital and he hates hospitals even more. For him hospitals are places where people die and he doesn't like to think about dying. Not surprising when the rest of your family have been wiped out in Auschwitz."

Now, turning away from her onto his back and staring up at the patterned silk on which the bedside lamp shed a soft glow, he said: "Have you spoken to Gerard yet?"

"No, not yet. I'll do that after the next board meeting."

"Look, Claudia, I want this shop. I need it. I've made it. Everything that's different about it is because of me. Old Simon can't sell it to someone else."

"I know. We'll have to see that he doesn't."

How strange it was, she thought, this urge to give, to satisfy the lover's every desire as if propitiating him for the burden of being loved. Or was there a deeper irrational belief that he deserved to get what he wanted when he wanted it simply by virtue of being lovable? And when Declan wanted something he wanted it with the insistence of a spoiled child, without reserve, without dignity, without patience. But she told herself that this particular want was adult and rational. The freehold comprising the two flats and all the shop would be a snip at £350,000. Simon wanted to sell, and wanted to sell to him, but he couldn't wait much longer.

She said: "Has he spoken to you recently? How much longer can we have?"

"He wants a decision by the end of October, but the sooner the better. He yearns to go and lay his old bones in the sun."

"But he wouldn't find another purchaser in a hurry."

"No, but he wants to put it on the market if we don't give him a definite answer by then. He'll ask more, of course, than he's asking from me."

Claudia said slowly: "I'm going to suggest to Gerard that he buys me out."

"You mean all your shares in the Peverell Press? Can he afford to?"

"Not without difficulty, but if he agrees he'll find the money."

"And there's no other way you can get it?"

She thought, I could sell the Barbican flat and move in here, but what sort of solution would that be to anything? She said: "I haven't got £350,000 sitting on deposit in the bank, if that's what you mean."

He persisted again: "Gerard's your brother. Surely he'll help."

"We aren't close. How could we be? After our mother died we were sent away separately to school. We hardly saw each other until we both started work at Innocent House. He'll buy my shares if he thinks it's to his advantage. Otherwise he won't."

"When will you ask him?"

"After the board meeting on October the fourteenth."

"Why wait until then?"

"Because then will be the best time."

They lay for minutes in silence.

Suddenly she said: "Look, Declan, let's go on the river on the fourteenth. Why don't you call for me at six-thirty and we'll take the launch down to the Thames Barrier. You've never seen it after dark."

"I haven't seen it at all. Won't it be cold?"

"Not particularly. Wear something warm. I'll bring a thermos of soup and the wine. It really is worth seeing, Declan, those great hoods rising out of the dark river towering over you. Do come. We could put in at Greenwich for a pub meal."

"All right," he said. "Why not? I'll come. I don't see why you have to fix it now, but I'll come as long as I don't have to meet your brother."

"I can promise you that."

"Six-thirty then at Innocent House. We could make it earlier if you like."

"Six-thirty is the earliest. The launch won't be free until then."

He said: "You make it sound important."

"Yes," she said. "Yes, it is important, important for both of us."

9

Gabriel left Frances as soon as the game was finished, a game he easily won. She saw with compunction that he looked very tired and wondered if he had come up out of compassion for her rather than from his own need for company. The funeral must have been worse for him than for the other partners. He was after all the only member of staff for whom Sonia had appeared to have any affection. Her own tentative attempts at friendship had been subtly rebuffed by Sonia, almost as if being a Peverell disqualified her for intimacy. Perhaps alone among the partners he was feeling a personal grief.

The game had stimulated her mind and she knew that to go to bed now would only result in one of those nights of alternate restlessness and brief periods of sleep which brought her to the morning more tired than if she had never been to bed. On impulse she went to the hall cupboard for her warm winter coat, then, putting out the light, opened the window and stepped outside onto the balcony. The night air smelled cold and clean with the familiar tang of the river. Grasping the rail, she felt as if she were suspended, disembodied in air. A cluster of low cloud lay over London, stained pink like a lint bandage which had soaked up the city's blood. Then, as she watched, the clouds moved slowly apart and she saw the clear blue-black of the night sky and a single star. A helicopter like a jewelled metallic dragonfly clattered upstream. This was how her father had stood night after night before going to bed. She would be busy in the kitchen after dinner and would come into the sitting-room to find it in darkness except for the one low lamp, and would see the dark shadow of that silent motionless figure standing there looking out over the river.

They had moved to number 12 in 1983, when the firm was expanding in one of its periods of comparative prosperity, and extra office space was needed at Innocent House. Number 12 had been let to a long-standing tenant who had conveniently died, freeing the property to be converted to provide a top flat for herself and her father and a smaller one at the bottom of the house for Gabriel Dauntsey. Her father had accepted the need to move philosophically, had indeed seemed almost to welcome it, and she suspected that it was only after she joined him in 1985, on leaving Oxford, that he began to find the flat restrictive, almost claustrophobic.

Her mother, never strong, had died suddenly and unexpectedly of viral pneumonia when Frances was five and she had spent all her childhood with her father and a nurse in Innocent House. Only in adult life had she realized how extraordinary those early years had been, how unsuitable the house as a family home, even for a family diminished by death, to the two of them, father and daughter. She had had no young companions; only a few remaining Georgian squares in the East End which had survived the bombing had become fashionable enclaves for the middle classes. Her playground was the glittering marble hall and the forecourt and here, despite the protective railings, she was always closely supervised, permitted no bicycle or ball games. The streets were unsafe for a child and she, with Nanny Bostock, was taken, occasionally by the firm's launch, across the river to a small private school in Greenwich where the emphasis was on gentility rather than the development of questioning intelligence, but where she had at least been given a good grounding. But on most days the launch was needed to pick up members of staff from the Thames pier and she and Nanny Bostock would be driven to the Greenwich foot tunnel, and always accompanied on their subterranean walk by the chauffeur or by her father for extra safety.

It never occurred to the adults that she found the foot tunnel terrifying and she would have died rather than tell them. She had known from early childhood that her father admired courage above all virtues. She would walk between them, holding their hands in a simulation of childish meekness, trying not to grasp the fingers too hard, keeping her eyes down so that they couldn't see that they were tightly closed, smelling the distinctive tunnel smell, hearing the echo of their feet and picturing above them that great weight of slopping water, terrifying in its power, which one morning would break the tunnel roof and begin to seep through, at first in heavy drops as the tiles cracked and then, suddenly, in a thundering wave, black and evil-smelling, sweeping them off their feet, swirling and rising, until there was nothing between their fighting bodies and screaming mouths but a few inches of space and air. And then not even that.

Five minutes later, they would come up by the lift into the daylight to see the gleaming magnificence of Greenwich Naval College with its twin cupolas and gold-tipped weathervanes. For the child it was like coming out of hell and having her eyes dazzled by the celestial city. Here, too, was the *Cutty Sark* with her tall masts and slender lines. Her father would tell her about the East India Company's monopoly of trade with the Far East in the eighteenth century and how these great clippers, built for speed, would vie with each other to bring to the British market in record time the perishable and valuable tea of China and India.

From her earliest years her father had told her stories of the river, which for him had been almost an obsession, a great artery, endlessly fascinating, constantly changing, bearing on its strong tide the whole history of England. He told her of the rafts and coracles of the first Thames voyagers, the square sails of the Roman ships bringing cargo to Londinium, the Viking long-boats with their curved prows. He would describe to her the river of the early eighteenth century, when London was the greatest port in the world and the wharfs and quays with their tall-masted ships looked like a wind-denuded forest. He told her of the raucous life of the waterfront and the many trades which drew their life from this bloodstream: the stevedores or lumpers, the water-men who worked the lighters which provisioned the vessels as they rode at anchor, suppliers of rope and tackle, boat-builders, ships' bakers, carpenters, rat-catchers, lodging-house keepers, pawnbrokers, publicans, marine-store dealers, rich and poor alike, drawing their life from the river. He had described for her the great occasions: Henry VIII in the gold-crested royal barge being rowed up-river to Hampton Court, the long oars sweeping upwards in salute; Lord Nelson's body taken up-river in 1806 from Greenwich in the barge originally built for Charles II; river festivities; floods and tragedies. She yearned for his love and approbation. She had listened dutifully, had asked the right questions, had instinctively known that this was an interest he assumed that she would share. But she realized now that the deception had only added guilt to her natural reserve and timidity, that the river had become the more terrifying because she could not acknowledge its terrors and her relationship with her father more distant because it was founded on a lie.

But she had made for herself another world and, lying awake at night in that glittering, un-cosy nursery, curled womb-like under the sheets, she would enter its gentle security. In this imaginary life she had a sister and brother and lived with them in a large country rectory. There was a garden with an orchard and a fruit cage and vegetables planted in rows separated by neat box hedges from the wide green lawns. Beyond the garden was a gentle stream, only inches deep, which they could leap across, and an old oak with a tree house, snug as a hutch, where they sat and read and scrunched apples. The three of them slept in the nursery, looking out over the lawn and rose garden to the church tower, and there were no raucous voices, no river smell, no image of terror, only tenderness and peace. There was a mother too; tall, fair, with a long blue dress and a half-remembered face, walking towards her across the lawn, arms outstretched for her to leap into because she was the youngest and the best-loved.

There was, she knew, the adult equivalent of this unfrightening world available to her. She could marry James de Witt and move into his charming house in Hillgate Village and have his children, the children she, too, wanted. She could rely on his love, be certain of his kindness, know that, whatever problems their marriage might bring, there would be no cruelty and no rejection. She might have taught herself, not to desire him, since that was not susceptible to the will, but to find in kindness and gentleness a substitute for desire, so that in time sex with him would become possible, even agreeable, at its lowest a price to be paid for his love, at its highest a pledge of affection and of belief that love could in time beget love. But for three months she had been Gerard Etienne's mistress. After that wonder, that astonishing revelation, she found that she couldn't even bear James to touch her. Gerard, taking her casually, discarding her equally casually, had deprived her even of the consolation of the second best.

It was always the terror of the river, not its romance or its mystery, which had held her imagination and, with Gerard's brutal rejection, these terrors, which she thought she had put away with childhood, reasserted themselves. This Thames was a dark tide of horror; that sodden algae-matted gate, leading into the fastness of the Tower, the thud of the axe, the tide lapping Wapping Old Stairs, where pirates were taken and tied to the piles at low water until three tides—the Grace of Wapping—had flowed over them; the stinking hulks lying off Gravesend with their fettered human cargo. Even the river steamers

butting upstream, their decks loud with laughter and brightly patterned
with holiday-makers, brought back to mind unbidden the greatest of
all Thames tragedies, when, in 1878, the paddle-steamer *Princess Alice*,
returning loaded from a trip to Sheerness, was mown down by a collier
and 640 people drowned. It seemed to her now that it was their screams
that she heard in the cries of the gulls and, looking down at night at
the dark river splattered with light, she could imagine the pale upward
faces of the drowned children torn from their mothers' arms floating
like frail petals on the dark tide.

When she was fifteen her father had taken her for her first visit to
Venice. He had said that fifteen was the earliest age at which a child
could appreciate Renaissance art and architecture, but she had suspected
even then that he preferred to travel alone and that taking her was a
duty which he could no longer reasonably defer, but a duty nevertheless
which held some promise of hope for both of them.

It was their first and last holiday together. She had expected bright,
hot sun, gaudily clad gondoliers on blue water, gleaming marble palaces,
dining alone with him in one of the new dresses chosen for her by the
housekeeper, Mrs. Rawlings, for the occasion, drinking wine at dinner
for the first time. She had longed desperately for the holiday to be a
new beginning. It had begun badly. They had had to travel in the school
holidays and the city was overcrowded. For the whole ten days the sky
had been leaden with intermittent rain, its heavy drops pitting canals
as brown as the Thames. Her impression was of constant noise, raucous
foreign voices, the terror of losing her father in the crush, of dimly lit
old churches in which the attendant would shuffle to switch on the light
and illumine a fresco, a painting, an altarpiece. The air would be heavy
with incense and the sour mustiness of wet clothes. Her father would
edge her to the front of the jostling tourists and whisper to her, explaining the paintings, above the noise of discordant tongues and the
distant calls of peremptory guides.

One picture remained strongly in memory. A mother nursing her
baby under a stormy sky, a solitary male watcher. She knew that there
was something to which she should respond, some mystery of subject
and intention, and she longed to share her father's excitement, to say
something which, if it couldn't be clever, would at least not cause him
to turn away with the silent disapproval to which she had become
accustomed. Always at the bad moments there were remembered words.
"Madam was never the same after the child was born. That pregnancy
killed her, no doubt about that. And now look what we've got landed
with." The woman, her name and purpose in the house now long

forgotten, had probably only meant that what they were faced with was a large unmanageable house without the controlling hand of a mistress, but to the child the meaning of the words had been plain and had remained plain. "She killed her mother and look what we've got in exchange."

Another memory of that holiday remained sharp in the years to follow. It was on their first visit to the Accademia and, holding her gently by the shoulder, he had led her to a picture by Vittore Carpaccio, *The Dream of St. Ursula*. They were, for once, alone, and, standing beside him, aware of the weight of his hand, she had found herself looking at her bedroom in Innocent House. Here were the twin rounded windows with their top half-moons filled with discs of bottle-glass, the corner door ajar, the two vases on the window-shelf so like those at home, the same bed, a delicate four-poster with a high carved headboard and a tasselled fringe. Her father had said: "See, you sleep in a fifteenth-century Venetian bedroom."

There was a woman in the bed, resting her head on her hand. Frances had asked, "Is that lady dead?"

"Dead? Why should she be dead?"

She had heard in his voice the familiar sharpness. She hadn't answered, had said no more. The silence between them lengthened until, with the hand still on her shoulder but pressing more heavily now, or so it seemed, he had turned her away. But she had failed him again. It had always been her fate to be sensitive to his every mood but without the skill or the confidence to meet that mood or respond to his need.

They were divided even by religion. Her mother had been a Roman Catholic, but how devout she neither knew nor had any means of discovering. Mrs. Rawlings, a co-religionist employed a year before her mother's death to be half housekeeper to the ailing woman, half child-minder, had been punctilious in taking her every Sunday to Mass but had otherwise ignored her religious education, giving the child the impression that religion was something her father couldn't understand and could barely tolerate, a feminine secret best not spoken of in his presence. They seldom went more than twice to any church. It was as if Mrs. Rawlings was a taster of religion, sampling the variety of ritual, architecture, music and sermons on offer, afraid of a premature commitment, of being recognized by the congregation, welcomed as a regular by the priest at the door, enticed into parish activities, perhaps even expected to receive visitors at Innocent House. As Frances grew older she suspected that finding a new church for Sunday-morning

Mass had become something of a private initiative test for Mrs. Rawlings, affording a sense of adventure and providing a measure of variety to her otherwise monotonous week and a lively subject of conversation on their way home.

"Not a very good choir, was it? Hardly up to Oratory standard. We must go to the Oratory again when I've got the energy. Too far for every Sunday but at least the sermon was short. I can't be doing with long sermons. Very few souls saved after the first ten minutes, if you ask me."

"I don't like that Father O'Brien. That's what he calls himself apparently. Very poor attendance. No wonder he was so friendly at the door. Wanted to entice us back next week, I don't wonder."

"Nice Stations of the Cross they've got. I like them carved. Those painted ones we saw at St Michael's last week were too gaudy by half. And at least the choirboys had clean surplices, someone did a good job of ironing there."

After one Sunday morning, when they had heard Mass at a particularly dull church where the rain had clattered like hailstones on the temporary tin roof ("Not our class of person. We won't be going there again."), Frances had asked: "Why do I have to go to Mass every Sunday?"

"Because your ma was RC. That's what your father agreed. The boys would be brought up C of E, the daughters RC. Well, he got you."

He had got her. The despised sex. The despised religion.

Mrs. Rawlings said: "There's plenty of religions in the world. Everyone can find something to suit them. All you have to remember is that ours is the only true one. But there's no point in thinking about it too much, not until you have to. I think we'll go back to the cathedral next week. It'll be Corpus Christi. They'll put on a grand show for that, I shouldn't wonder."

It was a relief to her father and to her when, at twelve, she was sent to the convent. He had come himself to collect her at the end of the first term and she had overheard the Mother Superior's words as she said goodbye to them at the door: "Mr. Peverell, the child has had virtually no instruction in her faith."

"In my wife's faith. Then, Mother Bridget, I suggest that you instruct her."

They had with gentle patience done that for her, and much more. They had given her a brief period of security, the sense that she was valued, that it was possible she could be loved. They had prepared her for Oxford, which she supposed she ought to consider a bonus since

Mother Bridget had frequently impressed on her that the intention of a true Catholic education was to prepare her for death. They had done that too, but she was less sure that they had prepared her for life. Certainly they hadn't prepared her for Gerard Etienne.

She turned back into the sitting-room, closing the window firmly behind her. The sound of the river became faint, a gentle susurration on the night air. Gabriel had said to her, "He can have no power over you unless you give it to him." Somehow she had to find the will and the courage to break that power finally and for ever.

10

Mandy's first four weeks at Innocent House, which began inauspiciously with a suicide and were to end dramatically in murder, seemed in retrospect one of the happiest months of her working life. As always, she adapted quickly to the daily routine of the office and with a few exceptions liked her fellow workers. She was given plenty to do, which suited her, and the work was more varied and more interesting than that which normally came her way.

At the end of her first week Mrs. Crealey had asked if she was happy and Mandy had replied that there were worse jobs and that she might as well stick it out for a bit longer, which was as far as she ever went in expressing satisfaction with a job. She had rapidly become accepted at Innocent House; youth and vitality combined with high efficiency are seldom resented for long. Miss Blackett, after a week of staring across at her with repressive severity, had apparently decided that she had known worse temps. Mandy, always quick to recognize her own interest, treated Miss Blackett with a flattering mixture of deference and confidence: fetching her coffee from the kitchen, asking her advice although with no intention of taking it and accepting some of the duller routine tasks with cheerful goodwill. Privately she thought the poor old thing was pathetic; you had to be sorry for her. It was obvious that Mr. Gerard for one couldn't stand the sight of her, and no wonder. Mandy's private opinion was that Miss Blackett was for the chop. They were, in any case, too busy to spend time considering how little they had in common and how much each deplored the other's clothes, hairstyle and attitude to senior staff. Nor was Mandy required to spend every day in Miss Blackett's office. She was frequently called to take shorthand from Miss Claudia or Mr. de Witt, and one Tuesday when George was away ill with a violent stomach upset she took over the reception desk and coped with the switchboard with no more than a few misdirected calls.

On the Wednesday and Thursday of her second week she spent two days in the publicity department helping to organize a couple of publicity tours and a signing session and was introduced by Maggie FitzGerald, Miss Etienne's assistant, to the foibles of authors, those unpredictable and oversensitive creatures on whom, as Maggie reluctantly conceded, the fortunes of Peverell Press ultimately depended. There were the frighteners, who were best left to Miss Claudia to cope with; the timid and insecure, who needed constant reassurance before they could utter even one word on a BBC chat-show and for whom the prospect of a literary luncheon induced a mixture of inarticulate terror and indigestion. Equally hard to handle were the aggressively overconfident, who, if not restrained, would break free of their minder and leap into any convenient shop with offers to sign their books, thus reducing the carefully worked-out publicity schedule to chaos. But the worst, Maggie confided, were the conceited, usually those whose books sold the least well, but who demanded first-class fares, five-star hotels, a limousine and a senior member of staff to escort them, and who wrote furious letters of complaint if their signings didn't attract a queue round the block. Mandy enjoyed her two days in publicity: the youthful enthusiasm of the staff, cheerful voices calling against the perpetual stridency of the telephone, salesmen vociferously welcomed, homing in for gossip and an exchange of news, the sense of urgency and impending crisis. She returned to her seat in Miss Blackett's room with reluctance.

She was less enthusiastic about requests that she take dictation from Mr. Bartrum, in charge of accounts, who, she confided to Mrs. Crealey, was boring, middle-aged, and treated her like something the cat had brought in. The accounts department was in number 10 and, after a stint with Mr. Bartrum, Mandy would escape upstairs for a few minutes of chat, flirtation and the ritual exchange of insults with the three packing-staff. They inhabited their private world of bare floors and trestle tables, of collapsible brown cartons, Sellotape and immense balls of twine, of the distinctive and exciting smell of books fresh from the press. She liked them all; Dave of the bush-ranger hat, who, despite his size, had arm muscles like footballs and could shift extraordinary weights; Ken, who was tall and lugubrious and silent; and Carl, the warehouse manager, who had been with the firm since he was a boy. "They'll do no good with this one," he would say, slapping a hand on a carton.

"He can't go wrong," confided Dave admiringly. "He can tell a best-seller from a dud just by smelling it. He don't even 'ave to read 'em."

Her willingness to make tea and coffee for the two PAs and the partners gave her the opportunity for a twice-daily gossip with the cleaner, Mrs. Demery. Mrs. Demery's domain was centred on the large kitchen and adjacent smaller sitting-room on the ground floor at the back of the house. The kitchen was furnished with a rectangular pine table, large enough to seat ten, one gas and one electric stove and a microwave oven, a double sink, a huge refrigerator and a wall fitted with small cupboards. Here, at any time between twelve and two, in a pungent aroma of discordant cooking smells, all but the senior staff ate their sandwiches, heated their foils of oven-ready pasta and curry, made omelettes, boiled eggs, grilled bacon for bacon rolls and brewed their tea and coffee. The five partners never joined them. Frances Peverell and Gabriel Dauntsey went next door to their separate flats at number 12 and the two Etiennes and James de Witt took the launch upstream to lunch in the city, or walked to the Prospect of Whitby or one of the pubs in Wapping High Street. The kitchen, without their inhibiting presence, was the centre of gossip. Here news was received, endlessly discussed, embroidered and disseminated. Mandy would sit in silence in front of her sandwich box, knowing that when she was present the middle-grade staff in particular were unusually discreet. Whatever their feelings about the new chairman or the possible future of the firm, loyalty and a sense of their status forbade open criticism in front of a temp. But when she and Mrs. Demery were alone brewing morning coffee or afternoon tea, Mrs. Demery had no such inhibitions.

"We thought Mr. Gerard and Miss Frances would marry. That's what she thought too, the poor kid. And then there's Miss Claudia and her toy boy."

"Miss Claudia with a toy boy! Come off it, Mrs. D."

"Well, maybe not a toy boy exactly, although he's young enough. Younger than her anyway. I saw him when he came to Mr. Gerard's engagement party. He's good-looking, I'll say that for him. Miss Claudia always had an eye for a good-looking chap. He's in antiques. You know, like the Antiques Road Show. They're supposed to be engaged but I notice she don't wear a ring."

"But she's quite old, isn't she? And people like Miss Claudia don't bother so much about rings."

"That Lady Lucinda's got one, though, hasn't she? A bloody great emerald set with diamonds. That must have cost Mr. Gerard a packet. I don't know why he wants to marry an earl's sister. Young enough to be his daughter, too. I don't think it's decent."

"Maybe he fancies a wife with a title, Mrs. D. You know, Lady Lucinda Etienne. Maybe he likes the sound of that."

"That don't count for as much as it did, Mandy, not with the way some of these old families behave nowadays. No better than the rest of us. It used to be different when I was a girl, you had some respect for them then. That brother of hers is nothing to write home about, earl or no earl, if you're to believe half of what you read in the papers. Ah well, them that lives longest will see most." It was Mrs. Demery's invariable way of ending a conversation.

On her first Monday, a day so sunny that she could almost believe they were back in the summer, she had watched with some envy while the first set of staff entered the launch at 5:30 to be taken to Charing Cross. On impulse she asked Fred Bowling, the waterman, if she could go for the ride. He made no objection and she jumped in. On the way there he had sat at the wheel in silence, as she suspected he always did. But when the party had disembarked and they turned for the journey downstream to Innocent House, she had started asking him questions about the river and had been amazed at his knowledge. There was no building which he couldn't identify, no history which apparently he didn't know, no fellow waterman whom he couldn't recognize and few boats which he couldn't name.

It was from him that she learned that Cleopatra's Needle was first erected about 1450 B.C. in front of the Temple of Isis at Heliopolis, and towed to England to be erected on the river bank in 1878. It was one of a twin and the other stood in Central Park, New York. She could picture the great container with its core of stone thrashing through the turbulent seas of the Bay of Biscay like a great fish. He pointed out Doggett's Coat and Badge public house next to Blackfriars Bridge, and told her about Doggett's Coat and Badge sculling race, which has been rowed since 1722 from the Old Swan Inn at London Bridge to the Old Swan Inn at Chelsea, the first single sculling race in the world. His nephew had rowed in it. As they butted under the great pillars of Tower Bridge he could tell her the length of each span and that the High Walk was 142 feet above high water. When they reached Wapping he told her about James Lee, a market gardener from Fulham, who in 1789 had noticed a fine flowering plant in a cottage window which had been brought back by a sailor from Brazil. James Lee bought it for £8 and planted cuttings, and next year made his fortune selling 300 plants at a guinea each.

"Now, what do you think that plant was?"

"I don't know, Mr. Bowling, I don't understand about plants."

"Go on, Mandy, have a guess."

"It couldn't be a rose?"

"A rose? 'Course it wasn't a rose! There have been roses in England for ever. No, that was a fuchsia."

Glancing up at him, Mandy saw that the brown creased face, still looking ahead, was quietly smiling. How odd people were, she thought. Nothing he had told her about the splendours and horror of the river was for him as sweetly remarkable as the discovery of that single flower.

As they neared Innocent House Mandy could see the figures of the last two passengers, James de Witt and Emma Wainwright, ready to embark. Darkness had fallen and the river had become as smooth and thick as oil, a black tide which broke into a fishtail of white foam as the launch chugged away. Mandy crossed the patio to her motor bike. She didn't linger. She wasn't superstitious or particularly nervous, but once darkness had fallen Innocent House became more mysterious and a little sinister, even with the two globes of light casting over the marble their soft warm light. She walked with her eyes ahead, willing herself not to look down in case she could see that fabled stain of blood or upwards to the top balcony from which that long-dead distracted wife had hurled herself to her death.

And so the days passed. Going from office to office, willing, consci-entious, quickly accepted, there was nothing which escaped Mandy's sharp experienced eyes: Miss Blackett's unhappiness, the casual con-tempt with which Mr. Gerard treated her; Miss Frances's taut white face, stoical in misery; George's anxious eyes following Mr. Gerard whenever he passed the reception desk; half-overheard conversations which broke off when she appeared. Mandy knew that the staff were anxious about the future. There hung over the whole of Innocent House an atmosphere of unease, almost foreboding, which she could sense and occasionally even slightly relish, since she felt, as she always did, that she was merely the privileged spectator, the outsider who was under no personal threat, who took her money by the week, owed allegiance to no one and could walk out when she chose. Sometimes at the end of the day, when the light began to fade and the river outside was a black tide, and footsteps echoed eerily on the marble of the hall, she would be reminded of the hours before a bad thunderstorm: the deepening darkness, the heaviness and sharp metallic smell of the air, the knowledge that nothing could break this tension but the first crash of thunder and a violent tearing of the skies.

11

It was Thursday 14 October. The partners' meeting at Innocent House was due to begin at ten o'clock in the boardroom and by 9:45, as was his habit, Gerard Etienne had already taken his seat at the oval mahogany table. He sat in the middle of the side which faced the window and the river. By ten o'clock his sister, Claudia, would be seated on his right and Frances Peverell on his left. James de Witt would be opposite him with Gabriel Dauntsey on his right. The seating hadn't changed since that day nine months earlier when he had formally taken over as chairman and managing director of Peverell Press. On that Thursday his four colleagues had loitered outside the boardroom as if each was reluctant to enter it alone. Joining them, he had unhesitatingly thrust open the double mahogany door and, striding confidently into the room, had taken his seat in Henry Peverell's old chair. Behind him the other four partners had entered together and silently seated themselves as if in obedience to some preordained plan which both established and reaffirmed their status in the firm. He had taken Henry Peverell's chair as if by right, and it was by right. Frances, he remembered, had sat pale-faced and almost silent throughout that short meeting and afterwards, drawing him aside, James de Witt had said: "Need you have taken her father's chair? He's only been dead ten days."

He felt again that mixture of surprise and mild irritation which the question had provoked at the time. Which chair was he expected to take? What did James want, to waste time while the five of them deferred politely to each other, discussing who should or should not have a river view, playing a kind of unaccompanied musical chairs around the table? The chair with the arms was the managing director's chair and he, Gerard Etienne, was managing director. How could it possibly matter how long old Peverell had been dead? Henry had used this chair, this place at the table, when he was alive, had occasionally raised his eyes to look out over the river in one of his irritating moments of private contemplation while the rest of them had waited patiently for the meeting to resume. But he was dead. James surely wasn't suggesting that the chair should be left permanently empty as a kind of memorial, that a suitable plaque should be attached to the seat.

He saw the incident as typical of James's overdeveloped and self-indulgent sensitivity, typical too of something else, which he found more perplexing and more interesting since it concerned himself. It sometimes seemed to him that the thought processes of other people were so radically different from his that he and they inhabited a different dimension of reason. Facts which to him were self-evident required from his four partners prolonged thought and discussion before, reluctantly, they were accepted; discussions were complicated by confused emotions and personal considerations which seemed to him as irrelevant as they were irrational. He told himself that, for them, reaching a decision was like achieving orgasm with a frigid woman, requiring a tedious amount of foreplay and the expenditure of disproportionate energy. He wondered occasionally whether to present them with the analogy but decided, inwardly smiling, that the pleasantry was best kept to himself. Frances, for one, would not find it amusing. But it would happen again this morning. The choices facing them were stark and inescapable. They could sell Innocent House and use the capital to establish and develop the firm; they could negotiate an arrangement with another publishing house whereby the name Peverell Press would at least be preserved; or they could go out of business. The second option was merely a longer and more tedious route to the last, beginning invariably with public optimism and ending in ignominious extinction. He had no intention of going down that well-trod path. The house must be sold. Frances had to realize, they all had to realize, that they couldn't both keep Innocent House and continue as independent publishers.

He got up from the table and moved over to the window. As he watched, a cruise ship suddenly and silently blocked his view, so close that for a moment he could look into a lighted porthole and see, in the half-circle of brightness, the head of a woman, delicate as a cameo, pale arms raised, running her fingers through an aureole of hair, and could imagine that their eyes met in a surprised and fleeting intimacy. He wondered briefly, and with no real curiosity, who it was who shared her cabin—husband, lover, friend?—and what plans they had for the evening. He had none. By established habit he worked late on Thursday nights. He wouldn't see Lucinda until Friday, when they had planned a concert on the South Bank followed by dinner at the Bombay Brasserie since Lucinda had expressed a preference for Indian food. He thought of the weekend without excitement but with quiet satisfaction. One of Lucinda's virtues was her decisiveness. Frances, asked where she preferred to eat, would have replied "Anywhere you like, darling," and if the meal disappointed and he complained, would have said, leaning against him, slipping her arm through his, beguiling him into a good humour, "It was perfectly edible, not bad really. And what does it matter, darling? We were together." Lucinda had never suggested that his company could compensate for or excuse a poorly cooked, ill-served dinner. Occasionally he wondered whether, in fact, it did.

12

E tienne said: "This is a private meeting, Miss Blackett. We have some confidential business to discuss. I'll take my own notes. There's plenty of typing to keep you occupied."

His voice was dismissive with a note of contempt. Miss Blackett flushed and gave a small, soundless intake of air. Her notebook slid from her fingers and she bent stiffly to pick it up, then rose and walked to the door with a pathetic attempt at dignity.

James de Witt said: "Was that kind? Blackie has taken the notes of the partners' meeting for over twenty years. She's always sat in."

"Wasting her time and ours."

Frances Peverell said: "You needn't have suggested that we don't trust her."

"I didn't. All the same, when we get to discussing the mischief here she has to be a suspect. I don't see why she should be treated differently from the rest of the staff. She has no alibi for any of the incidents. She has plenty of opportunity."

Gabriel Dauntsey said: "So do I, or any of the five of us here. And haven't we spent enough time discussing the practical joker? It never gets us anywhere."

"Perhaps. Anyway, that can wait. The important news first. Hector Skolling has upped his offer for Innocent House by another £300,000. Four and a half million. It's the first time in the negotiations that he's used the words 'final offer,' and when he says that he means it. It's a clear million more than I thought we would have to take. More than it's worth in purely commercial terms, but property is worth what someone is prepared to pay, and Hector Skolling likes the house. After all, his empire is in Docklands. There's a clear distinction between the property he develops for letting and the kind of house he's prepared to live in. I propose to accept verbally today and get the solicitors working on the details so that we can exchange within a month."

James de Witt said: "I thought we discussed it at the last meeting but didn't reach a decision. I think if you consult the minutes . . ."

"I don't need to. I'm not running this company on the basis of what Miss Blackett chooses to put in the minutes."

"Which, incidentally, you haven't yet signed."

"Exactly. I suggest that in the future we run this monthly meeting with a less formal agenda. You're always saying that this is a partnership of friends and colleagues and that I'm the one who insists on tedious procedures and unnecessary bureaucracy. So why all this formality, agenda, minutes, resolutions, when it comes to the monthly partners' meeting?"

De Witt said: "It has been found useful. And I don't think I, for one, have ever used the phrase 'friends and colleagues.' "

Frances Peverell had been sitting bolt upright, her face very white. Now she said: "You can't sell Innocent House."

Etienne didn't look at her but kept his eyes on his papers. "I can. We can. We have to sell if this business is to survive. You can't run an efficient publishing house from a Venetian palace on the Thames."

"My family has for a hundred and sixty years."

"I said an efficient publishing business. Your family didn't need to be efficient, they were cushioned with private incomes. Publishing in your grandfather's day wasn't even an occupation for gentlemen, it was a hobby for gentlemen. Today a publisher makes money, and makes it efficiently, or goes under. Is that what you want? I don't propose to go under. I intend to make the Peverell Press profitable and after that to make it large."

Gabriel Dauntsey said quietly: "So that you can sell it? Make your millions and get out?"

Etienne ignored him.

"I'm getting rid of Sydney Bartrum to begin with. He's a competent enough accountant, but what we want is someone a great deal more than that. I propose to appoint a financial director with the job of finding money for development and setting up a proper financial system."

De Witt said: "We have a perfectly good financial system. The auditors have never complained. Sydney has been here for nineteen years. He's an honest, conscientious, hard-working accountant."

"Exactly. That's what he is and it's all he is. As I said, we need something more. For example, I need to know the margin of profit over gross expenditure of every book we publish. Other houses have that information. How can we cut out the unproductive authors if we don't know who they are? We need someone who will make money for us, not just tell us each year how we spent it. I know how we spent it. If all we need is a competent accountant I can do that myself. I'd expect you to support him, James. He's pathetic, unprepossessing and not particularly efficient. Naturally that makes an immediate appeal. You needs must love the lowest when you see it. You should do something about your bleeding-heart syndrome."

James flushed, but said quietly enough: "I don't particularly like the man. I cringe every time he calls me Mr. de Witt. I suggested that he should say de Witt or James, but he looked at me as if I were proposing an indecency. But he's a perfectly competent accountant and he's been here for nineteen years. He knows the firm, he knows us, he knows the way we work."

"Used to work, James, used to work."

Frances said: "And he only married a year ago. They've got a new baby."

"What on earth has that to do with whether he's the right man for the job?"

De Witt asked: "Do you have someone in mind?"

"I've asked Patterson Macintosh, the head-hunters, to put forward some names."

"That will cost us a few quid. Head-hunters don't come cheap. Odd that nowadays we can't recruit staff without head-hunters, can't improve efficiency without time-and-motion-study experts and have to call in management consultants to tell us how to manage. Half the time these so-called experts are just front-men called in to cut down staff when the management haven't the guts to do it themselves. Have you ever known management consultants who didn't recommend sacking people? It's what they're paid to say, and a cushy little number they've made out of it for themselves."

Frances said: "We should have been consulted about all this."

"You are being consulted."

"In that case we can stop talking about it now. It isn't going to happen. Innocent House isn't going to be sold."

"It is if just one of you agrees to sell. That's all it takes. You've forgotten how many shares I own. And the house isn't yours, Fran. Your family sold it to the firm in 1940, remember. All right, they got it too cheap, but they probably didn't give much for its chance of survival, given the East End bombing. It was under-insured and, anyway, it couldn't have been replaced. Get this into your head, Fran, it isn't a Peverell house any more. Why are you so worried? You haven't a child. There's no Peverell to inherit."

Frances flushed and half rose from her chair, but de Witt said quietly: "Don't, Frances. Don't leave. We all need to discuss this."

"There's nothing to discuss."

There was a silence broken by Dauntsey's quiet voice. "Is my poetry required to earn its 8.5 per cent net or whatever?"

"We'll keep your volumes in print, Gabriel, naturally. There will be a few books we'll have to carry."

"I must hope that the burden of mine won't be too great."

"And selling this place will mean turning you out of number twelve. Skolling wants the whole property, the two houses as well as the main building. I'm sorry about that."

"But I have, after all, lived at number twelve at a ludicrously low rent for over ten years."

"Well that's the arrangement Henry Peverell agreed with you, and naturally you had a right to take what he gave." He paused, then added, "And to go on taking. But you must see, things can't be allowed to go on like this."

"Oh yes, I do see. Things can't be allowed to go on."

Etienne went on as if he hadn't heard.

"And it's time to get rid of George. We should have retired him years ago. The switchboard operator is the first contact that people have with the firm. You need a young, vital, attractive girl, not that sixty-eight-year-old man. He is sixty-eight, isn't he? And don't tell me he's been here for twenty-two years. I know how long he's been here, that's just the trouble."

Frances said: "He isn't just the switchboard operator. He opens the place up, sees to the burglar alarm, and he's a wonderful handyman."

"And he needs to be. There's always something going wrong with this house. It's time we moved into a modern, purpose-built, efficiently run building. And we haven't begun to take on board modern technology. You people thought you were being dangerously innovative when you replaced a few of the typewriters with word processors. And there's one other piece of good news. There's a chance that I may be able to entice Sebastian Beacher from his present publishers. He's not at all happy."

Frances cried out: "But he's an appallingly bad writer, and he's not much better as a human being."

"The business of publishing is to give people what they want, not to make moral judgements."

"You could argue that if you were manufacturing cigarettes."

"I would argue it if I were manufacturing cigarettes. Or whisky for that matter."

De Witt said: "It isn't a true analogy. You could argue that drink is positively beneficial if used in moderation. You can never argue that a bad novel is other than a bad novel."

"Bad for whom? And what do you mean by bad? Beacher tells a strong story, keeps the action moving, provides that mixture of sex and violence which people apparently want. Who are we to tell readers what is good for them? Anyway, haven't you always argued that the important thing is to get people reading? Let them begin with cheap romantic fiction and they may go on to Jane Austen or George Eliot. I don't see why they should—go on to the classics, I mean. That's your argument, not mine. What's wrong with cheap romantic fiction if that's what they happen to enjoy? It's a pretty condescending attitude to argue that popular fiction is only justified if it leads on to higher things. Well, what you and Gabriel happen to think are higher things."

Dauntsey said: "Are you saying that one shouldn't make value judgements? We make them every day of our lives."

"I'm saying you shouldn't make them for other people. I'm saying that I shouldn't make them as a publisher. Anyway, there's one unanswerable argument: if I'm not allowed to make a profit on popular books, good or bad, I can't afford to publish less popular books for what you see as the discerning minority."

Frances Peverell turned on him. Her colour was high and she found difficulty in controlling her voice. "Why do you keep on saying 'I'? It's always 'I'll do this, I'll publish that.' You may be chairman but you aren't the firm. We are. Collectively. The five of us. And we aren't meeting now as the Book Committee. That's next week. We're supposed to be talking about the future of Innocent House."

"We are. I propose that we accept the offer and put the negotiations in hand."

"And where do you propose we move to?"

"Offices in Docklands, on the river. Downstream possibly. We need to discuss whether we buy or take a long lease, but either's possible.

Prices have never been lower. Docklands has never been better value. And now that the Docklands Light Railway is working and the tube is to be extended, access will be easier. We shan't need the launch."

Frances said: "And sack Fred after all these years?"

"My dear Frances, Fred is a qualified waterman. Fred will have no problem in getting another job."

Claudia said: "It's too hurried, Gerard. I agree that the house will probably have to go, but we don't have to decide this morning. Put something on paper, the figures for example. Let's look at it when we've had time to consider."

Gerard said: "And lose the offer?"

"Is that likely? Come off it, Gerard. If Hector Skolling wants the house he isn't going to withdraw because he has to wait a week for an answer. Accept it if that makes you feel happier. We can always take it off the market if we have second thoughts."

James de Witt said: "I wanted to talk about Esmé Carling's new novel. At the last meeting you said something about turning it down."

"*Death on Paradise Island?* I have turned it down. I thought that was agreed."

De Witt said quietly and slowly as if to a recalcitrant child: "No, it wasn't agreed. It was briefly discussed and the matter deferred."

"Like so many of our decisions. You four remind me of that definition of a meeting—a collection of people who prefer to substitute the pleasure of talk for the responsibility of action or the ardour of decision. Something like that. I spoke to Esmé's agent yesterday and gave her the news. I confirmed it in writing with a copy to Carling. I take it that no one here is seriously arguing that Esmé Carling is a good novelist, or even a profitable one. Personally I prefer a writer to be one or the other, preferably both."

De Witt said: "We have published worse."

Etienne turned on him with a small explosion of derision. "God knows why you support her, James. You're the one who's keen to publish literary novels, Booker Prize candidates, sensitive little works to impress the literary mafia. Five minutes ago you were criticizing me for trying to get Sebastian Beacher. You're not suggesting that *Death on Paradise Island* is going to enhance the reputation of Peverell Press? I mean, I take it that you don't see it as the Whitbread Book of the Year. Incidentally, I'd be a great deal more sympathetic to your so-called Booker books if they occasionally made the Booker shortlist."

James said: "I agree it's probably time that we parted from her. It's the means, not the end I object to. I suggested at the last meeting, if you remember, that we should publish her latest and then tactfully say that we're closing the popular-mystery list."

Claudia said: "Hardly convincing. She's the only author on it."

James went on, speaking directly to Gerard. "The book will need careful editing but she'll take that if it's done tactfully. The plot needs strengthening and the middle section is weak. But the description of the island is good. She's excellent at evoking an atmosphere of menace. And the characterization is an improvement on her last. We won't lose on it. We've published her for thirty years. It's a long association. I'd like it to end with goodwill and generosity, that's all."

Gerard Etienne said: "It has ended. And we're a publishing house not a charity. I'm sorry, James, she's got to go."

De Witt said: "You could have waited until the Book Committee met."

"I probably would have waited if her agent hadn't rung. Carling was pressing to know if we had fixed publication day and what was proposed by way of a publication party. A party! A wake would have been more appropriate. There was no point in prevaricating. I told her that the book wasn't up to standard and that we didn't propose to publish. I confirmed that in writing yesterday."

"She'll take it badly."

"Of course she'll take it badly. Authors always take rejection badly. They equate it with infanticide."

"What about her back-list?"

"Now there we may be able to make a bit of money."

Frances Peverell suddenly spoke. "James is right. We did agree that we'd discuss it again. You had absolutely no authority to speak to Esmé Carling or to Velma Pitt-Cowley. We could perfectly well publish her latest and tell her gently that it had to be the last. Gabriel, you agree, don't you? You think we should have taken *Death on Paradise Island?*"

The four partners looked at Dauntsey and waited as if he were a final court of appeal. The old man had been studying his paper but now he looked up and smiled gently at Frances.

"I don't think that would have softened the blow, do you? You don't reject an author. What you reject is the book. If we publish this latest she'll present us with another and we'll be faced with the same dilemma. Gerard acted prematurely and I imagine not particularly tactfully, but I think the decision was right. A novel is either worth publishing or it isn't."

"I'm glad we've settled something." Etienne began shuffling his papers together.

De Witt said: "As long as you realize that's all that we've settled. No more negotiations about selling Innocent House until we've had another meeting and you've provided us with the figures and a full business plan."

"You've had a business plan. I gave you one last month."

"Not one we could understand. We'll meet a week today. It would be helpful if you could circulate the papers a day in advance. And we need alternatives. A business plan on the assumption that Innocent House is sold, a second on the assumption that it isn't."

Etienne said: "The second is easily provided. Either we do business with Skolling or we go bankrupt. And Skolling isn't a patient man."

Claudia said: "Keep him quiet with a promise. Tell him that if we decide to sell he will get first refusal."

Etienne smiled. "Oh no, I don't think I could make that kind of promise. Once his interest becomes public we could attract another £50,000. I don't think it's likely but you never know. The Greyfriars Museum is said to be looking for somewhere to house its collection of maritime paintings."

Frances Peverell said: "We're not going to sell Innocent House to Hector Skolling or anyone else. This house is sold over my dead body —or yours."

13

In the secretaries' office Mandy looked up as Blackie entered, stalked over red-faced to her desk, sat down at her word processor and began typing. After a minute curiosity overcame discretion and Mandy asked: "What's up? I thought you always took notes at the partners' meeting."

Blackie's voice was strange, at once harsh but with a small note of triumphant vindication: "Not any more apparently."

Chucked out, poor cow, Mandy thought. She said: "What's so secret then? What are they doing up there?"

"Doing?" Blackie's hands ceased their restless weaving over the keys. "They're ruining this firm, that's what they're doing. They're sweeping away everything Mr. Peverell worked for, cared for, stood for, for over thirty years. They're planning to sell Innocent House. Mr. Peverell loved this house. It's been in the family for over a hundred and sixty years. Innocent House is Peverell Press. If one goes they both go. Mr. Gerard's been planning to get rid of it ever since Mr. Etienne retired and now he's taken over there's no one to stop him. They don't care anyway. Miss Frances won't like it but she's in love with him, and no one takes much notice of Miss Frances. Miss Claudia is his sister and Mr. de Witt hasn't the guts to stop him. No one has. Mr. Dauntsey might, but he's too old now and past caring. None of them can stand up to Mr. Gerard. But he knows what I think. That's why he didn't want me there. He knows I disagree. He knows I'd stop him if I could."

Mandy saw she was close to tears, but they were tears of anger.

Embarrassed, anxious to comfort but uneasily aware that Blackie would later regret this unwonted confidence, she said: "He can be a right sod. I've seen the way he treats you sometimes. Why don't you leave, try a spot of temping? Ask for your cards and tell him where he can stuff his job."

Blackie, fighting for control, made an attempt to recover her dignity. "Don't be ridiculous, Mandy. I've no intention of leaving. I'm a senior personal secretary. I'm not a temp. I never have been and I never will be."

"There are worse things than temping. What about some coffee, then? I could make it now—no point in waiting—and a couple of chocolate digestives."

"All right then, but don't waste time gossiping with Mrs. Demery. I've got some copy-typing for you when you've finished those letters. And, Mandy, what I said is confidential. I spoke rather more freely than I should have done and I want it kept within these walls."

Fat chance, thought Mandy. Didn't Miss Blackett realize that it was gossiped about all over the building? She said: "I can keep my mouth shut. It's no skin off my nose, is it? I'll be gone by the time you move from here."

She was hardly on her feet when the telephone on her desk rang and she heard George's worried voice, but speaking with such conspiratorial quietness that she could hardly hear.

"Mandy, do you know where Miss FitzGerald is? I can't get Blackie out of a partners' meeting and I've got Mrs. Carling here. She's demanding to see Mr. Gerard and I don't think I can hold her much longer."

"It's OK, Miss Blackett's here." Mandy handed over the instrument. "It's George. Mrs. Carling is in reception screaming to see Mr. Gerard."

"Well she can't."

Blackie took the instrument, but before she could speak the door was flung open and Mrs. Carling burst in, thrust Mandy aside and strode straight through to the front office. Immediately she was back confronting them.

"Well, where is he? Where's Gerard Etienne?"

Blackie, attempting dignity, flipped open her desk diary. "I don't think you have an appointment, Mrs. Carling."

"Of course I haven't a bloody appointment! After thirty years with the firm I don't need an appointment to see my publisher. I'm not a rep trying to sell him advertising space. Where is he?"

"He's in the partners' meeting, Mrs. Carling."

"I thought that was only on the first Thursday."

"Mr. Gerard moved it to today."

"Then they'll have to interrupt it. They're in the boardroom I suppose."

She made for the door, but Blackie was quicker and, slipping past her, stood with her back against it.

"You can't go up, Mrs. Carling. Partners' meetings are never interrupted. I have instructions that even urgent telephone calls have to be held."

"In that case I'll wait until they're through."

Blackie, still standing, found her typing chair firmly occupied, but remained calm.

"I don't know when that will be. They could send down for sandwiches. And haven't you a signing in Cambridge this lunch hour? I'll let Mr. Gerard know that you called and no doubt he'll get in touch with you when he has a free moment."

The recent contretemps, the need to re-establish her status before Mandy, made her voice more authoritative than was tactful, but even so the ferocity of the response surprised them. Mrs. Carling rose from the chair at a speed which set it spinning and stood so that her face was almost touching Blackie's. She was three inches shorter but it seemed to Mandy that this difference made her more, not less, terrifying. The muscles of the stretched neck stood out like cords, the eyes blazed upwards and beneath the slightly hooked nose the mean little mouth, like a red gash, spat out its venom.

"When he has a free moment! You stupid bitch! You arrogant conceited little fool! Who do you think you're talking to? It's my talent which has paid your wages for the last twenty-odd years and don't you forget it. It's time you realized just how unimportant you are in this firm. Just because you worked for Mr. Peverell, and he indulged you and tolerated you and made you feel wanted, you think you can queen it over people who were part of Peverell Press when you were still a snotty-nosed school kid. Old Henry spoiled you, of course, but I can tell you what he really thought of you. And why? Because he told me, that's why. He was sick of you hanging about and gazing at him like a moonstruck cow. He was sick and tired of your devotion. He wanted you out, but he hadn't the guts to sack you. He never did have any guts, poor sod. If he'd had guts Gerard Etienne wouldn't be in charge now. Tell him I want to see him, and it had better be at my convenience, not his."

Blackie spoke through lips so white and stiff that it seemed to Mandy that they could hardly move. "It isn't true. You're lying. It isn't true."

And now Mandy was frightened. She was used to office rows. In over three years of temping she had witnessed some impressive squalls of temperament and like a stalwart little boat had bobbed happily among the strewn wreckage of tumultuous seas. Mandy rather enjoyed a good office row. There was no better antidote to boredom. But this was different. Here, she recognized, was genuine suffering, real adult pain, an adult malice welling out of a hatred which was terrifying. This was grief which could not be assuaged by fresh coffee and a couple of biscuits from the tin Mrs. Demery reserved for the partners only. She thought for a terrifying second that Blackie was going to throw back her head and howl with anguish. She wanted to hold out a hand in comfort but instinctively knew that there was no comfort she could give and that the attempt would later be resented.

The door banged. Mrs. Carling had swept out.

Blackie said again: "It's a lie. It's all lies. She doesn't know anything about it."

"Of course she doesn't," said Mandy sturdily. "Of course she's lying, anyone could see that. She's just a jealous bitch. I shouldn't take any notice of her."

"I'm just going to the bathroom."

It was apparent that Blackie was about to be sick. Again Mandy wondered whether she could go with her but decided against it. Blackie walked out as stiff as an automaton, almost colliding with Mrs. Demery as she came in carrying a couple of parcels.

Mrs. Demery said: "These came in the second post so I thought I'd bring them in. What's wrong with her?"

"She's upset. The partners didn't want her at the meeting and then Mrs. Carling arrived demanding to see Mr. Gerard and Blackie stopped her."

Mrs. Demery folded her arms and leaned against Blackie's desk. "I expect she got the letter this morning telling her that they don't want her new novel."

"How on earth do you know that, Mrs. Demery?"

"There's not much happens around here I don't get to know about. There'll be trouble about this, mark my words."

"If it's not good enough why doesn't she revise it or write another?"

"Because she doesn't think she can, that's why. That's what happens to authors when they get rejected. That's what they're terrified about all the time, losing their talent, writers' block. That's what makes them so tricky to deal with. Tricky, that's what writers are. You have to keep

on telling them how wonderful they are or they go to pieces. I've seen
it happen before more than once. Now old Mr. Peverell knew how to
deal with them. He had the right touch with authors, had Mr. Peverell.
With Mr. Gerard it's difficult. He's different. He doesn't see why they
can't get on with the job and stop whining."

It was a view with which Mandy had considerable sympathy. She
might tell Blackie—and indeed believe it—that Mr. Gerard was a sod,
but she found him difficult to dislike. She felt that, given the chance,
she could cope with Mr. Gerard. But further confidences were interrupted by the return of Blackie much sooner than Mandy had expected.
Mrs. Demery slipped away and Blackie, without a word, sat again at
her keyboard.

For the next hour they worked in an oppressive silence broken only
when Blackie issued orders. Mandy was sent to the copy room to make
three copies of a recently arrived manuscript which, judging by the first
three paragraphs, she thought was unlikely to appear in print, was
handed a pile of extremely dull copy-typing and then told to weed out
any papers more than two years old from the "Keep a Little While"
drawer. This useful compendium was used by the whole office as a
depository for papers for which no one could find an appropriate place
but which they were reluctant to throw away. There was little in it under
twelve years old and weeding the "Keep a Little While" drawer was a
deeply unpopular chore. Mandy felt that she was being unjustly punished for Blackie's burst of confidence.

The partners' meeting ended earlier than usual and it was only half
past eleven when Gerard Etienne, followed by his sister and Gabriel
Dauntsey, came briskly through the office and into his own room.
Claudia Etienne was pausing to speak to Blackie when the inner door
was flung open and he reappeared. Mandy saw that he was containing
his temper with difficulty. He said to Blackie: "Have you taken my
private diary?"

"Of course not, Mr. Gerard. Isn't it in your right-hand desk drawer?"

"If it were I should hardly be asking for it."

"I made it up to date on Monday afternoon and put it back in the
drawer. I haven't seen it since."

"It was there yesterday morning. If you haven't taken it you had
better discover who has. I presume you accept that looking after my
diaries is part of your responsibility. If you can't find the diary I should
be glad to have the pencil returned. It's gold and I'm rather attached
to it." Blackie's face was scarlet. Claudia Etienne looked on with an
amused sardonic lift of her eyebrow. Mandy, scenting battle, studied

the outlines in the shorthand notebook as if they had suddenly become incomprehensible.

Blackie's voice was hovering on the edge of hysteria. "Are you accusing me of theft, Mr. Gerard? I've worked in this office for twenty-seven years but—" Her voice broke off.

He said impatiently, "Don't be a little fool. No one's accusing you of anything." His eye hit on the snake curled over the handle of the filing cabinet. "And for God's sake get rid of that bloody snake. Chuck it in the river. It makes this office look like a kindergarten."

He went into his office and his sister followed. Without a word Blackie took the snake and shut it in her desk drawer.

She said to Mandy, "What are you staring at? If you haven't any typing to do I can soon find you some. In the mean time you can make me some coffee."

Mandy, armed with this new gossip for the delectation of Mrs. Demery, was happy to oblige.

14

Declan was to arrive for the river trip at half past six, and it was 6:15 when Claudia went in to her brother's office. They were the last two people in the building. Gerard invariably worked late on Thursdays, but it was the night when most of the staff planned to leave early and take advantage of Thursday late-night shopping. He was sitting at his desk in the pool of light from his lamp, but stood up as she entered. His manners to her were always formal, always impeccable. She used to wonder if this was one small ploy to discourage intimacy.

She seated herself opposite him and said without preamble: "Look, I'll support you about selling Innocent House. I'll go along with all your other plans, come to that. With my support you can easily out-vote the others. But I need cash: £350,000. I want you to buy half of my shares, all of them if you like."

"I can't afford to."

"You can when Innocent House is sold. Once the contracts are exchanged you can raise a million or so. With my shares you'll have a permanent overall majority. That will give you absolute power. It's worth paying for. I'll stay on in the firm but with fewer shares, or none."

He said quietly: "It's certainly worth thinking about, but not now. And I can't use the money from the sale. That belongs to the partnership. I'll need it anyway for the relocation and my other plans. But you could raise it. You could raise £350,000. If I can, so can you."

"Not as easily. Not without a great deal of trouble and delay. And I need it urgently. I need it by the end of the month."

"What for? What are you going to do?"

"Invest in the antique business with Declan Cartwright. He's got the chance of buying the business from old Simon: £350,000 for the four-storey freehold property and all stock. It's a very good price. The old man's devoted to him and would prefer him to have the business, but he can't wait to sell. He's old, he's sick and he's in a hurry."

"Cartwright's a pretty boy, but at £350,000, isn't he pricing himself rather high?"

"I'm not a fool. The money isn't going to be handed over. It will still be my money invested in a joint business. Declan isn't a fool either. He knows what he's doing."

"You're thinking of marrying him, are you?"

"I may do. Does it surprise you?"

"It does rather." He added: "I think you're fonder of him than he is of you. That's always dangerous."

"Oh, it's more equal than you think. He feels as much for me as he's capable of feeling, and I feel as much for him as I'm capable of feeling. Our capacities for feeling are unequal, that's all. We both give the other what we have to give."

"So you propose to buy him?"

"Isn't that how you and I have always got what we wanted, by buying it? And what about you and Lucinda? Are you so sure you're doing the right thing—for you I mean? I'm not worried about her. I'm not deceived by that air of virtuous fragility. She can take care of herself all right. Anyway, her class always do."

"I mean to marry her."

"Well you needn't sound so belligerent over it. No one's trying to stop you. Incidentally, are you proposing to tell her the truth about yourself—about us? More to the point, are you going to tell her family?"

"I shall answer reasonable questions. So far they haven't asked any, reasonable or unreasonable. We aren't in the age, thank God, when fathers are asked for their consent and fiancés have to produce some evidence of moral fitness and financial probity. Anyway, there's only her brother. He seems to assume I have a house for her to live in and enough money to keep her in reasonable comfort."

"But you haven't a house, have you? I can't see her living in the Barbican flat. Nothing like enough room."

"I think she rather fancies Hampshire. Anyway, we can discuss that nearer the date of the wedding. I shall keep on the Barbican flat. It's handy for the office."

"Well, I hope it works out. Frankly I give Declan and me the better chance of the two. We don't confuse sex with love. And you may not find this marriage easy to get out of. She'll probably develop religious scruples about divorce. Anyway divorce is vulgar, messy and expensive. OK, she couldn't prevent it after two years of separation but they'd be very uncomfortable years. You wouldn't enjoy public failure."

"I'm not even married. It's a bit early to start deciding how I'm going to cope with failure. It won't fail."

"Frankly, Gerard, I don't see what you expect to get out of it, except a beautiful wife eighteen years younger than you."

"Most people would think that was enough."

"Only the naïve. It's a recipe for disaster. You aren't royal, you don't have to marry a totally unsuitable virgin just to continue a dynasty. Or is that what this is all about, founding a family? Yes, I believe it is. You've turned conventional in middle age. You want a settled life, children."

"That seems the most sensible reason for marriage. Some might say the only sensible reason."

"You've had enough of playing the field so now you're looking for a young, beautiful and preferably well-born virgin. Frankly, I think you'd have been better off with Frances."

"That was never a possibility."

"It was for her. I can see how it happened, of course. Here's a virgin of nearly thirty obviously wanting sexual experience and who better to provide it than my clever brother. But it was a mistake. You've made an enemy of James de Witt and you can't afford that."

"He's never spoken to me about it."

"Of course he hasn't. That isn't how James operates. He's a doer, not a talker. A word of advice. Don't stand too near the balcony of the upper storeys of Innocent House. One violent death in this house is enough."

He said calmly: "Thank you for the warning, but I'm not sure James de Witt would be the chief suspect. After all, if anything happens to me before I marry and make a new will, you'll get my shares, my flat and my life-assurance money. You can buy quite a lot of antiques for the best part of two and a half million."

Claudia was at the door when he spoke again, coolly and without looking up from his paper.

"By the way, the office menace has struck again."

Claudia turned and said sharply: "What do you mean? How? When?"

"This afternoon, at twelve-thirty to be precise. Someone sent a fax from here to Better Books in Cambridge cancelling Carling's signing. She arrived to find the advertisements taken down, the table and chair removed, the hopefuls turned away and most of the books relegated to the back office. Apparently she was incandescent with rage. I rather wish I'd been there to see it."

"Christ! When did you learn this?"

"Her agent, Velma Pitt-Cowley, rang me at two-forty-five, when I got back from lunch. She'd been trying to reach me since one-thirty. Carling telephoned her from the shop."

"And you've kept quiet about it until now?"

"I've had more important things to do this afternoon than swan round the office asking people for alibis. Anyway, that's your job, but I shouldn't make too much of it. I've a good idea this time who was responsible. It's of small importance anyway."

Claudia said grimly: "Not to Esmé Carling. You can dislike her, despise her or pity her but don't underestimate her. She could prove a more dangerous enemy than you imagine."

15

The upstairs room at the Connaught Arms off Waterloo Road was crowded. Matt Bayliss, the licensee, had no doubt about the success of the poetry reading. Already by nine o'clock the bar takings were well up for a Thursday night. The small upstairs room was normally used for lunches—there was little demand for hot dinners at the Connaught Arms—but was also available for the occasional function, and it was his brother, who worked for an arts organization, who had persuaded him to cater for the Thursday-night event. The plan was for a number of published poets to read their works interposed with readings by any amateurs who cared to take part. A fee of £1 a head had been charged and Matt had set up a cash wine bar at the back of the room. He had no idea that poetry was so popular or that so many of his regulars had ambitions to express themselves in verse. The initial sale of tickets had been satisfactory but there was a steady stream of late arrivals and people from the bar, hearing of the entertainment overhead, were making their way up the narrow staircase, tankards in hand.

Colin's enthusiasms were varied and fashionable: Black Art, Women's Art, Gay Art, Commonwealth Art, Accessible Art, Innovative Art, Art for the People. This event was billed as Poetry for the People. Matt's personal interest was in beer for the people, but he had seen no reason why the two enthusiasms should not be profitably combined. Colin's ambition was to make the Connaught Arms a recognized centre for contemporary-verse speaking and a public platform for new poets. Matt, watching his relief barman busily opening bottles of Californian red, discovered in himself an unexpected interest in contemporary culture. He came up from the saloon bar from time to time to sample the entertainment. The verses were to him largely incomprehensible; certainly very few either rhymed or had a discernible metre, which was his definition of poetry; but all were enthusiastically applauded. As most of the amateur poets and the audience smoked, the stagnant air was heavy with the fumes of beer and tobacco.

The advertised star of the evening was Gabriel Dauntsey. He had asked to go on early but most of the poets before him had overstepped their time limits, the amateurs in particular not being susceptible to Colin's muttered hints, and it was nearly 9:30 before Dauntsey made his slow way to the rostrum. He was listened to in a respectful silence and loudly applauded, but Matt guessed that his poems of a war which, for the great majority of those present, was now history, had little relevance to their current preoccupations. Afterwards Colin had pushed his way through the throng to reach him.

"Do you really have to leave? A few of us are thinking of going out for a meal afterwards."

"I'm sorry, it will be too late for me. Where can I get a taxi?"

"Matt here could ring, but you'll probably get one quicker by walking to Waterloo Road."

He had slipped away almost unnoticed and unthanked, leaving Matt feeling that somehow they had done badly by the old man.

Dauntsey had hardly left when an elderly couple came up to him at the bar. The man said: "Has Gabriel Dauntsey gone? My wife has a first edition of his poems which she'd love him to sign. We can't see him anywhere upstairs."

Matt said: "Have you got a car?"

"Parked about three blocks away. It's the nearest we could get."

"Well he's only just left. He's on foot. If you hurry you could catch him up. You'll probably miss him if you wait to go for the car."

Hurriedly they left, the woman, book in hand, eager-eyed.

Within three minutes they were back. Across the bar Matt could see them coming in through the door, supporting Gabriel Dauntsey between them. He was holding a blood-stained handkerchief to his brow. Matt made his way across to them.

"What's happened?"

The woman, obviously shaken, said: "He's been mugged. Three men, two black and one white. They were bending over him, but ran off when they saw us. They got his wallet, though."

The man looked round for a vacant chair and settled Dauntsey into it. "We'd better ring the police and an ambulance."

Dauntsey's voice was stronger than Matt had expected. "No, no. I'm all right. I don't want either. It's only a graze where I fell."

Matt looked at him, undecided. He seemed more shaken than hurt. And what was the point of ringing the police? They didn't have a chance of catching the muggers and this would only be one more minor crime to add to their statistics of crimes reported but unsolved. Matt, while a strong supporter of the police, preferred on the whole not to see them too frequently in his bar.

The woman looked at her husband then said firmly: "We have to pass St Thomas's Hospital. We'll take him to the casualty department. That would be the wisest plan."

Dauntsey, apparently, was to have no say in the matter.

They want to get rid of the responsibility as soon as possible, thought Matt, and he didn't blame them. After they had left he made his way upstairs to check on the supply of wine and noticed on a table by the door a pile of slim volumes. He felt a spurt of pity for Gabriel Dauntsey. The poor devil hadn't even waited to sign his books. But perhaps that was just as well. It would have been embarrassing for everyone if he hadn't made a sale.

16

On the following morning, Friday 15 October, Blackie awoke to a weight of apprehension. Her first conscious thought was dread of the day and what might lie ahead. She put on her dressing-gown and went down to make the morning tea, wondering whether to wake Joan with the complaint that she had a headache, that she didn't think she'd go into the office today, asking Joan to telephone later with her regrets and promises to be back on Monday. She thrust the temptation aside. Monday would come only too quickly, bringing with it an even heavier weight of anxiety. And not to appear today would look suspicious. Everyone knew that she didn't take days off, that she was never ill. She must go in to work as if this were just an ordinary day.

She could eat no breakfast. Even the thought of eggs and bacon made her nauseous and the first spoonful of cereal clogged her mouth. At the station she bought her usual *Daily Telegraph* but clutched it unopened during the journey, staring out at the flashing kaleidoscope of the Kent suburbs with unseeing eyes.

The launch was five minutes late starting off from Charing Cross Pier. Mr. de Witt, usually so punctual, came running down the ramp just as Fred Bowling was deciding that he had to cast off.

Mr. de Witt said briefly, "Sorry, everyone, I overslept. Good of you to wait. I thought I'd have to take the second boat."

They were all there now, the usual first boatload: Mr. de Witt, herself, Maggie FitzGerald and Amy Holden from publicity, Mr. Elton

from rights and Ken from the warehouse. Blackie took her usual seat
in the prow. She would have liked to have removed herself to the stern
and sit alone, but that too might have looked suspicious. It seemed that
she was abnormally conscious of her every word and action, as if she
were already under interrogation. She heard James de Witt tell the
others that Miss Frances had rung him late the previous night to tell
him that Mr. Dauntsey had been mugged. It had happened after his
poetry reading. He had been quickly found by two people who had
been at the pub and who had taken him to the casualty department at
St Thomas's Hospital. He had suffered more from shock than from the
mugging and was all right now. Blackie didn't comment. This was just
one more minor mishap, one more piece of bad luck. It seemed
unimportant compared to the dragging weight of her own anxiety.

Usually she enjoyed the river trip. She had done it now for over
twenty-five years and it had never lost its fascination. But today all the
familiar landmarks seemed no more than stage-posts on the journey to
disaster: the elegant ironwork of Blackfriars Railway Bridge; Southwark
Bridge, with the steps on Southwark Causeway from which Christopher
Wren was rowed across the river when he supervised the building of St
Paul's Cathedral; London Bridge, where once the heads of traitors were
displayed on spikes at either end; Traitor's Gate, green with algae and
weed; and Dead Man's Hole under Tower Bridge, where, by tradition,
the ashes of the dead were scattered outside the city boundaries; Tower
Bridge itself, the white and pale blue of the high walkway with its
gleaming gold-tipped badge; HMS *Belfast* in its Atlantic colours. She
saw them all with uncaring eyes. She told herself that this anxiety was
ridiculous and unnecessary. She had only one small cause for guilt,
which perhaps, after all, wasn't really so important or so blameworthy.
She had only to keep her nerve and all would be well. But her anxiety,
which now amounted to active fear, grew stronger with every minute
which brought her closer to Innocent House and it seemed to her that
her mood infected the rest of the group. Mr. de Witt usually sat in
silence, often reading, on the river journey, but the girls were usually
cheerful chatterers. This morning all of them fell into silence as the
launch slowly rocked to its usual mooring ring to the right of the steps.

De Witt suddenly said: "Innocent House. Well, here we are. . . ."

His voice held a note of spurious jollity as if they had all returned
from a boat trip, but his face was stern. She wondered what was the
matter with him, what he was thinking. Then slowly, with the others,
she carefully made her way up the tide-washed steps onto the marble
patio, bracing herself to meet whatever the day had in store.

17

George Copeland, standing behind the protection of his reception desk in embarrassed ineptitude, heard the clatter of feet on the cobbles with relief. So the launch had arrived at last. Lord Stilgoe halted his angry pacing and they both turned to the door. The little group came through in a bunch with James de Witt at the front. Mr. de Witt gave one look at George's worried face and asked quickly: "What's wrong, George?"

It was Lord Stilgoe who answered. Without greeting de Witt he said grimly: "Etienne's missing. I had an appointment to meet him in his office at nine o'clock. When I arrived there was no one here but the receptionist and the cleaner. It's not the way I expect to be treated. My time is valuable even if Etienne's isn't. I have a hospital appointment this morning."

De Witt said easily: "How do you mean, missing? I expect he's got held up in the traffic."

George broke in: "He must be here somewhere, Mr. de Witt. His jacket is over the chair in his office. I looked there when he didn't reply to my ring. And the front door wasn't locked when I arrived this morning, not with the Banham. I got in with just the Yale. And the alarm hadn't been set. Miss Claudia's just arrived. She's checking now."

They all moved, as if driven by a common impulse, into the hall. Claudia Etienne, with Mrs. Demery at her shoulder, was coming out of Blackie's office.

She said: "George is right. He must be here somewhere. His jacket is over the chair and his bunch of keys in the top right-hand drawer." She turned to George. "You've checked at number ten?"

"Yes, Miss Claudia. Mr. Bartrum's arrived but there's no one else in the building. He had a look and rang back. He says that Mr. Gerard's Jaguar is there, parked where it was last night."

"How about the house lights? Were they on when you arrived?"

"No, Miss Claudia. There wasn't a light in his office either. Not anywhere."

At this moment Frances Peverell and Gabriel Dauntsey appeared. George saw that Mr. Dauntsey looked frail. He was walking with a stick and there was a small sticking-plaster on the right of his forehead. No one remarked on it. George wondered if anyone but him had even noticed.

Claudia said: "You haven't got Gerard at number twelve, have you? He seems to have disappeared."

Frances said: "He hasn't been with us."

Mandy, coming in behind and taking off her helmet, said: "His car is here. I saw it at the end of Innocent Passage when I drove past."

Claudia said repressively, "Yes, we know that, Mandy. I'll take a look upstairs. He must be somewhere in the building. The rest of you, wait here."

She made briskly for the staircase with Mrs. Demery at her back. Blackie, as if she hadn't heard the instruction, gave a little gasp and ran clumsily after them. Maggie FitzGerald said, "Trust Mrs. Demery to be in on the act," but her voice was uncertain and when no one commented she blushed as if wishing she hadn't spoken.

The little group moved quietly into a semicircle, almost, George thought, as if gently pushed by an invisible hand. He had switched on the lights in the hall and the painted ceiling glowed above them, seeming to mark with its splendour and permanence their puny preoccupations and unimportant anxieties. All their eyes were turned upwards. George thought that they looked like figures in a religious painting, staring up in anticipation of some supernatural visitation. He waited with them, uncertain whether his place was here or behind his counter. It wasn't for him to initiate action by joining the search. As always he did what he was told, but he was a little surprised that the partners waited with such docility. But why not? It was pointless for a whole crowd of them to go charging round Innocent House. Three searchers were more than enough. If Mr. Gerard was in the building Miss Claudia would find him. No one spoke or moved except James de Witt, who had stepped quietly to Frances Peverell's side. It seemed to George that they had been waiting, frozen, like actors in a tableau, for hours, although it could only have been for a few minutes.

Then Amy, her voice sharp with fear, said: "Someone's screaming. I heard a scream." She looked round at them, frantic-eyed.

James de Witt didn't turn to look at her but kept his eyes on the stairs. He said quietly: "No one screamed. You imagined it, Amy."

Then it came again, but this time louder and unmistakable, a high desperate cry. They moved forward to the bottom of the stairs but no further. It was as if no one dared to take that first upward step. There was a second's silence, and then the wailing began, at first a distant lament and then rising, getting closer. George, rooted in terror, couldn't identify the voice. It seemed to him as inhuman as the wail of a siren or the scream of a cat in the night.

Maggie FitzGerald whispered: "Oh my God! My God, what is it?"

And then, with dramatic suddenness, Mrs. Demery appeared at the top of the staircase. It seemed to George that she materialized out of the air. She was supporting Blackie, whose wails were now subsiding into low heaving sobs.

James de Witt's voice was low but very clear: "What is it, Mrs. Demery? What's happened? Where's Mr. Gerard?"

"In the little archives room. Dead! Murdered! That's what's happened. He's lying up there half-naked and stiff as a bloody board. Some devil has strangled him with that sodding snake. He's got Hissing Sid wound round his neck with its head stuffed in his mouth."

At last James de Witt moved. He sprang for the stairs. Frances made to follow him, but he turned and said urgently, "No, Frances, no," and pushed her gently aside. Lord Stilgoe followed him with an old man's ungainly waddle, grasping at the stair rail. Gabriel Dauntsey hesitated for a moment, then followed.

Mrs. Demery cried: "Give me a hand, can't you, someone? She's a dead weight."

Frances went immediately to her and placed an arm round Blackie's waist. Looking up at them, George thought that it was Miss Frances who needed support. They came down the stairs together almost carrying Blackie between them. Blackie was moaning and whispering, "I'm sorry. I'm sorry." Together they supported her across the hall towards the back of the house while the little group looked after them in appalled silence.

George went back to his desk, to his switchboard. This was his place. This was where he felt secure, in control. This was where he could

cope. He could hear voices. The awful sobbing was quieter now but he
could hear Mrs. Demery's high expostulations and a babble of female
voices. He shut them out of his mind. There was a job to be done: he
had better do it. He tried to unlock his security cupboard under the
counter but his hands were shaking so violently that he couldn't fit the
key into the lock. The telephone rang and he jumped violently, then
fumbled for the headpiece. It was Mrs. Velma Pitt-Cowley, Mrs. Carling's
agent, wanting to speak to Mr. Gerard. George, shocked into initial
silence, managed to say that Mr. Gerard wasn't available. Even to his
ears, his voice sounded high, cracked, unnatural.

"Miss Claudia, then. I suppose she's in."

"No," said George, "no."

"What's wrong? That's you, isn't it, George? What's the matter?"

George, appalled, switched off the call. Immediately the telephone
rang again, but he didn't answer and after a few seconds the noise
stopped. He gazed at it in trembling impotence. Never before had he
acted like this. Time passed, seconds, minutes. And then Lord Stilgoe
was towering over the desk and he could smell his breath and feel the
force of his triumphant anger.

"Get me New Scotland Yard. I want to speak to the Commissioner.
If he's not available, get me Commander Adam Dalgliesh."

Book Two

DEATH OF
A PUBLISHER

18

Detective Inspector Kate Miskin, nudging aside a half-empty packing case, opened the balcony door of her new Docklands flat and, grasping the rail of polished oak, gazed over the shimmering river, up to Limehouse Reach and down to the great curve round the Isle of Dogs. It was only 9:15 in the morning but already an early mist had cleared and the sky, almost cloudless, was brightening to an opaque whiteness with glimpses of soft clear blue. It was a morning more like spring than mid-October, but the river smell was autumnal, strong as the smell of damp leaves and rich earth overlaying the salty tang of the sea. It was full tide and beneath the pin-points of light which flicked and danced on the creased surface of the water like fireflies, she could imagine the strong tug of the flowing current, could almost sense its power. With this flat, this view, one more ambition had been achieved, one more step taken away from that dull box-sized flat at the top of Ellison Fairweather Buildings in which she had spent the first eighteen years of her life.

Her mother had died within days of her birth, her father was unknown and she had been cared for by a reluctant and elderly maternal grandmother, who resented the child who had made her a virtual prisoner in the high-rise flat she dared no longer leave at night to seek the conviviality, the glitter and the warmth of the local pub and who had grown increasingly embittered by her grandchild's intelligence and by a responsibility for which she was unsuited, by age, by health, by temperament. Kate had realized too late, only at the moment of her grandmother's death, how much she had loved her. It seemed to her now that in the moment of that death each had paid to the other a lifetime's arrears of love. She knew that she would never break completely free of Ellison Fairweather Buildings. Coming up to this flat in the large modern lift, surrounded by the carefully packed oil paintings which she herself had painted, she had remembered the lift at Ellison Fairweather, the smeared and filthy walls with their graffiti, the stink of urine, the cigarette ends, the discarded beer cans. It had been frequently vandalized and she and her grandmother had had to lug their shopping and washing up the seven storeys, pausing at the top of each flight for her grandmother to catch her breath. Sitting there surrounded by their plastic bags, listening to the old lady's wheezings, she had vowed: "When I'm grown-up I shall get out of this. I shall leave bloody Ellison Fairweather Buildings for ever. I shall never come back again. I shall never be poor again. I shall never have to smell this smell again."

She had chosen the police service through which to make her escape, resisting the temptation to enter the sixth form or try for university, anxious only to begin earning, to get away. That first Victorian flat in Holland Park had been the beginning. After her grandmother's death she had stayed on for nine months, knowing that to leave at once would be a desertion, although she was not sure from what, perhaps from a reality that had to be faced, knowing too that there was expiation to be made, things she had to learn about herself, and that this was the place in which to learn them. The time would come when it would be right to leave and she could close the door with a sense of completion, of putting behind her a past which couldn't be altered, but which could be accepted with its miseries, its horrors—yes, and its joys—reconciled and made part of herself. And now that time had come.

This flat, of course, wasn't what she had originally imagined. She had pictured herself in one of the great converted warehouses near Tower Bridge with high windows and huge rooms, the strong oak rafters and, surely, the lingering smell of spice. But even with a falling property market this had been beyond her means. And the flat which after careful searching she had chosen wasn't a poor second. She had taken the highest mortgage possible, believing that it was financially wise to buy the best she could afford. She had one large room, eighteen feet by twelve, and two smaller bedrooms, one with its shower en suite. The kitchen was large enough to eat in and well fitted. The south-facing balcony, which ran the whole length of the sitting-room, was narrow but still wide enough to take a small table and chairs. She could eat out there in the summer. And she was glad that the furniture originally bought for her first flat hadn't been cheap. The sofa and two chairs in real leather were going to look good and right in this modern setting. It was lucky that she had rejected black in favour of fawn. Black would have looked too smart. And the simple elm table and chairs looked right too.

And the flat had another great advantage. It was at the end of the building and with a double outlook and two balconies. From her bedroom she could see the wide gleaming panorama of Canary Wharf, the tower like an immense cellular pencil with its lead topped with light, the great white curve of the adjoining building, the still water of the old West India Dock and the overhead Docklands Light Railway with its trains like clockwork toys. This city of glass and concrete would become busier as new firms moved in. She would be able to look down on the multicoloured, ever-changing pageant of half a million scurrying men and women leading their working lives. The other balcony looked south-west over the river and the slower immemorial traffic of the Thames; barges, pleasure boats, the launches of the River Police and the Port of London Authority, the cruise liners making their way upstream to berth at Tower Bridge. She loved the stimulus of contrast and here in the flat she could move at will from one world to another, from the new to the old, from still water to the tidal river which T. S. Eliot had called a strong brown god.

The flat was particularly suitable for a police officer, with an entry-phone system on the main entrance and two security locks and a chain fitted to her front door. There was a basement garage to which the residents had their own keys. That, too, was important. And the journey to New Scotland Yard wouldn't be too difficult. She was, after all, on the right side of the river. But perhaps she might occasionally travel by river boat to Westminster Pier. She would get to know the river, become part of its life and history. She would wake in the morning to the cry of gulls and step out into this cool white emptiness. Standing now between the glitter of the water and the high, delicate blue of the sky, she felt an extraordinary impulse which had visited her before and which she thought must be as close as she could ever get to a religious experience. She was possessed by a need, almost physical in its intensity, to pray, to praise, to say thank you, without knowing to whom, to shout with a joy that was deeper than the joy she felt in her own physical well-being and achievements or even in the beauty of the physical world.

She had left the fitted bookshelves at the old flat, but new ones built to her specification covered the whole of the wall facing the window and on these, kneeling beside a packing case, Alan Scully was arranging her books. She had been surprised how many she had acquired since knowing him. None of these writers had she ever encountered at school but she was grateful now for Ancroft Comprehensive. It had done its best for her. The teachers whom she had once in her arrogance despised she now knew had been dedicated, struggling to impose discipline, to cope with large classes and a dozen different languages, to meet competing needs, to tackle the appalling home problems of some of the children and to get them through the examinations which would at least open the door to something better. But most of her education had happened since school. Behind its bicycle sheds and in its asphalt playground she had learned all that was unimportant about sex and nothing that was important. It was Alan who had done that for her, that and so much else. He had taught her about books, not condescendingly, not seeing himself as some kind of Pygmalion, but wanting to share with someone he loved the things that he loved. And now the time had come for that, too, to end.

She heard his voice: "If we're taking a break I'll make a coffee. Or are you just admiring the view?"

"Admiring the view. Gloating. What do you think of it, Alan?"

It was the first time he had seen the flat and she had displayed it with something of the pride of a child with a new toy.

"I shall like it when you're finally settled. That is, if I see it when you're finally settled. What about these books? Do you want to separate poetry, fiction, non-fiction? At present we've got Dalgliesh next to Defoe."

"Defoe? I didn't know I had a Defoe. I don't even like Defoe. Oh, separate I think. And then by author's name."

"The Dalgliesh is a first edition. Do you feel it necessary to buy him in hardback because he's your boss and you work with him?"

"No. I read his poetry to see if I can understand him better."

"And do you?"

"Not really. I can't relate the poetry to the man. And when I do, it's terrifying. He notices too much."

"Not signed, I notice. So you didn't ask."

"It would embarrass both of us. Don't fiddle with it, Alan. Just put it on the shelf."

She went over and knelt beside him. He had made no mention of her professional books and she saw that they were neatly piled beside the packing case. One by one she began placing them on the lowest shelf: a copy of the latest Criminal Statistics, the *Police and Criminal Evidence Act 1984,* Blackstone's *Guide to the Criminal Justice Act 1991,*

Butterworth's *Police Law*, Keane's *The Modern Law of Evidence*, Clifford Hogan's *Criminal Law*, the *Police Training Manual* and the Sheehy Report. She thought: The collection of a professional woman on the make, and wondered whether in placing them to one side and not mentioning them, Alan was making some kind of comment, perhaps even a subconscious judgement on more than her library. For the first time in years she saw that relationship through the eyes of a detached and critical observer. Here we have a professional woman, successful, ambitious, knowing where she wants to go. Coping every day with the messy detritus of undisciplined lives, she has carefully excluded messiness from her own. One necessary accoutrement of this well-organized self-sufficiency is a lover, intelligent, personable, available when needed, skilful in bed and undemanding out of it. For three years Alan Scully had admirably filled this need. She knew that, in return, she had given affection, loyalty, kindness, understanding; none of these things had been difficult to provide. But was it surprising that, having made his own commitment, he wanted to be more to her than the equivalent of a fashion accessory?

She ground the beans, relishing the fresh coffee smell. No drink ever tasted quite as good as the beans smelled. They drank the coffee sitting on the floor, their backs against a packing case as yet unopened. She said: "What flight are you taking next Wednesday?"

"The eleven o'clock, BA175. You haven't changed your mind?"

She almost said "No, I can't, Alan, it's impossible," but stopped herself. It wasn't impossible. She could perfectly well change her mind. The honest answer was that she didn't want to. They had talked over their problem many times before and she knew now that there could be no compromise. She understood what he felt and what he wanted. He wasn't trying to blackmail her. The chance had come for him to work for three years in Princeton and he was anxious to go. It was important to his career, to his future. But he would stay in London, would continue his present job at the library if she would make a commitment to him, would agree to marry him, or at least to live with him, and have his child. It wasn't that he thought her career less important than his; if necessary he would temporarily give up his job and stay at home while she worked. He had always granted her that essential equality. But he was tired of being on the periphery of her life. She was the woman he loved and wanted to spend his life with. He would give up Princeton, but not if it meant continuing as they were, seeing her only when the job permitted, knowing that he was her lover but would never be more.

She said: "I'm not ready for marriage or for motherhood. Perhaps

I never shall be, particularly not for motherhood. I wouldn't be any good at it. I've never had any training, you see."

"I don't think it requires training."

"It requires loving commitment. That's one thing I can't give. You can't give what you haven't had."

He didn't argue or attempt to persuade her. The time for talking was over.

He said: "At least we've got another five days and we'll have today. Unpacking all this morning, lunch at a riverside pub, maybe the Prospect of Whitby. There ought to be time for that. You've got to eat. What time are you expected back at the Yard?"

She said: "Two o'clock. I've only got the half-day. Daniel Aaron's on leave today so it isn't easy. I'll get off as early as I can and we'll have dinner here tonight. One meal out is enough. We can pick up a Chinese takeaway."

Alan was carrying the coffee mugs into the kitchen when the telephone rang. He called out: "Your first call. That's what comes of sending out change-of-address cards. You'll be pestered by friends wishing you luck."

But the call was short and Kate hardly spoke as she answered it. Putting down the receiver, she turned to him.

"It's the Squad. Suspicious death. They want me at once. It's on the river so AD is picking me up here in a Thames Division launch. Sorry, Alan." She seemed to have spent the last three years saying "Sorry, Alan."

They looked at each other in silence for a moment, then he said: "As it was in the beginning, is now and ever shall be. What do you want me to do, Kate, go on unpacking?"

Suddenly the thought of him here alone was intolerable. "No," she said. "Leave it. I'll do it later. It can wait."

But he continued unpacking as she changed her clothes from the jeans and sweatshirt, which had been suitable for the dusty job of moving in and then cleaning the flat, to a pair of fawn corduroy trousers, a well-cut tweed jacket and a polo-necked jumper in fine cream wool. She plaited her thick hair high at the back and secured the end of the plait with a slide.

On her return he gave her his usual quick appraising smile and said: "Your working clothes? I never know whether you dress for Adam Dalgliesh or for the suspects. Obviously it's not for the corpse."

She said: "This corpse isn't exactly lying in a ditch."

It was comparatively new, this jealousy of her boss, and was perhaps both a symptom and the cause of their changing relationship.

They left together in silence. It wasn't until Kate was double-locking the front door after them that he spoke again. He said: "Shall I see you again before I leave next Wednesday?"

"I don't know, Alan. I don't know."

But she did know. If this case was as important as it promised to be she would be working a sixteen-hour day, perhaps longer. She would look back on those few hours they had spent together in the flat with pleasure, even with sadness. But what she was feeling now was something more intoxicating, and she felt it whenever she was called to a new case. This was her job, one she had been trained for, one she did well, one she enjoyed. Already knowing that this might be the last time she saw him for years, she was moving in thought away from him, mentally bracing herself for the task ahead.

He had parked his car in one of the marked spaces to the right of the forecourt but he didn't get in. Instead he came and waited with her for the approach of the police launch. When its dark-blue sleek lines came into view he turned from her without a word and went back to the car. But still he didn't drive away. As the launch drew up Kate knew that he was still watching as the tall dark figure standing in the bow held out a hand to steady her on board.

19

The call came to Inspector Daniel Aaron just as he was approaching Eastern Avenue. He didn't need to stop the car to take it; the message was short and clear. A suspicious death at Innocent House, Innocent Walk. He was to go there immediately. Robbins would be bringing his murder bag.

The message couldn't have come at a better time. His first reaction was a surge of excitement that here at last was the major job he had been longing for. He had only replaced Massingham on the Special Squad three months ago and was anxious to prove himself. But there was another reason. He was on his way to his parents' house, in The Drive, Ilford. It was their fortieth wedding anniversary and a luncheon party had been arranged with his mother's sister and her husband. He had applied well in advance for a day's leave, knowing that this was one family occasion he couldn't reasonably ignore, but he hadn't been looking forward to it. The morning promised a pretentious but dull lunch at the popular store restaurant his mother had chosen, followed by an afternoon of boring family chat. He knew that his aunt regarded him as an uncaring son, an unsatisfactory nephew, a bad Jew. On this occasion she might not openly voice her disapproval but this brittle forbearance would hardly lighten the atmosphere.

He turned into a side road and stopped the car to telephone. It was going to be a difficult call and he preferred not to be driving while he made it. As he stabbed out the number he was aware of a confusion of emotions: relief that he had a valid excuse to miss the luncheon party, a strong disinclination to break the news, excitement that he was on his way to a case which promised to be a big one and the usual irrational and pleasure-destroying guilt. He had no intention of wasting time in argument or prolonged explanations. Kate Miskin might be already at the scene. His parents would have to accept that he had a job to do.

It was his father who answered the telephone. "Daniel, haven't you started out yet? You said you'd come really early, have a quiet time with us before the others arrive. Where are you?"

"I'm on Eastern Avenue. I'm sorry, Father, but I can't come. I've just had a call from the Squad. It's an urgent case. Murder. I have to drive straight to the scene."

And then his mother's voice as she took over the telephone. "What is it you're saying, Daniel? Did you say you're not coming? But you must come. You promised. Your aunt and uncle will be here. It's our fortieth wedding anniversary. What is a celebration if I can't have both my sons with me? You promised."

"I know that I promised. I wouldn't be on Eastern Avenue now if I hadn't intended to come. The call's just come through."

"But you're on leave. What's the point of having a rest day if they call you back like this? Can't someone else cope? Why does it always have to be you?"

"It doesn't always have to be me. It does today. It's an urgent case. Murder."

"Murder! And you'd rather be mixed up in murder than be with your parents. Murder. Death. Can't you give a thought to the living?"

"I'm sorry, I have to go now." He added grimly, "Have a good lunch," and replaced the receiver.

It had been worse than he had expected. He sat for a few seconds willing himself into calm, fighting down an irritation which was rising to anger. Then he slipped in the clutch, found a convenient driveway to reverse and joined the stream of traffic. He was part now of the morning rush hour, although the words seemed inappropriate to describe this grinding erratic progress. And he was unlucky with the traffic lights. The journey was punctuated by light after light glowing into red with maddening perversity. The scene of violent death to which he was driving with such tedious slowness could not yet even be imagined but, once there, the tasks would take all his thoughts and energies. Physically he was moving away from that Ilford house mile by painful mile, but now he could not banish it or its life from his thoughts.

The family had moved from the Whitechapel terraced house where

he was born when he was ten and David thirteen. He still thought of
27 Balaclava Terrace as home. It was one of the few streets not destroyed
by enemy bombing, stubbornly surviving while the surrounding flats
and houses were demolished in clouds of acrid dust and the great high
towers rose up like an alien city. It, too, would have gone but for the
eccentricity and determination of an old woman in a neighbouring
square whose efforts at preserving something of the old East End had
coincided with a shortage of local-authority money for their more
adventurous plans. So Balaclava Terrace still stood, now no doubt gentrified, a refuge from strident modernity for young executives, house-
men from the London Hospital and sharing medical students. None of
the family had ever returned. For his parents the move had been the
realization of a dream, a dream which was almost terrifying when it
promised to become reality, a matter for constant half-understood
conversations late into the night. His father, his accountancy examinations completed, had gained a promotion. It was to be a sloughing off
of the past, a move north-east which was also a move upwards, a few
more miles from that distant Polish village with its unpronounceable
name from which his great-grandfather had originally come. It would
mean a mortgage, a matter for anxious arithmetic, the weighing of
alternatives.

But all had been well. Within six months of moving, an unforeseen
death in the firm had meant further promotion and with it financial
security. There was a modern fitted kitchen in the Ilford house, a three-
piece suite for the sitting-room. The women who attended the local
synagogue were smartly dressed; now his mother was among the
smartest. Daniel suspected that he was the only member of the family
who regretted Balaclava Terrace. He was ashamed of the Ilford house
and ashamed of himself for despising what had been so hardly won.
He thought to himself that if ever he brought Kate Miskin home he
would prefer her to see Balaclava Terrace, not The Drive, Ilford. But
what on earth had Kate Miskin to do with where or how he lived?
There was no question of inviting her home. He had worked with her
in the Special Squad for only three months. What on earth had Inspector
Kate Miskin to do with his family's life?

He thought he knew the root of his discontent: it lay in envy. Almost
from early childhood he had known that his elder brother was his
mother's favourite son. She had been thirty-five when David was born
and had almost given up hope of a child. The overwhelming love she
had felt for her first-born had been a revelation of such intensity that
it had absorbed almost all she had to give in maternal affection. Com-

ing three years later, he was welcomed but never obsessively desired. He remembered as a fourteen-year-old seeing a woman gazing into a neighbour's pram at a new baby, and saying, "So he's number five? Still, they all bring their own love with them, don't they?" He had never felt that he had brought his.

And then, when David was eleven, he had had his accident. Daniel could still remember the effect on his mother. Her wild eyes as she clung to his father, her face bleached with terror and pain, suddenly the face of a wild stranger, her unbearable sobbing, the long hours spent at David's bedside in the London Hospital while he was left to the care of neighbours. In the end they had had to amputate David's left leg below the knee. She had brought home her maimed elder son with an exultant tenderness as if he had risen from the dead. But Daniel knew that he had no chance of competing. David had been courageous, uncomplaining, an easy child. He had been moody, jealous, difficult. He had also been intelligent. He suspected that he was cleverer than David but had early given up their academic rivalry. It was David who went to London University, read law, had been called to the Bar and had now found a place in a chambers which specialized in criminal cases. And it was as an act of defiance that at eighteen and straight from school he had joined the police.

He told himself, and half believed, that his parents were ashamed of his job. Certainly they never boasted of his successes as they did of David's. He remembered a snatch of conversation at his mother's last birthday dinner. Greeting him at the door she had said: "I haven't told Mrs. Forsdyke that you're a policeman. Of course I shall mention it if she asks what you do."

His father had said quietly: "And in Commander Dalgliesh's Special Squad, Mother, called in to crimes of particular sensitivity."

He had said with a bitterness which surprised even himself: "I'm not sure that will help disinfect the shame. And what will the old bat do anyway? Faint into her prawn cocktail? Why should the job worry her, unless her old man's on the fiddle?" Oh God, he had thought, I've started it all again. On her birthday, too. "Cheer up. You've got one respectable son. You can tell Mrs. Forsdyke that David spends his time lying to keep criminals out of gaol and I spend my time lying to get them in."

Well, they could enjoy criticizing him over their hors d'oeuvre. And Bella would be there, of course. Like David, she was a lawyer but she would have found time for his parents' anniversary. Bella the perfect daughter-in-law-to-be. Bella who was learning Yiddish, who visited

Israel twice a year and raised money to help immigrants from Russia and Ethiopia, who attended Beit Midrash, the Talmudic learning centre at the synagogue, who kept Sabbath; Bella who turned on him her dark reproachful eyes and worried about the state of his soul.

It was no use saying to them, "I don't believe in it any more." How much did they believe, either of his parents? Put them on oath in the witness box and ask them whether they really believed that God handed down the Torah to Moses at Sinai and that their lives depended on the right answer. What would they say? He had asked his brother that question and he still remembered the answer. It had surprised him at the time and did so now, opening the disconcerting possibility that there were subtleties in David which he had never understood.

"I should probably lie. There are some beliefs it is worth dying for and that doesn't depend on whether or not they are strictly true."

His mother, of course, would never bring herself to say, "I don't care whether you believe or disbelieve, I want you to be here with us on the Sabbath. I want you to be seen in the synagogue with your father and brother." And it wasn't intellectual dishonesty, although he tried to tell himself that it was. You could argue that few adherents of any religion believed all the dogma of their faith except the fundamentalists and, God knew, they were a bloody sight more dangerous than any non-believer. God knew. How natural it was and how universal to slip into the language of faith. And perhaps his mother was right, although she would never bring herself to speak the truth. The outward forms were important. To practise religion wasn't only a matter of intellectual assent. To be seen in the synagogue was to proclaim: This is where I stand, these are my people, these are the values by which I try to live, this is what generations of my forebears have made me, this is what I am. He remembered his grandfather's words, spoken to him after his bar mitzvah: "What is a Jew without his belief? What Hitler could not do to us shall we do to ourselves?" The old resentments welled up. A Jew wasn't even allowed his atheism. Burdened with guilt from childhood, he couldn't reject his faith without feeling the need to apologize to the God he no longer believed in. It was always there at the back of his mind, silent witness of his apostasy, that moving army of naked humanity, the young, the middle-aged, the elderly, flowing like a dark tide into the gas chambers.

And now, halted at yet another red light, thinking of the house that would never be home, seeing with his mind's clear eye the gleaming windows, the looped lace curtains with their bows, the immaculate front lawn, he thought: Why must I define myself by the wrongs others have done to my race? The guilt was bad enough; do I have to carry the burden of innocence also? I'm a Jew, isn't that enough? Do I have to represent to myself and others the evil of mankind?

He had at last reached The Highway and, mysteriously as is its habit, the traffic had eased and he was making good progress. With luck he would be at Innocent House within five minutes. This death wouldn't be commonplace, this mystery not easily solved. The team wouldn't have been called in to a routine case. For those intimately concerned, perhaps, no death was commonplace and no investigation purely routine. But this was his chance to prove to Adam Dalgliesh that he had been right to choose him as Massingham's replacement and he intended to seize it. There was no priority, personal or professional, which was higher than this.

20

The police launch butted upstream round the northerly bend of the river between Rotherhithe and Narrow Street against a strong current. The breeze was strengthening to a light wind and the morning was colder than it had seemed to Kate on her first wakening. A few clouds, thin trails of white vapour, drifted and dissolved against the pale blue of the sky. She had seen Innocent House before from the river, but when it appeared with dramatic suddenness as they rounded the bend of Limehouse Reach she gave a small gasp of wonder and, glancing up at Dalgliesh's face, caught his brief smile. In the morning sunlight it gleamed with such an unreal intensity that for a moment she thought it was floodlit. As the engine of the police launch died and it was skilfully manoeuvred to the row of hanging tyres to the right of the landing steps she could almost believe that the house was part of a film set, an insubstantial palace of hardboard and paste behind whose ephemeral walls the director, the actors, the lighting men were already busying themselves around the body of the corpse while the make-up girl darted forward to mop a glistening brow and apply a final dollop of artificial blood. The fantasy disconcerted her; she was not prone to play-acting or to flights of imagination, but the sense of a contrived occasion, of being at once an observer and a participant, was difficult to shake off and was strengthened by the posed immobility of the reception party.

There were two men and two women. The women stood a little to the front with a man on each side. They were grouped on the wide marble forecourt as motionless as statues watching the tying up of the launch with serious and, it seemed, critical faces. There had been time on the short journey for Dalgliesh to give her some briefing and Kate could guess who they were. The tall dark woman must be Claudia Etienne, the dead man's sister, with the last of the Peverells, Frances Peverell, on her left. The older of the two men, who looked well over seventy, would be Gabriel Dauntsey, the poetry editor, and the younger James de Witt. They looked as posed as if a director had carefully arranged them to suit the camera angles, but as Dalgliesh advanced the little group broke up and Claudia Etienne, hand outstretched, came forward to make the introductions. She turned and they followed her down a short cobbled lane and into the side door of the house.

An elderly man was seated at the switchboard behind the reception desk. With his pale smooth face an almost perfect oval, the cheeks splotched with small red circles under gentle eyes, he had the look of an elderly clown. He looked up at them as they entered and Kate saw in the luminous eyes a look of mingled apprehension and appeal. It was a look she had seen before. The police might be needed, even impatiently waited, but they were seldom greeted without anxiety, even by the innocent. For the first couple of seconds she wondered irrelevantly which professions were invited into people's homes without reservation. Doctors and plumbers came high on the list, midwives probably at the top. She wondered what it would feel like to be greeted with the heartfelt words, "Thank God you're here." The telephone rang and the old man turned to answer it. His voice was low and very attractive but held an unmistakable note of distress and his hands were shaking.

"Peverell Press. Can I help you? No, I'm afraid Mr. Gerard isn't available. Can I get someone else to ring you back later?" He looked up again, this time at Claudia Etienne, and said helplessly: "It's Matthew Evans's secretary from Fabers, Miss Etienne. He wants to talk to Mr. Gerard. It's about next Wednesday's meeting on literary piracy."

Claudia took the receiver. "This is Claudia Etienne. Please tell Mr. Evans I'll ring him back as soon as I can. We're going to close the office now for the rest of the day. I'm afraid there's been an accident. Tell him Gerard Etienne is dead. I know he'll understand that I can't speak now."

Without waiting for a response she replaced the receiver, then turned to Dalgliesh. "There's no point in trying to cover it up, is there? Death is death. It isn't a temporary embarrassment, a little local difficulty. You can't pretend it hasn't happened. Anyway the press will get hold of it soon enough."

Her voice was harsh; the dark eyes were hard. She looked like a woman possessed more by anger than grief. Turning to the receptionist, she said more gently: "Put a message on the answerphone, George, that the office is closed for the day. Then go and get yourself some strong coffee. Mrs. Demery is about somewhere. If any other staff arrive, tell them to go home."

George said: "But will they go, Miss Claudia? I mean, they won't want to take it from me surely?"

Claudia Etienne frowned: "Perhaps not. I suppose I ought to see them. Better still, we'll get Mr. Bartrum. He's here somewhere, isn't he, George?"

"Mr. Bartrum is in his own office in number ten, Miss Claudia. He said he had plenty of work to get on with and wanted to stay. He thought it would be all right as he's not in the main house."

"Ring him, will you, George, and ask him to have a word with me. He can cope with the latecomers. Some of them may have work they can take home. Tell them I shall be speaking to all of them on Monday."

She turned to Dalgliesh. "We've been doing that, sending staff home. I hope that's all right. It seemed better not to have too many people on the premises."

Dalgliesh said: "We shall need to see them all in time, but that can wait. Who found your brother?"

"I did. Blackie—Miss Blackett, my brother's secretary—was with me and so was Mrs. Demery, our cleaner. We went up together."

"Which of you entered the room first?"

"I did."

"Then if you could show me the way. Did your brother usually take the lift or the stairs?"

"The stairs. But he didn't normally go up to the top of the house. That's what's so extraordinary, his being in the archives office at all."

Dalgliesh said: "Then we'll take the stairs."

Claudia Etienne said: "I locked the room after we found my brother's body. Lord Stilgoe has the key. He asked for it so I gave it to him. Why not if it made him happy? I suppose he thought one of us might go back and interfere with the evidence."

But Lord Stilgoe was already pressing forward. "I thought it right to take charge of the key, Commander. I have to speak to you in private. I warned you. I knew that we should have a tragedy here sooner or later."

He held out the key but it was Claudia who took it. Dalgliesh said: "Lord Stilgoe, do you know how Gerard Etienne died?"

"Of course not, how could I?"

"Then we'll talk later."

"But I've seen the body, of course. I thought that was only my duty. Abominable. Well, I warned you. It's obvious that this outrage is part of the campaign against me and my book."

Dalgliesh said: "Later, Lord Stilgoe."

He was, as always, taking his time in viewing the body. Kate knew that, however speedily he responded to a murder call, he always arrived with the same unhurried calm. She had seen him put out a restraining hand to an over-enthusiastic detective sergeant with the quiet words, "Cool it, Sergeant. You're not a doctor. The dead can't be resuscitated."

Now he turned to Claudia Etienne. "Shall we go up?"

She turned to the three partners who, with Lord Stilgoe, were standing together in a silent group as if waiting for instructions, and said: "Perhaps you'd better wait in the boardroom. I'll join you as soon as I can."

Lord Stilgoe said in a voice more reasonable than Kate expected: "I'm afraid I can't stay any longer, Commander. That's why I made such an early appointment with Mr. Etienne. I wanted to discuss progress on my memoirs before I went into hospital for a minor operation. I'm due there at eleven. I don't want to risk losing the bed. I'll telephone either you or the Commissioner at the Yard from the hospital."

Kate sensed that this suggestion was greeted with relief by de Witt and Dauntsey.

The little group passed through the open doorway into the hall. Kate gave a silent gasp of admiration. For a second her step halted, but she resisted the temptation to let her eyes too obviously range. The police were always invaders of privacy; it was offensive to act as if she were a paying tourist. But it seemed to her that in that one moment of revelation she was aware simultaneously of every detail of the hall's magnificence, the intricate segments of the marble floor, the six mottled marble pillars with their elegantly carved capitals, the richness of the painted ceiling, a gleaming panorama of eighteenth-century London, bridges, spires, towers, houses, masted ships, the whole unified by the blue reaches of the river, the elegant double staircase, the balustrade curving down to end in bronzes of laughing boys riding dolphins and holding aloft the great globed lamps. As they mounted the magnificence was less intrusive, the decorative detail more restrained, but it was through dignity, proportion and elegance that they moved purposefully upwards to the stark desecration of murder.

On the third floor there was a green baize door which stood open. They mounted a narrow stairway, Claudia Etienne leading with Dalgliesh

at her shoulder and Kate at the rear. The stairs turned to the right
before the final half-dozen treads led them to a narrow hall about ten
feet wide, with the grille doors of a lift to the left. The right-hand wall
was without doors but there was a closed door on the left and one
immediately in front of them which stood open.

Claudia Etienne said: "This is the archives room, where we keep
our old records. The little archives office is through here."

The archives room had obviously once been two rooms, but the
central wall had been removed to produce one very long chamber
running almost the whole length of the house. The rows of wooden
filing racks at right angles to the door and reaching almost to the ceiling
were ranged so closely that there could hardly be room to move
comfortably between them. Between the rows hung a number of light
bulbs without shades. Natural light came from six long windows through
which Kate could glimpse the intricate stone carving of a balustrade.
They turned to the right, down the clear space about four feet wide
between the ends of the shelves and the wall, and came to another door.

Claudia Etienne silently handed Dalgliesh the key. Taking it, he
said: "If you can bear to come in I would like you to confirm that the
room and your brother's body look exactly as they did when you first
entered. If you find that too distressing, don't worry. It will help, but
it isn't essential."

She said: "It's all right. It's easier for me now than it would be
tomorrow. I still can't believe it's real. Nothing about it looks real,
nothing about it feels real. I suppose that by tomorrow I'll know that it
is real and that the reality is final."

It was her words which to Kate sounded unreal. There was a strain
of falsity, of histrionics in the balanced cadences, as if they had been
thought out in advance. But she told herself not to be over-hasty. It
was too easy to misinterpret the disorientation of grief. She more than
most surely knew how oddly inappropriate the first spoken reaction to
shock or bereavement could be. She remembered the wife of a bus
driver stabbed to death in an Islington pub, whose first reaction had
been to lament that he hadn't changed his shirt that morning or posted
the pools coupon. And yet the wife had loved her husband, and
genuinely grieved for him.

Dalgliesh took the key from Claudia Etienne. It turned easily in the
lock and he opened the door. A sour gaseous smell wafted out like a
contagion. The half-naked body seemed to leap up at them with the
stark theatricality of death and hang for a moment suspended in un-
reality, an image bizarre and powerful, staining the quiet air.

He was lying supine, his feet towards the door. He was wearing grey trousers and grey socks. The shoes of fine black leather looked new, the soles almost unscuffed. It was odd, Kate thought, how one noticed such details. The top of his body was naked and a white shirt was bunched in the extended fist of his outstretched right hand. The velvet snake was wound twice round his neck, the tail lying against his chest, the head jammed into the wide-stretched mouth. Above it his eyes, open and glazed, unmistakably the eyes of death, seemed to Kate to hold for a moment a look of outraged surprise. All the colours were strong, unnaturally bright. The rich dark brown of the hair, the face and torso stained an unnatural pinkish red, the stark whiteness of the shirt, the livid green of the snake. The impression of a physical force emanating from the body was so strong that Kate instinctively recoiled and felt the soft bump of her shoulder against Claudia's. She said, "I'm sorry," and the conventional apology sounded inadequate even if it referred only to that brief physical encounter. Then the image faded and reality reasserted itself. The body became what it was, dead bare flesh, grotesquely adorned, displayed as if on a stage.

And now in a swift glance, standing in the open doorway, she took in the details of the room. It was small, no more than twelve feet by eight, and bleak as an execution shed, the wooden floor uncovered, the walls bare. There was one high narrow window, closed tight shut, and a single white shaded bulb suspended from the middle of the ceiling. From the window frame hung a broken window cord no more than three inches long. To the left of the window was a small Victorian fireplace with coloured tiles of fruit and flowers. The grate had been removed and replaced by an old-fashioned gas fire. Against the opposite wall was a small wooden table holding a modern black angled reading lamp and two wire filing trays each holding a few shabby manila files. Aware that some small detail was incongruous, Kate looked for the remaining length of the window cord and saw it under the table, as if it had been casually kicked or thrown out of the way. Claudia Etienne was still standing at her shoulder. Kate was aware of her stillness, of her breathing, shallow and controlled.

Dalgliesh asked: "Is this how you found the room? Does anything strike you now which didn't then?"

She said: "Nothing's changed. Well how could it? I locked the door before we left. I didn't notice much about the room when I—when I found him."

"Did you touch the body?"

"I knelt by him and felt his face. He was very cold, but I knew he was dead before then. I stayed kneeling by him. When the others had gone, I think . . ." She paused, then went on resolutely, "I laid my cheek briefly against his."

"And the room?"

"It looks odd now. I'm not often up here—the last time was when I found Sonia Clements' body—but it looks different, emptier, cleaner. And there's something missing. It's the tape recorder. Gabriel—Mr. Dauntsey—dictates onto a tape and the recorder is usually left on the table. And I didn't notice that broken window cord when I first came in. Where's the end? Is Gerard lying on it?"

Kate said: "It's under the table."

Claudia Etienne looked at it and said: "How odd. You'd expect it to be lying by the window."

She swayed, and Kate put out a supporting hand but the girl shrugged it quickly away.

Dalgliesh said: "Thank you for coming up with us, Miss Etienne. I know it wasn't easy. That's all I wanted to ask now. Kate, will you . . . ?"

But before Kate could move, Claudia Etienne said: "Don't touch me. I'm perfectly capable of walking downstairs by myself. I'll be with the others in the boardroom if you need me again."

But her way down the narrow stairs was impeded. There was the sound of male voices, quick light footsteps. A few seconds later Daniel Aaron came swiftly into the room, followed by two scene-of-crime officers, Charlie Ferris and his assistant.

Aaron said: "I'm sorry I'm late, sir. The traffic was heavy on the Whitechapel Road."

His eyes met Kate's and he gave a shrug and a brief, rueful smile. She liked and respected him. She had no difficulty in working with him. He was in every way an improvement on Massingham, but like Massingham he was never happy to find that Kate had got to the scene of crime before him.

21

The four partners had moved together into the boardroom on the first floor less by deliberate intention than by an unspoken feeling that it was wiser to stay together, to hear what words were spoken by the others, to feel at least the spurious comfort of human comradeship, not to retreat to a suspicious isolation. But they were without occupation and each was unwilling to send for files, papers or reading matter in case this demonstrated a callous indifference. The house seemed curiously quiet. Somewhere, they knew, the few staff still on the premises would be conferring, discussing, speculating. There were things they too needed to discuss, a provisional reallocation of work to be agreed, but to do so now seemed as brutally insensitive as robbing the dead.

But at first their wait was not long. Within ten minutes of his arrival Commander Dalgliesh appeared with Inspector Miskin. As the tall dark figure moved quietly up to the table, four pairs of eyes turned and regarded him soberly as if his presence, at once desired and half-feared, was an intrusion into a common grief. They sat unmoving as he pulled out a chair for the woman police officer and then himself sat down, resting his hands on the table.

He said: "I'm sorry to have kept you waiting but I'm afraid that waiting and disruption are inevitable after an unexplained death. I shall need to see you separately and I hope to give those interviews before too long. Is there a room here with a telephone I could use without too great inconvenience? I shall need it only for the rest of the day. The incident room will be at Wapping Police Station."

It was Claudia who replied. "If you took over the whole house for a month the inconvenience would be slight compared with the inconvenience of murder."

De Witt broke in quietly, "If it is murder," and it seemed as if the room, already quiet, grew quieter as they waited for his reply.

"We can't be sure of the cause of death until after the post-mortem. The forensic pathologist will be here shortly and I shall then know when that's likely to be. Then there may be some laboratory investigations which will also take time."

Claudia said: "You can use my brother's office. That would seem appropriate. It's on the ground floor, the right-hand front room. You have to go through his PA's office to get to it but Miss Blackett can move out if that's inconvenient. Is there anything else you need?"

"I would like, please, a list of all staff presently employed and the rooms they occupy and the names of any who may have left but were here for the whole of the period during which your practical joker has been at work. I believe that you have already carried out an investigation into these incidents. I need details of the incidents and what, if anything, you have discovered."

De Witt said: "So you know about that?"

"The police had been told. It would be helpful too if I could have a plan of the building."

Claudia said: "There's one in the files. We had some interior alterations done a couple of years ago and the architect drew up new drawings of the interior and the exterior. The original designs for the house and for its decoration are in the archives, but I don't suppose your interest is primarily architectural."

"Not at present. What arrangements are there for securing the building? Who holds the keys?"

Miss Etienne said: "Each of the partners has a set of keys to all the doors. The formal entrance is from the terrace and the river but that door is only used now for big occasions, when most of the guests come by boat. We don't have many of those nowadays. The last one was the joint summer party and celebration of my brother's engagement on the tenth of July. The door from Innocent Walk is the main street door but it's rarely used. Because of the architectural oddity of the house it leads past the servants' quarters and the kitchen. It's always kept locked and bolted. It's still locked and bolted. Lord Stilgoe checked the doors before you arrived." She seemed about to make some comment on Lord Stilgoe's activities but checked herself and went on: "The door we use is the side one on Innocent Lane, by which you came in. That is normally left open during the day as long as George Copeland is on the switchboard. George has a key to that door, but not the back door or the river frontage. The burglar-alarm system is controlled from the panel beside the switchboard. The doors and the windows on three storeys are locked. The system is fairly rudimentary, I'm afraid, but burglary has never really been a problem. The house itself is, of course, almost priceless but few of the pictures, for example, are originals. There is a large safe in Gerard's office and after an incident when the page proofs of Lord Stilgoe's book were tampered with we installed additional locking cupboards in three of the offices and under the reception desk so that any manuscripts or important papers can be locked up at night."

Dalgliesh asked: "And who normally arrives first in the morning and unlocks?"

Gabriel Dauntsey said: "Usually it's George Copeland. He's due to start work at nine o'clock and he's usually on the switchboard by then. He's very reliable. If he does get held up—he lives south of the river —it could be Miss Peverell or me. We each have a flat in number twelve, that's the house to the left of Innocent House. It's a bit haphazard. Whoever arrives first unlocks and switches off the alarm system. The door on Innocent Lane has a Yale and one security lock. This morning George arrived first as usual and found that the security lock hadn't been used. He was able to open the door with the Yale. The alarm system was also switched off so he naturally assumed that one of us had already arrived."

Dalgliesh asked, "Which of you four last saw Mr. Etienne?"

Claudia said: "I did. I went into the office to talk to him before I left, just before half past six. He usually worked late on Thursday nights. He was still at his desk. There may have been other people in the building at the time but I think they had all gone. Obviously I didn't check or make a search."

"Was it generally known that your brother worked late on Thursdays?"

"It was known within the office. Probably other people knew as well."

Dalgliesh said: "He seemed as usual? He didn't tell you that he intended to work in the little archives office?"

"He seemed perfectly as usual, and he never mentioned the little archives office. As far as I know it wasn't a room he ever visited. I have no idea why he went up there or why he died there—if, in fact, that is where he died."

Again the four pairs of eyes looked intensely into Dalgliesh's face.

He didn't comment. After formally asking the expected question whether they knew of anyone who might wish Etienne dead and receiving their short and equally expected answers, he got up from his chair and the woman officer, who hadn't spoken, got up too. Then he thanked them quietly and she stood a little aside so that he moved first out of the door.

After they had left there was a silence for half a minute, then de Witt said: "Not exactly the kind of copper from whom one asks the time. Personally I find him terrifying enough to the innocent, so God knows what he does to the guilty. Do you know him, Gabriel? After all you're in the same line of business."

Dauntsey looked up and said, "I know his work, of course, but I don't think we've ever met. He's a fine poet."

"Oh, we all know that. I'm only surprised you've never tried to wean him away from his publisher. Let's hope he's an equally good detective."

Frances said: "It's odd, though, isn't it, he never asked us about the snake?"

Claudia said sharply: "What about the snake?"

"He didn't ask us whether we knew where to find it."

"Oh he will," said de Witt. "Believe me, he will."

22

In the little archives room Dalgliesh asked: "Did you manage to speak to Dr. Kynaston, Kate?"

"No, sir. He's in Australia visiting his son. Doc Wardle's coming. He was in his lab so he shouldn't be long."

It was an unpropitious start. Dalgliesh was used to working with Miles Kynaston, whom he both liked as a man and respected as probably the country's most brilliant forensic pathologist. He had, perhaps unreasonably, taken it for granted that it would be Kynaston who would be squatting by this body, Kynaston's stubby-fingered hands in the latex gloves, fine as a second skin, which would be moving about the corpse with as much gentleness as if these stiff limbs could still tense under his probing hands. Reginald Wardle was a perfectly capable forensic pathologist; he wouldn't otherwise have been employed by the Met. He would do a good job. His report would be as thorough as Kynaston's and would come on time. He would be as effective in the witness box, if it came to that, cautious but definite, unshakable under cross-examination. But Dalgliesh had always found him irritating and suspected that the mild antipathy, not strong enough to be called dislike or to prejudice their co-operation, was mutual.

Wardle, when called out, came promptly to the murder scene—no one could fault him there—but would invariably stroll in with leisurely unconcern as if to demonstrate the unimportance of violent death, and this corpse in particular, in his private scheme of things. He was apt to

sigh and tut-tut over the body, as if the problem it presented was irritating rather than interesting and one which hardly justified the police
in dragging him away from the more immediate concerns in his
laboratory. He provided the minimum of information at the scene,
perhaps from natural caution, but too often giving the impression that
the police were unreasonably pressing him for a premature judgement.
His most common words spoken over the corpse were: "Better wait,
better wait, Commander. I'll get him on the table soon enough and
then we'll know."

He was, too, a self-publicist. At the scene he might give the impression
of a boring and reluctant colleague but, surprisingly, he was a brilliant
after-dinner speaker and probably enjoyed more free meals than most
of his profession. Dalgliesh, who found it astonishing that a man could
actually volunteer for, let alone enjoy, a protracted and usually poor
hotel dinner for the satisfaction of getting on his feet afterwards,
privately added this fact to the list of Wardle's mild delinquencies. Once
in his autopsy room, however, Doc Wardle was a different man. Here,
perhaps because this was his acknowledged kingdom, he seemed to take
a pride in demonstrating his considerable skills and was ready enough
to share opinions and propound theories.

Dalgliesh had worked with Charlie Ferris before and was glad to see
him. His nickname of "the Ferret" was rarely used to his face but it was
perhaps too appropriate a soubriquet to be always avoided. He had
pale-lashed sharp little eyes, a long nose sensible to every variety of
smell and tiny fastidious fingers which could pick up small objects as if
by magnetism. He presented an eccentric and occasionally bizarre
appearance when on the job, his preferred clothes for a search being
tight-fitting cotton shorts or trousers, a sweatshirt, surgeon's latex gloves
and a plastic swimming cap. His professional creed was that no murderer
left the scene of his crime without depositing some physical evidence
and it was his business to find it.

Dalgliesh said: "Your usual search, Charlie, but we'll need a gas
engineer to take out that gas fire and make a report. Tell them it's
urgent. If there's rubble blocking the flue I want that sent to the lab
with samples of any loose pieces of the chimney lining. It's a very old
nursery gas fire with a removable tap. I don't know whether we'll get a
useful print from there, almost certainly not. All surfaces of the fire
need testing for prints. The window cord is important. I'd like to know
if it snapped because of natural wear and tear or was deliberately
frayed. I doubt whether you'll get more than an opinion but the lab
may be able to help."

Leaving them to it, he knelt by the body, studied it intently for a moment, then, putting out his hand, touched the cheek. Was it his imagination and the ruddiness of the skin which made it feel slightly warm to the touch? Or was it that the warmth of his own fingers had for a few seconds given a spurious life to the dead flesh? He moved his hand to the jaw, taking care not to dislodge the snake. The flesh was soft, the bone moved under his gentle urging.

He said to Kate and Dan: "See what you make of the jaw. Be careful. I want the snake in place until after the PM."

They knelt in turn, Kate first, touched the jaw, looked closely into the face, put their hands to the naked torso.

Daniel said: "Rigor mortis is well established in the top part of the body but the jaw is free."

"Which means?"

It was Kate who replied. "That someone broke the rigor in the jaw some hours after death. Presumably it was necessary in order to stuff the snake into the mouth. But why bother? Why not wind it round his neck? That would make the point just as well."

Daniel said: "But less dramatically."

"Maybe. But forcing open the jaw proves that someone visited the body hours after death. It could have been the murderer—if this is murder. It could have been someone else. We'd never have suspected that there was a second visit to the scene if the snake had been merely wrapped round the neck."

Daniel said: "Perhaps it's precisely what the murderer wanted us to know."

Dalgliesh looked carefully at the snake. It was about five feet long and was obviously intended as a draught excluder. The top of the body was of striped velvet, the bottom of some tougher brown material. Under the softness of the velvet, it felt grainy to his touch.

There were leisurely footsteps approaching through the archives room. Daniel said: "It sounds as if Doc Wardle has arrived."

He was over six feet three inches tall, his impressive head jutting above wide bony shoulders from which his ill-fitting and thin jacket drooped as if from a wire coat-hanger. With the beaked, mottled nose, barking voice and keen darting eyes under bushy brows so luxuriant and vigorous that they seemed to have a life of their own, he looked and sounded like the stereotype of an irascible colonel. His height could have been a disadvantage in a job where corpses often lay inconveniently concealed in ditches, culverts, cupboards and makeshift graves, but the long body could insinuate itself with unexpected ease, even grace, into the most unaccommodating place. Now he gazed round the room, deploring its stark simplicity and the uninviting business which had dragged him from his microscope, then knelt by the body and let out a lugubrious sigh.

"You'll want the approximate time of death, of course, Commander. That's always the first question after 'Is he dead?' and, yes, he is dead. That's the one fact we can all agree about. Body cold, rigor mortis fully established. One interesting exception, but we'll get on to that later. Suggests he's been dead about thirteen to fifteen hours. The room's warm, unnaturally so for the time of the year. Taken the temperature, have you? Sixty-eight degrees. That and the fact that metabolism was probably fairly pronounced at the time of death could delay the onset of rigor. You've already discussed the interesting anomaly, no doubt. Still, tell me about it, Commander. Tell me about it. Or you, Inspector. I can see you're longing to."

Dalgliesh almost expected him to add, "It's too much to hope that you could keep your hands off him." He looked at Kate, who said: "The jaw is slack. Rigor mortis begins in the face, jaw and neck at five to seven hours after death and is fully established at about twelve hours. It passes off in the same sequence. So either it is already passing off in the jaw, which would put the time of death earlier by some six hours, or the mouth was forcibly opened. I'd say almost certainly the latter. The facial muscles aren't slack."

Wardle said: "I sometimes wonder, Commander, why you bother to call out a pathologist."

Undeterred, Kate went on: "Which means that the snake's head was put in the mouth not at the time of death but at least five to seven hours later. So the cause of death can't be suffocation, at least not with the snake. But then we never thought that it was."

Dalgliesh said: "The staining and the position of the body suggest that he died face-downwards and was subsequently turned over. It would be interesting to know why."

Kate suggested: "Easier to arrange the snake, stuff the head in his mouth?"

"Perhaps."

Dalgliesh said no more, while Doc Wardle continued his examination. He had already encroached on the pathologist's territory more than was prudent. He had little doubt about the cause of death and wondered whether it was perversity rather than caution which was keeping Wardle silent. It wasn't the first case either of them had seen of carbon-monoxide poisoning. The post-mortem lividity, more pronounced than usual because of the blood's slower liquidation, the cherry-red colour-ation of the skin, so bright that the body looked as if it had been painted, were unmistakable and surely definitive.

Wardle said: "Copy-book, isn't it? Hardly needs a forensic pathologist and a commander of the Met to diagnose carbon monoxide. But don't let's get too excited. Let's get him on the table, shall we? Then the lab leeches can take their blood samples and give us an answer we can rely on. Do you want that snake kept in the mouth?"

"I think so. I'd prefer to leave it undisturbed until the autopsy."

"Which you'll want done, no doubt, immediately if not sooner."

"Don't we always?"

"I can do it this evening. We were due at a dinner party which our hostess has cancelled. Sudden attack of 'flu, or so she claims. Six-thirty at the usual mortuary if you can make it. I'll give them a ring, tell them to expect us. Is the meat wagon on the way?"

Kate said: "It should arrive any moment."

Dalgliesh was aware that the PM would go ahead whether or not he could make it, but of course he would be there. Wardle was being unexpectedly co-operative, but then he reminded himself that when the chips were down Wardle invariably was.

23

As soon as he saw Mrs. Demery Dalgliesh knew that he would have no trouble with her; he had dealt with her kind before. The Mrs. Demerys, in his experience, had no hang-ups about the police, whom they assumed in general to be beneficent and on their side, while seeing no reason to treat them with inordinate respect or to credit male officers with more sense than was commonly found in the rest of the sex. They were, no doubt, as ready to lie as other witnesses when it came to protecting their own, but, being honest and unburdened by imagination, preferred to tell the truth, as being on the whole less trouble, and, having told it, saw no reason to torture their consciences with doubts about their own motives or the intentions of other people. They were obstinately firm, unshakable and occasionally irreverent under cross-examination. Dalgliesh suspected that they found men slightly ridiculous, particularly when dressed in gowns and wigs and given to pontificating in arrogant voices over other people's heads, and had no intention of being lectured to, browbeaten or put down by those irritating creatures.

Now the latest example of this excellent species settled herself opposite him and gave him a frank appraisal from bright intelligent eyes. Her hair, obviously recently dyed, was a bright orange-gold worn in a style seen in Edwardian photographs: swept up firmly at the back and sides and with a fringe of frizzy curls low on the forehead. With her sharp nose and bright, slightly exophthalmic eyes, she reminded Dalgliesh of an exotic and intelligent poodle.

Without waiting for him to begin the conversation she said: "I knew yer dad, Mr. Dalgliesh."

"Did you, Mrs. Demery? When was that? During the war?"

"Yes, that's right. My twin brother and I was evacuated to your village. Remember the Carter twins? Well, of course, you wouldn't. You wasn't even a glint in yer dad's eye then. Oh, he was a lovely gentleman! We wasn't billeted at the rectory, they had the unmarried mothers. We was with Miss Pilgrim in her cottage. Oh God, Mr. Dalgliesh, that was a terrible place, that village. I don't know how you put up with it when you was a kid. Put me off the country for life, that village did. Mud, rain and that awful stink you get from the farmyard. And talk about boredom!"

"Not much, perhaps, for a city child to do."

"I wouldn't say that. There was things to do all right, but start doing them and you were in dead trouble."

"Like damming the village stream?"

"So you heard about that? How was we to know that it would flow into that Mrs. Piggott's back kitchen and drown her old cat? Fancy you knowing about that, though." Mrs. Demery's face expressed the liveliest gratification.

"You and your brother are part of the folklore of the village, Mrs. Demery."

"Are we now? That's nice. Remember Mr. Stuart's piglets?"

"Mr. Stuart does. He's well over eighty now, but there are some events that are branded on the memory."

"A proper race, that was going to be. We got the little buggers lined up, more or less, but after that they was all over the place. Well, mostly all over the Norwich road. But, oh God! That village was a terrible place. The quiet of it! We'd lie awake listening to it, that silence. It was like being dead. And the dark! I never knew darkness like that. Pitch-black it was. It was like a great black woolly blanket being pressed down on you until you felt suffocated. Billy and I couldn't stand it. We never had a nightmare till we was evacuated. When our mum came to visit we used to bawl all the time. I can remember those visits, Mum dragging us along that boring old lane and Billy and I howling that we wanted to come home. We told her that Miss Pilgrim wasn't giving us any food and was always after us with the slipper. It was true about the food too, we never had a decent chip the whole time we was there. In the end Mum brought us back home to get a bit of peace. We was all right then. We had a lovely time, especially after the bombing started. We had one of those Anderson shelters in the garden and we were all snug in it with Mum and Gran and Auntie Edie and Mrs. Powell from number forty-two when she got bombed out."

Dalgliesh asked: "Wasn't it dark in the Anderson shelter?"

"We had our torches, didn't we? And when the raids weren't actually on you could go outside and watch the searchlights. Lovely crisscross patterns they made in the sky. And talk about noise! Those anti-aircraft guns, well it was like a giant tearing up corrugated iron. Well, as Mum said, if you give your kids a happy childhood there's not much life can do to them after that."

Dalgliesh felt that it would be unproductive to argue this sanguine view of child rearing. He was about tactfully to suggest that it was time they got down to business when Mrs. Demery forestalled him.

"Well, that's enough about the good old days. You'll be wanting to ask me about this murder."

"So that's how it strikes you, Mrs. Demery?"

"Stands to reason. He didn't put that snake around his own neck. Strangled, was he?"

"We shan't know how he died until we get the result of the PM."

"Well, he looked strangled to me, with his face all pink and that snake's head stuffed in his mouth. Mind you, I've never seen a healthier-looking corpse. Looked better dead than he did alive, and he looked pretty good alive. He was a good looker all right. I always thought he looked a bit like the young Gregory Peck."

Dalgliesh asked her to describe exactly what had happened since her arrival at Innocent House.

"I come in every weekday except Wednesday from nine until five. On Wednesdays they're supposed to have the whole place thoroughly cleaned by the Superior Office Cleaning Company. At least that's what they call themselves. Inferior Cleaning Company would be more like it. I suppose they do the best they can, but it's not like taking a personal interest in the place. George comes thirty minutes early and lets them in. They're usually through by ten."

"Who lets you in, Mrs. Demery? Do you have keys?"

"No. Old Mr. Etienne suggested I did but I didn't want the responsibility. Too many keys in my life already. George usually opens up. Or it could be Mr. Dauntsey or Miss Frances. Just depends who's earlier. This morning Miss Peverell and Mr. Dauntsey weren't here, but George was and he let me in. Well, I got on quietly enough with my cleaning back in the kitchen. Nothing happened until just before nine, then this Lord Stilgoe turned up, saying he'd got an appointment with Mr. Gerard."

"Were you there at the time?"

"I was as it happened. I was having a bit of a chat with George. Lord Stilgoe was none too pleased to find no one there but the receptionist and me. George had rung round the office trying to find Mr. Gerard, and he was suggesting that Lord Stilgoe should wait in the reception area when Miss Etienne arrived. She asked George if Mr. Gerard was in his office and George said he'd rung but there was no reply. So she went across the hall to the office and Lord Stilgoe and I followed her. Mr. Gerard's jacket was over his chair and the chair was pulled back from the desk, which seemed a bit odd. Then she put her hand in the right-hand drawer and found his keys. Mr. Gerard always kept his keys there when he was in his office. The bunch was rather heavy and he hated it dragging on his jacket pocket. Miss Claudia said, 'He must be here somewhere. Perhaps he's in number ten with Mr. Bartrum.' So we went back to the reception room and George said he'd rung number ten. Mr. Bartrum had arrived but he hadn't seen Mr. Gerard though his Jag was there. Mr. Gerard always parked his car in Innocent Passage because it was safer. So Miss Claudia said, 'He must be here somewhere. We'd better start looking for him.' By then the first boat had arrived and then Miss Frances and Mr. Dauntsey."

"Did Miss Etienne sound worried?"

"More puzzled, if you know what I mean. I said, Well I've been through most of the back of the house and on the ground floor, so he isn't in the kitchen. And Miss Claudia said something about well he'd hardly likely to be would he, and started up the stairs with me and Miss Blackett just behind her."

"You didn't say that Miss Blackett was there."

"Didn't I? Well she'd arrived all right with the launch. Of course you tend to overlook her now that old Mr. Peverell's dead. Anyway she was there, although she was still wearing her coat, and she came up the stairs with us."

"Three of you to search for one man?"

"Well, that's how it was. I suppose I went out of curiosity. It was a kind of instinct really. I don't know why Miss Blackett went. You'll have to ask her. Miss Claudia said, 'We'll start searching at the top of the house,' so that's what we did."

"So she went straight to the archive room?"

"That's right, and then on to the little room beyond. The door wasn't locked."

"How did she open it, Mrs. Demery?"

"How do you mean? She opened it same way you always open a door."

"Did she fling it wide? Open it gently? Did she seem at all apprehensive?"

"Not that I noticed. She just opened it. And, well, there he was. Lying on his back with his face all pink and that snake wound round his neck with the head stuffed in his mouth. His eyes were open and staring. Horrible they was! Mind you, I could see he was dead at once, though, like I said, I've never seen him looking better. Miss Claudia went over and knelt beside him. She said, 'Go and phone the police. And get out of here, both of you.' Kind of sharp, she was. Still, it was her brother. I know when I'm not wanted so I got out. I wasn't that anxious to stay."

"What about Miss Blackett?"

"She was just behind me. I thought she was going to scream but instead of that she made a kind of high wailing noise. I put my arms round her shoulders. She was shaking something terrible. I said, 'Come on, dearie, come on, there's nothing you can do here.' So we went down the stairs. I thought it would be quicker than the lift, which is always getting stuck. But maybe the lift would've been better. I had some trouble getting her down the stairs, she was shaking so much. And once or twice her legs almost gave way. Once I thought I'd just have to dump her and go for help. When we got to the bottom flight there was Lord Stilgoe and Mr. de Witt and the rest of them standing there looking up at us. I suppose they saw from my face and the state Miss Blackett was in that something awful had happened. So then I told them. Seemed like they couldn't take it in for a moment, and then Mr. de Witt started running up the stairs with Lord Stilgoe and Mr. Dauntsey behind him."

"What happened then, Mrs. Demery?"

"I helped Miss Blackett to her chair and went off to find her some water."

"You didn't ring the police?"

"I thought I'd leave that to the rest of them. The body wasn't going to go away, was it? What was the hurry? Anyway, if I had rung I'd only have done the wrong thing. Lord Stilgoe came back. He went straight to the reception desk and said to George, 'Get me New Scotland Yard. I want the Commissioner. Failing him, Commander Adam Dalgliesh.' Straight to the top for him, of course. Then Miss Claudia asked me to go and make some strong coffee, so that's what I did. White as a sheet she was. Well, you couldn't wonder, could you?"

Dalgliesh said: "Mr. Gerard Etienne took over as chairman and managing director fairly recently, didn't he? Was he well liked?"

"Well he wouldn't have been carried out of here in a body bag if he was a little ray of sunshine about the place. Someone didn't like him, that's for sure. Of course, it wasn't easy for him taking over from old Mr. Peverell. Everyone respected Mr. Peverell. He was a lovely man. But I got on all right with Mr. Gerard. I didn't worry him and he didn't worry me. I don't reckon, though, that many about the place will be crying for him. Still, murder is murder and it'll be a shock, no doubt about it. Won't do much good for the firm either, I shouldn't wonder. Now here's an idea. See how this grabs you. Maybe he did it himself, then this joker we've got about the place put the snake round his neck afterwards to show what they thought of him. Might be worth thinking about."

Dalgliesh didn't say that it had been thought about. He asked: "Would it surprise you to hear that he had killed himself?"

"Well it would, to tell you the truth. Too pleased with himself for that, I'd have said. Anyway, why should he? OK, so the firm's in a bit of trouble, but what firm isn't? He'd have come through all right. I can't see Mr. Gerard doing a Robert Maxwell. Still, who'd have thought it of Robert Maxwell, so there's no knowing really, is there? Mysterious, that's what people are, mysterious. I could tell you a thing or two about the mysteriousness of people."

Kate broke in: "Miss Etienne must have been terribly distressed finding him like that. Her own brother."

Mrs. Demery transferred her attention to Kate but seemed none too pleased at this intrusion of a third person into her tête-à-tête. "Ask a straight question and you'll get a straight answer, Inspector. How distressed was Miss Claudia? That's what you want to know, isn't it? You'll have to ask her. I don't know. She was at the side of the body bending over it and she never turned her face all the time Miss Blackett and I were in the room, which wasn't long. I don't know what she was feeling. I only know what she said."

" 'Get out of here both of you.' Rather harsh."

"Shock, maybe. You work it out for yourselves."

"Leaving her alone with the body."

"That's the way she wanted it seemingly. Anyway, I couldn't have stayed. Someone had to help Miss Blackett down the stairs."

Dalgliesh asked: "Is it a good place to work, Mrs. Demery? Are you happy here?"

"As good as I'm likely to get. Look, Mr. Dalgliesh, I'm sixty-three. OK, that's no great age and I've still got my eyes and legs, and I'm a damned sight better worker than some I could name. But you don't start looking for a new job at sixty-three, and I like work. I'd die of boredom stuck at home. And I'm used to this place, been here nigh on twenty years. It's not everyone's cup of tea, but it suits me. And it's handy—well, more or less. I'm still in Whitechapel. Got a nice little modern flat now."

"How do you get here?"

"Tube to Wapping, then walk. It's no distance. I'm not afraid of London streets. Been walking London streets before you was thought of. Old Mr. Peverell said that he'd send a taxi for me any morning if the journey worried me. He would have too. He was a very special gentleman, was Mr. Peverell. That showed what he thought of me. It's nice to be appreciated."

"It is indeed. Tell me, Mrs. Demery, about the cleaning of the archives room, the large one and the small office where Mr. Etienne was found. Is that your responsibility, or does the cleaning company do it?"

"I do. The outside cleaners never go as high as the top floor. That started with old Mr. Peverell. There's all that paper up there, you see, and he was afraid of them smoking and starting a fire. Besides, those files are confidential. Don't ask me why. I've had a peek at one or two and they're only full of a lot of old letters and manuscripts as far as I can see. It's not as if they keep the staff records there, or anything private like that. Still, Mr. Peverell set great store by the archives. Anyway, he agreed I'd be responsible for those two rooms. No one hardly ever goes up there, except Mr. Dauntsey, so I don't bother overmuch. No point in it. I usually go up once a month on a Monday and give it a quick dust."

"Do you vacuum the floor?"

"Might give it a quick go-round if it looked as if it needed it. Might not. As I said, there's only Mr. Dauntsey uses it and he doesn't make much mess. There's enough to do in the rest of the house without lugging the vacuum cleaner all the way up there and spending time where it isn't needed."

"I can see that. When did you last clean the little room?"

"I gave it a quick dust three weeks ago last Monday. I'll be up there again next Monday. Leastwise that's what I normally do, but I expect you'll be keeping the door locked."

"For the time being, Mrs. Demery. Shall we go up?"

They took the lift, which was slow but smooth enough. The door of the small archives office was open. The gas-company engineer hadn't yet arrived but the two scene-of-crime officers and the photographers were still there. At a sign from Dalgliesh they slipped past him and stood waiting.

Dalgliesh said: "Don't go in, Mrs. Demery. Just stand at the door and tell me if you see any change."

Mrs. Demery surveyed the room slowly. Her eyes rested briefly on the white-chalked outline of the absent body but she made no comment. With only a few seconds' pause, she said: "Your chaps been giving it a clean-up then, have they?"

"We've done no cleaning, Mrs. Demery."

"Someone has. There's not three weeks' dust here. Look at that mantelpiece and the floor. That floor's been vacuumed. Bloody hell! So he cleaned the room before he did his killing, and with my Hoover!"

She turned to Dalgliesh and he saw in her eyes a dawning mixture of outrage, horror and superstitious awe. Nothing so far about Etienne's death had affected her so deeply as this cleaned and prepared death-cell.

"How do you know, Mrs. Demery?"

"The Hoover's kept in the utility room on the ground floor, next to the kitchen. When I went to take it out this morning I said to myself, 'Someone's been using this.' "

"How could you tell?"

"Because it was set for cleaning a smooth floor, not a carpet. There's two settings, you see. When I put it away it was set for cleaning the carpet. The last job I'd done was those carpets in the boardroom."

"Are you sure, Mrs. Demery?"

"Not to swear in a court of law. There are things you can swear to and things you can't. I suppose I could have changed the setting accidentally like. All I know is that when I took it out this morning I said to myself, 'Someone's been using this.' "

"Did you ask anyone if they had been using it?"

"No one here to ask then, was there? Besides, it wouldn't be any of the staff here. Why would any of them be wanting the Hoover? That's my job, not theirs. I thought it might be someone from the cleaning company, but that would be odd too. They bring all their own equipment."

"Was the vacuum cleaner in its usual place?"

"Yes it was. And the flex wound round crossed, just like I left it. But the setting wasn't the same."

"Is there anything else about this room that strikes you?"

"Well the window cord's gone, hasn't it? I suppose you chaps have taken that away. It was getting a bit old and frayed. I said to Mr. Dauntsey when I put my head round the door on Monday that it ought to be replaced and he said he'd have a word with George. George does all the odd jobs around here. Very handy is George. Mr. Dauntsey had the window half-open at the time. He usually keeps it like that. He didn't seem much worried but, like I said, he was going to have a word with George about it. And that table's been moved. I never move the table when I dust up here. Look for yourself. It's a couple of inches to the right. You can see by that faint line of dirt on the wall where it usually was. And Mr. Dauntsey's tape recorder's gone. There used to be a bed here once, but they took that away after Miss Clements killed herself. A nice thing that was too. Two deaths we've had in this room, Mr. Dalgliesh. I reckon it's time they locked it up for good."

Before they had finished with Mrs. Demery, Dalgliesh asked her to say nothing to anyone about the possible use made of her vacuum cleaner, but with little hope that she would keep the news to herself for long.

After she had left, Daniel said: "How reliable is that piece of evidence, sir? Could she really tell if the room has been recently cleaned? It could be her imagination."

"She's the expert, Daniel. And Miss Etienne remarked on the cleanness of the room. On Mrs. Demery's admission she doesn't usually bother with the floor. This floor is dustless, even in the corners. Someone has cleaned it recently and it wasn't Mrs. Demery."

24

In the boardroom the four partners still waited. Gabriel Dauntsey and Frances Peverell sat at the oval mahogany table, close but not touching. Frances had her head bowed but was absolutely still. De Witt was at the window, one hand pressed to the pane as if he needed support. Claudia stood intently examining the large copy of a Canaletto of the Grand Canal which hung beside the door. The magnificence of the room both diminished and formalized the burden each bore of fear, grief, anger or guilt. They were like actors in an over-designed play in which a fortune had been lavished on the extravagant set but in which the players were amateurs, the dialogue half-learned, the moves stiff and unpractised. When Dalgliesh and Kate had left the room Frances Peverell had said, "Leave the door open," and de Witt, without a word, had gone back to leave it ajar. They needed the sense of a world outside, the sound of distant voices however faint, however occasional. The closed door would be too like the vacant chair at the middle of the table, one awaiting Gerard's impatient entry, the other his presiding presence.

Without looking round, Claudia said: "Gerard always disliked this picture. He thought Canaletto overrated, too precise, too flat. He said he could picture the apprentices carefully painting in the waves."

De Witt said: "It wasn't Canaletto he disliked, just that picture. He said he was bored with constantly having to explain to visitors that it's only a copy."

Frances's voice was indistinct. "He resented it. It reminded him that Grandfather had sold the original at a bad time and for about a quarter of what it was worth."

"No," said Claudia firmly. "He disliked Canaletto."

De Witt moved slowly from the window. He said: "The police are taking their time. Mrs. Demery is enjoying herself, I imagine, giving her favourite impersonation of a cockney charwoman, good-natured but sharp-tongued. I hope the Commander appreciates it."

Claudia turned from her concentrated examination of the painting. "Since that is what she is you can hardly describe it as an impersonation. Still, she does become garrulous when excited. We must take care that we don't. Become garrulous. Talk too much. Tell the police things they don't need to know."

De Witt said: "What things had you in mind?"

"That we weren't precisely united about the future of the firm. The police think in clichés. Since most criminals act in clichés that is probably their strength."

Frances Peverell raised her head. No one had seen her weep but her face was drained and bloated, the eyes were dull under swollen lids, and when she spoke her voice sounded cracked and a little querulous.

"What does it matter if Mrs. Demery does talk? What does it matter what we say? No one here has anything to hide. It's obvious what happened. Gerard died of natural causes or an accident and someone, the same person who's been playing tricks in this place, found the body and decided to make a mystery of it. It must have been terrible for you, Claudia, finding him like that, seeing the snake around his neck. But it's all fairly straightforward surely. It has to be."

Claudia turned on her as vehemently as if they were in the middle of a quarrel. "What sort of accident? You're suggesting Gerard had an accident? What sort of accident?"

Frances seemed to shrink in her chair but her voice was firm. "I don't know. I wasn't there when it happened, was I? It was just a suggestion."

"A bloody stupid one."

"Claudia." De Witt's voice was more loving than censorious. "We mustn't quarrel. We have to keep calm and we have to stay together."

"How can we stay together? Dalgliesh will want to see us separately."

"Not physically together. Together as partners. Together as a team."

As if he hadn't spoken, Frances said: "Or a heart attack. Or a stroke. He could have had either. It happens to the healthiest of people."

Claudia said: "Gerard had a perfectly sound heart. You don't climb the Matterhorn if you've got a weak heart. And I can't imagine any less likely subject for a stroke."

De Witt's voice was conciliatory. "We don't know yet how he died. We can't until after the post-mortem. In the mean time what happens here?"

Claudia said: "We carry on. Of course we carry on."

"Provided we have the staff. People may not want to stay, especially if the police suggest that Gerard's death wasn't straightforward."

Claudia's laugh was harsh as a sob. "Straightforward! Of course it wasn't straightforward. He was found dead, half-naked with a toy snake wound round his neck and its head stuffed in his mouth. Even the least suspicious policeman would hardly call that straightforward."

"I meant, of course, if they suspect murder. We've all got the word in our minds. Someone may as well speak it."

Frances said: "Murdered? Why should anyone murder him? And there wasn't any blood, was there? You didn't find a weapon. And no one could have poisoned him. Poisoned him with what? When could he have taken it?"

Claudia said: "There are other ways."

"You mean he was strangled with Hissing Sid? Or suffocated? But Gerard was strong. You'd have to overpower him to do that." Then, as no one replied, she said, "Look, I don't know why you're both so anxious to suggest Gerard was murdered."

De Witt came and sat down beside her. He said gently: "Frances, no one is suggesting it, we're just facing the possibility. But you're right of course. It's much better to wait until we know how he died. What puzzles me is why he was in the little archives office. I can't remember him ever going up to the top floor, can you, Claudia?"

"No, and he couldn't have been working up there. If he decided to do that he wouldn't have left his keys in his desk drawer. You know how punctilious he was about security. The keys were only in that drawer when he was working at his desk. If he left the office for any length of time he'd slip on his jacket and put the bundle of keys back in his pocket. We've all seen him do that often enough."

De Witt said: "The fact that he was found in the archives office doesn't necessarily mean that he died there."

Claudia seated herself opposite him and leaned forward over the table. "You mean he could have died in his office?"

"Died or been killed there and moved subsequently. He could have died quite naturally at his desk, a stroke or heart attack as Frances suggests, and the body moved later."

"But that would need considerable strength."

"Not if you used one of the book trolleys and took the body up by the lift. There's nearly always a trolley waiting at the lift."

"But surely the police can tell whether a body has been moved after death."

"Yes, if it's found outdoors. You get traces of soil, twigs, flattened grass, signs of dragging. I'm not sure that it would be so easy with a body discovered in a building. It's one of the possibilities they'll be considering. I suppose they'll condescend to tell us something sooner or later. They're certainly taking their time up there."

The two of them were talking as if there was no one else in the room. Frances suddenly said: "Do you have to discuss it as if Gerard's death was some kind of a puzzle, a detective story, something we'd read or seen on television? This is Gerard we're talking about, not a stranger, not a character in a play. Gerard is dead. He's upstairs with that ghastly snake round his neck and we're sitting here as if we didn't care."

Claudia turned on her a speculative gaze tinged with contempt. "What do you expect us to do? Sit around in silence? Read a good book? Ask George if the newspapers have been delivered? I think it helps to talk. He was my brother. If I can stay reasonably calm, so can you. You shared his bed, at least temporarily, but you never shared his life."

De Witt said quietly, "Did you, Claudia? Did any of us?"

"No, but when this death really hits me, when I really believe what's happened, I shall mourn for him, never fear. I shall mourn for him but not yet, not now and not here."

Gabriel Dauntsey had been sitting gazing ahead out of the window towards the river. Now he spoke for the first time, and the others turned and looked at him as if suddenly remembering that he was there.

He said quietly: "I think he may have died of carbon-monoxide poisoning. The skin was very pink—that's one of the signs apparently —and the room was unnaturally warm. Didn't it strike you, Claudia, that the room was very warm?"

For a moment there was silence, then Claudia said: "Very little struck me except seeing Gerard and that snake. You mean he could have been gassed?"

"Yes. I'm saying that he could have been gassed."

The word hissed on the air. Frances said: "But isn't the new North Sea gas harmless? I thought you couldn't poison yourself any more by putting your head in a gas oven."

It was de Witt who explained. "It isn't poisonous to breathe. It's perfectly safe if properly used. But if he lit the gas fire and the room wasn't adequately ventilated the fire could malfunction and produce carbon monoxide. Gerard could have become disorientated and unconscious before he realized what was happening."

Frances said: "And afterwards someone found the body, turned off the gas and put the snake round his neck. As I said, it was an accident."

Dauntsey spoke quietly and calmly. "It isn't quite as simple as that. Why did he light the fire? It wasn't particularly cold last night. And if he did light it, why did he shut the window? It was shut when I saw his body and I left it open when I last used the room, on Monday."

De Witt said: "And if he was planning to spend the evening working in the archives long enough to need a fire, why did he leave his jacket and keys in his office? None of it makes sense."

In the silence that followed Frances suddenly spoke. "We've forgotten Lucinda. Someone's got to tell her."

Claudia said, "God yes! One tends to forget the Lady Lucinda. Somehow I don't imagine that she'll hurl herself into the Thames with grief. There was always something odd about that engagement."

De Witt said: "All the same, we can't let her read it in tomorrow's papers or hear it on the South East News. One of us had better ring Lady Norrington. She can break the news to her daughter. It would come best from you, Claudia."

"I suppose so, as long as I'm not expected to go round and administer comfort. I'd better do it now. I'll ring from my own office, that is if the police aren't in occupation. Having the police here is like having mice in the house. You can sense them scrabbling away even when you don't actually hear or see them and once they're in you feel you'll never get rid of them."

She got up and walked out, her head held unnaturally high but her step uncertain. Dauntsey tried to get to his feet, but his stiffened limbs seemed unable to respond and it was de Witt who moved quickly to her side. But she shook her head and gently pushed away his supporting arm and was gone.

Less than five minutes later she returned. She said: "She wasn't in. It's hardly the kind of message you can leave on the answerphone. I'll try again later."

Frances said: "What about your father? Isn't he more important?"

"Of course he's more important. I shall drive down to see him to-night."

The door opened without a preliminary knock, and Detective Sergeant Robbins put his head in.

"Mr. Dalgliesh is sorry that he's keeping you waiting longer than he expected. He would be grateful if Mr. Dauntsey could come now to the archives office."

Dauntsey at once got up, but his stiffness after long sitting had made him clumsy. His stick, dislodged from the back of his chair, clattered to the ground. He and Frances Peverell knelt simultaneously to retrieve it and, after what sounded to the others like a short scuffle and a few almost conspiratorial whispers, Frances laid hands on it and, rising red-faced from under the table, handed it to Dauntsey. He leaned on it for a few seconds, then hung it again on the back of the chair and moved towards the door without its aid, slowly but firm-footed.

When he had left, Claudia Etienne said: "I wonder why Gabriel gets the privilege of going first."

James de Witt answered: "Probably because he uses the little archives office more than most of us."

Frances said: "I don't think I've ever used it. The last time I was there was when they took the bed away. You don't go up there either, do you, James?"

"I've never worked up there, at least not for more than half an hour. The last time was about three months ago. I went up to find Esmé Carling's original contract with us. I couldn't find it."

"You mean you couldn't find her old file?"

"I found her file. I took it into the little archives room to study it. The original contract wasn't there."

Claudia said, without particular interest: "That's not surprising. We've had her on the list for thirty years. It was probably misfiled twenty years ago." And then, with sudden energy: "Look, I don't see why I should waste time just because Adam Dalgliesh wants to chat with a fellow poet. We don't have to stay in this room."

Frances sounded doubtful. "He said he wanted to see us together."

"Well, he has seen us together. Now he's seeing us separately. When he wants me he'll find me in my office. Tell him that, will you."

After she had left, James said: "She's right, you know. We may not feel like working but it's worse sitting and waiting, looking at that empty chair."

"But we haven't been looking at it, have we? We've been carefully not looking at it, keeping our eyes elsewhere, almost as if Gerard were an embarrassment. I can't work, but I would like some more coffee."

"Then let's find it. Mrs. Demery must be about somewhere. I'd rather like to hear her version of her interview with Dalgliesh. If that doesn't lighten the atmosphere nothing will."

They moved together to the door. As they reached it Frances turned to him. "James, I feel so frightened. I ought to be feeling grief and shock and the horror of it. We were lovers. I did love him once and now he's dead. I ought to be thinking of him, of the awful finality of his death. I ought to be praying for him. I did try but it came out as meaningless words. What I'm feeling is totally selfish, totally ignoble. It's fear."

"Fear of the police? Dalgliesh isn't a bully."

"No, it's worse than that. Fear of what's going on here. That snake —whoever did that to Gerard is evil. Don't you find it, the presence of evil in Innocent House? I think I've been feeling it for months. This just seems like the inevitable end, something all the petty mischiefs have been leading up to. My mind ought to be full of grief for Gerard. It isn't, it's full of terror, terror and an awful foreboding that this isn't the end."

James said gently: "There aren't any right or wrong emotions. We feel what we feel. I doubt whether any of us feels intense grief, even Claudia. Gerard was a remarkable man but he wasn't lovable. What I try to persuade myself is grief, is probably no more than that universal and impotent sadness one always feels at the death of the young, the talented, the healthy. Even that is overlaid by a fascinated curiosity spiced with apprehension." He turned to her and said: "I'm here, Frances. When you need me and if you need me, I'm here. I shan't be a nuisance. I shan't thrust myself on you just because shock and fear have made us both vulnerable. I'm just offering you whatever you need when you need it."

"I know. Thank you, James."

She put out her hand and for a second laid it against his face. It was the first time she had ever voluntarily touched him. Then she turned to the door and, in turning, missed the spreading radiance of joy and triumph on his face.

25

Twenty years previously Dalgliesh had heard Gabriel Dauntsey reading his poetry in the Purcell Room on the South Bank. He had no intention of telling Dauntsey so, but as he waited for the old man the event came back to him with such clarity that he listened to the approaching footsteps through the archives room with something of the excited expectation of youth. Of the two world wars it was the first which had produced the greater poetry and sometimes he occupied his mind by wondering why this should be so. Was it that the year 1914 had seen the death of innocence, that the cataclysm had swept away more than a brilliant generation? But for a few years—was it only three?—it had seemed that Dauntsey might be the Wilfred Owen of his own time, his very different war. But the promise of those first two volumes had never been fulfilled and he had published nothing more. Dalgliesh told himself that the word promise, with its suggestion of a talent as yet unrealized, was hardly appropriate. One or two of those early poems had represented achievement at a level which few post-war poets had reached.

After that reading Dalgliesh had discovered as much as Dauntsey wanted known of his history: how, living in France, he had been in England on business when war was declared, leaving his wife and two children trapped by the invading Germans; how they had totally disappeared from knowledge and official records so that it was only after years of searching after the war that he had discovered that all three, living under a false name to avoid internment, had been killed in a British bomber raid on occupied France. Dauntsey himself had served in RAF Bomber Command but had been spared the ultimate tragic irony; he had not taken part in that raid. His had been the poetry of modern war, of loss and grief and terror, comradeship and courage, cowardice and defeat. The strong sinuous brutal verses were lit by passages of lyrical beauty, like shells bursting in the mind. The great Lancasters lifting themselves like ponderous beasts with death in their bellies, the dark and silent skies exploding in a cacophony of terror, the boyish crew for whom he, little older, was responsible, climbing clumsily accoutred into that frail metal shell night after night, knowing the arithmetic of survival, that this could be the night when they would fall from the sky like flaming torches. And always the guilt, the sense that this nightly terror, both dreaded and welcomed, was an expiation, that there was a betrayal for which only death could atone, personal betrayal mirroring a greater universal desolation.

And now he was here, an ordinary old man if any old man could be described as ordinary, not bent, but holding himself with disciplined effort as if endurance and courage could successfully overcome the ravages of time. Old age either produces a soft plumpness obliterating character in crinkled nonentity or, as here, strips the face so that the bones stand out like a skeleton temporarily clothed in flesh dry and delicate as paper. But the hair, although grey, was still strong, the eyes as black and darting as Dalgliesh remembered. Now they fixed on him a questioning ironic stare.

Dalgliesh swung round the chair from the table and placed it near the door. Dauntsey sat.

Dalgliesh said: "You came up with Lord Stilgoe and Mr. de Witt. Did anything strike you about this room apart from the presence of the body?"

"Not at first, apart from a disagreeable smell. A corpse, half-naked, grotesquely decorated as that corpse was, assaults the senses. After a minute, perhaps less, I did notice other things, and with unusual clarity. The room struck me as different—odd. It looked stripped, although it wasn't, unnaturally clean, warmer than usual. The body looked so—so disordered; the room so very ordered. The chair was precisely in place, the files as neatly on the table. I noticed, of course, that the tape recorder was missing."

"Were the files as you had left them?"

"Not as I remember. The two filing trays have been reversed. The tray with the smaller number of files should be on the left. I had two piles, the right higher than the left. I work from left to right with six to ten files at a time, depending on their size. When I finish with a file I transfer it to the right. When all six have been dealt with I return them to the main archives room with a ruler inserted to show how far I've got."

Dalgliesh said: "We noticed the ruler in a space on the bottom shelf of the second row. Does that mean that you've only completed one row?"

"It's very slow work. I tend to get interested in old letters even if they aren't worth preserving. I've found quite a lot that are—letters from twentieth-century writers and others who corresponded with Henry Peverell and his father, even if the firm didn't publish them. There are letters from H. G. Wells, Arnold Bennett, members of the Bloomsbury group, some even earlier."

"What is your system?"

"I dictate a description of the contents of each file and my recommendation either for Destruction, Doubtful, Preserve or Important on the tape recorder. A typist then types a list and periodically the board goes through it. Nothing has actually been thrown out yet. Until we know the future of the firm it seemed unwise to destroy anything."

"When did you last use this room?"

"On Monday. I worked here all day. Mrs. Demery put her head round the door at about ten o'clock but said that she wouldn't disturb me. The place only gets cleaned about one week in four and then superficially. She told me about the frayed window cord and I said I'd mention it to George and get him to do the repair. I haven't spoken to him yet."

"You hadn't noticed it yourself?"

"I'm afraid not. The window has been open for weeks. I prefer it that way. I suppose I would have noticed when the weather gets colder."

"How do you heat the room?"

"Always with an electric fire. Actually it belongs to me. I prefer it to the gas fire. I don't mean that I thought the gas fire was unsafe, but I don't smoke so I never seem to have matches when I need them. It was easier to bring the electric reflector fire over from my flat. It's very light and I either carry it back to number twelve with me or leave it here if I propose to work next day. On Monday I took it home."

"And the door was unlocked when you left the room?"

"Oh yes. I never lock the door. The key is kept in the lock, usually on this side, but I've never used it."

Dalgliesh said: "The lock looks comparatively new. Who had it fitted?"

"Henry Peverell. He liked to work up here occasionally. I don't know why, but he was a solitary man. I suppose he thought fitting a lock gave him an added sense of security. But it isn't really new—much newer than the door, of course, but I think the key has been there for at least five years."

Dalgliesh said: "But it hasn't been unused for five years. The lock has been kept oiled, the key turns easily."

"Does it? I don't use it so I haven't noticed. But it's odd about the oiling. Mrs. Demery may have done it but it seems unlikely."

Dalgliesh said: "Did you like Gerard Etienne?"

"No, but I respected him. Not for qualities which necessarily deserve respect; I respected him for being so different from me. He had the virtues of his defects. And he was young. He could hardly claim credit or responsibility for that, but it gave him an enthusiasm which most of us here no longer have and which I think the firm needs. We may have complained about what he did or disliked what he proposed to do, but at least he knew where he was going. I suspect we shall feel rudderless without him."

"Who will take over as managing director?"

"Oh, his sister, Claudia Etienne. The job here goes to the person with the greatest number of shares. As far as I know she will inherit his. That will give her an overall majority."

Dalgliesh said: "To do what?"

"I don't know. You'll have to ask her. I doubt whether she knows herself. She's just lost a brother. I doubt whether she's spending much time thinking about the future of Peverell Press."

Dalgliesh went on to ask Dauntsey how he had spent the previous day and night. Dauntsey looked down with a small wry smile. He was too intelligent not to know that what he was being asked for was his alibi. He was silent for a little time as if marshalling his thoughts. Then he said: "I was in the partners' meeting from ten o'clock until eleven-thirty. Gerard liked to get it over within two hours, but yesterday we stopped earlier than usual. After the meeting he had a few words with me coming down from the boardroom about the future of the poetry list. I think, too, he was trying to enlist my support for his plan to sell Innocent House and move the firm down-river to Docklands."

"You saw that as desirable?"

"I saw it as necessary." He paused, then said, "Unfortunately." Again he paused, then continued, speaking slowly and deliberately but with little emphasis, occasionally pausing as if to select one word over another, from time to time frowning as if memory were painful or uncertain. Dalgliesh listened in silence to the monologue.

"After I left Innocent House I went back to my flat to get ready for a luncheon appointment. When I say get ready, I mean merely to run a comb through my hair and wash my hands. I wasn't there long. I took a young poet, Damien Smith, to lunch at the Ivy. Gerard used to say that James de Witt and I spent money on entertaining authors in inverse proportion to their importance to the firm. I thought the boy might enjoy the Ivy. I was due there at one o'clock and was taken by launch to London Bridge and then caught a taxi to the restaurant. We spent two hours over lunch and I was back at my flat about half past three. I made myself a pot of tea and returned to my office here at four. I worked for about an hour and a half.

"The last time I saw Gerard was when I went to the ground-floor lavatory. It's the one at the back of the house, next to the shower room. The women usually use the lavatory on the first floor. Gerard was coming out as I went in. We didn't speak but I think he nodded or smiled. There was some kind of passing acknowledgement, that's all. I didn't see him again. I came back to my flat and spent the next two hours in reading over the poems I'd selected for the evening, thinking about them, making coffee. I listened to the BBC six o'clock news. Shortly afterwards Frances Peverell rang me to wish me good luck. She had offered to go with me. I think she thought that someone from the firm ought to be there. We had spoken about it a few days earlier and I managed to dissuade her. One of the poets due to read was Marigold Riley. She's not a bad poet but much of her verse is scatological. I knew that Frances wouldn't enjoy the poetry, the company or the atmosphere. I told her that I would prefer to be on my own, that having her there would make me nervous. It wasn't entirely a lie. I hadn't read my verse for fifteen years. Most of the people there would assume that I was dead. I was already wishing I hadn't agreed to go. Having Frances there, wondering whether she was unhappy, how much she was disliking it all, would only have increased the trauma. I rang for a taxi and left shortly after half past seven."

Dalgliesh asked: "How shortly?"

"I rang for the taxi to be in the lane by seven-forty-five, and I suppose I kept him waiting a few minutes, not more." He paused again, then went on: "What happened at the Connaught Arms will hardly interest you. There were enough people there to confirm my presence. I suppose the reading went rather better than I expected, but it was too crowded and too noisy. I hadn't realized that poetry had become a spectator sport. There was a great deal of drinking and smoking and some of the poets were rather self-indulgent. It all went on too long. I meant to ask the landlord to telephone for a taxi but he was busy talking to a group of people and I slipped out more or less unnoticed. I thought I could pick up a cab at the end of the road, but before I got there I was mugged. There were three of them, I think, two black and one white, but I won't be able to identify them. I was just aware of rushing figures, the strong shove from the back, of hands grabbing at my pockets. It wasn't even a necessary assault. If they had asked I would have handed over my wallet. What else could I do?"

"They got it?"

"Oh yes, they got it. At least it was missing when I looked. The fall stunned me for a moment. When I came to, a man and a woman were bending over me. They had been at the reading and were trying to catch me up. I had banged my head when I fell and it was bleeding slightly. I took out my handkerchief and held it to the wound. I asked them to bring me home but they said that they had to drive past St Thomas's Hospital and insisted on leaving me there. They said that I ought to have an X-ray. I could hardly insist that they drove me home or found a cab. They were being very kind, but I don't think they wanted to go too far out of their way. At the hospital I had to wait quite a time. There were more urgent cases in the casualty department. Eventually a nurse dressed the wound on my head and said that I must wait to have an X-ray. That meant another wait. The result of that was satisfactory but they wanted to keep me in for a night's observation. I assured them that I would be well looked after at home and told them that I wasn't prepared to be admitted. I asked them to ring Frances and let her know what had happened and call a taxi. I thought she would probably be watching out for me to hear how the evening went and might be worried when I wasn't back by eleven. It was about half past one when I did get home, and I rang Frances at once. She wanted me to go up to her flat, but I told her I was perfectly all right and what I needed most was a bath. As soon as I'd had one I gave her another ring and she came down at once."

Dalgliesh said: "And she didn't insist on coming down to your flat as soon as you returned?"

"No. Frances never intrudes if she thinks someone wants to be alone, and I did want to be alone at least for a little time. I wasn't quite ready to give explanations, hear expressions of sympathy. What I needed was a drink and a bath. I had both and then rang Frances. I knew she was anxious and I didn't want to keep her waiting until the morning to learn what had happened. I thought the whisky would make me feel better, but in fact it made me feel rather sick. I suppose I had some kind of delayed shock. By the time she knocked on the door I wasn't feeling too good. We sat up together for a little time and then she insisted that I went to bed. She said she would stay in the flat in case I needed something in the night. I think she was afraid that I might be a great deal more ill than I made out and that she ought to be at hand to telephone a doctor if anything went wrong. I didn't try to dissuade her, although I knew that all I needed was a night's rest. I thought she would sleep in my spare room but I believe she wrapped herself in a blanket and stayed next door in the sitting-room. When I woke in the morning she was dressed and had made me a cup of tea. She insisted that I should stay at home, but I was feeling a great deal better by the time I was dressed and decided to go into Innocent House. We arrived together in the main hall just after the first launch of the day had arrived. That's when we were told that Gerard was missing."

Dalgliesh said: "And that was the first you knew of it?"

"Yes. It was his habit to work later than most of us, particularly on Thursdays. He was usually in later in the morning, except on the days when we had a partners' meeting, when he liked to begin promptly at ten. I'd assumed, of course, that he had gone home at about the time I left for my reading."

"But you didn't see him when you left for the Connaught Arms?"

"No, I didn't see him."

"Or see anyone entering Innocent House?"

"No one. I saw no one."

"And when you were given the news that he was dead the three of you went up to the little archives office?"

"Yes, we went up together, Stilgoe, de Witt and myself. It was a natural response to the news, I suppose, the need to see for oneself. James got there first. Stilgoe and I couldn't keep up with him. Claudia was still kneeling by her brother's body when we arrived. She got up and faced us and spread out one arm towards us. It was a curious gesture. It was as if she were displaying this enormity to public gaze."

"And how long were you in the room?"

"It could only have been less than a minute. It seemed longer. We were bunched together just inside the door, looking, staring, unbelieving, appalled. I don't think anyone spoke. I know I didn't. Everything in the room was extremely vivid. The shock seemed to have jarred my eyes into an extraordinary keenness of perception. I saw every detail of Gerard's body and of the room itself with astonishing clarity. Then Stilgoe spoke. He said: 'I'll telephone the police. We can do nothing here. This room must be locked at once and I'll keep the key.' He took over. We left together and Claudia locked the door after us. Stilgoe took the key. The rest you know."

26

During the innumerable discussions of the tragedy which were to occupy the following weeks and months, it was generally agreed by the staff of the Peverell Press that the experience of Marjorie Spenlove had been singular. Miss Spenlove, senior copy editor, had arrived at Innocent House punctually at her usual hour of 9:15. She had murmured a "good morning" to George, who, sitting stricken at his switchboard, hadn't noticed her. Lord Stilgoe, Dauntsey and de Witt were in the little archives room with the body, Mrs. Demery was ministering to Blackie in the ground-floor cloakroom surrounded by the rest of the staff and the hall was for a few minutes empty. Miss Spenlove went straight up to her room, took off her jacket and settled down to work. When working, she was oblivious to everything except the text before her. It was claimed by Peverell Press that no work copy-edited by Miss Spenlove ever contained an undetected error. She was at her best working on non-fiction, occasionally finding it difficult, with young modern novelists, to distinguish between grammatical mistakes and their cultivated and much-praised natural style. Her expertise went beyond details of the words; no geographical or historical inaccuracy went unchecked, no inconsistencies of weather, topography or dress unnoticed. Authors valued her even though their session with her to approve the final text left them feeling that they had undergone a particularly traumatic session with an intimidating headmistress of the old school.

Sergeant Robbins and a detective constable had searched the premises soon after their arrival. The search had been a little perfunctory; no one could seriously expect that the murderer was still on the premises unless he or she was a member of the staff. But Sergeant Robbins, perhaps excusably, had neglected to look in the small lavatory on the second floor. Descending to fetch Gabriel Dauntsey, his sharp ears detected the sound of a cough from the adjoining office and, opening the door, he found himself confronting an elderly lady working at a desk. Regarding him sternly above her half-moon spectacles, she enquired: "And who may you be?"

"Detective Sergeant Robbins of the Metropolitan Police, madam. How did you get in?"

"Through the door. I work here. This is my office. I am the senior copy editor of Peverell Press. As such I have a right to be here. I very much doubt whether that could be said of you."

"I'm here on duty, madam. Mr. Gerard Etienne has been found dead under suspicious circumstances."

"You mean someone has murdered him?"

"We can't be sure of that yet."

"When did he die?"

"We shall know more after the forensic pathologist has reported."

"How did he die?"

"We don't yet know the cause of death."

"It seems to me, young man, that there is very little you do know. Perhaps you had better come back when you are better informed."

Sergeant Robbins opened his mouth, then shut it firmly, just managing to prevent himself saying, "Yes, miss. Very good, miss." He disappeared, closing the door behind him, and was halfway down the stairs before realizing that he hadn't asked the woman's name. He would, of course, learn it in time. It was a small omission in a brief encounter which, he admitted, hadn't gone well. Being honest and given to mild speculation, he also admitted that part of the reason was the woman's uncanny resemblance in appearance and voice to Miss Addison, who had been his first teacher when he moved up from the infants' school and who had believed that children do best and are happiest when they know from the start who is boss.

Miss Spenlove was more shaken by the news than she had let him see. After completing work on the page, she telephoned the switchboard.

"George, could you find Mrs. Demery for me?" In seeking information, she believed in going to an expert. "Mrs. Demery? There's a young man roaming the building who claims to be a detective sergeant of the Metropolitan Police. He told me that Mr. Etienne is dead, possibly murdered. If you know anything about it, perhaps you could come up and enlighten me. And I'm ready for my coffee."

Mrs. Demery, abandoning Miss Blackett to the ministrations of Mandy, was only too eager to oblige.

27

Dalgliesh, with Kate, conducted the remaining interviews with the partners in Gerard Etienne's office. Daniel was occupied in the little archives room, where the gas man was already at work dismantling the fire, and, when this was completed and samples of any chimney debris despatched to the lab, would go on to Wapping Police Station to set up the incident room. Dalgliesh had already spoken to the station superintendent, who had accepted philosophically the need for the intrusion and the temporary use of one of his offices. Dalgliesh hoped that it wouldn't be for long. If this was murder, and he now had no doubt in his own mind that it was, then the number of possible suspects was unlikely to be great.

He had no wish to sit at Etienne's desk, partly because of sensitivity to the feelings of the partners, but principally because a confrontation across four feet of pale oak invested any interview with a formality which was more likely to inhibit or antagonize a suspect than elicit helpful information. There was, however, a small conference table in the same wood, with six chairs, close to the windows, and they seated themselves there. The long walk from the door would be intimidating for all but the most self-possessed, but he doubted whether it would worry Claudia or James de Witt.

The room had obviously once been a dining-room but its elegance had been desecrated by the end partition, which cut across the oval stucco decorations on the ceiling and bisected one of the four tall windows which looked out on Innocent Passage. The magnificent marble fireplace with its elegant carving was in Miss Blackett's office. And here in Etienne's office the furniture—desk, chairs, conference table and filing cabinets—was almost aggressively modern. They might have been chosen to be deliberately at odds with the marble pilasters and porphyry entablatures, the two magnificent chandeliers, one almost touching the partition, and the gilt of picture frames against the pale green of the walls. The pictures were conventional rural scenes, almost certainly Victorian. They were well but a little over-painted, too sentimental for his taste. He doubted whether these were the pictures which had originally hung here and he wondered what portraits of the Peverells had once graced these walls. There was still one piece of the original furniture: a marble-and-bronze wine-table, obviously Regency. So one reminder of past glories, at least, was still in use. He wondered what Frances Peverell thought of the room's desecration and whether now, with Gerard Etienne dead, the partition would be taken down. He wondered, too, if Gerard Etienne had been insensitive to all architecture or only disregarding of this particular house. Was the partitioning, the discordant modern furnishing, his comment on the unsuitability of the room for his purposes, a deliberate rejection of a past which had been dominated by Peverells, not Etiennes?

Claudia Etienne walked across the thirty feet towards him with confident grace and seated herself as if she were conferring a favour. She was very pale, but had herself well under control, although he suspected that her hands, plunged in the pockets of her cardigan, would have been more revealing than her taut grave face. He offered his condolences simply and, he hoped, sincerely but she cut him short.

"Are you here because of Lord Stilgoe?"

"No. I'm here because of your brother's death. Lord Stilgoe did get in touch with me indirectly through a mutual friend. He had received an anonymous letter which greatly upset his wife; she saw it as a threat to his life. He asked for an official assurance that the police have no suspicion of foul play in the three deaths concerned with Innocent House, two authors and Sonia Clements."

"Which you were, of course, able to give."

"Which the police divisions concerned were able to give. He should have received that assurance about three days ago."

"I hope it satisfied him. Lord Stilgoe's self-absorption amounts to paranoia. Still, he can hardly suppose that Gerard's death is a deliberate attempt to sabotage his precious memoirs. I still find it strange, Commander, that you are here personally, and in such impressive force. Are you treating my brother's death as murder?"

"As an unexplained and suspicious death. That is why I need to trouble you now. I would be grateful for your co-operation, not only personally, but in explaining to your staff that some invasion of their privacy and interference with their work is inevitable."

"I think they will understand that."

"We shall need to take fingerprints for the purpose of elimination. Any not needed in evidence will be destroyed when the case is complete."

"That will be a new experience for us. If it is necessary, of course, we must accept it. I assume that you will be requiring all of us, particularly the partners, to provide an alibi."

"I need to know what you were doing, Miss Etienne, and who you were with from six o'clock last night."

She said: "You have the unenviable task, Commander, of expressing sympathy at my brother's death while requiring an alibi to prove that I didn't murder him. You do it with some grace. I congratulate you; but then you've had plenty of practice. I was on the river with a friend, Declan Cartwright, last night. When you check with him he'll probably describe me as his fiancée. I prefer to use the word lover. We started off shortly after six-thirty, when the launch returned from taking staff to Charing Cross Pier. We were on the river until about ten-thirty, perhaps a little later, when we returned here and I drove him back to his flat off Westbourne Grove. He lives above an antique shop which he manages for the owner. I shall, of course, give you the address. I was with him until two o'clock, then drove back to the Barbican. I have a flat there, on the floor beneath that of my brother."

"It was a long time to spend on the river on an October night."

"A fine October night. We went downstream to see the Thames Barrier and then returned and put in at Greenwich Pier. We had dinner at Le Papillon in Greenwich Church Street. We booked for eight o'clock and I suppose we were there for about an hour and a half. Then we went upstream, beyond Battersea Bridge, and returned and, as I've said, were back here shortly after ten-thirty."

"Did anyone see you, other, of course, than the staff of the restaurant and the other diners?"

"The river wasn't very busy. Even so, plenty of people must have seen us, but that doesn't mean they'll remember us. I was in the wheelhouse and Declan was with me most of the time. We saw at least two police launches on the river. I dare say they will have noticed us. That's their job, isn't it?"

"Did anyone see you when you embarked or on your return?"

"Not as far as I know. We saw and heard no one."

"And you can think of no person who wished your brother dead?"

"You asked that question before."

"I'm asking it again now that we're here in private."

"Are we? Is anything one says to a police officer really private? The answer is the same. I know of no one who hated him enough to kill him. There are probably people who won't be sorry he's dead. No death is universally regretted. Every death advantages someone."

"Who will be advantaged by this death?"

"I shall. I'm Gerard's heir. That would, of course, have changed once he was married. As it is I inherit his shares in the firm, his Barbican flat, the proceeds of his life insurance. I didn't know him very well, we weren't brought up to be loving siblings. We went to different schools, different universities, had different lives. My Barbican flat is underneath his but we didn't make a habit of dropping in on each other. It would have seemed an invasion of privacy. But I liked him, I respected him. I was on his side. If he was murdered I hope that his killer rots in prison for the rest of his life. He won't, of course. We're so quick to forget the dead and forgive the living. Perhaps we need to show mercy because we're uncomfortably aware that one day we may need it. Incidentally, here are his keys. You asked for a set. I've taken off his car keys and the keys to his flat."

"Thank you," said Dalgliesh, taking them. "I don't need to assure you that they will stay in my possession, or be held by one of my team. Has your father been told that his son is dead?"

"Not yet. I'm going to drive down to Bradwell-on-Sea late this afternoon. He lives as a recluse and doesn't take incoming calls. In any case I would prefer to break it to him personally. Do you want to see him?"

"It's important I do. I'd be grateful if you would ask him if I could see him tomorrow at any time convenient for him."

"I'll ask but I'm not sure whether he'll agree. He has a strong dislike of visitors. He lives with an elderly Frenchwoman who looks after him. Her son is his chauffeur. He's married to a local girl and I imagine they'll take over when Estelle dies. She certainly won't retire. She regards it as a privilege to devote her life to a hero of France. Father, as always, has his life well organized. I tell you this so that you'll know what to expect. I don't think you will be welcome. Is that all?"

"I need, too, to see the next-of-kin of Sonia Clements."

"Sonia Clements? What possible connection can there be between her suicide and Gerard's death?"

"None as far as I know at present. Does she have next-of-kin, or was there someone she lived with?"

"Only her sister, and they didn't live together for the last three years of her life. She's a nun, a member of a community at Kemptown, outside Brighton. They run a hostel for the dying. I think it's called St Anne's Convent. I'm sure the Reverend Mother will allow you to see her. After all the police are like the VAT inspectors, aren't they? However disagreeable or inconvenient their presence, when they call on you, you have to let them in. Is there anything else you want from me?"

"The little archives room will be sealed and I should also like to lock the archives room itself."

"For how long?"

"For as long as necessary. Will that be very inconvenient?"

"Of course it will be inconvenient. Gabriel Dauntsey is working on the old records. The job is already well behind schedule."

"I realize that it will be inconvenient. I asked if it will be very inconvenient. The work of the firm can continue without access to those two rooms?"

"Obviously, if you think it important, we shall have to manage."

"Thank you."

He ended by asking her about the practical joker at Innocent House and the means taken to discover the culprit. The investigation seemed on the whole to have been as superficial as it was unsuccessful.

She said: "Gerard more or less left it to me, but I didn't get very far. All I could do was to list the incidents as they happened and the number of people who were on the premises at the time or could have been responsible. That meant practically everyone except staff who were off sick or on holiday. It was almost as if the joker deliberately chose times when all the partners and most of the staff were here and could have been responsible. Gabriel Dauntsey has an alibi for the last incident, the fax that was sent yesterday from this office to Better Books in Cambridge—he was on his way at the time to lunch with one of our authors at the Ivy—but the other partners and the senior staff were here. Gerard and I took the launch to Greenwich and had a pub lunch at the Trafalgar Tavern, but we didn't leave here until twenty past one. The fax was sent at twelve-thirty. Carling was due to begin signing at one o'clock. The most recent incident, of course, is the stealing of my brother's diary. That could have been taken from his desk drawer any time on the Wednesday. He missed it yesterday morning."

Dalgliesh said: "Tell me about the snake."

"Hissing Sid? Goodness knows when that first appeared here. About five years ago, I think. Someone left it after a staff Christmas party. It used to be used by Miss Blackett to prop open the door between her room and Henry Peverell's. It's become something of an office mascot. Blackie's attached to it for some reason."

"And yesterday your brother told her to get rid of it."

"Mrs. Demery told you that, I suppose. Yes, he did. He wasn't in a particularly good mood after the partners' meeting and for some reason the sight of the thing irritated him. She put it in the desk drawer."

"You saw her do that?"

"Yes. Myself, Gabriel Dauntsey and our temporary shorthand-typist, Mandy Price. I imagine that the news got round the office pretty fast."

Dalgliesh said: "Your brother came out of the meeting in a bad temper?"

"I didn't say that. I said he wasn't in a particularly good mood. None of us were. It's no secret that the Peverell Press is in trouble. We have to face up to selling Innocent House if we're to have any hope of staying in business."

"That must be a distressing prospect for Miss Peverell."

"I don't think any of us welcomes it. The suggestion that any of us tried to prevent it by harming Gerard is ludicrous."

Dalgliesh said: "It was not a suggestion that I have made."

Then he let her go.

She had just reached the door when Daniel put his head round. He opened it for her and waited to speak until she had left the room.

"The gas engineer is ready to go, sir. It's what we expected. The flue is badly blocked. It looks like rubble from the chimney lining, but there's been a lot of falling grit over the years. He'll provide an official report but he hasn't any doubt about what happened. With the flue in the state it is, that fire was lethal."

Dalgliesh said: "Only in a room without adequate ventilation. We've been told that often enough. The lethal combination was the burning fire and the unopenable window."

Daniel said: "There was one particularly large piece of rubble wedged against the flue. It could have fallen naturally from the lining of the chimney or been deliberately dislodged. There's really no way of telling. You'd only have to prod parts of that lining and chunks would fall away. Do you want to have a look, sir?"

"Yes, I'll come now."

"And you want the fire as well as the rubble to go to forensics?"

"Yes, Daniel, all of it." He had no need to add "And I want prints, photographs, the lot." He was, as always, working with experts in violent death.

As they made their way upstairs, he asked: "Any news of the missing tape recorder or Etienne's diary?"

"Not so far, sir. Miss Etienne made a fuss about checking the desk drawers of the staff who'd been sent home or who are on leave today. I didn't think you'd want to apply for a search warrant."

"Not necessary at present. I doubt whether it will be. The search can take place on Monday, when all the staff are here. If that tape recorder was taken by the murderer for a specific reason it's probably at the bottom of the river. If the office joker took it, it could turn up anywhere. The same goes for the diary."

Daniel said: "The recorder was the only one of its kind in the office, apparently. It belonged personally to Mr. Dauntsey. All the others are larger and are AC/battery cassette recorders which take the usual two-and-a-half-by-four-inch cassettes. Mr. de Witt wonders if you'll see him fairly soon, sir. He has a seriously sick friend living with him and promised that he'd be home early."

"All right, I'll take him next."

The gas engineer, already in his coat and ready to go, was vocal in his disapproval, obviously torn between an almost proprietorial interest in the appliance and professional outrage at its misuse.

"Haven't seen a fire of this type for nearly twenty years. It should be in a museum. But there's nothing wrong with the functioning of the fire itself. It's well made, sturdy. It's the type they used to install in nurseries. The tap's removable, you see, so that the children couldn't accidentally turn it on. You can see plainly enough what happened here, Commander. The flue's totally blocked. This grit must have been coming down for years. God knows when this appliance was last serviced. This was a death waiting to happen. I've seen it before, you too no doubt, and we'll see it again. People can't say they haven't been warned often enough. Gas appliances need air. Without ventilation what you get is malfunctioning and a build-up of carbon monoxide. Gas is a perfectly safe fuel if it's used properly."

"He'd have been all right with the window open?"

"Should have been. The window is high and rather narrow, but if it'd been properly open he'd have been all right. How did you find him? Asleep in a chair, I suppose. That's usually how it happens. People get a bit dozy, fall asleep and don't wake up."

Daniel said: "There are worse ways of going."

"Not if you're a gas engineer there aren't. It's an insult to the product. You'll be needing a report I suppose, Commander. Well, you'll get it soon enough. He was a young chap, wasn't he? Well, that makes it worse. I don't know why it should but it always does." He opened the door and looked round the room. "I wonder why he came up here to work. Odd place to choose. You'd think there'd be plenty of offices in a building this size without wanting to come up here."

28

James de Witt closed the door behind him and paused for a moment nonchalantly against it as if wondering whether he would after all bother to enter, then walked across the room in easy strides and pulled the empty chair to one side of the table.

"Is it all right if I sit here? Confronting you across the board in this adversarial way is rather intimidating. It brings back unpleasant memories of interviews with one's tutor." He was casually dressed in dark-blue jeans and a loose-fitting ribbed sweater with leather patches on the elbows and shoulders which looked like army surplus. On him it looked almost elegant.

He was very tall, certainly over six feet, and loose-limbed with a suggestion of gawkiness in the long bony wrists. His face, with something of the melancholy humour of a clown, was lean and intelligent, his cheeks flat under the jutting bones. A heavy strand of light-brown hair fell across the high forehead. His eyes were narrow, sleepy under heavy lids, but they were eyes which missed little and gave nothing away. When he spoke the soft agreeable drawl was oddly inappropriate to his words.

"I've just seen Claudia. She looks desperately tired. Did you really need to interrogate her? She has, after all, lost an only brother in appalling circumstances."

Dalgliesh said: "It was hardly an interrogation. If Miss Etienne had asked us to stop, or if I thought she was too distressed, we would obviously have deferred the interview."

"And Frances Peverell? It's just as ghastly for her. Can't her interview wait until tomorrow?"

"Not unless she's too distressed to see me now. In this kind of investigation we need to get as much information as possible as soon as possible."

Kate wondered whether his real concern had been for Frances Peverell rather than Claudia Etienne.

He said: "I suppose I'm taking Frances's turn. Sorry about that. It's just that my arrangements have temporarily broken down and my friend, Rupert Farlow, will be alone if I don't get back by half past four. Actually, Rupert Farlow is my alibi. I'm assuming that the main purpose of this interview is for me to provide one. I went home yesterday by the launch, at five-thirty, and was at Hillgate Village by half past six. I took the Circle Line from Charing Cross to Notting Hill Gate. Rupert can confirm that I was at home with him for the whole evening. Nobody called and, unusually, no one telephoned. It would be helpful if you could make an appointment before you check with him. He's seriously ill now and some days are better for him than others."

Dalgliesh asked him the usual question, whether he knew anyone who might wish Gerard Etienne dead. He asked: "Any political enemies for example, using that word in the widest sense?"

"Good God no! Gerard was impeccably liberal, in talk if not in actions. And after all it's the talk that matters. All the correct liberal opinions. He knew what can't be spoken or published in Britain today and he didn't speak it or publish it. He may have thought it, like the rest of us, but that's hardly a crime yet. Actually, I doubt whether he was much interested in political or social affairs, not even as they affected publishing. He'd pretend to a concern if it were expedient but I doubt whether he felt it."

"What did concern him? What did he feel deeply about?"

"Fame. Success. Himself. The Peverell Press. He wanted to head one of the largest—the largest—and most successful private publishing house in Britain. Music: Beethoven and Wagner in particular. He was a pianist and played rather well. It's a pity his touch with people wasn't as sensitive. His current woman, I suppose."

"He was engaged?"

"To Earl Norrington's sister. Claudia has telephoned the Dowager. I expect she's broken the news to her daughter by now."

"And there was no problem about the engagement?"

"Not that I am aware of. Claudia might know but I doubt it. Gerard was reticent about Lady Lucinda. We've all met her, of course. Gerard gave a joint engagement and birthday party for her here on the tenth of July instead of our usual summer bash. I believe he met her in Bayreuth last year but I gained the impression—I could be wrong—that it wasn't Wagner who had taken her there. I think she and her mother were visiting some continental cousins. I really know little else about her. The engagement was surprising, of course. One didn't think of Gerard as socially ambitious, if that's what it was all about. It's not as if Lady Lucinda was bringing money into the firm. Lineage but not lolly. Of course, when these people complain that they are poor they only mean that there is a slight temporary difficulty about paying the heir's fees at Eton. Still, Lady Lucinda certainly counts as one of Gerard's interests. And then there's mountaineering. If you had asked Gerard about his interests he would probably have added mountaineering. To my knowledge he only climbed one mountain in his life."

Kate asked unexpectedly: "Which mountain?"

De Witt turned to her and smiled. The smile was unexpected and transformed his face. "The Matterhorn. That probably tells you as much about Gerard Etienne as you need to know."

Dalgliesh said: "Presumably he intended to make changes here. They can't all have been popular."

"That didn't mean they weren't necessary, still are necessary I suppose. Maintaining this house has been eating up the annual profit for decades. I suppose we could stay on if we halved the list, sacked two-thirds of the staff, took a 30-per-cent cut in our own pay and contented ourselves with the back-list and being a very small cult publisher. That wouldn't have suited Gerard Etienne."

"Or the rest of you?"

"Oh, we grumbled and kicked against the pricks at times but I think we recognized that Gerard was right; it was expand or go under. A publishing house today can't survive on trade publishing. Gerard wanted to take over a firm with a strong legal list—there's one ripe for plucking—and to go into educational publishing. It was all going to take money, not to say energy and a certain amount of commercial aggression. I'm not sure that some of us had the stomach for it. God knows what will happen now. I imagine that we'll have a partners' meeting, confirm Claudia as chairman and MD and defer all disagreeable decisions for at least six months. That would have amused Gerard. He would have seen it as typical."

Dalgliesh, anxious not to detain him too long, ended by asking him briefly about the practical joker.

"I've no idea who's responsible. We've wasted a lot of time in the monthly partners' meetings talking about it but we've got nowhere. It's odd really. With a total staff of only thirty, you'd imagine that we'd have got some clue by now if only by a process of elimination. Of course, the great majority of the staff have been with the Press for years and I'd have said that all of them, old and new, were beyond suspicion. And the incidents have happened when practically everyone has been there. Perhaps that was the joker's idea, to make elimination difficult. Most serious, of course, were the disappearance of the artwork for the non-fiction book on Guy Fawkes and the alteration of Lord Stilgoe's proofs."

Dalgliesh said: "But neither, in fact, proved catastrophic."

"As it happens, no. This last business with Hissing Sid seems to be in a different category. The others were directed against the firm, but stuffing the head of that snake into Gerard's mouth was surely an act of malice against him personally. To save you asking, I may as well say that I knew where to find Hissing Sid. I imagine most of the office did by the time Mrs. Demery had finished her rounds."

Dalgliesh thought that it was time to let him go. He said: "How will you get to Hillgate Village?"

"I've ordered a taxi, it'll be too slow by launch to Charing Cross. I'll be in at half past nine tomorrow if there's anything else you want to know. Not that I think I can help. Oh, I may as well say now that I didn't kill Gerard, nor did I put that snake round his neck. I could hardly hope to persuade him of the virtues of the literary novel by gassing him to death."

Dalgliesh said: "So that's how you think he died?"

"Didn't he? Actually it was Dauntsey's idea, I can take no credit for it. But the more I think about it the more credible it appears."

He left with the same unhurried grace as that with which he had entered.

Dalgliesh reflected that questioning suspects was rather like inter-viewing candidates as a member of a selection board. There was always the temptation to assess the performance of each and to put forward a tentative opinion before the next applicant was summoned. Today he waited in silence. Kate, as always, sensed that it was wise to keep her counsel, but he suspected that there were one or two pungent comments she would have liked to have made about Claudia Etienne.

Frances Peverell was the last. She came into the room with something of the docility of a well-trained schoolchild but her composure broke when she saw Etienne's jacket still hanging across the back of his chair.

She said: "I didn't think this was still here," and began to move towards it, her hand outstretched. Then she checked herself and turned towards Dalgliesh and he saw that her eyes had brimmed with tears.

He said: "I'm sorry. Perhaps we should have taken it away."

She said: "Claudia might have removed it, perhaps, but she's had other things to think about. Poor Claudia. I suppose she'll have to cope with all his belongings, all his clothes."

She sat down and looked at Dalgliesh like a patient, waiting for a consultant's opinion. Her face was gentle, the light-brown hair with strands of gold was cut in a fringe above straight eyebrows and blue-green eyes. Dalgliesh suspected that the look of strained anxiety in them was more long-standing than a response to the present trauma and he wondered what Henry Peverell had been like as a father. The woman before him had none of the petulant self-absorption of a spoiled only daughter. She looked like a woman who all her life had responded to the needs of others, more used to receiving implied criticism than praise. She had none of Claudia Etienne's self-possession or de Witt's dégagé elegance. She was wearing a skirt in a soft blue-and-fawn tweed with a blue jumper and matching cardigan, but without the usual string of pearls. She could, he thought, have worn exactly the same in the 1930s or 1950s, the unexceptional day clothes of the English gentle-woman: unexciting, conventional, expensive good taste, giving offence to no one.

Dalgliesh said gently: "I always think that's the worst job after someone dies. Watches, jewellery, books, pictures—these can be given to friends and it seems right and appropriate. But clothes are too intimate to be given as gifts. Paradoxically it seems that we can only bear to think of them being worn not by people we know, but by strangers."

She said with eagerness, as if grateful that he understood: "Yes, I felt that after Daddy died. In the end I gave all his suits and shoes to the Salvation Army. I hope they found someone who needed them, but it was like clearing him out of the flat, clearing him out of my life."

"Were you fond of Gerard Etienne?"

She looked down at her folded hands and then straight into his eyes. "I was in love with him. I wanted to tell you myself because I'm sure you'll find out sooner or later and it's better coming from me. We had an affair but it ended a week before he became engaged."

"By common consent?"

"No, not by common consent."

He didn't need to ask her what she had felt at this betrayal. What she had felt, and was still feeling, was written plainly on her face.

He said: "I'm sorry. Talking about his death can't be easy for you."

"Not as painful as being unable to talk. Please tell me, Mr. Dalgliesh, do you think that Gerard was murdered?"

"We can't be certain yet but it is a probability rather than a possibility. That's why we have to question you now. I'd like you to explain exactly what happened last night."

"I expect Gabriel—Mr. Dauntsey—has explained about the mugging. I didn't go with him to his poetry reading because he was adamant he wanted to be alone. I think he felt I wouldn't enjoy it. But someone from Peverell Press should have gone with him. It was the first time he'd read for about fifteen years and it wasn't right that he should be alone. If I'd been with him perhaps he wouldn't have been mugged. I received the telephone call from St Thomas's at about eleven-thirty saying he was there and would have to wait for an X-ray, and asking if I would be with him if they sent him home. Apparently he was more or less demanding to come back and they wanted to be sure he wouldn't be alone. I was watching out for him from my kitchen window but I missed hearing the taxi. His front door is in Innocent Lane but I think the driver must have turned at the bottom and left him there. He must have rung as soon as he got in. He said he was all right, that there was no fracture and he was going to have a bath. After that he'd be glad if I'd come down. I don't think he really wanted me, but he knew I couldn't be happy if I hadn't made sure he was all right."

Dalgliesh asked: "You haven't a key to his flat, then? You couldn't wait for him there?"

"I do have a key and he has a key to my flat. It's a sensible precaution in case there's a fire or flood and we need to gain access when the other is away. But I wouldn't dream of using it unless Gabriel had asked me."

Dalgliesh asked: "How long was it before you joined him?"

The answer was, of course, of vital importance. It was possible for Gabriel Dauntsey to have killed Etienne before he set off for the poetry reading at 7:45. The timing would have been tight but it could have been done. But it seemed that the only chance he would have had to return to the scene was after one in the morning.

He asked again: "How long was it before Mr. Dauntsey rang to call you down? Can you be fairly precise?"

"It can't have been long. I suppose about eight or ten minutes, maybe a little shorter. About eight minutes, I'd say, just long enough for him to have a bath. His bathroom is under mine. I can't hear it when he runs his bath but I do hear the water running away. Yesterday I was listening for that."

"And it was about eight minutes before you heard it?"

"I wasn't watching the time. Why should I have been? But I'm sure it wasn't unduly long." She said, as if the possibility had suddenly struck her: "But you can't really mean that you suspect Gabriel, that you think he went back to Innocent House and killed Gerard?"

"Mr. Etienne was dead long before midnight. What we are considering now is the possibility that the snake was put round his neck some hours after he died."

"But that would mean that someone went up to the little archives office specially, knowing that he was dead, knowing that he was lying there. But the only person who knew that would be the murderer. You're saying you thought the murderer went back later to the little archives room."

"If there was a murderer. We can't be sure of that yet."

"But Gabriel was ill, he'd been mugged! And he's old. He's over seventy. And he's rheumatic. He usually walks with a stick. He couldn't possibly have done it in the time."

"Are you absolutely sure of that, Miss Peverell?"

"Yes, I'm sure. Besides, he did have a bath. I heard the water running away."

Dalgliesh said gently: "But you couldn't tell if it was his bath water."

"What else could it have been? He didn't just leave his tap running, if that's what you're suggesting. If he had I should have heard it immediately. This water didn't begin running away until about eight minutes after he rang and said he was ready for me. When I went down he was wearing his dressing-gown. I could tell he had had a bath. His hair and face were damp."

"And after that?"

"He'd already had some whisky and didn't want anything else, so I insisted that he went to bed. I was determined to stay the night so he told me where the clean sheets were for the spare bed. I don't think anyone had slept in that room for years and I didn't make up the bed. He fell asleep very quickly and I settled myself in the armchair in the sitting-room in front of the electric fire. I left the door open so that I could hear him, but he didn't wake. I woke before him, shortly after seven, and made a cup of tea. I tried to be quiet but I think he must have heard me moving around. It was about eight o'clock when he woke. Neither of us was in a hurry. We knew that George would open Innocent House. We both had a boiled egg for breakfast and went across shortly after nine o'clock."

"And you didn't go up to see Mr. Etienne's body?"

"Gabriel did. I didn't. I waited with the others at the bottom of the stairs. But when we heard that horrible high wailing, I think I knew that Gerard was dead."

Dalgliesh could see that she was again becoming distressed. He had learned all he needed for the present. He thanked her gently and let her go.

After she had left them they were silent for a moment, then Dalgliesh said: "Well Kate, we've been presented with more disinterested and convincing alibis: Claudia Etienne's lover, de Witt's sick house-guest and Frances Peverell, who's obviously incapable of believing that Gabriel Dauntsey could be guilty of a malicious act, let alone murder. She's trying to be honest about the length of time between his coming home and calling her down. She's an honest woman, but I'd guess that her eight minutes was an underestimate."

Kate said: "I wonder if she realized that he was giving her an alibi as well as she providing one for him. But of course it isn't important, is it? She could have gone over to Innocent House and done that business with the snake any time before Dauntsey arrived home. And she had every opportunity to kill Etienne. She's got no alibi for earlier yesterday evening. She was quick to pick up that point about the bath water, that he couldn't just have turned on the tap and let it run."

"No, but there is another possibility. Think about it, Kate."

Kate thought, then said: "Of course, it could have been done that way."

"Which means that we need to know the capacity of that bath. And we need to test the timing. Don't use Dauntsey. Robbins will have to imagine he's a rheumatic seventy-six-year-old. See how long it takes to get from Dauntsey's door in Innocent Lane up to the little archives room, do what had to be done there and get back."

"Using the stairs?"

"Time it using both stairs and the lift. With that lift the stairs are probably quicker."

As they began putting their papers together Kate thought about Frances Peverell. Dalgliesh had been gentle with her, but when was he ever brutal in interrogation? He had been sincere in that comment about the clothes of the dead. All the same it had been remarkably effective in gaining Frances Peverell's confidence. He was probably sorry for the woman, possibly even rather liked her; but no personal feelings would influence him in his investigation. And what about me? Kate asked herself, not for the first time. Wouldn't he show a similar detachment, a comparable ruthlessness, in all aspects of his professional life? She thought: He respects me, he's glad to have me in the team, he trusts me, sometimes I can believe that he likes me. But if I fell down badly on the job, how long would I last?

Dalgliesh said: "I need to go back to the Yard now for a couple of hours. I'll meet you and Daniel at the mortuary for the PM but I may not be able to stay until it's completed. I've a meeting with the Commissioner and the Minister in the House of Commons at eight o'clock. I don't know when I'll get away from that but I'll come on straight to Wapping and we'll review progress so far."

It was going to be a long night.

29

It was two minutes to three and Blackie was sitting alone at her desk. She was oppressed by a listlessness which was partly the result of delayed shock, partly fear, but which made any action seem an intolerable exertion. She supposed she could go home, although no one had told her so. There was filing to be done, letters which Gerard Etienne had dictated still to be typed, but it seemed somehow indecent as well as pointless to file papers for which he would now never call and type letters his hand would never sign. Mandy had left half an hour earlier, presumably told that she was no longer wanted. Blackie had watched while she took her red crash-helmet from the bottom drawer of her desk and zipped up her tight leather jacket. Topped with that glittering dome, with her skinny body, the long legs clad in black ribbed leggings, she had been instantly transformed as always into the caricature of an exotic insect.

Her last words to Blackie, spoken with a trace of embarrassed sympathy, had been: "Look, don't you go losing any sleep over him. I won't, and I quite liked him, what I saw of him. But he was a proper bastard to you. Are you going to be all right, going home, I mean?"

She had replied: "Yes thank you, Mandy. I'm perfectly all right now. It was the shock. After all, I was his PA. You've only known him for a few weeks and as a temporary typist."

The words, a clumsy attempt to restore her dignity, had sounded even to her own ears repressive and pompous. They had been greeted with a shrug and Mandy had left without another word, her loud goodbyes to Mrs. Demery echoing across the hall.

Mandy had been notably cheered by her interview with the police and had immediately gone off to discuss it with Mrs. Demery, George and Amy in the kitchen. Blackie would have liked to have joined them but had felt that it would be inappropriate to her status to be found gossiping with the junior staff. She knew, too, that they wouldn't have welcomed her intrusion into their confidences and speculations. On the other hand, she hadn't been invited to join the partners when they were closeted in the boardroom and had been seen by no one except Mrs. Demery when they rang for more coffee and sandwiches. It seemed to her that there was no place in Innocent House where she was wanted or could any longer feel at home.

She thought about Mandy's last words. Was that what Mandy had told the police, that Mr. Gerard had treated her, Blackie, like a proper bastard? But of course she had. Why should Mandy keep quiet about anything that had happened at Innocent House, Mandy who was the outsider, who had arrived long after the series of practical jokes had begun, who could take a detached, almost pleasurable, interest in all the excitement, secure in the knowledge of her own innocence, unmoved by personal affections, untouched by personal loyalties. Mandy, whose sharp little eyes missed nothing, would have been a gift to the police. And she had been with them a long time, nearly an hour, longer, surely, than her importance in the firm could justify. Once more, and fruitlessly, since nothing now could be changed, Blackie thought over her own interview. She hadn't been among the first to be called. She had had time to prepare herself, to think about what she would say. And she had thought about it. Fear had sharpened her mind.

It had taken place in Miss Claudia's office and only two of the police had been there, the woman detective inspector and a sergeant. Somehow she had expected to see Commander Dalgliesh and his absence had disconcerted her so that she had answered the first questions uncertain whether the interview had really begun, and half expecting him to come in at the door. She was surprised, too, that the interview wasn't being tape-recorded. The police almost always did that in the detective series which were her cousin's favourite viewing at Weaver's Cottage, but perhaps that came later, when they had a prime suspect and were questioning him or her under caution. And then, of course, she would have a lawyer present. Now she was alone. This time there had been no caution, no suggestion that this was anything but an informal preliminary chat. The woman detective inspector had asked most of the questions while the sergeant had made notes, but he had intervened

from time to time without deferring to his senior officer and with the
quiet assurance which suggested to her that they were used to working together. Both had been very polite, almost gentle, with her but
she hadn't been deceived. They were still interrogators and even their
formal expressions of sympathy, their gentleness, were part of their
technique. She was surprised, looking back on it, how she had known
this and known them for the enemies they were even in the tumult of
her fear.

They had begun by asking simple preliminary questions about her
length of service in the firm, the method of locking the premises at
night, the people who had keys and could control the burglar alarms,
the general shape of her day, even her arrangements for lunch. Answering them, she had begun to feel more at ease even while she knew
that they were designed for just that purpose.

Then Detective Inspector Miskin had said: "You worked for Mr.
Henry Peverell for twenty-seven years until he died, then transferred
to Mr. Etienne when he took over as chairman and managing director
in January this year. That must have been a difficult change for you
and for the firm."

She was expecting that. She had her answer ready.

"It was different, of course. I had worked for old Mr. Peverell for
so long that naturally he confided in me. Mr. Gerard was younger and
had different methods of working. I had to adapt to a different
personality. Every PA does that when she gets a change of boss."

"You were happy to work for Mr. Etienne? You liked him?" This
was the sergeant, uncompromising dark eyes compelling her own.

She said: "I respected him."

"That's not quite the same thing."

"You can't always like your boss. I think I was getting used to him."

"And he to you? What about the rest of the firm? He was making
changes, wasn't he? Change always causes some pain, particularly in a
long-established organization. We know that at the Yard. Weren't there
sackings, threats of sackings, a possible move down-river to new premises, the proposal to sell Innocent House?"

She had said: "You'll have to ask Miss Claudia. Mr. Gerard didn't
discuss house policy with me."

"Unlike Mr. Peverell. The change from confidante to ordinary
secretary can't have been agreeable."

She didn't reply. Then Inspector Miskin leaned forward and said
confidingly, almost as if they were girls together ready to share a feminine secret: "Tell us about the snake. Tell us about Hissing Sid."

So she had told them how the snake had been brought into the office about five years previously at Christmas by a temporary shorthand-typist whose name and address no one now could remember. She had left it behind after the Christmas party and it hadn't been discovered until six months later, stuffed into the back of the drawer of her desk. Blackie had used it to wind round the handles of the door between her office and that of Mr. Peverell. He liked the door to be kept ajar so that he could call for her when he wanted her. Mr. Peverell had never liked using the telephone. Hissing Sid had become something of a house mascot, taken on the river outing in the summer and to the Christmas party, but she no longer used the snake to keep the door ajar. Mr. Etienne preferred it closed.

The sergeant asked: "Where was the snake usually kept?"

"Usually curled on top of the left-hand filing cabinet. Sometimes it would be hung or curled round one of the handles."

"Tell us what happened yesterday. Mr. Etienne objected, didn't he, to seeing the snake in the office?"

She said, trying to keep her voice calm, "He came out of his room and saw Hissing Sid drooping from the handle of the top filing cabinet. He thought it looked inappropriate in an office and told me to get rid of it."

"And what did you do?"

"I put it in my top right-hand drawer."

Detective Inspector Miskin said: "This is very important, Miss Blackett, and I'm sure you are intelligent enough to know why. Who was in the office when you put the snake into the drawer?"

"Only Mandy Price, who shares the office with me, Mr. Dauntsey and Miss Claudia. Afterwards she went with her brother into his office. Mr. Dauntsey gave Mandy a letter to type, then left."

"And no one else?"

"No one else in the room but I expect some of the people who were mentioned what had happened. I don't think that Mandy would have kept quiet. And anyone looking for the snake would probably have thought of my right-hand drawer. I mean, that was the natural place to put the snake."

"And you didn't think of throwing it away?"

Thinking back on it, she knew now that she had reacted too forcibly to the suggestion, that there had been in her voice a note of angry resentment.

"Get rid of Hissing Sid? No, why should I? Mr. Peverell used to like the snake. He found it amusing. It wasn't doing any harm in the office. After all, my office isn't a place where the public normally come. I just put it in the top drawer. I thought perhaps I might take it home."

They had asked about the earlier visit of Esmé Carling and her insistence on seeing Mr. Etienne. She realized that someone must have talked, that none of this was new to them, so she told the truth, or as much of the truth as she could bear to speak.

"Mrs. Carling isn't one of our easiest authors and she was extremely angry. I think her agent had told her that Mr. Etienne didn't wish to publish her latest book. She was insistent on seeing him but I had to explain that he was in the partners' meeting and that it was impossible to disturb them. She retaliated by being extremely offensive about Mr. Peverell and our confidential relationship. I think she thought that I had exerted too much influence in the firm."

"Did she threaten to come back and see Mr. Etienne later in the day?"

"No, nothing like that. Of course, she might have insisted on staying until the meeting was over, but she had a signing at a bookshop in Cambridge."

"Which was, of course, cancelled by a fax from this office sent at twelve-thirty. Did you send that fax, Miss Blackett?"

She stared straight into the grey eyes. "No, I didn't."

"Do you know who did send it?"

"I have no idea. It was during our usual lunch hour. I was in the kitchen heating up a Marks & Spencer packet of spaghetti bolognese for my lunch. People were in and out all the time. I can't remember where anyone was at twelve-thirty precisely. I only know I wasn't in the office."

"And your office wasn't locked?"

"Of course not. We never lock offices during the day."

And so it had gone on. Questions about the previous practical jokes, questions about when she had left the office the previous night, her journey home, the time she had arrived, how she had spent the evening. None of that was difficult. Eventually Detective Inspector Miskin had brought the interview to an end but with no sense that it had really finished. When it was over, Blackie had found that her legs were trembling and she had had to grasp the side of her chair firmly for a few seconds before she could be confident of walking to the door without staggering.

She had tried twice to ring Weaver's Cottage but there had been no reply. Joan must be somewhere in the village or shopping in the town; but perhaps that was just as well. This was news best broken in person, not over the telephone. She wondered whether there was any point in ringing again to say that she would be home early, but even picking up the receiver seemed too much effort. While she was trying to rouse herself to action, the door opened and Miss Claudia put her head round.

"Oh, you're still here. The police are happy for people to go now. Didn't anyone tell you? The office is closed anyway. Fred Bowling is ready to take you to Charing Cross in the launch." Seeing Blackie's face, she added: "Are you all right, Blackie? I mean, do you want someone to go home with you?"

The thought appalled Blackie. Who was there anyway? Mrs. Demery, she knew, was still on the premises making endless jugs of coffee for the partners or the police, but she certainly wouldn't welcome being detailed to make an hour-and-a-half journey into Kent. Blackie could picture that journey, the chatter, the questions, arriving together at Weaver's Cottage, Mrs. Demery reluctantly escorting her as if she were a delinquent child or a prisoner under surveillance. Joan would probably feel that she had to give Mrs. Demery tea. Blackie imagined the three of them in the cottage sitting-room, Mrs. Demery giving her highly coloured version of the day's events, garrulous, vulgar, solicitous in turn, almost impossible to get rid of. She said: "I'm perfectly all right, thank you, Miss Claudia. I'm sorry I was so stupid. It was just the shock."

"It was a shock for all of us."

Miss Claudia's voice was colourless. Perhaps the words weren't meant as a rebuke; they only sounded like one. She paused as if there was something else she needed to say, or perhaps felt she should say, then she added: "Don't come in on Monday if you still feel distressed. There's no real need. If the police want you again they know where to find you." And then she was gone.

It was the first time that they had been alone together, however briefly, since the discovery of the body and Blackie wished she had found something to say, some word of sympathy. But what was there to say that was at once truthful and sincere? "I never liked him and he didn't like me, but I'm sorry he's dead." And was that really true?

At Charing Cross she was used to being borne along on the rush-hour stream of commuter traffic, purposeful and confident. It was strange to be there in the mid-afternoon with a concourse surprisingly quiet for a Friday and a muted air of indecisive timelessness. An elderly couple, overclad for the journey, the woman obviously in her best, were anxiously scanning the departure board, the man dragging a large suitcase on wheels, the case heavily strapped. At a word from the woman he jerked it closer and immediately it thudded over. Blackie watched for a time, as they tried unsuccessfully to right it, then moved across to help them. But even as she grappled with its unwieldy top-heavy bulk she was aware of their anxious and suspicious eyes, as if fearing that she had designs on their underwear. The task completed, they murmured their thanks and moved off, supporting the case between them and from time to time patting it as if pacifying a recalcitrant dog.

The board showed that Blackie had half an hour to wait, just comfortable time for a coffee. Sipping it, smelling the familiar aroma, comforting her hands around the cup, she thought that this unexpected and early journey would normally have been a small indulgence, the unfamiliar emptiness of the station reminding her not of rush-hour discomforts but of childhood holidays, the leisure for coffee, the reassuring certainty of getting home before dark. But all pleasure was now overburdened by the memory of horror, by that nagging, insistent amalgam of fear and guilt. She wondered whether she would ever again be free of it. But at last she was on her way home. She hadn't made up her mind how far she would confide in her cousin. There were things that she couldn't and mustn't tell her, but at least she would be sure of Joan's common-sense reassurance, of the familiar ordered peace of Weaver's Cottage.

The train, half-empty, left on time, but later she could recall nothing of the journey or of unlocking the car in the car park at East Marling, nor of the drive to West Marling and the cottage. All she remembered later was driving up to the front gate and what then met her eyes. She stared in unbelieving horror. In the autumnal sunshine the garden lay before her, violated, desolate, physically torn up, ripped and thrown aside. At first, disorientated by shock, confused by a memory of the great storms of earlier years, she thought that Weaver's Cottage had been struck by a bizarre and localized tornado. But the thought was momentary. This destruction, more petty, more discriminate, was the work of human hands.

She got out of the car, her limbs seeming no longer part of her, and walked stiffly to the gate, clutching at it for support. And now she could see each separate barbarity. The flowering cherry to the right of the gate, its autumn palettes of bright red and yellow staining the air, had been stripped of all its lower branches, the scars on the bark raw as open wounds. The mulberry tree in the middle of the lawn, Joan's special pride, had been similarly violated and the white slatted bench round the trunk smashed and splintered as if jumped on by heavy boots. The rose bushes, perhaps because of the spikiness of their branches, had been left whole but torn up by their roots and thrown into a heap, and the bed of early Michaelmas daisies and white chry-

santhemums, which Joan had planned as a pale drift against the dark
hedge, lay in swathes over the path. The rose over the porch had
defeated them, but they had ripped down both the clematis and the
wistaria, making the front of the cottage look oddly naked and defenceless.

The cottage was empty. Blackie went from room to room calling
Joan's name long after it was obvious that she wasn't at home. She was
beginning to feel the first prick of real anxiety when she heard the bang
of the front gate and saw her cousin wheeling her bicycle down the
path. Running from the front door to meet her, she cried out: "What
happened? Are you all right?"

Her cousin showed no surprise at seeing her home hours before the
usual time. She said grimly: "You can see what happened. Vandals.
Four of them on motor bikes. I nearly caught them at it. They were
roaring off as I got back from the village but they were away before I
could get their numbers."

"You've rung the police?"

"Of course. They're coming from East Marling and taking their
time. This wouldn't have happened if we'd still had our village policeman. There's no point in their hurrying. They won't catch them. No
one will. And if they do, what will happen to them? Nothing but a small
fine or a conditional discharge. My God, if the police can't protect us,
they'd better let us arm ourselves. If I'd only had a gun."

Blackie said: "You can't shoot people just because they've vandalized
your garden."

"Can't you? I could."

As they moved into the cottage Blackie saw with amazement and
embarrassment that Joan had been crying. The signs were unmistakable:
the eyes, unnaturally small and lifeless, still bloodshot, her blotched face
an unhealthy grey mottled with raw red patches. This had been a
violation against which all her customary calmness and stoicism were
powerless. She could more easily have borne an attack on her person.
But anger had now taken over from grief and Joan's anger was formidable.

"I've been back to the village to see what else they've done. Nothing
much, apparently. They went into the Moonraker's Arms for lunch but
got so noisy that Mrs. Baker refused to serve them further and Baker
pushed them out. Then they began riding round in circles on the village
green until Mrs. Baker went across and told them it wasn't allowed. By
then they were being extremely offensive and jeering, revving up their
bikes and making a great deal of noise. However, they did eventually

leave when Baker went out and threatened to phone the police. I suppose this was their revenge."

"Suppose they come back?"

"Oh, they won't come back. Why should they? They'll look for something else beautiful to destroy. My God, what sort of generation have we bred? They're better fed, better educated, better looked after than any previous generation and they behave like vicious louts. What's happened to us? And don't talk to me about unemployment. They may have been unemployed but they could afford expensive motor bikes, and two of them had cigarettes hanging out of their mouths."

"They're not all like that, Joan. You can't judge a whole generation by the few."

"You're right, of course. I'm glad you're home."

It was the first time in their nineteen years together that she had expressed a need for Blackie's support and comfort. She went on: "It was good of Mr. Etienne to let you get away early. What happened? Did someone from the village telephone you to tell you? But they couldn't have. You must've been on your way about the time it happened."

And then Blackie, concisely but vividly, told her.

The news of this bizarre horror had at least the merit of diverting Joan's mind from the violation of her garden. She sank into the nearest chair as if her legs had given way, but she listened in silence, making no exclamations of disgust or surprise. When Blackie had finished she got up and gazed fixedly for a long quarter of a minute into her cousin's eyes as if to reassure herself that Blackie was still in her right mind. Then she said briskly: "You'd better stay sitting down. I'll put a match to the fire. We've both had a bad shock and it's important to keep warm. And I'll get the whisky. We need to talk this over."

As Joan settled her more comfortably into the fireside chair, plumping up the cushions and pulling over the footrest with a solicitude rare to her, Blackie couldn't help noticing that her cousin's voice and face expressed less outrage than a certain grim satisfaction and reflected that there was nothing like the vicarious horror of murder to divert attention from one's own less egregious misfortunes.

Forty minutes later, sitting in front of the crackle of the wood fire, soothed by the warmth and the bite of the whisky which she and her cousin kept for emergencies, she felt for the first time distanced from the traumas of the day. On the rug Arabella delicately stretched and curled her paws in ecstasy, her white fur ruddy from the dancing flames. Joan had lit the oven before they settled down together and

Blackie could detect the first savoury smell of lamb casserole seeping through the kitchen door. She realized that she was actually hungry, that it might even be possible to enjoy a meal. Her body felt light, as if a weight of guilt and fear had been physically lifted from her shoulders. Despite her resolution she found herself confiding about Sydney Bartrum.

"You see, I knew he was due for the sack. I typed the letter from Mr. Gerard to this head-hunting firm. Of course I couldn't directly tell Sydney what was being planned—I've always regarded a PA's job as highly confidential—but it didn't seem right not to warn him. Only married just over a year ago and now they've got a baby daughter. And he's over fifty. He must be. It won't be easy for him to get another job. So I left a copy of the letter on my desk when I knew he was due to see Mr. Gerard about the estimates. Mr. Gerard always kept him waiting, so I went out of the office and gave him his chance. I felt sure he'd read it. It's human instinct to glance at a letter if it's there in front of you."

But her action, so alien to her character and normal behaviour, hadn't been prompted by pity. She knew that now, and wondered why she hadn't realized it before. What she had felt was a common cause with Sydney Bartrum; they were both victims of Mr. Gerard's barely concealed disdain. She had made her first small gesture of defiance. Was it that which had given her courage for that later, more disastrous rebellion?

Joan said: "But did he read it?"

"He must have done. He didn't give me away—at least Mr. Gerard never mentioned the matter to me or rebuked me for my carelessness. But next day Sydney made an appointment to see him and I think asked if his job was safe. I didn't hear their voices but he wasn't in there long, and when he came out he was crying. Think of that, Joan, a grown man crying." She added, "That's why I didn't tell the police."

"About the crying?"

"About the letter. I didn't tell them any of it."

"And is that all you didn't tell them?"

"Yes," lied Blackie, "that's all."

"I think you were right." Mrs. Willoughby, strong legs planted apart, hand reaching for the whisky bottle, was judicial. "Why volunteer information which may be irrelevant and even misleading? If they ask you directly, of course, you'll have to tell the truth."

"That's what I thought. And we can't even be sure yet that it was murder. I mean he could have died from natural causes, a heart attack maybe, and someone put the snake around his neck afterwards. That's what most people seem to think. It's exactly the kind of thing the office prankster would do."

But Mrs. Willoughby immediately rejected this convenient theory. "Oh, I think we can be reasonably sure that it was murder. Whatever happened to the body afterwards, you wouldn't have had the police there for so long, and at such senior level, if they had any real doubt. This Commander Dalgliesh, I've heard of him. They wouldn't send an officer of his seniority if they thought it was a natural death. You say, of course, that Lord Stilgoe was the one who telephoned New Scotland Yard. Perhaps that may have influenced the police. A title still has some power. There's always suicide or accident, of course, but neither seems likely from what you've told me. No, if you ask me, this was murder, and an inside job."

Blackie said: "But not Sydney. Sydney Bartrum wouldn't hurt a fly."

"Maybe. But he might swat something a great deal larger and more dangerous. Anyway, the police will check up on all your alibis. It's a pity you went late-night shopping in the West End yesterday and didn't come straight home. I suppose there's no one at Liberty or Jaeger who can speak for you?"

"I don't think so. You see I didn't buy anything. I was only looking, and the stores were very crowded."

"It's ludicrous, of course, to think that you had anything to do with it, but the police have to treat everyone on the same footing, at least initially. Oh well, there's no point in worrying until we know the exact time of death. Who saw him last? Has that been established?"

"Miss Claudia, I think. She's usually among the last to leave."

"Except, of course, for his murderer. I wonder how he managed to entice the victim up to the little archives office. I suppose it is where he died. Assuming he was strangled or suffocated with Hissing Sid, then the murderer must have overpowered him first. A strong young man doesn't lie down meekly allowing himself to be murdered. He could have been drugged, of course, or perhaps stunned by a blow sufficiently powerful to knock him out, but not strong enough to break the skin."

Mrs. Willoughby, an avid reader of detective stories, was familiar with fictional murderers adept at this difficult procedure. She went on: "The drug could have been administered in his afternoon tea. It would need to be tasteless and very slow-acting. Difficult. Or, of course, he could have been throttled with something soft which wouldn't leave a mark, a pair of tights or a stocking. It would be no use for the murderer to use a cord, the mark would show very plainly under the snake. I expect the police have thought of all that."

"I am sure, Joan, that they have thought of everything."

Sipping her whisky, Blackie reflected that there was something strangely reassuring about Joan's uninhibited interest in and speculation about the crime. Not for nothing were there those five shelves of crime paperbacks in her bedroom, Agatha Christie, Dorothy L. Sayers, Margery Allingham, Ngaio Marsh, Josephine Tey and the few modern writers whom Joan considered fit to join those Golden Age practitioners in fictional murder. After all, why should Joan feel a personal grief? She had only been to Innocent House once, three years previously, when she had attended the staff Christmas party. She knew few of the staff except by name. And as she cogitated, the horror of Innocent House began to seem unreal, unfrightening, an elegant literary concoction, without grief, without pain, without loss, the guilt and horror disinfected and reduced to an ingenious puzzle. She stared into the leaping flames from which the image of Miss Marple seemed to rise, handbag protectively clutched to her bosom, the gentle wise old eyes gazing into hers, assuring her that there was nothing to be afraid of, that everything would be all right.

The fire and the whisky combined to induce a somnolent contentment, so that her cousin's voice, fitfully heard, seemed to be coming from a long distance. If they didn't begin dinner soon she would be asleep. Rousing herself, she said: "Isn't it time we thought about eating?"

30

They had met at 6:15 on the steps leading down to the river by Greenwich Station between a high wall and the ramp of a boathouse. It was a good and private place to meet. There was a small gritty beach and now, driving home and far from the river, he could still hear the gentle splash of the small spent waves, the grinding and tinny clatter of the pebbles, the backward suck of the tide. Gabriel Dauntsey had arrived first for the assignation but hadn't turned as Bartrum moved up beside him. When he spoke his voice was gentle, almost apologetic.

"I thought we ought to talk, Sydney. I saw you letting yourself into Innocent House yesterday evening. My bathroom window overlooks Innocent Lane. I looked out by chance and glimpsed you. It was about six-forty."

Sydney had known what he was going to hear and now, when the words were spoken, he heard them with something very like relief.

He had said, willing Dauntsey to believe him: "But I came out again almost at once. I swear it. If you'd waited, if you'd been watching for only a minute more, you would have seen me. I didn't get any further than the reception room. I lost my nerve. I told myself that it wouldn't have been any use arguing and pleading. Nothing would have moved him, nothing would have done any good. I swear to you, Mr. Dauntsey, that I never set eyes on him last night after I left my office."

"Yes, it wouldn't have done any good. Gerard wasn't susceptible to pleading." He added, "Or to threats."

"How could I threaten him? I was powerless. He could sack me the next week and I couldn't stop him. And if I did anything more to antagonize him he'd have given me one of those cunningly worded references which you can't contest but which make sure that you never get another job. He had me in his power. I'm glad he's dead. If I were a religious man I'd go down on my knees and thank God that he's dead. But I didn't kill him. You have to believe me. If you don't, Mr. Dauntsey, my God, who will?"

The figure at his side didn't move or speak but stood staring out over the black waste of the river. At last, humbly, he had asked: "What are you going to do?"

"Nothing. I had to see you to find out whether you've told the police, whether you propose to tell them. I was asked, of course, whether I'd seen anyone going into Innocent House. We all were. I lied. I lied and I'm proposing to go on lying, but it will be pointless if you've told them or are likely to lose your nerve."

"No, I didn't tell them. I said I got home at the usual time, just before seven. I rang my wife as soon as I heard the news, before the police arrived, and told her to confirm that I was home on time if anyone rang to ask. It was lucky I was the first one in. I had the office to myself. I hated having to ask her to lie but she didn't think it mattered. She knew that I was innocent, that I hadn't done anything to be ashamed of. I'll explain more fully to her tonight. She'll understand."

"You rang her before you knew that his death might be murder?"

"I thought it was murder from the start. The snake, that half-naked body. How could that be a natural death?" He added simply: "Thank you for keeping silent, Mr. Dauntsey. I won't forget this."

"You don't need to thank me. It's the sensible thing to do. I'm not doing you a favour. You don't have to be grateful. It's a matter of common sense, that's all. If the police waste time suspecting the innocent they'll have less chance of catching the guilty. And I haven't quite the confidence I once had that they don't make mistakes."

He had said, greatly daring: "And you care about that? You want them to catch the guilty?"

"I want them to find out who put that snake round Gerard's neck and stuffed its head in his mouth. That was an abomination, a desecration of death. I prefer the guilty to be convicted and the innocent vindicated. I suppose most people do. That, after all, is what we mean by justice. But I don't feel personally outraged by Gerard's death, not by any death, not any longer. I doubt whether I have the capacity to feel strongly about anything. I didn't murder him; I have done more than my share of killing. I don't know who did, but this murderer and I have something in common. We didn't have to look our victim in the eyes. There's something particularly ignoble about a murderer who doesn't even have to face the reality of what he has done."

He had brought himself to the final humiliation: "My job, Mr. Dauntsey. Do you think it's safe now? It is important to me. You don't know what Miss Etienne has in mind—what any of the partners has in mind? I know that there have to be changes. I could learn new methods if you think it necessary. And I don't mind if you bring someone in over my head if he's better qualified. I can work loyally as a subordinate." He added with bitterness: "That's all Mr. Gerard thought I was good for."

Dauntsey had said: "I don't know what will be decided but I dare say we'll make no major changes for at least six months. And if I have anything to do with it, your job will be safe."

Then they had turned together and walked without speaking to the side road where both had parked their cars.

31

The house which Sydney and Julie Bartrum had chosen, and which he was buying on the highest mortgage obtainable, was close to Buckhurst Hill Station, on a sloping narrow road which was more like a country lane than a suburban street. It was a conventional 1930s house with a front bay window and porch and narrow back garden. Everything in it he and Julie had chosen together. Neither had brought anything from the past except memories. It was this home, this hard-won security, which Gerard Etienne had threatened to take from him with so much else. If he lost his job at fifty-two, what hope would there be of an equal salary? His lump sum would drain away, month after month, until even paying the mortgage became an impossible burden.

She came out of the kitchen as soon as she heard his key in the lock. As always she put out both arms and kissed him on the cheek, but tonight her arms were taut and she clung to him almost desperately.

"Darling, what is it? What's happened? I didn't like to phone you back. You said not to ring."

"No, that wouldn't have been wise. Darling, there's nothing for you to worry about. Everything is going to be all right."

"But you said that Mr. Etienne is dead. Killed."

"Come into the sitting-room, Julie, and I'll tell you."

She sat very close to him and very still while he spoke. Afterwards she said: "They can't think you had anything to do with it, darling. I mean, that's ridiculous, that's stupid. You wouldn't hurt a soul. You're kind, good, gentle. They can't believe that."

"Of course they won't. But innocent people do sometimes get harassed, questioned and put under suspicion. Sometimes they even get arrested and tried. It does happen. And I was the last person to leave the office. I had some important work to do and stayed a little late. That's why I rang as soon as I heard the news. It seemed sensible to tell the police that I was home at the usual time."

"Of course it was, darling. You're right. I'm glad you did."

He was a little surprised that his request to her to lie had caused her no unease, no guilt. Perhaps women lied more easily than men provided they believed the cause was just. He needn't have worried that he was causing her a crisis of conscience. Like him, she knew where her allegiance lay.

He said: "Has anyone been in touch—anyone from the police?"

"Someone rang. He said he was a Sergeant Robbins. He just asked what time you got back last night. Nothing else. He didn't give me any information or say that Mr. Gerard was dead."

"And you didn't let on that you knew?"

"Of course not. You'd warned me. I did ask what it was all about and he said you would explain when you got home, that you were all right and that I wasn't to worry."

So the police had been quick off the mark. Well, that was to be expected. They had wanted to check before he had had time to arrange an alibi.

He said: "You see what I mean, darling. It really was wise to be prepared."

"Of course it was. But you don't really think Mr. Gerard was murdered?"

"They don't seem to know how he died. Murder's a possibility, but only one. He could have had a heart attack and the snake been put round his neck afterwards."

"Darling, how terrible! That's a horrible thing for anyone to do. It's wicked."

He said: "Don't think about it. It's nothing to do with us. It can't touch us. If we stick to our story, there's nothing anyone can do."

She had no idea how closely it touched them. This death was his salvation. He hadn't confided in her about the risk to his job or his hatred and fear of Etienne. This had partly been because he didn't want to worry her, but he knew that the main motive had been pride. He needed her to believe that he was successful, respected, invaluable to the firm. Now she need never know the truth. He decided, too, to say nothing of the earlier interview with Dauntsey. Why worry her? Everything was going to be all right.

As usual before supper, they went up together to look at their sleeping daughter. The baby was in the nursery at the back of the house, which he with Julie's help had decorated. She had been recently promoted from the basket crib to the railed cot and lay, as always, pillowless and supine. Julie had explained that this was the recommended position. She didn't speak the words "to avoid cot death," but both of them knew what she meant. That anything should happen to the child was their greatest unspoken horror. He put out a hand and touched the downy head. It was incredible that any human hair could feel so soft, any scalp so vulnerable. Overcome with love, he wanted to pick up the child and hold her against his cheek, to enfold mother and daughter in an embrace that was strong, eternal and unbreakable, to shield them against all the terrors of the present and all the terrors to come.

This house was his kingdom. He told himself that he had won it by love but he felt for it some of the fierce possessiveness of a conqueror. It was his by right and he would kill a dozen Gerard Etiennes before he lost it. No one before Julie had ever found him lovable. Plain, scrawny, humourless, and shy, he knew that he wasn't lovable, the years in the children's home had taught him that. Your father didn't die, your mother didn't walk out on you, if you were lovable. The staff at the home had done their best according to the received wisdom of the time, but the children hadn't been loved. The caring, like the food, had been carefully allocated to go round. The children knew that they were rejects. He had taken in that knowledge with his porridge. After the children's home there had been a succession of landladies, of bed-sitting-rooms, of small rented flats, of evening classes and examinations, watery cups of coffee, solitary meals in inexpensive restaurants, breakfast cooked in a shared kitchen, of solitary pleasures, solitary, unsatisfying, guilt-inducing sex.

He felt now like a man who all his life had been living underground in partial darkness. With Julie he had come up into the sunlight, his eyes dazed by an unimagined world of light and sound and colour and sensation. He was glad that Julie had been previously married, but in their love-making she managed to make him feel that it was she who was inexperienced, who was finding fulfillment for the first time. He told himself that perhaps she was. Sex with her had been a revelation. He could never have believed that it was at once so simple and so marvellous. He was glad, too, with a half-guilty relief, that her first marriage had been unhappy and that Terry had walked out on her. He need never fear that she was comparing him with a first love romanticized and immortalized by death. They spoke rarely of the past; for both of them, the people who lived and walked and spoke in that past were different people. Once, early in their marriage, she had said to him: "I used to pray that I could find someone to love, someone I could make happy and who could make me happy. Someone who would give me a child. I had almost given up hope. And then I found you. It seems like a miracle, darling, the answer to a prayer." Her words had exalted him. He felt for a moment as if he was the agent of God himself. He who all his life had known only what it was to feel powerless was filled with an intoxication of power.

He had been happy at Peverell Press until Gerard Etienne took over. He knew himself to be a valued, conscientious accountant. He worked long hours of unpaid overtime. He did what was required of him by Jean-Philippe Etienne and Henry Peverell; and what they required was well within his powers. But then one had retired and the other died, and the young Gerard Etienne had taken his seat in the managing director's chair. He had played little part in the firm for the previous few years but he had been watching, learning, biding his time, taking his Master's degree in business administration, formulating plans which didn't include a fifty-two-year-old accountant with minimal qualifications. Gerard Etienne, young, successful, handsome, rich, who through all his privileged life had grasped what he wanted without compunction, had been going to take from him, Sydney Bartrum, everything which made his life worthwhile. But Gerard Etienne was dead, lying in a police mortuary with a snake stuffed into his mouth.

He tightened his arm around his wife and said: "Darling, let's go down to supper. I'm hungry."

32

The street entrance to Wapping Police Station is so unobtrusive that it can easily be missed by the uninitiated. From the Thames its agreeable and unpretentious brick façade and the domestic note of a bay window overlooking the river suggest an old and accommodating utility, the residence of an eighteenth-century merchant, with a preference for living above his warehouse. Standing at the window of the incident room, Daniel looked down at the wide ramp, the three bays of the floating pier with its flotilla of police launches and the discreetly sited stainless-steel bath trolley for the reception and hosing-down of drowned bodies, and reflected that few perceptive travellers by water would fail to recognize the function of the house.

He had been busy since he and Sergeant Robbins had arrived, passing through the vehicle parking lot and up the iron staircase into the subdued busyness of the station. He had set up the computers, cleared desks for Dalgliesh, himself and Kate, had spoken to the coroner's officer about arrangements for the post-mortem and the inquest and had liaised with the forensic-science laboratory. The photographs taken at the scene had been pinned to the noticeboard, their stark shadowless clarity seeming to reduce horror to an exercise in photographic technique. He had also spoken to Lord Stilgoe in his private room at the London Clinic. Happily the effect of a general anaesthetic, the cosseting of the nurses and the number of his visitors had temporarily diverted Lord Stilgoe's attention from the murder and he had received Daniel's report with surprising equanimity and had not, as expected, demanded Dalgliesh's immediate appearance at his bedside. Daniel had also put the Met's Press Bureau in the picture. When the story broke they would be responsible for setting up press conferences and for liaison with the media. There were a number of details which the police in the interests of their enquiry had no intention of divulging, but the bizarre use of the snake would be known to everyone at Innocent House by tomorrow at the latest and would be round the publishing houses of London and into the papers within hours. The Press Bureau was likely to be busy.

Robbins had moved up beside him, obviously taking his senior's inactivity as the justification for a break. He said: "It's interesting to be here, isn't it? The oldest police station in the United Kingdom."

"If you're itching to tell me that the River Police were established in 1798, thirty-one years before the Met, then I know."

"I don't know whether you've seen their museum, sir. It's in the carpenter's shop of the old boatyard. I was taken round it when I was at Preliminary Training School. They've got some interesting exhibits. Leg irons, police cutlasses, old uniforms, a surgeon's chest, early-nineteenth-century records and accounts of the *Princess Alice* disaster. It's a fascinating collection."

"That probably accounts for the less than enthusiastic welcome. They probably suspect the Met curator of wanting to get his hands on it, or suspect we might nick the choicest exhibits. I like their new toys, though."

Below them the river had erupted into foaming tumult. A couple of high-speed semi-rigid inflatables, bright orange, black and grey, with their crew of two in crash-helmets and fluorescent green jackets, skimmed, veered and circled the police launches like dangerous adult playthings before roaring downstream.

Robbins said: "No seats. I should think those back rolls are hard on the muscles. They must be doing close on forty knots. Do you think there will be time to have another look at the museum, sir?"

"I shouldn't rely on it."

In Daniel's opinion Sergeant Robbins, who had come into the police service straight from his red-brick university, with a second-class degree in history, was almost too good to be true. Here surely was the epitome of every mother's favourite son: fresh-faced, ambitious without being ruthless, a devout Methodist, engaged, so it was rumoured, to a girl from his church. No doubt after a virtuous engagement they would marry and produce admirable children who would go to the right schools, pass the right exams, cause no grief or pain to their parents and eventually end up interfering with people for their own good, as teachers, social workers and possibly even policemen. In Daniel's book Robbins should have long ago resigned, disillusioned by a macho ethos which could so easily degenerate into violence, by the necessary compromises and fudges, and by the job itself with its daily evidence of the sleaziness of crime and man's inhumanity to man. Instead he was apparently both unshockable and idealistic. Daniel supposed that he had a secret life; most people did. It was hardly possible to live without one. But Robbins was singularly adept at keeping his hidden. Daniel reflected that it would pay the Home Office to parade him round the country to persuade idealistic school-leavers of the advantages of a police career.

They settled back to work. There was very little time before they were due at the mortuary, but there was no justification for wasting it. Daniel sat down to go through Etienne's papers. Even at his first and cursory glance he had been surprised at the amount of work Gerard Etienne had taken on. The firm published about sixty books a year with a total staff of thirty. Publishing was an alien world to him. He had no idea whether this was average but the administrative structure seemed odd and Etienne's load disproportionate. De Witt was the editorial director with Gabriel Dauntsey assisting him as poetry editor but otherwise, apparently, doing little except for his job in the archives. Claudia Etienne was responsible for sales and publicity, including personnel, and Frances Peverell for contracts and rights. Gerard Etienne, as chairman and managing director, had overseen production, accounts and the warehouse and had had by far the heaviest load.

Daniel was interested, too, in how far Etienne had pushed forward his plans to sell Innocent House. The negotiations with Hector Skolling had been under way for some months and were now advanced. Looking through the minutes of the monthly partners' meetings, he could see little reference to much that was happening. While Dalgliesh and Kate had been busy with the formal interviews, he had learned almost as much by listening to Mrs. Demery's gossip and talking to George and the few staff who were in the building. The partners might wish to present the picture of a generally united board with a common purpose, but the evidence so far showed a very different reality.

The phone rang. It was Kate. She was going back to her flat to change. AD had been called to the Yard. They would both see Daniel at the mortuary.

33

The local-authority mortuary had recently been modernized but the exterior remained unaltered. It was a single-storey building of grey London brick approached from a short cul-de-sac, the forecourt bounded by an eight-foot wall. Neither noticeboard nor street number proclaimed its function; those who had business there knew how to find it. It presented to the curious an impression of some dull and not particularly flourishing enterprise where goods were delivered in plain vans and unpacked with discretion. To the right of the door was a garage, large enough to accommodate two undertaker's vans, from which double doors led to a small reception area with a waiting-room to the left. Here Dalgliesh, arriving a minute before 6:30, found Kate and Daniel already waiting. An attempt had been made to make the waiting-room welcoming with a low round table, four comfortable chairs and a large TV set which Dalgliesh had never found turned off. Perhaps its purpose was less entertainment than therapy; the lab technicians in their unpredictable spells of leisure needed to exchange, however momentarily, the silent corruption of death for the bright ephemeral images of the living world.

He saw that Kate had exchanged her usual tweed jacket and trousers for denim jeans and jacket, and that her thick plait of blonde hair had been tucked inside a peaked jockey cap. He knew why. He too was informally dressed. The half-sweet, half-citrus smell of the disinfectant became almost unnoticeable after the first half-hour but lingered for days in the clothes, permeating his wardrobe with the smell of death. He had early learned to wear nothing that couldn't be thrown into the washing machine, while he obsessively showered, lifting his face under the power-jet as if the sting of the water could physically wash away more than the smell and the sights of the last two hours. He was due to meet the Commissioner at the Minister's room in the House of Commons at eight o'clock. Somehow he must find time to get back to his Queenhithe flat to shower before then.

He remembered vividly—how could he not?—the first post-mortem he had attended as a young detective constable. The murder victim had been a twenty-two-year-old prostitute and there had, he recalled, been difficulty over the formal identification of the body since the police had been unable to trace either relatives or close friends. The white under-nourished body stretched out on the tray, with the weals of the lash purple as stigmata, had seemed in its pale frigidity the ultimate mute witness to male inhumanity. Looking round at the crowded PM room, the phalanx of officialdom, he had reflected that Theresa Burns was receiving in death a great deal more attention from the agents of the state than she had received in life. The pathologist then had been Doc McGregor, one of the old school of egregious individualists, a rigid Presbyterian who had insisted on conducting all his post-mortems in the spiritual, if not the physical, odour of sanctity. Dalgliesh remembered his rebuke to a technician who had responded with a brief laugh to a colleague's muttered witticism. "I'll have no laughter in my mortuary. It's no a frog I'm dissecting here."

Doc McGregor would have no secular music while he worked and had a preference for the metrical psalms, whose lugubrious tempo tended to slow down the speed of the work as well as depressing the spirits. But it had been one of McGregor's post-mortems—that of a murdered child—accompanied by Fauré's *Pie Jesu* that had given Dalgliesh one of his best poems, and he supposed that for this he should be grateful. Wardle cared little what music was played while he worked, so long as it wasn't pop, and today they were to listen to the familiar anodyne melodies of Classic FM.

There were two post-mortem rooms, one with four dissecting tables and a single room. It was this which Reginald Wardle preferred for murder cases, but the room was small and there was the inevitable crush as the experts in violent death jostled for space: the pathologist and his assistant, the two mortuary technicians, four police officers, the laboratory liaison officer, the photographer and assistant, the scene-of-crime officer and fingerprint men and a trainee pathologist whom Dr. Wardle introduced as Dr. Manning and announced would take the notes. He had a dislike of using the overhead microphone. In their fawn cotton overalls the group looked, thought Dalgliesh, like a cluster of dilatory removal men. Only the plastic overshoes suggested that theirs might be a more sinister assignment. The technicians were wearing their head-straps but with the visors still up. Later, when they received the organs into the bucket and weighed them, the visors would be down, protection against AIDS and the more common risk of hepatitis B. Dr. Wardle as usual wore only his pale-green apron over slacks and shirtsleeves. Like most forensic pathologists he was cavalier about his own safety.

The body, parcelled and sealed in its plastic shroud, lay on the trolley in the outer room. At a word from Dalgliesh the technicians slashed the plastic and tore it aside. There was a small explosion of air like an expelling sigh, and the plastic crackled like a charge of electricity. The body lay exposed like the contents of some great Christmas cracker. The eyes were duller now; only the snake taped to the cheek, its head gagging the mouth, seemed to have life or vitality. Dalgliesh was visited by a strong desire to see it removed—only then could the body be re-stored to some dignity—and he wondered briefly why it was that he had been insistent it remained in place until the autopsy. It was all he could do to prevent himself from reaching down and tearing it away. Instead he made his formal identification establishing the chain of evidence.

"This is the body I first saw at nine-forty-eight on Friday the fifteenth of October at Innocent House, Innocent Walk, Wapping."

Dalgliesh had a considerable respect for Marcus and Len, both as men and as mortuary technicians. There were some people, a number of them police officers, who found it difficult to believe that a man could voluntarily work in a mortuary unless to satisfy some eccentric if not sinister psychological compulsion, but Marcus and Len seemed blessedly free even from the crude graveyard humour which some professionals used as a defence against horror or distaste, and did their work with a matter-of-fact competence, quietness and dignity which he found im-pressive. He had seen, too, how much trouble they took to make a body presentable before the next-of-kin came to view. Many of the bodies they watched being clinically dismembered would be those of the old, diseased, or dead by natural causes, small tragedies, perhaps, to a loved one, but hardly a cause for distress to a stranger. But how, he wondered, did they cope psychologically with the murdered young, the violated, the victims of accident or violence? In an age when every sorrow, even those natural to the human condition, could not apparently be endured without counselling who, if anyone, counselled Marcus and Len? But at least they would be free from the temptation to deify the popular, the rich and the famous. Here in the mortuary was the final equality. What mattered to Marcus and Len was not the number of eminent doctors who had clustered around the deathbed, nor the splendour of the planned obsequies, but the state of decay and whether the corpse would need to be accommodated in the obese refrigerator.

The tray holding the now naked body had been placed on the floor so that the photographer could more easily move around it. When he nodded his satisfaction with the first shots the two technicians gently turned the corpse over, taking care not to dislodge the snake. Finally, with the body face-upwards, the tray was lifted and placed on the supports at the foot of the dissecting table, the round hole over the drain. Doc Wardle made his usual general examination of the body, then turned his attention to the head. He stripped away the tape, gently removed the snake as if it were a biological specimen of extraordinary interest and began his examination of the mouth, looking, thought Dalgliesh, like an over-enthusiastic dentist. He remembered what Kate Miskin had once confided to him when she had first started working for him and confidence came more easily to her: that it was this part of the autopsy, not the later systematic removal and weighing of all the main organs, that made her squeamish, as if the dead nerves were merely quiescent and could still react as they had in life to the gloved, probing fingers. He was aware of Kate standing a little behind him, but did not glance at her. He could be sure that she wouldn't faint, either now or later, but he guessed that, like him, she was feeling something more than a professional interest in the dismemberment of what had been a young and healthy man—and felt again a small ache of regret that police work demanded so much of gentleness and innocence.

Suddenly Doc Wardle gave a low grunt that was almost a growl, his distinctive noise when he found something of interest.

"Take a look at this, Adam. On the roof of the mouth. A distinct scratch. Post-mortem by the look of it."

At the scene it had been "Commander" but now, king of his domain, at ease as always with his work, he had reverted to Dalgliesh's Christian name.

Dalgliesh bent low. He said: "It looks as if something sharp-edged was forced in or out of the mouth after death. I'd say out by the look of the mark."

"Difficult to be 100 per cent sure, of course, but that's what it looks like to me. The direction of the scratch is from the back of the palate almost to the top teeth." Doc Wardle stood aside so that Kate and Daniel could take their turn at peering into the mouth. He added: "Impossible to say exactly when it happened, of course, except that it was after death. Etienne may have put the thing—whatever it was—in his mouth but someone else took it out."

Dalgliesh said: "And with some force, and possibly in a hurry. If it had happened before rigor mortis set in the removal would have been quicker and easier. How much strength would it take to force open the jaw after rigor was established?"

"It's not difficult, of course, and easier if the mouth were partly open and he could get his fingers in and use both hands. A child couldn't do it, but then you aren't looking for a child."

Kate said: "If the snake-head was pushed in immediately the sharp object was removed and soon after death, couldn't we expect some visible blood stain on the fabric? How much seeping of blood would there have been after death?"

Doc Wardle said: "Immediately after death? Not a lot. But he wasn't alive when that mark was made."

They peered at the snake's head together. Dalgliesh said: "This thing has been played about with at Innocent House for nearly five years. It's easier to imagine a stain than to see it. There's no obvious blood. The lab may give us something. If it was placed in the mouth as soon as the object was pulled out there should be some biological evidence."

Daniel asked: "Any idea, Doc, of the kind of object?"

"Well, there are no other marks on the soft tissues or the back of the teeth that I can see, which suggests that it was something that he could fairly easily fit into his mouth, though why the hell he would have wanted to beats me. Still, that's your department."

Daniel said: "If it was something he wanted to conceal, why not slip it into his trouser pocket? Hiding it in his mouth meant keeping silent. He could hardly speak normally even with a small object between his tongue and the roof of his mouth. But suppose he knew that he was going to die. Suppose he was trapped in that room with the gas pouring out, the key to the gas tap missing, a window he couldn't open. . . ."

Kate broke in: "But the object would be found on the body later even if he only put it in his pocket."

"Unless his murderer knew it was there and came back for it. Then hiding it in the mouth made sense, even if it was something the murderer didn't know existed. Putting it in his mouth made sure that it would be found at the PM if not before."

Kate said: "But he did know—the murderer I mean. He came back to look for it and I think he found it. He forced open the jaw to get it out, then used the snake to make it look like the work of the practical joker."

She and Daniel were concentrated on each other. The room could have been empty except for those two. Daniel said: "But could he really expect that we wouldn't find the scrape?"

"Oh come on, Daniel. He didn't know that he'd scratched the mouth. What he did know was that he had to break the rigor and that we wouldn't miss that. So he used the snake. And if it hadn't been for that scratch we would have fallen for it. We're looking for a murderer who knew something about the timing of rigor and expected the body to be found relatively soon. If the body was to lie undisturbed for another day the snake wouldn't have been necessary."

They were, Dalgliesh knew, in danger of theorizing in advance of all the facts. The autopsy hadn't yet been completed. There was still no confirmation of the cause of death but he felt reasonably sure, and so, he knew, did Doc Wardle, what the cause of death would prove to be.

Kate asked: "What kind of object? Something small, sharp-edged? A key? A bunch of keys? A small metal box?"

Dalgliesh said quietly, "Or the cassette of a small tape recorder?"

Dalgliesh left before the post-mortem was completed. Doc Wardle was explaining to his assistant that the blood samples for the lab must be taken from the femoral vein, not the heart, and why. Dalgliesh doubted whether there was anything further to learn from the autopsy, and if there was he would be told soon enough. There were papers he needed to look over before the meeting at eight o'clock in the House and time was tight. It would have been pointless to go first to the Yard before going to his flat and his driver, William, had collected his briefcase from his office and was waiting now in the forecourt, his amiable chubby face displaying carefully controlled anxiety.

The heavy rain of the afternoon had abated to a thin continuous drizzle and with the window half-open he tasted the salt tang of the Thames. The traffic lights on the Embankment smudged the air with crimson and, waiting for them to change, a police horse, its flanks gleaming, stamped its delicate hoofs on the shining tarmac. Darkness had come striding over the city, transforming it into a phantasmagoria of light in which the streets and squares shivered into moving necklaces of white, red and green. He opened his briefcase and drew out his papers for a quick reading of the salient arguments. It was time to shift the gears of his mind to a more immediate—and perhaps in the end more important—preoccupation. Usually he did not find this difficult, but now the earlier images of the mortuary persisted.

Something small, something sharp, had been wrenched out of Etienne's mouth after rigor had set in in the top part of the body. It was possible that object had been a cassette; the removal of the tape recorder certainly suggested that possibility. The inference was that Etienne had dictated the name of his murderer and the killer had later returned to remove the evidence. But his mind rejected this simple hypothesis. Etienne's murderer had taken care that nothing should remain in the room which would enable him to leave a message. The floor and the mantelpiece had been cleaned, all the papers had been removed, Etienne's diary with the gold pencil attached had been stolen the day before. The killer had thought even of that. Etienne hadn't even been able to scrawl his or her name on the bare wooden floor. Why then should the murderer have been so stupid as to leave a tape recorder ready for his victim's use?

There was, of course, another explanation. The tape recorder could have been there for a specific purpose, and if it had been then the case promised to be even more puzzling and more intriguing than it had at first appeared.

34

It was after 10:30 before Dalgliesh returned to the Wapping incident room, and Robbins had been sent off duty. Kate and Daniel had bought sandwiches on their drive back from the mortuary and made do with them and coffee as the night wore on. They had already worked a twelve-hour day but it wasn't over yet. Dalgliesh would want to assess progress and have a clear idea where they were going before they entered on the next stage of the enquiry.

He sat for ten minutes studying the papers Daniel had brought from Gerard Etienne's study, then, closing the file without comment, looked at his watch and said: "Right. So what tentative conclusions have you reached from the facts as far as we know them?"

Daniel broke in immediately as Kate had expected him to. That didn't worry her. They were of equal rank but she had seniority in service and felt no need to emphasize it. There was an advantage in going first; it prevented other people from taking credit for your ideas and showed keenness. On the other hand, there was a certain wisdom in biding one's time. Daniel was taking care over his spiel; probably, she thought, he had been mentally practising it since their return from the mortuary.

He said: "Natural death, suicide, accident or murder? The first two are out. We don't need the laboratory reports to be sure that this was carbon-monoxide poisoning, the post-mortem told us that. Told us too that, otherwise, he died healthy. There is absolutely nothing to indicate suicide, so I don't think we need waste time on that.

"So we come to accident. If this is an accidental death, what are we expected to believe? That Etienne decided for some reason to work up in the archives office, left his jacket on the chair downstairs and his keys in his desk drawer. That he felt cold, lit the fire with matches which we've no evidence he had on him, then got so engrossed in his work that he didn't realize that the fire had started to malfunction until too late. Apart from the obvious inconsistencies, if it happened that way, I suggest that he'd have been found slumped over the table, not lying half-naked on his back with his head towards the fire. At this stage I'm not taking account of the snake. I think we have to make a clear distinction between what happened at the time of death and what happened to the body afterwards. Obviously someone found him after rigor had set in to the top part of the body, but there's no evidence that the person who stuffed the snake in his mouth took off his shirt or moved him from the table to where he was found."

Kate said: "He must have taken off his own shirt. It was clutched in his right hand. It looked as if he had taken it off with some idea of using it to put out the fire. I mean, look at the photograph. The right hand is still holding part of the shirt, the rest of it trails across the body. It looks to me as if he died on his face and his killer turned over the body, perhaps using his foot, and then prised open the mouth. Look at the position of the knees, slightly bent. He didn't die in that position. It's consistent with the post-mortem findings that he died on his face. He was crawling across the room towards the fire."

"OK, I agree. But he couldn't have hoped to put it out, not that way. The shirt would have caught fire."

"I know he couldn't, but that's what it looks like. Snuffing out the fire may have seemed possible to his confused mind."

Dalgliesh didn't intervene but listened while they argued it out.

Daniel said: "That suggests he knew what was happening to him. But if he did, the obvious thing was to open the door and let in air, then turn off the gas."

"But suppose the door had been locked on the outside and the tap removed from the gas fire. When he tried to open the high window the cord snapped because someone had frayed it to make damned sure it would as soon as it was tugged with any force. The murderer must have first moved out the chairs and table so that Etienne couldn't climb on them to reach the window and break the glass. The window was stuck fast. He couldn't have opened it if he had, not unless he had something to bash it with."

Daniel said: "The tape recorder perhaps?"

"Too small, too fragile. All the same, I agree he would have tried.

He could have battered the glass with his hands, but there was no evidence of bruising of the knuckles. I think that the furniture must have been moved before he entered the room. We know from the marks on the wall that the table was normally a few inches to the left."

"That isn't proof. The cleaner could have moved it."

"I didn't say that it was proof, but it is significant. Both Gabriel Dauntsey and Mrs. Demery said that the table wasn't in the usual position."

"That doesn't let them out as suspects."

"I didn't say that it did. Dauntsey is an obvious suspect. No one had better opportunity than he. But if Dauntsey moved out the chairs and table, surely he would have taken trouble to place the table back precisely where it was. Unless, of course, he was in a hurry." She broke off, then turned to Dalgliesh excitedly. "And of course, sir, he was in a hurry. He had to be back in the time it would take to bath."

Daniel said: "We're going too fast. It's all conjecture."

"I'd call it logical deduction."

Dalgliesh spoke for the first time. "Kate's theory is reasonable; it conforms with all the facts as we know them. But what we haven't got is a scintilla of hard evidence. And don't let's forget the snake. How far have you got with finding out who knew that it was in Miss Blackett's desk drawer, apart of course from Miss Blackett, Mandy Price, Dauntsey and the two Etiennes?"

It was Kate who replied. "The news was round the office by the afternoon, sir. Mandy told Mrs. Demery that Etienne had told Miss Blackett to get rid of it when they were making coffee together in the kitchen, shortly after eleven-thirty. Mrs. Demery admits that she may have told one or two people when she took round the afternoon tea trolley. 'One or two people' probably means every room in the building. Mrs. Demery was a bit vague about what she actually said, but Maggie FitzGerald in publicity is quite certain that they were told that Mr. Gerard had instructed Miss Blackett to get rid of the snake and that she'd put it in her desk drawer. Mr. Sydney Bartrum in accounts claims that he didn't know. He said that he and his staff had no time to gossip with the office domestics and that they wouldn't have the opportunity anyway. Their department is in number ten and they make their own afternoon tea. De Witt and Miss Peverell have admitted that they knew. Miss Blackett's drawer was the natural place for anyone to look anyway. She had a sentimental affection for Hissing Sid and wouldn't have thrown it away."

Daniel said: "Why did Demery bother to pass on the news? It was hardly a major office scandal."

"No, but it obviously caused a stir. Most of the staff knew or suspected that Gerard Etienne wouldn't be sorry to see the back of Miss Blackett. They were probably wondering how long she'd hold out, whether she'd chuck the job before she was sacked. Any fresh spat between those two was news."

Dalgliesh said: "You see the importance of the snake. Either it was wound round Etienne's neck and stuffed into his mouth by the murderer, probably to explain the breaking of the rigor of the jaw, or the joker stumbled on the body and saw the chance of a particularly revolting piece of malice. If the murderer did it, is he or she also the joker? Were these pranks part of a carefully laid plan which goes back as far as the first incident? That would tie up with the frayed window cord. If that was deliberate it was done over a period of time. Or did the murderer realize the significance of the loose jaw and use the snake on impulse to conceal the fact that he'd actually removed some object from Etienne's mouth?"

Daniel said: "There's another possibility, sir. Suppose the joker finds the body, thinks it's a natural or accidental death, then decides to stir things up by making it look like murder. It could have been he or she who moved the table out of place as well as putting the snake round Etienne's neck."

Kate objected. "He couldn't have weakened the window cord, that must have been done earlier. And why bother to shift the table? That could only confuse the issue and make the death look like murder if the joker already knew that Etienne had died from carbon-monoxide poisoning."

"He must have known. He turned off the gas fire."

Kate said: "He'd have done that anyway. That small room must have been like a furnace." She turned to Dalgliesh. "Sir, I think there's only one theory that fits all the facts. This was intended to look like an accidental death from carbon-monoxide poisoning. The murderer planned to be the one to find the body and to find it on his own. All he had to do then was to replace the tap and turn off the gas—a natural reaction anyway—then put back the table and chair, take away the tape and raise the alarm. But he couldn't find the tape, and when he did he couldn't get his hands on it without breaking the rigor in the jaw. He knew that this wouldn't be missed by a competent detective or the forensic pathologists, so he used the snake to suggest that this was an accidental death complicated by the malice of the office joker."

Daniel objected. "Why take the tape recorder? I'm talking about the murderer now."

"Why leave it? He had to remove the tape, he might as well take the

recorder. Look, the natural thing would be to chuck it in the Thames."
She turned to Dalgliesh. "Do you think there's any chance an underwater
search could find it, sir?"

Dalgliesh said: "Extremely unlikely. And if it did the tape wouldn't
be intact. The murderer would certainly have erased any messages. I
doubt whether the expense of a search would be justified, but you'd
better have a word with the people here. Find out what the bottom of
the river is like at Innocent House."

Daniel said: "There's something else, sir. If the killer wanted to leave
a message for his victim, why use the tape? Why not write it? He had
to recover it anyway. It would have been as easy to recover a piece of
paper, perhaps easier."

Dalgliesh said: "But not as safe. If Etienne had time enough before
unconsciousness supervened, he could tear up the paper and hide the
separate pieces. But if he didn't tear it, paper is easier to conceal than
a tape. The murderer knew that he might not have much time. He
needed to retrieve that message and find it quickly. And there's another
point: a speaking voice can't be ignored, a written message can. The
interesting thing about this whole case is why he needed to leave a
message at all."

Daniel said: "To gloat. To have the last word. To show how clever
he was."

Dalgliesh said: "Or to explain to someone why he had to die. If that
was the reason then the motive for this murder may not be obvious. It
may lie in the past, even in the distant past."

"But if so, why wait until now? If the murderer is here at Innocent
House, Etienne could have been killed any time during the last twenty
years or so. He's been part of the firm since he left Cambridge. What
has happened recently to make this death necessary?"

Dalgliesh said: "Etienne took over as chairman and MD, he proposed
to force the sale of Innocent House, and he became engaged."

"Do you think the engagement could be relevant, sir?"

"Anything could be, Kate. I'm going to see Etienne's father tomorrow
morning. Claudia Etienne drove down to Bradwell-on-Sea early this
evening to break the news to him and to ask him to agree to a meeting.
She won't be staying the night. I've asked her to meet you at Etienne's
flat in the Barbican tomorrow. But the first priority is to check all the
alibis, starting with the partners and staff at Innocent House. Daniel,
you and Robbins had better see Esmé Carling. Find out where she went
when she left Better Books in Cambridge. There was Gerard Etienne's
engagement party on the tenth of July. We need to check the guest list

and interview people who were there. You're going to need tact. The line to take, of course, is whether they did wander through the house and whether they saw anything odd or suspicious. But we concentrate on the partners. Did anyone see Claudia Etienne and her companion on the river, and at what time? Check with St Thomas's Hospital what time Gabriel Dauntsey was brought in and when he left, and on his alibi. I'll be leaving early for Bradwell-on-Sea but I should be back by early afternoon. For the present I think we'd better call it a day."

35

The partners spent Friday night apart. Standing at her kitchen table, trying to summon the energy to decide what to eat, Frances reflected that this wasn't surprising. They led separate lives away from Innocent House and it sometimes seemed to her that they made a deliberate attempt to distance themselves outside the office, almost as if they wanted to demonstrate that all they had in common was work. They seldom discussed their social engagements and she would occasionally be a guest at the party of another publisher and be surprised to see Claudia's sleek head momentarily appearing in a gap of yelling faces, or be at the theatre with a friend from her convent-school days and see Dauntsey painfully edging his way along the row ahead. Then they would greet each other as politely as acquaintances. Tonight she sensed that something stronger than habit was holding them apart, that they had grown increasingly reluctant to discuss Gerard's death as the day progressed and that the frankness of that hour closeted together in the boardroom had been displaced by a wary distrust of intimacy.

James, she knew, had no choice. He needed to go home to Rupert, and she envied him the necessity of obligation. She had never met his friend, never been invited to his house since Rupert's arrival there, and she wondered now about their life together. But at least he would have someone with whom he could share the distresses of the day, a day which now seemed inordinate in length. They had, by common unspoken consent, left Innocent House early and she had waited while Claudia locked the door and set the alarm. She had asked, "Will you be all right,

Claudia?" and, even as she spoke, had been struck by the futility, the banality of the question. She had wondered if she ought to offer to go home with Claudia, but was afraid that this might only be seen as a confession of weakness, her own need for company. And Claudia, after all, had her fiancé—if he was her fiancé. She was more likely to turn to him than to Frances.

Claudia had replied: "All I want at the moment is to get home and be alone." Then she had added, "What about you, Frances? Will you be all right?"

The same meaningless, unanswerable question. She wondered how Claudia would have replied if she'd said, "No, I'm not all right. I don't want to be alone. Stay with me tonight, Claudia. Sleep in my spare room."

She could, of course, telephone Gabriel. She wondered what he was doing, what he was thinking, in that plain underfurnished apartment beneath her. He too had said, "Will you be all right, Frances? Ring me if you need company." She wished that he had said, "Do you mind if I come up, Frances? I don't want to be alone." Instead he had placed the onus on her. To ring for him was to confess a weakness, a need, which he might not welcome. What was it about Innocent House, she wondered, that made it so difficult for people to express a human need or to give each other a simple reciprocal kindness?

In the end she opened a carton of mushroom soup and boiled herself an egg. She felt extraordinarily tired. Curled last night in Gabriel's chair, her broken hours of fitful sleep hadn't been the best preparation for a day of almost continuous trauma. But she knew that she wasn't ready for sleep. Instead, after washing up her supper things, she went into the room which had been her father's bedroom and which she had now made into a small sitting-room and sat herself in front of the television. The bright images passed in front of her eyes: the news, a documentary, a comedy, an old film, a modern play. As she pressed the buttons, flicking from channel to channel, the changing faces, grinning, laughing, serious, magisterial, the mouths continually opening and closing were a visual drug, meaning nothing, evoking no emotion but at least providing a spurious companionship, a fleeting and irrational solace.

At one o'clock she went to bed, taking with her a glass of hot milk laced with a little whisky. It was effective and she slipped away into unconsciousness with the last thought that she was, after all, to enjoy the benison of sleep.

The nightmare returned to her in the early hours, the old familiar nightmare but in a new guise, more terrible, more intensely real. She

was walking along the Greenwich tunnel between her father and Mrs.
Rawlings. They were holding her hands but their grasp was an impris-
onment, not a comfort. She couldn't run away and there was nowhere
to run. Behind her she could hear the cracking of the tunnel roof but
she dared not turn her head because she knew that even to look back
would be disaster. In front of her the tunnel stretched longer than in
life, with a circle of bright sunlight at the end. As they walked the
tunnel lengthened and the circle became gradually smaller, until it was
only a small gleaming saucer and she knew that soon it would recede
into a pin-point of light, then disappear. Her father was walking very
upright, not looking at her, not speaking. He was wearing the tweed
coat with the short cape which he always wore in winter and which she
had given to the Salvation Army. He was angry that she had given it
away without consulting him, but he had found it and got it back. She
wasn't surprised to see the snake wound round his neck. It was a real
snake, immense as a cobra, expanding and contracting, draped round
his shoulders, hissing with its evil life, ready to crush the breath out of
him. And overhead the tiles of the roof were wet and the first large
drops were already falling. But she saw that they weren't drops of
water, but of blood. And now suddenly she broke free and began to
run, screaming, towards that unobtainable pin-point of light while the
roof ahead cracked and fell and there rolled towards her, shutting out
the last light, the black obliterating wave of death.

She woke to find herself slumped against the window, her hands
beating the glass. With consciousness came relief, but the horror of the
nightmare remained like a stain on the mind. But at least she knew it
for what it was. She went over to her bed and turned on the lamp. It
was nearly five o'clock. There was no point now in trying to sleep again.
Instead she put on her dressing-gown, drew the curtains and opened
the windows. With the darkened room behind her she could see the
luminous glimmer of the river and a few high stars. The terror of her
dream was passing but it gave way to that other terror, from which she
had no hope of waking.

Suddenly she thought of Adam Dalgliesh. His flat, too, was on the
river, at Queenhithe. She wondered how she knew where he lived, and
then remembered some of the press coverage of his last and successful
book of poetry. He was a very private man but that fact at least had
emerged. It was odd that their lives were linked by this dark tide of
history. She wondered if he, too, was wakeful, whether a mile or two
upstream his tall dark figure was standing looking out over the same
dangerous river.

Book Three

WORK IN PROGRESS

36

On Saturday 16 October Jean-Philippe Etienne took his morning walk as usual at nine o'clock. Neither the time nor the route varied, whatever the season or the weather. He would walk along the narrow ridge of rock between the marshes and the ploughed fields on which the Roman fort of Othona was said to have stood, past the Anglo-Celtic chapel of St-Peter-on-the-Wall and round the headland to the Blackwater estuary. It was rare for him to meet anyone on his morning perambulation, even in summer, when a visitor to the chapel or a bird-watcher might be abroad early, but if he did he would say a courteous good morning, but no more. The locals knew that he had come to Othona House for solitude and had no wish to violate it. He accepted no incoming telephone calls, received no visitors. But this morning, at half past ten, a visitor would come who could not be refused.

Now, in the strengthening light, he looked across the calm straits of the estuary to the lights on Mersea Island and thought about this unknown Commander Dalgliesh. The message he had sent to the police by Claudia had been unambiguous; he had no information to offer about his son's death, no theories to propose, no possible explanations of the mystery to put forward, no suspect he could name. His own view was that Gerard had died by accident, however odd or suspicious some of the circumstances. Accidental death seemed likelier than any other explanation, certainly far likelier than murder. Murder. The heavy consonants of horror thudded in his mind, evoking nothing but repugnance and disbelief.

And now, standing as still as if petrified on the narrow strip of gritty beach where the minuscule waves spent themselves in a thin smudge of dirty foam, and watching the lamps across the water die one by one as the day brightened, he paid his son the reluctant tribute of memory. Most of the memories were troubling, but since they besieged his mind and could not be repelled it was perhaps better that they should be accepted, made sense of and disciplined. Gerard had grown to adolescence with one central assurance: he was the son of a hero. That was important to a boy, to any boy, but particularly one as proud as he. He might resent his father, feel himself inadequately loved, undervalued, neglected, but he could do without the love if he had the pride, pride in the name and in what that name stood for. It had always been important to him to know that the man whose genes he carried had been tested as had few of his generation and had not been found wanting. The decades were passing and memories fading, but a man could still be judged by what he had done in those turbulent years of war. Jean-Philippe's reputation was secure, inviolable. The reputation of other heroes of the Resistance had been sullied by the revelations of later years, but never his. The medals that he never now wore had been honestly earned.

Jean-Philippe had watched the effect of that knowledge on Gerard: the compelling need for his father's approbation and respect, the need to compete, to justify himself in his father's eyes. Wasn't that what climbing the Matterhorn when he was twenty-one had been all about? He had never before shown any interest in mountaineering. The exploit had been time-consuming and expensive. He had employed the best Zermatt guide, who, reasonably, had decreed a period of some months' hard training before the climb was attempted and had laid down his strict conditions. The party would turn back before the final assault on the summit if he judged Gerard a danger to himself or to others. But they hadn't turned back. The mountain had been conquered. That was something Jean-Philippe hadn't achieved.

And then there was the Peverell Press. Here in his last years Jean-Philippe knew that he had been little more than a passenger, tolerated, undisturbed, no trouble to anyone. Gerard, when power passed into his hands, would transform Peverell Press. And Jean-Philippe had given him that power. He had transferred twenty of his shares in the firm to Gerard, and fifteen to Claudia. Gerard had only to keep the support of his sister to be sure of majority control. And why not? The Peverells had had their day; it was time for the Etiennes to take over.

And still Gerard had come, month after month, to give his account as if he were a steward reporting to his master. He asked for no advice, no approbation. It wasn't for advice or approbation that he came. Sometimes it seemed to Jean-Philippe that the journey was a form of reparation, a penance voluntarily imposed, a filial duty undertaken now, when the old man was past caring and letting slip from his stiffened hands those frail cords which bound him to family, to the firm, to life. He had listened, had occasionally commented, but had never brought himself to say: "I don't want to hear. I'm no longer concerned. You can sell Innocent House, move to Docklands, sell the firm, burn the archives. The last of my interest in Peverell Press was cast from me when I dropped those grains of crushed bone into the Thames. I am as dead to your busy concerns as is Henry Peverell. We are both now beyond caring. Don't think because I can speak to you, still perform some of the functions of a man, that I am alive." He would sit immobile, and from time to time stretch out a shaking hand for his tumbler of wine, the glass, with its heavy base, so much easier now to manage than a wineglass. His son's voice had come from a distance.

"It's difficult to know whether to buy or rent. In principle I'm for buying. The rents are ridiculously low but they won't be when the leases run out. On the other hand it makes sense to take a short lease for the next five years and free the capital for acquisitions and development. Publishing is about books, not property. For the past hundred years Peverell Press have squandered resources on maintaining Innocent House as if the house was the firm. Lose the house and you lose the Press. Bricks and mortar elevated to a symbol, even on the writing paper."

Jean-Philippe had said: "Stone and marble." To Gerard's quick enquiring frown he added, "Stone and marble, not bricks and mortar."

"The rear façade is brick. The house is an architectural bastard. People say how brilliantly Charles Fowler wedded late-Georgian elegance to fifteenth-century Venetian Gothic, but he'd have done better not to try. Hector Skolling is welcome to Innocent House."

"Frances will be unhappy."

He had said it for something to say. He was untouched by Frances's unhappiness. The wine was strong in his mouth. It was good that he could still taste the robust reds.

Gerard had said: "She'll get over it. All the Peverells feel compelled to love Innocent House, but I doubt if she greatly cares." Following the association of ideas, he added: "You saw the announcement of my engagement in last Monday's *Times*?"

"No. I no longer bother with newspapers. The *Spectator* has a summary of the week's main news. That half-page is sufficient to reassure me that the world goes on much as it always has. I hope you'll be happy in your marriage. I was."

"Yes, I always thought that you and Mother seemed to hit it off rather well."

Jean-Philippe could smell his embarrassment. The comment in its gross inadequacy had hung between them like a wisp of acrid smoke. Jean-Philippe said quietly: "I wasn't thinking of your mother."

And now, gazing across the stretch of quiet water, it seemed to him that only in those turbulent and confused days of war had he been truly alive. He had been young, passionately in love, exhilarated by constant danger, stimulated by the ardours of leadership, exalted by a simple and unquestioning patriotism which for him had become a religion. Among the confused loyalties of Vichy France his own had been clear and absolute. Nothing since had touched the wonder, the excitement, the glamour of those years. Never again had he lived every day with such intensity. Even after Chantal had been killed, his resolution hadn't faltered although he was confused by the realization that he blamed the Maquis as much as the occupying Germans for her death. He had never believed that the most effective resistance lay in armed action or in the murder of German soldiers. And then, in 1944, had come liberation and triumph, and with it a reaction so unexpected and so strong that it left him demoralized, almost apathetic. Only then, in the moment of triumph, had he space and time to grieve for Chantal. He felt like a man emptied of all capacity for emotion except for this overwhelming grief which in its sad futility seemed part of a greater, a universal grieving.

He had had little stomach for revenge and had watched with sick disgust the shaving of the heads of women accused of "sentimental relations with the enemy," the vendettas, the purges by the Maquis, the summary justice which executed thirty people in the Puy-de-Dôme without formal trial. He was glad, as was most of the population, when the due process of law was established, but he took no satisfaction in the proceedings or in the verdicts. He had no sympathy for those collaborators who had betrayed the Resistance, or who had tortured or murdered. But in those ambiguous years many collaborators with the Vichy regime had done what they believed right for France, and if the Axis powers had won, perhaps it would have been right for France. Some were decent men who had chosen the wrong side for motives not wholly ignoble, others were weak, some motivated by a hatred of communism, others seduced by fascism's insidious glamour. He could hate none of them. Even his own fame, his own heroism, his own innocence became repugnant to him.

He had needed to get away from France and had come to London. His grandmother had been English. He spoke the language faultlessly and was familiar with the peculiarities of English customs, all of which helped to soothe his self-imposed banishment. But he hadn't come to England out of any special affection for the country or its people. The countryside was beautiful, but then he had had France. It had been necessary to leave and England was the obvious choice. It was in London at a party—he couldn't now remember which or where—that he had been introduced to Henry Peverell's cousin Margaret. She was pretty, sensitive and appealingly childlike, and had fallen romantically in love with him, in love with his heroism, with his nationality, even with his accent. He had found her uncritical adulation flattering, and it was difficult not to respond with at least affection and a protective warmth for what he saw as her vulnerability. But he had never loved her. He had only loved one human being. With Chantal had died his capacity for any feeling warmer than affection.

But he had married her, taken her for four years to Toronto, and when that self-imposed banishment grew irksome they had returned to London, now with two babies. At Henry's invitation he had joined the Peverell Press, invested his considerable capital in the firm, taken his shares and spent the rest of his working life in that extravagant folly on a northern alien river. He supposed that he had been reasonably content. He knew people thought him rather dull; that didn't surprise him, he bored himself. The marriage had endured. He had made his wife Margaret Peverell as happy as she was capable of being. He suspected that the Peverell women weren't capable of much happiness. She had desperately wanted children and he had dutifully provided her with the son and daughter for which she had hoped. That was how, then and now, he thought of parenthood: the giving of something necessary for his wife's happiness if not for his own and for which, having provided it as he might a ring, a necklace or a new car, he need take no further responsibility since responsibility was handed over with the gift.

And now Gerard was dead and this unknown policeman was coming to tell him that his son had been murdered.

37

Kate and Daniel's appointment to see Rupert Farlow had been fixed
for ten o'clock. They knew it would be almost impossible to park
in Hillgate Village so left the car at Notting Hill Gate Police Station and
walked up the gentle hill under the high limes of Holland Park Avenue.
Kate thought how strange it was to be back so soon in this familiar part
of London. She had left her flat only three days earlier but it seemed
that she had moved away from the area in imagination as well as in fact
and that now, coming up to Notting Hill Gate, she saw the raucous
urban conglomeration through the eyes of a stranger. But nothing, of
course, had changed: the discordant undistinguished 1930s architecture,
the plethora of street signs, the railings which made her feel like a
herded animal, the long concrete flower beds with their straggling and
dust-grimed evergreens, the shop fronts spilling their names in rivers
of garish light red, green and yellow, the ceaseless grind of the traffic.
There was even the same beggar outside the supermarket with his large
Alsatian slumped on a rug at his feet, murmuring to passers-by his
appeal for change to buy a sandwich. Behind this busyness lay Hillgate
Village in its stuccoed multicoloured calm.

As they passed the beggar and stood waiting to cross at the traffic
lights, Daniel said: "We've got a few like that where I live. I'd be tempted
to pop into the supermarket and buy him a sandwich if I wasn't afraid
of provoking a breach of the peace and if he and the dog didn't already
look over-fed. Do you ever give?"

"Not to his kind, and not often. Sometimes. I disapprove of myself but I do it. Never more than a quid."

"To be spent on drink and drugs."

"A gift should be unconditional. Even a quid. Even to a beggar. And OK, I do know that it's conniving at an offence."

They had crossed the road at the traffic lights when abruptly he spoke again.

"I ought to go to my cousin's bar mitzvah next Saturday."

"Then go, that is if it's important."

"AD won't welcome an application for leave. You know how he is once we're on a case."

"It doesn't take all day, does it? Ask him. He was very decent when Robbins wanted that day off after his uncle died."

"That was for a Christian funeral, not a Jewish bar mitzvah."

"What other kind of bar mitzvah is there? And don't be unfair. He isn't like that and you know it. Like I said, if it's important ask, if it isn't don't."

"Important to whom?"

"How do I know? To the boy I suppose."

"I hardly know him. I doubt whether he'll care much either way. But we're a small family, he's only got the two cousins. I suppose he'd like me to be there. My aunt would probably prefer me not to be. That way she'll be given another grievance against my mother."

"You can hardly expect AD to decide whether pleasing your nephew is more important than disobliging your aunt. If it's important to you then go. Why make such a big thing about it?"

He didn't reply, and as they made their way up Hillgate Street she thought, Perhaps it's because, for him, it is a big thing. Thinking back on it, the brief conversation surprised her. This was the first time he had even tentatively opened the door to his private life. And she had thought that, like her, he guarded with almost obsessive watchfulness that essentially inviolate portal. In the three months since he had joined the Squad they had never spoken of his Jewishness, nor indeed of much else except work. Was he genuinely seeking advice or using her to clear his thoughts? If he needed advice it was surprising that he sought it from her. She had from the first been aware of a defensiveness in him which if not tactfully handled could become tricky, and she slightly resented the need for tact in a professional relationship. Police work was stressful enough without the need to propitiate or accommodate a colleague. But she liked him or, it might be truer to say, was beginning to like him without being sure why. He was sturdily built, hardly taller than she, strong-featured, fair-haired, and with slate-grey eyes which shone like polished pebbles. When he was angry they could darken almost to black. She recognized both his intelligence and an ambition which mirrored her own. And at least he had no hang-up about working with a woman senior to himself or, if he had, was more skilful than most of his colleagues at concealing it. She told herself, too, that she was beginning to find him sexually attractive, as if this formal and regular recognition of the fact could guard her against the follies of propinquity. She had seen too many colleagues make a mess of their private and professional lives to risk that kind of involvement, always so much easier to begin than to end.

She said, wanting to match his confidence and fearing that she had been too dismissive: "There were a dozen different religions among the children at Ancroft Comprehensive. We seemed always to be celebrating some kind of feast or ceremony. Usually it required making a noise and dressing up. The official line was that all religions were equally important. I must say that the result was to leave me with the conviction that they were equally unimportant. I suppose if you don't teach religion with conviction it becomes just one more boring subject. Perhaps I'm a natural pagan. I don't go in for all this emphasis on sin, suffering and judgement. If I had a God I'd like Him to be intelligent, cheerful and amusing."

He said: "I doubt whether you'd find him much of a comfort when they herded you into the gas chambers. You might prefer a god of vengeance. This is the street, isn't it?"

She wondered if he had wearied of the subject or was warning her off his private ground. She said: "Yes. It looks as if the high numbers are at the other end."

There was an entryphone at the left of the door. Kate pressed the bell and when a masculine voice responded said: "This is Inspector Miskin and Inspector Aaron. We've come to see Mr. Farlow. He is expecting us."

She listened for the buzz which would indicate that the door lock had been released, but instead the same voice said: "I'll be down."

The wait of a minute and a half seemed longer. Kate had looked at her watch a second time when the door was opened and they found themselves confronted by a stocky young man, barefoot and wearing tightly fitting trousers in a blue-and-white check and a white sweatshirt. His hair was cut in very short spikes, giving the round head the look of a bristled brush. His nose was wide and chubby and the short round arms with their patina of brown hair looked as softly plump as a child's.

Kate thought that he had the snug compactness of a toy bear, needing only a price tag dangling from the earring in his left ear to complete the illusion. But the pale-blue eyes meeting hers were initially wary, then changed as she met them to frank antagonism, and when he spoke there was no welcome in his voice. Ignoring the proffered warrant card, he said: "You'd better come up."

The narrow hall was very warm, the air permeated with an exotic smell, part floral, part spicy, which Kate would have found agreeable if it had been less strong. They mounted the narrow stairs behind their guide and found themselves in a sitting-room which ran the whole length of the house. A curved archway showed where once there must have been the dividing wall. At the rear a small conservatory had been built out to overlook the garden. Kate, who thought that she had brought to an art the ability to take in details of her surroundings without betraying too obvious a curiosity, now noticed nothing but the man they had come to see. He was lying propped up on a single bed to the right of the conservatory and he was obviously dying. She had seen the extremity of emaciation often enough pictured on her television screen, viewing almost routinely in her sitting-room the dead eyes and shrivelled limbs of starvation. But now, encountering it for the first time, she wondered how any human being could be so diminished and still breathe, how the great eyes, which seemed to be floating free in their sockets, could hold her with such a look of intense, slightly ironic amusement. He was enveloped in a dressing-gown of scarlet silk but it could give no glow to the sickly yellow skin. There was a card table close to the head of the bed with a facing chair and two packs of cards ready on the green baize top. It looked as if Rupert Farlow and his companion were about to begin a game of canasta.

His voice was not strong but it did not waver; the essential self was still alive, still heard in its high clear tones. "Forgive me if I don't get up. The spirit is willing but the flesh is weak. I'm conserving my energies for ensuring that Ray doesn't get a sight of my cards. Do sit down if you can find a seat. Would you like a drink? I know you're not supposed to drink on duty but I insist on regarding this as a social call. Ray, where did you hide the bottle?"

The boy, seated at the card table, made no move. Kate said: "We won't drink, thank you. And this shouldn't take long. It's about Thursday evening."

"I thought it might be."

"Mr. de Witt says that he came straight home from the office and was here with you all the evening. Could you confirm that?"

"If that's what James told you then it's true. James never lies. That's one of the things about him that his friends find so trying."

"And is it true?"

"Naturally. Hasn't he said so?"

"What time did he arrive home?"

"The usual time. About six-thirty, isn't it? He'll tell you. He has told you, surely."

Kate, who had pushed a heap of magazines to one side, had seated herself on a Victorian sofa opposite the bed. She said: "How long have you lived here with Mr. de Witt?"

Rupert Farlow turned on her his immense, pain-filled eyes, moving his head slowly as if the weight of his denuded skull had become too great for his neck to bear. He said: "Are you asking how long I've shared this house as opposed, shall we say, to sharing his life, sharing his bed?"

"Yes, that's what I'm asking."

"Four months, two weeks, three days. He took me in from the hospice. I'm not sure why. Perhaps being with the dying turns him on. It does some people. There was no shortage of visitors at the hospice, I assure you. We're the one charity they can always get volunteers for. Sex and death, a great turn-on. We weren't lovers, incidentally. He's in love with that boringly conventional woman, Frances Peverell. James is depressingly heterosexual. You needn't be frightened to shake his hand or even indulge in more intimate physical contact if you like to try your luck."

Daniel said: "He arrived here from work at six-thirty. Did he go out later?"

"Not as far as I know. He went up to bed at about eleven and he was here when I woke at three-thirty and four-fifteen and five-forty-five. I made a careful note of the hours. Oh, and he did various messy things for me at about seven o'clock in the morning. He certainly wouldn't have had time between these hours to get back to Innocent House and dispose of Gerard Etienne. But I may as well warn you that I'm not particularly reliable. I would say that anyway. It isn't exactly in my interest to have James carted off to prison, is it?"

Daniel said: "Nor in your interest to be an accessory to murder."

"That isn't the worry. If you take James you may as well take me. I should be more of an inconvenience to the criminal-justice system than you would be to me. That's the advantage of dying. It hasn't a lot to be said for it but it does put you beyond the power of the police. Still, I must try to be helpful, mustn't I? There is one piece of corroborative evidence. You rang and spoke to James, didn't you, Ray, at about seven-thirty?"

Ray had taken up a second pack of cards and was expertly shuffling them. "Yeah, that's right, seven-thirty. Rang to enquire. He was here then."

"There you are then. Wasn't it clever of me to remember?"

Kate said impulsively: "Are you—surely you must be—the Rupert Farlow who wrote *The Fruit Cage?*"

"Have you read it?"

"A friend gave it to me last Christmas. He managed to find a hardback. Apparently they're rather sought after. He told me that the first edition was sold out and that they didn't reprint."

"A literate cop. I thought you only got them in fiction. Did you like it?"

"Yes, I liked it." She paused, then added: "I thought it was wonderful."

He raised his head and looked at her. His voice changed and he spoke so softly she could hardly hear the words. "I was quite pleased with it myself."

Looking into his eyes, she saw, appalled, that they were glistening with tears. The frail body in its crimson shroud trembled and she had an impulse, so strong that she had almost physically to fight it, to move forward and take him in her arms. She looked away and said, trying to make her voice sound normal: "We won't tire you any more but we may have to come back and ask you to sign a statement."

"You'll find me at home. Or if I'm not, you'll be unlikely to get a statement. Ray will see you out."

The three of them walked down the stairs in silence. At the door Daniel turned and said: "Mr. de Witt has told us that no one telephoned this house on Thursday evening, so one of you is either lying or mistaken. Is it you?"

The boy shrugged. "OK, maybe I was mistaken. That's no great deal. It could have been another night."

"Or no night? It's dangerous to lie in a murder investigation. Dangerous for you and the innocent. If you have any influence over Mr. Farlow you should tell him that the best way he can help his friend is by telling the truth."

Ray had his hand on the door. He said: "Don't give me that crap. Why should I? That's what the police always say, that you help yourself and the innocent by telling the truth. Telling the truth to the fuzz is in the fuzz's interest. Don't try telling us it's in ours. And if you want to come back, you'd better ring first. He's too weak to be badgered."

Daniel opened his mouth, restrained himself and said nothing. The door closed firmly behind them. They walked into Hillgate Street without speaking. Then Kate said: "I shouldn't have said that about his novel."

"Why not? What's the harm—that is if you were being honest."

"It's because I was being honest that I did the harm. It upset him." She paused, then said: "What do you think that particular alibi is worth?"

"Not much. But if he sticks to it, and my guess is he will, we're in trouble, no matter what else we manage to grub up about de Witt."

"Not necessarily. It'll depend on the strength of any further evidence. And if we find the alibi unconvincing so will a jury."

"If you ever get that chap in front of a jury."

Kate said: "There's one thing, though. It might just have been chance but I wonder. Obviously that friend of his, Ray, was lying, but how did Farlow know that the alibi was needed for around seven-thirty? Or was it just a lucky guess?"

38

Dalgliesh's appointment with Jean-Philippe Etienne, conveyed by Claudia Etienne, had been made for 10:30, a time which necessitated a comfortably early start from London. The time of the appointment had been surprisingly specific for a man whose day was presumably his own. Dalgliesh wondered if it had been chosen to ensure that, even if the interview were more protracted than expected, Etienne would feel under no obligation to invite him to lunch. This, too, suited him. To lunch alone in a strange place where he was unknown and unrecognized, even if the food proved disappointing, a place where he could eat in the assurance that no one in the world knew who he was and that no telephone could reach him, was a rare pleasure, and he intended after the interview to make the most of it. He had a meeting at the Yard at four o'clock and then would go straight to Wapping to hear Kate's report. There would be no time for a solitary walk or for exploring an interesting-looking church. But after all, a man had to eat.

It was dark when he set out and the day lightened into a dry but sunless morning. But as he shook off the last eastern suburbs and drove between the muted colours of the Essex countryside, the grey canopy lightened into a white transparent haze with the promise that the sun might eventually break through. Beyond the cropped hedges spiked with the occasional wind-distracted tree, the ploughed fields of autumn, stippled with the first green shoots of winter wheat, stretched to the far horizon. He felt a sense of liberation under the wide East Anglian sky, as if the weight of an old and familiar burden had been temporarily lifted.

He thought about the man he was to meet. He was coming to Othona House with few expectations but he was not coming totally unprepared. There had been no time for detailed research into the man's history. He had spent some forty minutes in the London Library and had talked on the telephone to an ex-member of the Resistance living in Paris, whose name had been supplied by a contact at the French Embassy. He now knew something of Jean-Philippe Etienne, hero of the Resistance in Vichy France.

Etienne's father had owned a flourishing newspaper and printing press in Clermont-Ferrand and had been one of the earliest and most active members of the Organisation de Résistance de l'Armée. He had died of cancer in 1941 and his only son, recently married, had both inherited the business and taken over his father's role in the struggle against the Vichy authorities and the German occupiers. Like his father, he was a fervent Gaullist and strongly anti-Communist, distrustful of the Front National because it was founded by Communists, even though many of his own friends, Christians, socialists, intellectuals, were members of the Front. But he was by nature a loner and worked best with his own small, secretly recruited band. Without quarrelling openly with the major organizations, he had concentrated on propaganda rather than on armed struggle, circulating his own underground paper, distributing Allied leaflets dropped by air, providing London with regular and invaluable information and attempting even to suborn and demoralize German soldiers by infiltrating propaganda into their camps. His family newspaper continued, but now less a paper of record than a literary journal, its careful, non-political stance enabling Etienne to retain more than his share of printer's ink and paper, all rationed and closely supervised. By careful husbandry and subterfuge he was able to divert resources to his underground press.

For four years he had lived a double life so successfully that he was never suspected by the Germans nor denounced as a collaborator by his fellow résistants. His deep distrust of the Maquis had been reinforced when, in 1943, his wife had been killed in a train blown up by one of the more active groups. He had ended the war as a hero, not as well known as Alphonse Rosier, Serge Fischer or Henri Martin, but his name could be found in the index of books on the Vichy Resistance. He had earned his medals and his peace.

Less than two hours after leaving London, Dalgliesh had turned off

the A12 south-east to Maldon, then east through flat unexciting countryside, and had entered the attractive village of Bradwell-on-Sea with
its square-towered church and pink, white and ochre clapboard cottages,
the doorways hung with baskets of late chrysanthemums. He marked
down the King's Head as a possible place for lunch. A narrow road was
signposted to the chapel of St-Peter-on-the-Wall and soon it came into
view, a distant high rectangular building standing against the sky. It
looked now as it had when he had first been brought there by his father
as a ten-year-old, as simply and crudely proportioned as a child's doll's
house. There was a rough footpath leading to the chapel separated
from the road by a fixed wooden barrier, but the track to Othona
House, a few hundred yards to the right, was open. A signpost, the
wood beginning to split and the words almost indecipherable, bore the
painted name of the house, and that and the distant sight of the roof
and chimneys confirmed that the lane was the only access. Dalgliesh
reflected that Etienne could hardly have devised a more effective
deterrent to visitors and for a moment he wondered whether to walk
the half-mile rather than risk his suspension. Glancing at his watch, he
saw that it was 10:25. He would arrive precisely on time.

The track to Othona House was deeply rutted, the pot-holes still
holding water from the previous night's rain. It was bounded on one
side by ploughed fields stretching as far as the eye could see, hedgeless
and with no sign of habitation. On the left was a wide ditch bordered
by a tangle of blackberry bushes heavy with berries, and beyond them
a broken row of gnarled trunks thickly leached with ivy. On both sides
of the path the tall dry grasses, already weighted with seed pods, stirred
fitfully in the breeze. Under his careful handling the Jaguar lurched
and shuddered and he was beginning to regret not parking in the
entrance to the land when the track became less pot-holed, the crevasses
less deep, and he was able to accelerate for the last hundred yards.

The house, bounded by a high curved wall in brick which looked
comparatively modern, was still invisible except for the roof and
chimneys, and it was apparent that the entrance faced the sea. He drove
round to the right and saw the place clearly for the first time.

It was a small, agreeably proportioned house in mellowed red brick,
the façade almost certainly Queen Anne. The central bay was capped
with a Dutch parapet, its curve echoing that of the elegant portico of
the front door. On either side stretched identical wings with their eight-
paned windows under a stone cornice, decorated with carved scallop
shells. These were the only indication that the house had been built on
the coast but it still seemed oddly out of place, its dignified symmetry

and mellow calm more appropriate to a cathedral close than to this
bleak and isolated headland. There was no immediate access to the sea.
Between the breaking waves and Othona House stretched a hundred
yards or so of salt marsh, crossed by innumerable small streams, a
sodden and treacherous carpet of soft blues, greens and greys with
patches of acid green in which the pools of sea water gleamed as if the
marshland had been set with jewels. He could hear the sea, but on this
calm day, with only a light wind rustling the reeds, it came to him as
gently as a soft expiring sigh.

He rang the bell and heard its muffled peal within the house, but it
was over a minute before his ears caught the shuffle of approaching
footsteps. There was a rasp of a drawn bolt and he heard the key turn
before, slowly, the door was opened.

The woman who stood regarding him with blank incuriosity was
old—probably, he thought, nearer eighty than seventy—but there was
nothing frail about her full-fleshed solidity. She was wearing a black
dress, high-buttoned to the throat and fastened with an onyx brooch
surrounded with dull seed pearls. Her legs bulged above black laced
boots and her breasts were carried high, shapeless as a bolster over a
voluminous white starched apron. Her face was broad, the colour of
suet, the cheekbones sharp ridges under the creased, suspicious eyes.
Before he could speak, she said: "Vous êtes le Commandant Dalgliesh?"

"Oui, madame, je viens voir Monsieur Etienne, s'il vous plaît."

"Suivez-moi."

Her pronunciation of his name was so bizarre that at first he couldn't
recognize it, but her voice was strong and deep, and with a note of
confident authority. She might be a servant at Othona House but she
was not servile. She stood aside to let him enter and he waited while
she closed and secured the door. The bolt above her head was heavy,
the key large and old-fashioned, and she had some difficulty in turning
it. The veins on her age-blanched and speckled hands stood out like
purple cords and the strong work-worn fingers were gnarled.

She led him down a panelled hall to a room at the rear of the house.
Pressing her back against the open door as if he were infectious, she
announced "Le Commandant Dalgliesh," then closed the door firmly
as if anxious to dissociate herself from this unwanted guest.

The room was surprisingly light after the darkness of the hall. Two
tall windows, multi-paned and fitted with shutters, looked out over a
treeless garden dissected with stone paths and apparently given over to
vegetables and herbs. The only colour was from late geraniums planted
in the large terracotta pots which lined the main path. The room was
obviously both a library and a sitting-room. Three walls were fitted with

bookshelves to a height comfortable to reach, with prints and maps ranged above them. There was a drum table in the middle of the room, its top laden with books. To the left was a stone fireplace with a simple but elegant overmantel. A small fire of wood crackled in the basket-grate.

Jean-Philippe Etienne was sitting in a high buttoned green leather chair to the right of the fire, but made no move until Dalgliesh had almost reached it, when he got to his feet and held out his hand. Dalgliesh felt for no more than two seconds the clasp of the cold flesh. Time, he thought, can reduce all individuality to stereotype. It can soften and plump the aging features into bland childishness, or strip them to the bone and muscle so that mortality already stares out from the shrivelled eyes. It seemed to him that he could see the outline of every bone, the twitch of every muscle in Etienne's face. His spare figure was still upright, although he walked stiffly, and his dapper elegance held no hint of decrepitude. The grey hair was sparse, brushed back from a high forehead, the jutting nose was long above a wide, almost lipless mouth, the large ears lay flat against the skull and the veins under the high cheekbones looked as if they were about to bleed. He was wearing a velvet jacket with frogged fastening, reminiscent of a Victorian smoking-jacket, above black tightly fitting trousers. Just so might a nineteenth-century landowner have risen stiffly to greet a guest, but this guest, Dalgliesh at once knew, was as little welcome in this elegant library as he had been on arrival.

Etienne motioned him to the chair opposite his own and seated himself, then he said: "Claudia handed me your letter, but please spare me any renewal of your condolences. They can hardly be sincere. You did not know my son."

Dalgliesh said: "It isn't necessary to know a man to feel regret that he should die too young and needlessly."

"You are, of course, right. The death of the young is always em-bittered by the injustice of mortality, the young go, the old live on. You will take something? Wine? Coffee?"

"Coffee, please, sir."

Etienne walked into the passage, closing the door behind him. Dalgliesh could hear him call out, he thought in French. There was an embroidered bell rope to the right of the fireplace, but apparently Etienne did not choose to use it in his relationship with his household. Returning to his chair, he said: "It was necessary for you to come, I realize that. But there is nothing I can say to help you. I have no idea why my son died, unless it was, as seems most likely, by accident."

Dalgliesh said: "There are a number of oddities about his death which suggest that it could have been deliberate. I know that this must be painful for you and I'm sorry."

"What are those oddities?"

"The fact that he died of carbon-monoxide poisoning in a room he rarely visited. A broken window cord which could have snapped when it was tugged so that the window couldn't be opened. A missing tape recorder. A removable tap on the gas fire which could have been removed after the fire was lit. The position of the body."

Etienne said: "Nothing you have told me is new. My daughter was here yesterday. The evidence is surely entirely circumstantial. Were there any prints on the gas tap?"

"Only a smudge. The surface is too small for anything useful."

Etienne said: "Even taken together these suppositions are less— 'odd' was the word you used?—than the suggestion that Gerard was murdered. Oddities are not evidence. I am ignoring the matter of the snake. I know that there is a malicious prankster at Innocent House. His or her activities scarcely warrant the attention of a commander of New Scotland Yard."

"They do, sir, if they complicate, or obscure, or are connected with a murder."

There were footsteps in the passage. Etienne went at once to the door and opened it for the housekeeper. She came in with a tray bearing a cafetière, a brown jug, sugar and one large cup. She placed the tray on the table and, after a glance at Etienne, immediately left the room. Etienne poured the coffee and brought it over to Dalgliesh. It was apparent that he himself was not to drink, and Dalgliesh wondered if this was a not-very-subtle ploy to put him at a disadvantage. There was no small table by his chair so he placed the coffee cup on the hearth.

Returning to his chair, Etienne said: "If my son was murdered I want his murderer brought to justice, inadequate as that justice may be. It is not perhaps necessary that I say this, but it is important that I do say it and that you believe me. If you find me unhelpful it is because I have no help to give."

"Your son had no enemies?"

"I know of none. No doubt he had professional rivals, discontented authors, colleagues who disliked, resented or were envious of him. That is common for any successful man. I know of no one who would wish to destroy him."

"Is there anything in his past, or yours? Some old or imagined wrong or injustice that could have caused long-standing resentment?"

Etienne paused before replying, and Dalgliesh was aware for the first time of the silence of the room. Suddenly the wood fire crackled with a small explosion of flame and a shower of sparks fell on to the hearth. Etienne looked into the fire. He said: "Resentment? The enemies of France were once my enemies and I fought them in the only way I could. Those who suffered may have sons, grandsons. It seems to me ludicrous to imagine they are exacting a vicarious revenge. And then there are my own people, the families of Frenchmen who were shot as hostages because of the activity of the Resistance. Some would say they had a legitimate grievance, but surely, not against my son. I suggest you concentrate your attention on the present, not the past, and on those people who normally had access to Innocent House. That would seem the obvious line of enquiry."

Dalgliesh picked up his coffee cup. The coffee, black as he wanted, was still too hot to drink. He replaced it in the hearth and said: "Miss Etienne has told us that your son visited you regularly. Did you discuss the firm?"

"We discussed nothing. He apparently felt the need to keep me informed of what was happening, but he asked for no advice and I offered none. I have no longer any interest in the firm and I had little for the last five years I worked there. Gerard wanted to sell Innocent House and move to Docklands. There is, I think, no secret about that. He saw it as necessary, and no doubt it was. No doubt it still is. I have a confused memory of our conversations; there was talk of money, acquisitions, staff changes, leases, a possible purchaser for Innocent House. I'm sorry my memory is not more precise."

"But your years with the firm were not unhappy?"

The question, Dalgliesh saw, was regarded as an impertinence. He had ventured on forbidden ground. Etienne said: "Neither happy nor unhappy. I made a contribution although, as I say, in the last five years it was an increasingly unimportant one. I doubt whether any other job would have suited me better. Henry Peverell and I went on too long. The last time I visited Innocent House was to help scatter Peverell's ashes in the Thames. I shall not return again."

Dalgliesh said: "Your son planned a number of changes, some, no doubt, unwelcome."

"All change is unwelcome. I am glad to have placed myself beyond its reach. Some of us who dislike aspects of the modern world are fortunate. We need no longer live in it."

Looking across at him while he at last sipped his coffee, Dalgliesh saw that the man was as tense in his chair as if about to spring from it. He realized that Etienne was a true recluse. Human company, except that of the few people with whom he lived, was intolerable to him for more than a brief span and he was nearing the end of his endurance. It was time to go; nothing else would be learned.

Moments later, as Etienne was accompanying him to the front door, a courtesy which Dalgliesh hadn't expected, he commented on the age and architecture of the house. It was the only thing he had said which stimulated his host to an interested response.

"The façade is Queen Anne, as I expect you know, but the interior is largely Tudor. The original house on this site was much earlier. Like the chapel, it is built on the walls of the old Roman settlement of Othona, hence the name of the house."

"I thought I might visit the chapel, if I could leave my car here."

"Of course."

But the permission was not gracious. It was as if even the presence of the Jaguar on his forecourt was a disturbing intrusion. Dalgliesh was no sooner out of the door when it was firmly closed behind him and he heard the rasp of the lock.

39

Dalgliesh wondered if he would find the chapel door locked but it opened to his hand, and he entered into its silence and simplicity. The air was very cold and smelled of earth and mortar grit, an un-ecclesiastical smell, domestic and contemporary. The chapel was sparsely furnished. There was a stone altar with a Greek crucifix above it, a few benches, two large jars of dried flowers, one on each side of the altar, and a rack of pamphlets and guides. He folded a note and put it in the box, then took one of the guidebooks and sat on a bench to study it, wondering why he should feel this sense of emptiness and mild depression. The chapel was, after all, among the earliest church buildings in England, perhaps the oldest, the sole surviving monument of the Anglo-Celtic Church in this part of England, the foundation of St. Cedd, who had landed here at the old Roman fort at Othona as early as 653. It had stood here confronting the cold and inhospitable North Sea for thirteen centuries. Here, if anywhere, he should surely have heard the dying echoes of plainsong and the vibration of 1,300 years of muttered prayer.

Whether one found the building holy or empty of holiness was a matter of personal perception, and his failure in this moment to experience more than the out-flowing of tension he could always feel when totally alone was a failure of imagination, not of the place itself. He wished that, sitting there quietly, he could hear the sea, with a need that was almost a longing—that ceaseless rise and fall which, more than

any other natural sound, touched mind and heart with a sense of time's
inexorable passing, of the centuries of unknown and unknowable human
lives with their brief miseries and even briefer joys. But he had come
here not to meditate but to think about murder and of murder's more
immediate degradations. He put down the guidebook and mentally
reviewed the recent interview.

It had been an unsatisfactory visit. His journey had been necessary
but it had proved even more unproductive than he had feared. Yet he
couldn't shake off the conviction that there was something of importance
to be learned at Othona House which Jean-Philippe Etienne hadn't
chosen to tell him. It was possible, of course, that Etienne hadn't told
him because it was something he had forgotten, something he thought
insignificant, even something which he didn't realize that he knew.
Dalgliesh thought again about the central fact of the mystery, the
missing tape recorder, the scratches in Gerard Etienne's mouth. This
murderer had needed to talk to his victim before he died, to talk to
him even while he was dying. He or she had wanted Etienne dead, but
had also wanted Etienne to know why he was dying. Was it no more
than a murderer's overwhelming vanity, or had there been another
reason buried in Etienne's past life? And if so, part of that life was here
present in Othona House and he had failed to find it.

He wondered what had brought Etienne at the last to this soggy
bulge of an alien country, to this drear, wind-scoured coast where
the marsh lay like a sour, disintegrating sponge sopping up the
fringes of the cold North Sea. Did he ever long for the mountains of
his native province, for the jabber of French voices in street and café,
for the sound, the scents and colours of rural France? Had he come
to this desolate place to forget the past or to relive it? What had
these old unhappy far-off things to do with the death nearly fifty
years later of his son, a son by an English mother, born in Canada,
murdered in London? What tentacles, if any, had stretched out from
those momentous years to wind themselves round Gerard Etienne's
neck?

He glanced at his watch. It was still a minute short of 11:30. He
would make time to visit the monuments in St George's church in
Bradwell, but after that brief visit there would be no possible excuse
for not driving back to London to lunch at New Scotland Yard.

He was still sitting, guidebook held loosely in his hand, when the
door opened and two elderly women entered. They were shod and
dressed for walking, and each carried a small knapsack. They looked
disconcerted and a little apprehensive to see him and, thinking that

they might not welcome the presence of a solitary male, he said a quick "Good morning" and left. Turning briefly at the door, he saw that they were already on their knees and wondered what it was they found in this quiet place and whether, if he had come with more humility, he might have found it also.

40

Gerard Etienne's flat was on the eighth floor of the Barbican. Claudia Etienne had said that she would be there to meet them at four o'clock and when Kate rang the door it was opened promptly and, without speaking, she stood aside to let them in.

The day was beginning to darken but the large rectangular room was still full of light, as a room will hold warmth when the sun has set. The long curtains in what looked like fine cream linen were drawn back to reveal, beyond the balcony, an attractive view of the lake and the elegant spire of a city church. Daniel's first response was to wish the flat was his, his second that in all his visits to the homes of murder victims he had never seen one so impersonal, so ordered, so uncluttered with the detritus of the dead life. This place looked like a show flat, carefully furnished to attract a purchaser. But it would be a rich purchaser; nothing in this apartment had been inexpensive. And he was wrong to see it as impersonal, it spoke as clearly of its owner as the most overfurnished suburban sitting-room, or any tart's bedroom. He could have played that television game: "Describe the owner of this apartment." Male, young, rich, discriminating, organized, unmarried; there was nothing feminine about this room. Obviously musical; the expensive stereo equipment might be expected in any flat of a well-to-do bachelor, but not the grand piano. All the furniture was modern, pale unpolished wood elegantly fashioned into cupboards, bookcases, a desk. At the end of the room, close to a door obviously leading to the kitchen, was a round dining table with six matching chairs. There was no fireplace. The focus of the room was the window, and a long sofa and two armchairs in soft black leather were grouped to face it round a coffee table.

There was only one photograph. On the top of a low bookcase, in a silver frame, was the studio portrait of a girl, presumably Etienne's fiancée. Fine fair hair fell from a central parting to frame a long, delicately boned face, large-eyed, the mouth a little too small but with a full, beautifully curved upper lip. Was this too, Daniel wondered, an acquired expensive object? Feeling that it might be offensive to study it too closely, he turned to the only painting, a large oil of Etienne and his sister hanging on the wall facing the window. In winter, with the curtains drawn, this vivid picture would be the focus of the room, colours, form, brushwork almost aggressively proclaiming the artist's mastery. Perhaps this week or next the sofa and the chairs would have been swung round to face it and for Etienne winter would have officially begun. This identification with the routine of the dead man's life seemed to Daniel irrational and a little disturbing. There was, after all, no evidence here of Etienne's presence, none of the small but pathetic leavings of a life unexpectedly ended: the half-finished meal, the open book placed face-downwards, the unemptied ashtray, the little messes and muddles of ordinary life.

He saw that Kate was studying the oil painting. That was natural enough, she was known to like modern art. She turned to Claudia Etienne. "This is a Freud, isn't it? It's wonderful."

"Yes. My father had it painted as a present for Gerard on his twenty-first birthday."

It was all there, thought Daniel, moving up beside her: the arrogant good looks, the intelligence, the confidence, the assurance that life was his for the taking. Beside the central figure his sister, younger, more vulnerable, looked at the painter with wary eyes as if defying him to do his worst.

Claudia Etienne said: "Would you like coffee? It won't take long. One could never rely on finding food here—Gerard mostly ate out—but there was always wine and coffee. You can come into the kitchen if you like, but there's nothing to see there. All Gerard's papers are in that bureau. It opens at the side, a concealed catch. You're welcome to look, but you won't get any joy out of prying. Any papers of importance were kept by the bank and all his business papers are at Innocent House. You've got those. Gerard always lived as if he expected to die overnight. There is one thing, though. I found this unopened on the mat. It's dated the thirteenth of October, so probably arrived on Thursday by the second post. I saw no reason not to read it."

She handed over a plain white envelope. The paper inside was of the same high quality, the address embossed. The handwriting was large, a girlish scrawl. Daniel read it over Kate's shoulder.

Dear Gerard.
This is to tell you that I want to end our engagement. I suppose I ought to say that I'm sorry to hurt you, but I don't think you will be hurt except in your pride. I shall mind more than you, but not very much and not for long. Mummy thinks that we ought to put a notice in *The Times* since we did announce the engagement, but that doesn't seem very important at present. Look after yourself. It was fun while it lasted, but not as much fun as it could have been.

Lucinda.

Underneath there was a postscript: "Let me know if you want me to return the ring."

Daniel thought that it was as well the letter had been found unopened. If Etienne had received it, it could have been used by a defence counsel to show a motive for suicide. As it was, it was of small importance to their enquiry.

Kate said to Claudia: "Had your brother any idea that Lady Lucinda was about to break their engagement?"

"Not as far as I know. She's probably regretting that she wrote that letter. She can hardly pose now as the broken-hearted fiancée."

The desk was modern, plain and outwardly unpretentious, but with an interior cleverly designed with numerous drawers and cubby-holes. It was all in immaculate order: bills paid, a few bills still outstanding, chequebooks for the previous two years bound together with a rubber band, a drawer with a portfolio of his investments. It was obvious that Etienne kept only what was necessary, clearing his life as it went along, shedding inessentials, conducting his social life, such as it was, by telephone, not by letter. They had been at the task for only a few minutes when Claudia Etienne returned carrying a tray with a cafetière and three mugs. She placed the tray on the low table and they came over to take up their mugs. They were still standing, Claudia Etienne with her mug in her hand, when there was the sound of a key in the lock.

Claudia gave an extraordinary sound—something between a gasp and a moan—and Daniel saw that her face had become a mask of terror. The coffee mug dropped from her hands and the brown stain spread over the carpet. She bent down to pick it up, her hands scrabbling over the soft surface and shaking so violently that she couldn't replace the mug on the tray. It seemed to Daniel that her terror infected him and Kate so that they, too, gazed with horrified eyes at the closed door.

It was slowly opened and the original of the photograph came into the room. She said: "I'm Lucinda Norrington. Who are you?" Her voice was high and clear, a child's voice.

Instinctively Kate had moved to steady Claudia, and it was Daniel who answered. "Police. Detective Inspector Miskin, and I'm Detective Inspector Aaron."

Claudia had quickly managed to control herself. Clumsily, refusing Kate's help, she got to her feet. Lucinda's letter lay beside the tray on the coffee table. It seemed to Daniel that every eye was on it.

Claudia's voice was harshly guttural. "Why did you come here?"

Lady Lucinda moved further into the room. "I came for that letter. I didn't want people to think Gerard had killed himself because of me. After all he didn't, did he? Kill himself I mean."

Kate said quietly: "How can you be sure of that?"

Lady Lucinda turned on her her immense blue eyes. "Because he liked himself too much. People who like themselves don't commit suicide. Anyway he wouldn't kill himself because I chucked him. He didn't love me, he only loved an idea of me."

Claudia Etienne had found her normal voice. She said: "I told him that the engagement was foolish, that you were a selfish, over-bred and rather silly girl, but I think I may have been unfair. You're not as silly as I thought. Actually, Gerard never received your letter. I found it here unopened."

"Then why did you open it? It isn't addressed to you."

"Someone had to open it. I could have returned it to you but I didn't know who had sent it. I'd never seen your handwriting before."

Lady Lucinda said: "May I have my letter?"

Kate replied: "We should like to keep it for the time being, if we may."

Lady Lucinda seemed to regard this as a statement rather than a request. She said: "But it belongs to me. I wrote it."

"We may only need to keep it for a little time and we don't intend to publish it."

Daniel, uncertain what the law said about ownership of a letter, wondered whether they had, in fact, any right to take it, and what Kate would do if Lady Lucinda pressed the matter. He wondered, too, why Kate was so anxious to have it. It wasn't as if Etienne had received it. But what proof had they of that? They had only his sister's word that she had found it on the mat unopened. Lady Lucinda made no further objection. She shrugged and turned to Claudia.

"I'm sorry about Gerard. It was an accident, wasn't it? That's the impression you gave Mummy on the telephone. But this morning some of the papers are hinting it could be more complicated. He wasn't murdered, was he?"

Kate said: "He could have been."

Again the blue eyes were turned consideringly on her. "How bizarre. I don't think I've ever known anyone who was murdered, known them personally, I mean."

She walked over to her photograph and took it in her hands, studying it closely as if she hadn't seen it before and was none too pleased with what the photographer had made of her features. Then she said: "I'll take this. After all, you won't want it, Claudia."

Claudia said: "Strictly speaking, none of his possessions should be moved except by his executors or the police."

"Well the police won't want it either. I don't want it to be here in the empty flat, not if Gerard was murdered."

So she was not without superstition. The discovery intrigued Daniel. It sat oddly with her cool self-possession. He watched as she studied the photograph and ran a long pink-nailed finger caressingly over the glass as if testing it for dust. Then she turned and said to Claudia: "I suppose there's something I can use to wrap this?"

"There may be a plastic bag in the kitchen drawer, you'd better look. And if there's anything else which belongs to you, now might be a good time to take it."

Lady Lucinda didn't even trouble to cast her eyes round the room. She said: "There's nothing else."

"If you want a coffee bring in another mug. It's freshly made."

"I don't want coffee, thank you."

They waited in silence until, in less than a minute, she returned carrying the photograph in a Harrods plastic bag. She was walking to the door when Kate said: "Lady Lucinda, I wonder if we could ask you a few questions? We would in any case have asked to see you, but now that you're here it will save time for both of us."

"How much time? I mean, how long is it going to take?"

"Not very long." Kate turned to Claudia. "You don't mind if we use this flat for the interview?"

"I don't see how I can prevent you. I suppose you don't expect me to retire to the kitchen?"

"That won't be necessary."

"Or to the bedroom? That might be more comfortable."

She was looking fixedly at Lady Lucinda, who said calmly: "I can't tell you. I've never been in Gerard's bedroom."

She sat in the nearer of the two armchairs and Kate seated herself opposite. Daniel and Claudia sat between them on the sofa.

Kate said: "When did you last see your fiancé?"

"He isn't my fiancé. He was at the time, though. I saw him last Saturday."

"Saturday ninth October?"

"I suppose so, if last Saturday was the ninth. We were going to Bradwell-on-Sea to visit his father but the day was wet and Gerard said his father's house was gloomy enough without arriving in the rain and we'd go another time. Instead we went to the Sainsbury Wing at the National Gallery in the afternoon because Gerard wanted to look again at the Wilton Diptych, and then on to the Ritz for tea. I didn't see him that evening because Mummy wanted me to drive down to Wiltshire with her to spend the night and Sunday with my brother. She wanted to talk about marriage settlements before we saw the lawyers."

"And how was Mr. Etienne when you met him on the Saturday, apart from being depressed about the weather?"

"He wasn't depressed about the weather. There wasn't any hurry to see his father. Gerard didn't get depressed about things he couldn't change."

Daniel said: "And the things he could change, he changed?"

She turned and looked at him, and suddenly smiled. "That's right." She added, "That was the last time I saw him but it wasn't the last time I spoke to him. We talked on the telephone on Thursday night."

Kate's voice was carefully controlled: "You spoke to him two days ago, on the night he died?"

"I don't know when he died. He was found dead yesterday morning, wasn't he? I spoke to him on his private line on the previous evening."

"At what time, Lady Lucinda?"

"At about twenty past seven, I suppose. It might have been a little later but it was certainly before half past seven because Mummy and I were supposed to leave the house at seven-thirty to go to dinner with my godmother and I was already dressed. I thought I would just have time to ring Gerard. I wanted an excuse to make it a short conversation. That's how I can be so sure of the time."

"What about? You'd already written to break off the engagement."

"I know. I thought he would have got the letter that morning. I wanted to ask him whether he agreed with Mummy that we ought to put a notice in *The Times* or whether he preferred for us to write to our personal friends and just let the news get around. Of course Mummy now wants me to destroy my letter to Gerard and say nothing. I shan't do that. I can't anyway now you've seen it. But at least she doesn't have to worry about the notice in *The Times*. That will save her a few pounds."

The pin-prick of venom was so sudden and so quickly withdrawn that Daniel could almost believe he'd missed it. As if she hadn't heard, Kate asked: "What did he say about the notice, about your broken engagement? Didn't you ask him if he'd received your letter?"

"I didn't ask him anything. We didn't talk at all. He said he couldn't speak then because he had a visitor with him."

"You're sure of that?"

The high bell-like voice was almost expressionless. "I'm not sure that he had a visitor. I mean, how could I be? I didn't hear anyone or speak to anyone except Gerard. Perhaps that was just an excuse for not talking to me, but I'm sure that's what he told me."

"And in those precise words? I want to be absolutely clear about this, Lady Lucinda. He didn't say he wasn't alone or that he had someone with him? He used the word visitor?"

"I've told you. He said he had a visitor with him."

"And that was between, say, seven-twenty and seven-thirty?"

"Nearer seven-thirty. The car came round for Mummy and me at half past seven."

A visitor. By an effort of will Daniel prevented himself from glancing at Kate but he knew that their thoughts were in harness. If Etienne had indeed used that word—and the girl seemed positive about it—it surely implied that Etienne was with someone from outside the firm. He would hardly have used the word for a partner or a member of staff. Wouldn't it then be more natural to say "I'm tied up," or "In a meeting," or "I'm busy with a colleague"? And if someone had called on him that night, invited or uninvited, he or she hadn't yet come forward. Why not, if the visit had been innocent, if he'd left Etienne alive and well? There had been no note of any arranged meeting in Etienne's office diary, but that wasn't conclusive. The visitor could have rung him on his private line any time during the day or early evening, or come uninvited and unexpected. But the evidence, such as it was, was circumstantial, like so much evidence in this increasingly baffling case.

But Kate was pressing on, asking Lady Lucinda when she had last been at Innocent House.

"Not since the party on the tenth of July. It was partly for my birthday—I was twenty—and partly as an engagement party."

Kate said: "We have the list of guests. I suppose they were free to wander all over the house if they wanted?"

"Some of them did, I think. You know how couples are at parties, they like to get away on their own. I don't think any of the rooms were locked although Gerard said that the staff had been told to put away all their papers safely."

"You didn't happen to see anyone going to the top of the house, towards the archives room?"

"Well I did actually. It was rather funny. I needed to go to the loo but the one on the first floor, which was being used for the women guests, was occupied, and then I remembered there was a small one on the top floor and I decided to use that. I went up by the stairs and I saw two people coming down. Not at all the people you'd expect. They looked so guilty, too. It really was weird."

"Who were they, Lady Lucinda?"

"George, the old man who works on the switchboard in reception, and that dull little woman who's married to the accountant, I forget his name, Sydney Bernard or something like that. Gerard introduced me to all the staff and their wives. It was a terrible bore."

"Sydney Bartrum?"

"That's right, his wife. She was wearing an extraordinary dress in pale-blue taffeta with a pink sash." She turned to Claudia Etienne. "You remember, don't you, Claudia? A very full skirt covered with pink net and puffed sleeves. Gruesome!"

Claudia said shortly: "I remember."

"Did either of them say what they were doing on the top floor?"

"The same as I was, I suppose. She went scarlet and muttered something about using the toilet. They looked extraordinarily alike, the same round faces, the same embarrassment. George looked as if I'd discovered them pilfering the petty cash. It was odd, though, wasn't it? Those two together I mean. George wasn't a guest, of course. He was only there to help with the men's coats and repel gatecrashers. And if Mrs. Bartrum wanted the loo, why didn't she ask Claudia or one of the women staff?"

Kate asked: "Did you mention this to anyone afterwards, to Mr. Etienne, for example?"

"No, it wasn't that important, just odd. I'd almost forgotten about it until now. Look, is there anything else you want to know? I think I've been here long enough. If you want to speak to me again you'd better write and I'll try to arrange a meeting."

Kate said: "We'd like a statement, Lady Lucinda. Perhaps you could call in at Wapping Police Station as soon as convenient."

"With my solicitor?"

"If you prefer it, or think it necessary."

"I don't suppose it is. Mummy said that I might need a solicitor to watch my interests at the inquest, if it came out about the broken engagement, but I don't think I have any interests now, not if Gerard died before he got my letter."

She got to her feet and shook hands formally with both Kate and Daniel but made no move towards Claudia Etienne. But at the door she turned and it was to Claudia that she spoke.

"He never bothered to make love to me when we were engaged so I don't think the marriage would have been much fun for either of us, do you?" Daniel suspected that, had neither police officer been present, she would have used a coarser expression. She added, "Oh, you'd better have this," and laid a key on the coffee table. "I don't suppose I shall see this flat again."

She went out, closing the door firmly, and a second later they heard the front door close with equal finality.

Claudia said: "Gerard was a romantic. He divided women into those you have affairs with and those you marry. Most men get over that sexual illusion before they're twenty-one. He was probably reacting against too many sexual conquests made too easily. I wonder how long that marriage would have lasted. Well, there's one disillusionment he's been spared. Will you be much longer?"

Kate said: "Not much longer now."

Minutes later they were ready to go. Daniel's last picture of Claudia Etienne was of a tall figure standing and looking out over the balcony at the darkening spires of the city. She answered their goodbyes without turning her head and they left her to the silence and emptiness of the flat, quietly closing the doors behind them.

41

eaving Hillgate Street, Daniel and Kate had picked up the car at Notting Hill Gate Police Station and driven the short distance to Declan Cartwright's shop. It was open, and in the front room an elderly bearded man, wearing a skull-cap and a long black coat, verdigrised with age, was showing a customer a Victorian writing desk, his skeleton-yellow fingers caressing the marquetry on the lid. He was apparently too occupied to hear their entrance even with the clang of the bell, but the customer turned, and the old man looked round.

Kate said: "Mr. Simon? We have an appointment to see Mr. Declan Cartwright."

Even before she could take out her warrant card, he said, "He's in the back. Straight through. He's in the back," and turned quickly again to the writing desk, his hands shaking so violently that the fingers clattered on the lid. Kate wondered what it was in his past that had produced such fear of authority, such terror of the police.

They made their way through the shop, down three steps and into a kind of conservatory at the back. Among a clutter of miscellaneous objects Declan Cartwright was conferring with a customer. The man was large, very swarthy and wearing a coat with an astrakhan collar topped with a rakish trilby, and was studying a cameo through an eyeglass. Kate could only assume that a man who chose to look so like a caricature of a crook would hardly dare actually to be one. As soon as they appeared, Cartwright said: "Charlie, why don't you buy yourself a drink and think it over? Come back in about half an hour. This is the fuzz arriving. I've got myself mixed up in a murder. Don't look so worried, I didn't do it. It's just that I have to give an alibi for someone who might have done."

The customer, with a glance at Kate and Daniel, made a nonchalant exit.

Kate again took out her warrant card, but Declan waved it aside. "That's all right, don't bother. I can recognize the police when I see them."

He must, she thought, have been an exceptionally pretty child and there was still something childlike in the gamin face with its cluster of undisciplined curls above the high forehead, the huge eyes and the beautifully formed but petulant mouth. But there was a very adult sexuality in the appraisal he gave both her and Daniel. She felt Daniel stiffen at her side and thought: "Not his type, and certainly not mine."

Like Farlow, he answered their questions with a half-mocking insouciance, but there was an essential difference. With Farlow they had been aware of an intelligence and a force still dominating the pathetically emaciated body. Declan Cartwright was both weak and frightened, as frightened as old Simon had been but for a different reason. His voice was brittle, his hands were restless and his attempts at banter were as unconvincing as his accent. He said: "My fiancée told me that you would be coming. I don't suppose you're here to look at antiques but I've got some nice little pieces of Staffordshire just come in. All legally acquired. I could do you a very good price if you don't think that would be suborning the police in the execution of their duty."

Kate asked: "You and Miss Etienne are engaged to be married?"

"I'm engaged to her, but I'm not sure if she's engaged to me. You'll have to ask her. With Claudia being engaged is a fluctuating state. It rather depends on how she's feeling at the time. But we were engaged —at least I think we were—when we went on the river on Thursday night."

"When did you arrange this trip?"

"Quite a time ago, actually. On the night of Sonia Clements' funeral. You've heard about Sonia Clements, of course."

Kate said: "A bit odd, wasn't it, to arrange a river trip so far in advance?"

"Claudia likes to arrange things a week or so ahead. She's a very well-organized woman. Actually there was a reason. Thursday the fourteenth of October was the morning of the partners' meeting. She was going to tell me all about it."

"And did she tell you all about it?"

"Well she told me that the partners were going to sell Innocent House and move downstream to Docklands and that they were going to sack someone, the accountant I think. I can't remember the details. It was all rather boring."

Daniel said: "Hardly worth the trouble of a river trip."

"Oh, but there are other things you can do on the river than discuss business, even if the cabin is a little cramped. Those great steel hoods of the Thames Barrier are very erotic. You two should borrow a police launch. You might surprise yourselves."

Kate said: "When did you begin the trip and when did it end?"

"It began at six-thirty, when the launch came back from Charing Cross and we took over. It ended at about ten-thirty, when we got back to Innocent House and Claudia drove me home. I suppose we got back here at about eleven o'clock. As I expect she told you, she didn't leave here until two o'clock."

Daniel said: "I suppose Mr. Simon will be able to confirm that? Or doesn't he live here?"

"Actually, I'm afraid he won't. Sorry about that. The poor old darling is getting dreadfully deaf. We always creep up the stairs so as not to disturb him but it's a totally unnecessary precaution. Actually, he might be able to confirm when we arrived. He could have had his door ajar. He sleeps more soundly when he knows the boy is home and safely tucked up. But I doubt whether he heard anything after that."

Kate said: "You didn't take your own car, then, to Innocent House?"

"I don't drive, Inspector. I deplore the pollution caused by motor cars and I don't add to it. Isn't that public-spirited of me? There's also the fact that when I tried to learn I found the whole experience so terrifying that I had to keep my eyes permanently closed, and none of the instructors would take me on. I went to Innocent House by tube. Very tedious. I took the Circle Line from Notting Hill Gate to Tower Hill and then picked up a cab. It's easier to go by the Central Line to Liverpool Street and take a cab from there but, in fact, I didn't, if it's of the slightest importance."

Kate asked him for details of the evening and was unsurprised when he confirmed Claudia Etienne's account.

Daniel said: "So you were together the whole evening, from six-thirty until the early hours of the morning?"

"That's right, Sergeant—you are a sergeant, aren't you? If not, I'm so sorry. It's just that you look so very like a sergeant. We were together from six-thirty until about two in the morning. I don't suppose you're interested in what we were doing between, say, eleven o'clock and two. If you are, you'd better ask Miss Etienne. She'll be able to give an account suitable for your chaste ears. I suppose you'll be wanting all this in the form of a statement?"

It gave Kate considerable satisfaction to say that they would indeed and that he could come to Wapping Police Station to make it.

Under questioning by Kate so gentle and patient that it seemed only to increase his terror, Mr. Simon confirmed that he had heard them come in at eleven. He had been listening for Declan because he always slept more soundly knowing that there was someone in the house. That was partly why he had suggested to Mr. Cartwright that he should live on the premises. But once he had heard the door, he had settled to sleep. He wouldn't have heard if either of them had subsequently gone out.

Unlocking the car, Kate said: "Shit-scared, wasn't he? Cartwright I mean. D'you think he's a rogue or a fool or both, or just a pretty boy with a taste for baubles? What on earth does an intelligent woman like Claudia Etienne see in him?"

"Oh come on, Kate. Since when has intelligence had anything to do with sex? I'm not sure they aren't incompatible, sex and intelligence I mean."

"They aren't for me. Intelligence turns me on."

"Yes I know."

"What do you mean?" she asked sharply.

"Nothing. I find I do best with pretty, good-natured, obliging women who aren't very bright."

"Like most of your sex. You should try to train yourself out of it. How much do you think that alibi's worth?"

"About as much as Rupert Farlow's. Cartwright and Claudia Etienne could have killed Etienne, taken the launch straight over to Greenwich Pier and easily been in the restaurant by eight. There's not a lot of traffic on the river after dark, the chances of anyone seeing them aren't great. Another boring job of checking."

Kate said: "He has a motive—both of them have. If Claudia Etienne is fool enough to marry him he'll be getting a wealthy wife."

Daniel said: "Do you think he's got the bottle to kill anyone?"

"It didn't need much bottle, did it? All he had to do was entice Etienne into that killing room. He didn't have to stab or bludgeon or strangle. He didn't even have to face his victim."

"One of them would have had to go back later and do that business with the snake. That would have taken some guts. I can't see Claudia Etienne doing that, not to her brother."

"Oh I don't know. If she was prepared to kill him, why balk at desecrating the body? Do you want to drive or shall I?"

While Kate took the wheel, Daniel telephoned Wapping. It was apparent that there was news. Replacing the receiver after a few minutes, he said: "The lab report is in. I've just heard the blood analysis from Robbins in boring detail. There was a blood saturation of 73 per cent. He probably died pretty quickly. Seven-thirty seems about right for the time of death. You get dizziness and headache at 30 per cent, incoordination and mental confusion at 40 per cent, exhaustion at 50 per cent and unconsciousness at 60 per cent. Weakness may come on suddenly because of muscular suboxia."

Kate asked: "Anything on the rubble blocking the flue?"

"It came from the chimney. It's the same stuff. But we expected that."

Kate said: "We already know that the gas fire isn't defective and we've got no significant prints. What about the window cord?"

"That's rather more difficult. The likelihood is that it was deliberately frayed with some bluntish implement and over a period of time, but they can't be 100 per cent sure. The fibres were crushed and broken, not cut. The rest of the cord was old and in parts weak, but they could see no reason why it should have snapped at that point unless it had been deliberately interfered with. Oh, and there's one other finding. There was a minute stain of mucus on the head of the snake. That means that it was rammed into the mouth immediately or very soon after the sharp object was removed."

42

On Sunday 17 October Dalgliesh decided to take Kate with him to interview Sonia Clements' sister, Sister Agnes, at her Brighton convent. He would have preferred to go alone, but a convent, even an Anglican one, and even for the son of a rector with High Church tendencies, was unfamiliar ground, to be approached with circumspection. Without a woman as chaperon he might not be permitted to see Sister Agnes except in the presence of the Mother Superior or another nun. He wasn't sure what he expected to get from the visit but his instinct, which he sometimes distrusted but had learned not to ignore, told him that there was something to be learned. The two deaths, so very different, were linked by more than that bare upper room in which one person had chosen to die, the other had fought to live. Sonia Clements had worked at Peverell Press for twenty-four years; it was Gerard Etienne who had sacked her. Was that ruthless decision a sufficient reason for the suicide? And if not, why had she chosen to die? Who, if anyone, might have been tempted to avenge that death?

The weather held. An early mist lifted to promise another day of mellow if fitful sunshine. Even the London air held something of the sweetness of the summer and a light breeze dragged tatters of thin cloud across an azure sky. Making his tedious and circuitous way through the suburbs of South London with Kate at his side, Dalgliesh, with the return of a boyish longing for the sight and sound of the sea, found himself hoping that the convent would be situated on the coast. They spoke little on the journey. Dalgliesh preferred to drive in silence and Kate could tolerate even taciturnity without the need to chat. It was, he reflected, not the least of her virtues. He had called for her at her new flat but had waited in the Jaguar for her to appear rather than taking the lift and ringing her doorbell, when she might have felt an obligation to invite him in. He valued his own privacy too much to risk invading hers. She had appeared precisely on time as he had expected. She looked different and he realized how seldom he saw her wearing a skirt. He smiled inwardly, wondering whether she had hesitated over the choice before deciding that her usual trousers might be seen as inappropriate for a visit to a convent. He suspected that, despite his sex, he might be more at home there than Kate.

His hope, never realistic, of stealing five minutes for a brisk walk along the edge of the beach was due to be frustrated. The convent stood on rising ground above a dull but busy main road, separated from it by an eight-foot brick wall. The main gate stood open and, turning in, they saw an ornate building in harsh red brick, obviously Victorian and as obviously designed as an institution, probably to house the first sisters of the order. The four storeys of identical windows placed closely together and ranged with precision reminded Dalgliesh uncomfortably of a prison, a thought which may have occurred to the architect, since the incongruous addition of a thin spire at one end of the building and a tower at the other looked like afterthoughts, designed as much to humanize as to embellish. A wide sweep of gravel curved upwards to a front door of almost black oak banded with iron, which would have been more appropriate as the entrance to a Norman keep. To their right they could glimpse a brick-built church, large enough to serve a parish, with a graceless spire and narrow lancet windows. To the left was contrast: a low modern building with a covered terrace and small formal garden, which he guessed was the hospice for the dying.

There was only one car, a Ford, standing in front of the convent and Dalgliesh parked neatly beside it. Pausing outside the car for a moment, he glanced back over the terraced lawns and could at last glimpse the English Channel. Short streets of small coloured houses, pale blue, pink and green, their roofs patterned with a frail geometry of television aerials, ran down in parallel lines to the layered blue of the sea, their precisely ordered domesticity contrasting with the heavy Victorian pile at his back.

There was no sign of life from the main building but, as he turned to lock the car door, he saw a nun turn the corner of the hospice with a patient in a wheelchair. The patient wore a striped white-and-blue cap with a red bobble and was covered with a rug drawn up to the chin. The nun bent to whisper and the patient laughed, a thin falling trickle of joyous notes on the quiet air.

He pulled the iron chain to the left of the door and heard its echoing clangour even through the thick iron-bounded oak. The square grille slid open and a gentle-faced nun looked out. Dalgliesh gave his name and held out his warrant card. At once the door was opened and the nun, wordless, but still smiling, gestured them to enter. They found themselves in a wide hall which smelled not unpleasantly of mild disinfectant. The floor was chequered with black and white tiles which looked freshly scrubbed and the walls were bare except for a sepia portrait, obviously Victorian, of a formidable grave-faced nun whom Dalgliesh assumed to be the foundress of the order, and a reproduction of Millais's *Christ in the Carpenter's Shop* in an ornate carved wood frame. The nun, still smiling, still wordless, ushered them into a small room to the right of the hall and with a somewhat theatrical gesture silently invited them to sit. Dalgliesh wondered if she was deaf and dumb.

The room was sparsely furnished but was not unwelcoming. The central table, highly polished, held a bowl of late roses and there were two easy chairs covered with faded cretonne set in front of the double windows. The walls were plain except for a large and ornate wood-and-silver crucifix of horrific realism to the right of the fireplace. It looked, Dalgliesh thought, Spanish and as if it must once have hung in a church. Over the fireplace was a copy in oil of a Madonna offering a bunch of grapes to the Christ Child which it took him some time to identify as Mignard's *La Vierge à la Grappe*. A brass plaque bore the name of the donor. There were four upright dining chairs set in an uninviting line against the right-hand wall, but Dalgliesh and Kate remained standing.

They were not kept waiting long. The door opened and a nun entered with brisk self-assurance and held out her hand.

"You are Commander Dalgliesh and Inspector Miskin? Welcome to St Anne's. I am Mother Mary Clare. We spoke when you telephoned, Commander. Would you and the Inspector care for some coffee?"

The hand which briefly grasped his was plump but cool. He said: "No thank you, Mother. That is kind of you but we hope not to inconvenience you for too long."

There was nothing intimidating about her. Her short and sturdy body was dignified by the long blue-grey habit bound with a leather belt, but she looked as comfortable in it as if the formal garb were workaday clothes. A single heavy cross in dark wood hung from a cord round her neck and her face, soft and pale as dough, bulged like a baby's from the constricting wimple. But the eyes behind the steel spectacles were shrewd, and the little mouth, for all its delicate softness, held the promise of an uncompromising firmness. Dalgliesh knew that he and Kate were subject to a scrutiny as keen as it was unobtrusive.

Then, with a little nod, she said: "I'll send Sister Agnes to you. It's a lovely day, perhaps you would care to walk together in the rose garden."

It was, Dalgliesh recognized, a command, not a suggestion, but he knew that in that first brief encounter they had passed some private test. Had she been less than satisfied he had no doubt that the interview would have taken place in this room and under her supervision. She tugged at the bell-cord and the little smiling nun who had let them in again appeared.

"Will you ask Sister Agnes to be good enough to join us?"

Again they waited in silence, still standing. In less than two minutes the door opened and a tall nun entered alone. The Mother Superior said: "This is Sister Agnes. Sister, this is Commander Dalgliesh of New Scotland Yard and Inspector Miskin. I have suggested that you might like to walk outside in the rose garden."

With a valedictory nod but no formal goodbye she was gone.

The nun who confronted them with wary eyes could not have been more different from the Mother Superior. The habit was the same, except that her cross was smaller, but on her it conferred a hieratic dignity, remote and a little mysterious. The Mother Superior had looked dressed for a stint at the kitchen stove; it was difficult to imagine Sister Agnes except at the altar. She was very thin, long-limbed and strong-featured, the wimple emphasizing the high cheekbones, the strong line of the eyebrows and the uncompromising set of the wide mouth.

She said: "Then shall we look at the roses, Commander?" Dalgliesh opened the door and he and Kate followed her out of the reception room and through the hall on almost silent feet.

She led the way down the grand path to the terraced rose garden. The beds were in three long rows divided by parallel gravel paths, each path four stone steps down from the one above. There would be just room for the three of them to walk abreast, first along the top path, then down the steps, then back along the second path to the second flight of steps and the forty yards of the lowest path before turning, a bleak perambulation carried out in full view of all the convent windows. He wondered if there was a more private garden at the rear of the convent. Even if there was they were not, apparently, expected to walk there.

Sister Agnes paced between them, almost as tall as his six feet two inches, her head held high. She was wearing a long grey cardigan over her habit and with each hand thrust deeply into the opposite cuff as if for warmth. With her bound arms held tightly against her body she reminded Dalgliesh uncomfortably of old pictures he had seen of mental patients in strait-jackets. It seemed that she walked between them like a prisoner under escort, and he wondered if that was how the three of them would appear to any secret watcher from the high windows. The thought, and it was not agreeable, apparently also entered Kate's mind, for, muttering an excuse, she dropped a little behind and, kneeling, appeared to be tying the shoelace of her brogues. When she caught up with them she took her place next to Dalgliesh.

It was Dalgliesh who broke the silence. He said: "It is good of you to see us. I'm sorry to have to trouble you, particularly as it must seem an intrusion on private grief. I need to ask you about the death of your sister."

" 'Intrusion on private grief.' That was the telephone message I received from Mother Superior. I suppose they are words you often have to use, Commander."

"Intrusion is sometimes inseparable from my job."

"And have you specific questions you hope I can answer, or is this a more general intrusion?"

"A little of both."

"But you know how my sister died. Sonia killed herself, there is no possible doubt about that. She left a note at the scene. She also posted a letter to me on the morning she died. She didn't think the news was worth a first-class stamp. I received it three days later."

Dalgliesh said: "Would you mind telling me what was in the note? I know, of course, what was in the note to the coroner."

She didn't speak for a few seconds which seemed much longer, then spoke without emphasis as if reciting a piece of prose learned by heart. " 'What I am about to do will seem a sin in your eyes. Please try to understand that what you see as sinful is to me both natural and right. We have made different choices but they lead to the same end. After the vacillating years at least I can be absolute for death. Try not to grieve for me too long; grief is only an indulgence. I could not have had a better sister.' "

She said: "Is that what you want to hear, Commander? It is hardly relevant, surely, to your present enquiry."

"We have to look at anything which happened at Innocent House in the months before Gerard Etienne died which could have had a bearing even remotely on that death. One is your sister's suicide. The gossip in London literary circles and at Innocent House seems to be that Gerard Etienne drove her to that act. If he did, her friend—a particular friend—might have wished him harm."

She said: "I was Sonia's particular friend. She had no particular friends except me, and I had no reason to wish Gerard Etienne dead. I was here on the day or night when he died. That is a fact you can easily check."

Dalgliesh said: "I was not suggesting, Sister, that you were in any way personally concerned with Gerard Etienne's death. I am asking if you knew of any other person close to your sister who could have resented the way she died."

"None except myself. But I resented it, Commander. Suicide is the final despair, the final rejection of God's grace, the ultimate sin."

Dalgliesh said quietly: "Then perhaps, Sister, it will receive the ultimate mercy."

They had reached the end of the first path and together they descended the steps and turned left. Suddenly she said, "I dislike roses in autumn. They are essentially summer flowers. The December roses are the most depressing, brown and shrivelled buds on a tangle of prickles. I can hardly bear to walk here in December. Like us, roses don't know when to die."

He said: "But today we can almost believe it is summer." He paused, then added: "I expect you know that Gerard Etienne died from carbon-monoxide poisoning and in the same room as your sister. It is unlikely in his case to have been suicide. It could be accidental death, a blocked flue which caused the gas fire to malfunction, but we have to consider a third possibility, that the fire was deliberately tampered with."

She said: "You're saying that you believe he was murdered?"

"It can't be ruled out. What I have to ask you is whether you have any reason to believe that your sister could have interfered with the fire. I'm not suggesting it was a plot to kill Etienne. But is it possible that she might have planned a suicide which would look like accidental death and then changed her mind?"

"How can I possibly tell you that, Commander?"

"It was a very long shot, but I had to ask. If anyone is brought to trial for murder it is a possibility that the defence counsel will certainly put forward."

She said: "It would have saved a great deal of distress for other people if she had troubled to make her death look like an accident, but suicides so seldom do. It is, after all, the supreme act of aggression and what satisfaction is there in aggression if it hurts only oneself? To make suicide look accidental wouldn't have been so very difficult. I could think of ways, but they don't include dismantling a gas fire and blocking the flue. I'm not sure that Sonia would have known how to do that. She wasn't mechanically minded in life; why should she be so in death?"

"And the note she sent you, that was all? No reason, no explanation?"

"No," she said. "No reason, no explanation."

Dalgliesh went on: "It seems to have been assumed that your sister killed herself because Gerard Etienne had told her that she had to go. Does that seem likely to you?"

She didn't reply, and after a minute he gently persisted. "As her sister, as someone who knew her well, does that explanation satisfy you?"

She turned to him and, for the first time, looked him full in the face. "Is that question relevant to your enquiry?"

"It could be. If Miss Clements knew something about Innocent House, or about one of the people who worked there, something so distressing to her that it contributed to her death, that something could also be relevant to the death of Gerard Etienne."

Again she turned. She said: "Is there any question of reopening the manner of my sister's death?"

"Formally? None at all. We know how Miss Clements died. I would like to know why, but the verdict of the inquest was correct. Legally that is the end of it."

They paced in silence. She seemed to be considering a course of action. He was aware of, or perhaps imagined, the muscles taut with tension of the arm which briefly brushed his own. When she spoke her voice was harsh.

"I can satisfy your curiosity, Commander. My sister died because the two people she cared for most, perhaps the only two people she ever cared for, left her and left her finally. I took my vows the week before she killed herself; Henry Peverell died eight months earlier."

Until now Kate had been silent. She said: "You're saying that she was in love with Mr. Peverell?"

Sister Agnes turned and looked at her as if noticing her presence for the first time. Then she again turned her head and with an almost imperceptible shiver clasped her arms more tightly across her breast. "She was his mistress for the last eight years of his life. She called it love. I called it an obsession. I don't know what he called it. They were never seen together in public. The affair was kept deeply secret at his insistence. The room in which they made love was the one in which she died. I always knew when they had been together. Those were the nights when she stayed late at the office. When she came in I could smell him on her."

Kate protested: "But why the secrecy? What was he afraid of? Neither was married, they were both adults. This was no one's business but their own."

"When I asked that question she had her answers ready, or rather his. She said that he had no wish to marry again, that he wanted to stay faithful to the memory of his wife, that he disliked the idea of his private affairs being the subject of office gossip, that the relationship would distress his daughter. She accepted all the excuses. It was enough for her that he apparently needed what she could provide. It may, of course, have been quite simple, that she was adequate to satisfy a physical need but not sufficiently beautiful or young or rich enough to tempt him to marry her. And for him, I think the secrecy added an additional frisson to the affair. Perhaps this was what he enjoyed, humiliating her, testing the limits of her devotion, stealing up to that drab little room like a Victorian employer pleasuring his parlour-maid. It was not the sinfulness of the relationship which distressed me most, it was the vulgarity."

He had not expected such openness, such confidence. But, perhaps, it was not so surprising. She must have endured months of self-imposed silence and now, to two strangers whom she need never see again, the pent-up bitterness was released. She said: "I am the elder by only eighteen months. We were always very close. He destroyed that. She couldn't have him and her religion so she chose him. He destroyed the confidence between us. How could there be confidence when each of us despised the other's god?"

Dalgliesh said: "She had no sympathy with your vocation?"

"She had no understanding of it. Nor had he. He saw it as a retreat from the world and from responsibility, from sexuality and from involvement, and what he believed she believed. She had known for some time, of course, what I had in mind. I suppose that she hoped no one would have me. There are not many communities which welcome middle-aged postulants. A convent isn't intended as a refuge for the unsuccessful and disillusioned. And she knew, of course, that I had no practical skills to offer. I was—I am—a book-restorer. Reverend Mother still releases me from time to time to work in libraries in London, Oxford and Cambridge, provided that there is a suitable house—I mean a convent—in which I can be lodged. But that work is becoming infrequent. It takes a great deal of time to restore and rebind a valuable book or manuscript, more time than I can be spared for."

Dalgliesh recalled a visit three years previously to the library at

Corpus Christi College in Cambridge when he had been shown the Jerusalem Bible, taken under escort to Westminster Abbey for successive coronations, together with one of the earliest illuminated copies of the New Testament. The recently rebound treasure, lifted lovingly from its special box, had been placed on the padded V-shaped lectern, the pages turned with a wooden spatula to avoid handling. He had looked in wonder across five centuries at the meticulous drawings, still as bright as when the colours had flowed with such gentle precision from the artist's pen, drawings which, in their beauty and essential humanity, had brought him close to tears.

He said: "Your work here is regarded as more important?"

"It is judged by different criteria. And here my lack of the more commonplace practical skills is no disadvantage. Anyone with a little training can operate a washing machine, wheel patients to the bathroom, give out bedpans. I can't be sure how long even these services will be required. The priest who is our chaplain here is converting to Roman Catholicism following the decision of the Church of England to ordain women. Half of the sisters want to follow him. The future of St Anne's as an Anglican order is in doubt."

They had now walked the length of the three paths and, turning, began the journey again. Sister Agnes said: "Henry Peverell wasn't the only person who came between us in the last years of my sister's life. There was Eliza Brady. Oh you needn't trouble to look for her, Commander, she died in 1871. I read about her in a report of an inquest in a Victorian newspaper which I found in a second-hand bookshop in Charing Cross Road and which unhappily I passed over to Sonia. Eliza Brady was thirteen years old. Her father worked for a coal merchant and her mother had died in childbirth. Eliza became the mother to four younger brothers and sisters and the baby. Her father gave evidence at the inquest that Eliza was mother to them all. For fourteen hours a day she worked. She washed, she made the fire, she cooked, she shopped, she cared for the whole of that little family. One morning, when she was drying the baby's napkins on a guard in front of the fire, she leaned on the guard and it collapsed into the flames. She was horribly burnt and died in agony three days later. The story affected my sister powerfully. She said, 'So this is the justice of your so-called loving God. This is how he rewards the innocent and the good. He wasn't satisfied with killing her. She had to die horribly, slowly and in agony.' My sister became almost obsessed with Eliza Brady. She made her into a kind of cult figure. If she had had a picture of the child she would probably have prayed in front of it, although I don't know to whom."

Kate protested: "But if she'd wanted a reason to disbelieve in God why go back to the nineteenth century? There are plenty of contemporary tragedies. She'd only got to look at the television or read the newspaper. She'd only got to think of Yugoslavia. Eliza Brady has been dead for over a hundred years."

Sister Agnes said: "That is what I told her, but Sonia replied that justice had nothing to do with time. We shouldn't allow ourselves to be dominated by time. If God is eternal, then His justice is eternal. And so is His injustice."

Kate asked: "Before your estrangement from your sister, did you often visit Innocent House?"

"Not often, but I went there occasionally. Actually there was a possibility, months before I decided that I had a vocation, that I might have worked part-time at Innocent House. Jean-Philippe Etienne was very anxious that the archives should be examined and catalogued and apparently he thought I might be a suitable person to do it. The Etiennes have always had an eye for a bargain and he probably guessed that I would work as much for interest as for money. However, Henry Peverell put a stop to that, and, of course, I understood why."

Dalgliesh asked: "You knew Jean-Philippe Etienne?"

"I got to know all the partners reasonably well. The two old men, Jean-Philippe and Henry, seemed to be almost wilfully hanging on to a power neither seemed able or willing to exercise. Gerard Etienne was obviously the young Turk, the heir apparent. I never got on particularly well with Claudia Etienne but I liked James de Witt. De Witt is an example of a man who lives a good life without the help of religious belief. There are those who are apparently born with a deficiency of original sin. Goodness in them is hardly a merit."

Dalgliesh said: "Surely religious belief isn't necessary to a good life."

"Perhaps not. Belief in religion may not influence behaviour. The practice of religion surely should."

Kate said: "You weren't, of course, at the last party they held. Did you go to any of the earlier parties? Were the visitors able to wander where they wanted throughout the house?"

"I only went to two of the parties. They held one in the summer and one in the winter. There was certainly nothing to prevent visitors from wandering round the house. I don't think many people did. It is hardly courteous to take the opportunity of a party to explore rooms which are generally held to be private. Of course, Innocent House is now mainly offices and perhaps that makes a difference. But the Innocent House parties were fairly formal affairs. The guest list was controlled and Henry Peverell greatly disliked having more than eighty people in the house at one time. Peverell Press has never gone in for the ordinary kind of literary party—too many people invited in case any of their writers are offended at being left out; overcrowded, overheated rooms with guests trying to balance plates of cold food and drink lukewarm inferior white wine while bawling at each other. The majority of guests came by water, so it was fairly easy, I imagine, to repel gatecrashers."

There was little else to be learned. By common consent they turned at the end of the next path and retraced their steps. In silence they returned with Sister Agnes to the front door, then said their goodbyes without re-entering the convent. She looked at Dalgliesh and Kate with great intensity, holding their eyes, compelling them to a moment of concentrated attention as if by a force of will she could compel them to respect her confidence.

They had hardly turned out of the drive and were waiting at the first red traffic light when Kate's pent-up resentment burst out.

"So that's why the bed was there in the little archives room, why the door had a bolt and lock. My God, what a bastard! Sister Agnes was right, he did sneak up to that room like some Victorian petty despot. He did humiliate her, make use of her. I can imagine what went on up there. The man was a sadist."

Dalgliesh said quietly: "You've no evidence for that, Kate."

"Why the hell did she put up with it? She was an experienced, well-regarded editor. She could have left."

"She was in love with him."

"And her sister in love with God. She's looking for peace. I didn't get the impression that she's found it. Even the future of the convent is at risk."

"The founder of her religion didn't promise it. 'I came not to send peace but a sword.' " Glancing at her, he saw that the text meant nothing to her. He said: "It was a useful visit. We know now why Sonia Clements died and it was nothing—or little—to do with Gerard Etienne's treatment of her. There is apparently no one living with a motive to avenge her death. We already knew that visitors to Innocent House could wander at will through the house, but it's useful to have Sister Agnes's confirmation. And then there's the interesting piece of information about the archives. According to Sister Agnes it was Henry Peverell who was anxious that she shouldn't be given the job of working on them. It was only after his death that Jean-Philippe Etienne agreed that Gabriel Dauntsey should undertake the job."

Kate said: "It would have been more interesting if it had been the Etiennes who wanted the archives left undisturbed. It's obvious why

Henry Peverell didn't want Sonia Clements' sister working up there. It would have upset his little arrangements with his mistress."

Dalgliesh said: "That's the obvious explanation, and like most obvious explanations it's probably the right one. But there might be something else in the archives that Henry Peverell wanted to leave undisturbed, something he either knew or suspected was there. It's difficult to see, even so, why that should be relevant to Gerard Etienne's death. As you say, it would have been more interesting if it had been the Etiennes who were insisting that the archives were left undisturbed. Even so, I think we're going to have to take a look at those papers."

"All of them, sir?"

"If necessary, Kate. All of them."

43

It was now half past nine on Sunday evening and Daniel and Robbins were working together at the top of Innocent House searching through the files. They were using the desk and chair in the little archives room. The method Daniel had decided upon was for both of them to work their way along the shelves, pulling out any file which looked hopeful and then taking it into the little archives room for further investigation. It was a discouraging task since neither knew what he was looking for. Daniel had estimated that the task would take weeks with two of them working but they were making better progress than he had expected. If AD's hunch was right and there were papers which could throw a light on Etienne's murder someone must surely have consulted them fairly recently. This meant that the very old nineteenth-century files, many of which had obviously been untouched for a hundred years, could safely be ignored, at least for the present. There was no problem about the light; the unshaded overhead bulbs were only a few feet apart. But the job was dusty, tiring and boring and he did it without hope.

Soon after half past nine he decided that enough was enough for one night. He was aware of a disinclination to go back to his Bayswater flat, a reluctance so strong that almost any alternative seemed preferable. He had spent as little time in it as possible since Fenella had departed for the States. They had bought their flat together just eighteen months ago and he had known within weeks of their living together that this commitment to a joint mortgage and a shared life had been a mistake.

She had said: "We'll have separate rooms, of course, darling. We both need our privacy."

Later he was to wonder whether he had actually heard the words. Not only did Fenella not need her privacy, she had no intention of allowing him his, less, he thought, from wilful denial than from a total lack of understanding of what the word meant. He recalled too late what should have been a salutary childhood lesson: a friend of his mother's telling her complacently, "We've always respected books and learning in our home," while her six-year-old son, unrebuked, systematically tore to pieces the pages of Daniel's copy of *Treasure Island*. That should surely have taught him that what people believed about themselves seldom bore resemblance to how they behaved in reality. Even so, Fenella had set a record in the irreconcilability of belief and action. The flat was always crowded; friends dropped in, were fed in his kitchen, quarrelled and were reconciled on his sofa, took baths in his bathroom, made international calls on his telephone, raided his refrigerator and drank his beer. The flat was never quiet, the two of them were never alone. His bedroom became their shared bedroom, largely because Fenella's was usually temporarily occupied by a homeless chum. She drew people to her like a lighted doorway. Hers was the attraction of unbreakable good humour. She would probably have captivated his mother if he had ever allowed them to meet, no doubt by immediately promising to convert to Judaism. Fenella was nothing if not obliging.

Her compulsive gregariousness went with an untidiness which had never ceased to amaze him during their eighteen months together and which he could never reconcile with her fussiness about small items of décor. He remembered her holding up against the sitting-room wall three small prints, vertically mounted on a length of ribbon and surmounted by a bow. "Just here, darling, or another two inches to the left? What do you think?"

It scarcely seemed to matter when they had a kitchen sink full of unwashed dishes, a bathroom whose door had to be pushed open against the weight of a heap of dirty and malodorous towels, unmade beds and clothes strewn over the bedroom. With this sluttishness over domestic detail went a compulsive need to bathe and to wash her clothes. The flat was perpetually noisy with the thump and whirl of the washing machine and the hiss of the shower.

He recalled how she had announced the end of their relationship: "Darling, Terry wants me to join him in New York. Next Thursday, actually. He's sent a first-class ticket. I didn't think you'd mind. We haven't been having a lot of fun together recently, have we? Don't you think that something fundamental has gone out of the relationship? Something precious we once had has been lost. Don't you feel that something has just drained away?"

"Apart from my savings."

"Oh darling, don't be mean. It's so unlike you."

He had asked: "What about your job? How will you work in the States? It isn't easy getting a green card."

"Oh, I shan't bother about a job, not at once. Terry's loaded. He says I can amuse myself decorating his apartment."

Their parting had been unacrimonious. It was almost impossible, he found, to quarrel with Fenella. He was resigned, even wryly amused, to discover that this amiability went with a keener commercial sense than he had expected.

"Darling, I think you'd better buy me out at half what we paid for the flat, not half what it's worth now. It's gone down terribly, everything has. I'm sure you can get a higher mortgage. And if you pay me my half of what the furniture cost, I'll leave it all for you. You must have something to sit on, sweetie."

It seemed hardly worthwhile pointing out that he had paid for, although not chosen, most of the furniture and liked none of it. He noticed, too, that the more valuable of her small acquisitions disappeared with her and were presumably now in New York. The tat remained, and he had neither the time nor the will to dispose of it. She had left him with a crippling mortgage, a flat full of furniture he disliked, an outrageous telephone bill consisting mainly of calls to New York and a lawyer's bill he could only hope to pay by instalments. It was the more irritating to find how much he occasionally missed her.

There was a small washroom and lavatory off the landing outside the archives room. While Robbins was washing the dirt of decades from his hands Daniel, on impulse, telephoned Wapping Police Station. Kate wasn't there. He waited, thought for less than a second, then rang her home number.

She answered, and he said: "What are you doing?"

"Arranging papers. What about you?"

"Disarranging papers. I'm still at Innocent House. Would you care for a drink?"

She hesitated for a couple of seconds, then said: "Why not. Where do you suggest?"

"The Town of Ramsgate. It's convenient for us both. I'll meet you there in twenty minutes."

44

Kate parked her car at the bottom of Wapping High Street and walked the fifty yards or so to the Town of Ramsgate. As she approached, Daniel appeared from the alleyway leading to Wapping Old Stairs.

He said: "I've been looking at Execution Dock. D'you suppose the pirates were alive when they tied them to the piles at low tide and left them until they'd been washed by three tides?"

"I shouldn't think so. They probably hanged them first. The eighteenth-century penal system was barbaric but not that barbaric."

They pushed open the pub door and were received into the multicoloured glitter and Sunday-night conviviality of a London pub. The narrow seventeenth-century tavern was crowded and Daniel had to edge and push his way through the throng of regulars to get his pint and Kate's half-pint of Charrington's Ale. A man and woman were getting up from two seats at the end of the room close to the door into the garden and Kate quickly secured them. If Daniel had come primarily to talk rather than to drink, this was as good a place as any. The pub was orderly but the noise level high. Against this background babble of voices and sudden guffaws of laughter they could talk with as much privacy as if the bar had been empty.

He was, she sensed, in an odd mood and she wondered whether, in ringing her, he had been looking for a sparring partner rather than a drinking companion. But the call had been welcome. Alan hadn't telephoned and, with the flat now almost in order, the temptation to ring him, to see him once more before he left, had been too strong for comfort. She was glad to be out of the flat and away from temptation.

Daniel's temper had probably been soured by his frustrating evening in the archives. She would take her turn the next evening and probably with as little expectation of success. But if the object wrenched from Etienne's mouth had indeed been a cassette, if this murderer had needed to tell the victim why he had been lured to his death, then the motive might well lie in the past, even in the distant past: an old evil, an imagined wrong, a hidden danger. The decision to examine the old records might be one of AD's famous hunches but, like all his hunches, it was rooted in reason.

Looking down into his beer, Daniel said: "You worked with John Massingham, didn't you, on the Berowne case. Did you like him?"

"He was a good detective, although not as good as he thought. No, I didn't like him. Why?"

He left the question unanswered. "Nor do I. He and I were detective sergeants together in H Division. He called me a Jew-boy. I wasn't meant to hear, of course, he would have thought that was rather bad form, insulting a chap to his face. Admittedly his actual words were 'our clever little Jew-boy,' but somehow I don't think it was meant as a compliment."

When she didn't comment, he went on: "When Massingham uses the expression 'when I succeed,' you know he isn't talking about making Chief Superintendent. What he's talking about is inheriting his dad's title. Chief Constable, the Lord Dungannon. It won't do him any harm. He'll get there before either of us."

Certainly before me, thought Kate. For her, ambition had to be governed by reality. Someone had to be the first woman Chief Constable. It could be she, but it was folly to count on it. She had probably entered the force ten years too soon.

She said: "You'll make it, if you really want it."

"Perhaps. It's not easy being a Jew."

She could have retorted that it wasn't easy being a woman in the macho world of the police, but that was a common complaint and she had no intention of whining to Daniel. She said: "It's not easy being illegitimate."

"Are you? I thought that was fashionable."

"Not my kind of illegitimate. And so is being a Jew—prestigious anyway."

"Not my kind of Jew."

"How is it difficult?"

"You can't be a cheerful atheist like other people. You feel the need to keep explaining to God why you can't believe in him. Then you have a Jewish mother. That is absolutely essential, it comes with the package. If you haven't got a Jewish mother then you aren't a Jew. Jewish mothers want their sons to marry nice Jewish girls, produce Jewish grandchildren and be seen with them in the synagogue."

"You could do that last occasionally without too much violence to your conscience, if atheists have one."

"Jewish atheists do. That's the trouble. Let's go and look at the river."

There was a small garden at the rear of the tavern overlooking the river which, on warm summer nights, could become uncomfortably crowded. But on an October night few of the regulars had any inclination to carry their drinks outside and Kate and Daniel walked out into a cool river-scented silence. The one lamp shining from the wall shed a soft glow over the upturned garden chairs and the tubs of woody-stemmed tangled geraniums. They moved together and rested their glasses on the river wall.

There was a silence. Then Daniel said abruptly: "We're not going to get this chap."

She said: "Why so sure? And why chap? It could be a woman. And why so defeatist? AD is probably the most intelligent detective in Britain."

"More likely a man. Dismantling and replacing that gas fire is more likely to be the work of a man. Let's assume he's a man anyway. We shan't get him because he's as intelligent as AD and he's got one big advantage: the criminal-justice system is on his side, not ours." This was a familiar gripe. Daniel's almost paranoid distrust of lawyers was one of his obsessions, like his dislike of having his name shortened to Dan. She was used to his complaint that the criminal-justice system was less concerned with convicting the guilty than in devising an ingenious and lucrative obstacle course for lawyers to demonstrate their cleverness.

She said: "That's nothing new. The criminal-justice system has favoured criminals for the last forty years. That's a fact we live with. Fools try to get over it by improving the evidence when they know damn well their man is guilty. All that does is discredit the police, set guilty men free and produce more legislation which tips the balance against convictions still further. You know that, we all know it. The answer is to get good honest evidence and make it stick in court."

"Good evidence in a really serious case is often the evidence of informers and undercover agents. For God's sake, Kate, you know that.

Now we have to feed that to the defence in advance, so we can't use it without putting lives at risk. Do you know how many major cases we've had to abandon in the last six months in the Met alone?"

"That won't happen in this case, will it? When we get the evidence we'll produce it."

"But we aren't going to get it, are we? Not unless one of them cracks, and they won't. It's all circumstantial. We haven't a single fact which we can link with one of the suspects. Any of them could have done it. One of them did. We could put a case together against any of them. It wouldn't even get to court. The DPP would throw it out. And if it did get to court, can't you imagine what the defence would make of it? Etienne could have gone up to that room for his own purposes. We can't prove that he didn't. He could have been looking for something in the archives, checking an old contract. He doesn't expect to stay long so he leaves his coat and keys in his office. Then he comes upon something which is more interesting than he expects and settles down to study it. He feels cold so he shuts the window, breaking the window cord, and lights the fire. By the time he realizes what's happening he's too disorientated to get to the fire to turn it off. So he dies. Then, hours later, the firm's mischief-maker finds the body and decides to add a note of morbid mystery to what is, in fact, an unfortunate accident."

Kate said: "We've gone over all that. It doesn't really stand up, does it? Why did he collapse next to the fire? Why not go out of the door? Etienne was intelligent, he must have known the risks from a gas fire in a badly ventilated room, so why shut the window?"

"All right, he was trying to open it, not shut it, when the cord broke."

"Dauntsey says it was open when he last used the room."

"Dauntsey is the chief suspect; we can ignore that evidence."

"His counsel won't. You can't build a case by ignoring inconvenient evidence."

"All right, he was trying either to shut or open the window. We'll leave that."

"But why light the fire in the first place? It wasn't that cold. Where are these records that so intrigued him? The ones on the table were old contracts from fifty years ago, the writers dead, unremembered. Why should he want to look at those?"

"The mischief-maker changed them. We've no way of knowing what records he was actually looking at."

"Why should he change them? And if Etienne went to the room to work, where was his pen, his pencil, his Biro?"

"He went to read, not to write."

"He couldn't write, could he? He couldn't even scribble the name of his killer. He had nothing to write with. Someone had stolen his diary with the pencil attached. He couldn't even write the name in dust. There was no dust. And what about that scratch on his palate? That's incontrovertible, that's fact."

"Connected to no one. We won't be able to prove how that was made unless we can produce the object that made it. And we don't know what made it. We probably never shall know. All we've got is suspicion and circumstantial evidence. We haven't even enough to put one of the suspects under surveillance. Can't you imagine it, the outcry, if we did? Five respectable people, not one of them with a criminal record. And two of them with alibis."

Kate said: "Neither of them worth a damn. Rupert Farlow admitted frankly that he'd swear de Witt was with him, true or not. And that story of needing him during the night, he was careful to give us the precise times, wasn't he?"

"I imagine you tend to notice the precise time when you're dying."

"And Claudia Etienne claims she was with her fiancé. He's going to marry a very rich woman, a bloody sight richer than she was a week ago. Do you think he'd hesitate to lie for her if she asked him?"

Daniel said: "OK. It's easy to disbelieve the alibis, but can we disprove them? And they could be telling the truth, both of them. We can't assume they're lying. And if they are, then Claudia Etienne and de Witt are in the clear. Which leads us back to Gabriel Dauntsey. He had the means and the opportunity and he has no alibi for the half-hour before he left for that pub reading."

Kate said: "But that goes equally for Frances Peverell and she's the one with a motive. Etienne chucked her for another woman, proposed to sell Innocent House over her head. She had more reason to wish him dead than anyone. And try convincing a jury that a rheumatic man of seventy-six could get up those stairs or take that slow creaking lift, do what he had to do in the little archives room and get back to his flat in about eight minutes. OK, Robbins did that trial run and it was just about possible but not if he had to go down to the ground floor to fetch the snake."

"We've only Frances Peverell's word for it that it was eight minutes. And they could be in it together. That's always been one of our possibilities. And the bath water running away means nothing. I've seen that bath, Kate. It's the big old-fashioned solid kind. You could drown a couple of adults in it. All he had to do was to leave the tap on very slowly so that the bath filled up while he was away. Then he steps into it to get himself convincingly wet and rings for Frances Peverell. But my guess is they were fellow conspirators."

"Daniel, you're not thinking clearly. It's that story about the bath water which puts Frances Peverell in the clear. If they were fellow conspirators why concoct a complicated story about baths, running water and eight minutes? Why not merely say that she was looking out for his taxi, was worried because he was late, and when she saw that he'd arrived she took him up to her own flat and kept him there for the night. She's got a spare room, hasn't she? This is murder, after all. She's not going to be worried about the possibility of gossip."

"We could prove he hadn't slept in that bed. If she'd told that story we would have got forensic on to it. You can't sleep all night in a bed without some evidence, from hair or sweat."

"Well, I think she's telling the truth. That alibi is too complicated not to be genuine."

"That's probably what we're meant to believe. My God, this murderer is clever. Clever and lucky. Think about Sonia Clements for a moment. She killed herself in that room. Why couldn't she have frayed the window cord, bunged up the gas-fire flue?"

Kate said: "Look, Daniel, AD and I have checked that this morning, as far as we could anyway. Her sister says she was mechanically inept. And why should she tamper with the fire? In the hope that someone, weeks later, would mysteriously light it, entice Etienne upstairs and lock him in to be poisoned with carbon monoxide?"

"Of course not. But she could have planned to kill herself that way, wanting it to look like an accident, hoping to protect Peverells. Perhaps she had that in mind from the moment old Peverell died. Then, when Gerard Etienne sacked her so brutally . . ."

"If he was brutal."

"Assume he was. After that she no longer cares whether or not she harms the firm, probably wanted to harm it, or at least to harm Etienne. So she no longer bothers to make her death look accidental, kills herself in a more agreeable way with drugs and drink and leaves a suicide note. Kate, I like that. It has a kind of crazy logic about it."

"More crazy than logical. How would the murderer know that Clements had interfered with the gas? She's hardly likely to have told him. All you've done is to make the accidental-death theory more plausible. Your theory is just another gift for the defence. You can hear defence counsel making the most of it. 'Ladies and gentlemen of the jury, Sonia Clements had just as much chance as my client of interfering with that gas fire, and Sonia Clements is dead.' "

Daniel said: "OK, let's be optimistic. We catch him, and then what will happen to him? Ten years in prison if he's unlucky, fewer if he behaves himself."

"You wouldn't want to sling him up by the neck?"

"No. Would you?"

"No I wouldn't want hanging back. I'm not sure, though, that my position is particularly rational. I'm not even sure that it's honest. I happen to believe that the death penalty does deter, so what I'm saying is that I'm willing for innocent people to take a greater chance of being murdered so that I can salve my conscience by saying that we no longer execute murderers."

Daniel said: "Did you watch that TV programme last week?"

"The one about the U.S.A. correctional institute?"

"Correctional. That's a good word. The inmates were corrected all right. Killed with lethal injection after God knows how many years on death row."

"Yes, I saw it. You could argue that they got a damn sight easier end than their victims. An easier end than most human beings get, come to that."

"So you approve of revenge killing?"

"Daniel, I didn't say that. It's just that I couldn't feel much pity. They killed in a state with the death penalty and then seemed aggrieved that the state proposed to carry out what it had legislated for. Not one of them mentioned his victim. No one spoke the word 'remorse.'"

"One did."

"Then I must have missed it."

"That's not all you missed."

"Are you trying to quarrel?"

"Just trying to find out what you believe."

"What I believe is my business."

"Even on matters which concern the job?"

"Particularly on matters which concern the job. Anyway, this doesn't concern the job except indirectly. The programme was intended to make me feel outrage. OK, it was skilfully made. The producer didn't labour the point. You couldn't say it was unfair. But at the end they gave a number to the viewers so that they could ring to express disgust. All I'm saying is that I didn't feel quite the disgust they obviously intended. Anyway, I dislike television programmes which try to tell me what I ought to feel."

"In that case you'd better stop watching documentaries."

A police launch, sleek and fast, came into view travelling upstream, its prow searchlight raking the darkness, its wake a white fishtail of foam. Then it was gone and the dishevelled surface subsided into a gentle heaving calm on which the reflected lights of the river pubs threw shining pools of silver. Small beads of foam floated out of the darkness to break against the river wall. A silence fell. They were standing about two feet apart, each looking out over the river. Then simultaneously they turned and their eyes met. Kate couldn't see his expression from the one wall-lamp but she could feel his force and hear his quickened breathing. Suddenly she felt a charge of physical longing so strong that she had to put out a hand and steady herself against the wall to prevent herself from stepping forward into his arms.

He said "Kate," and made a quick move towards her, but she had known what was coming and she turned quickly aside. The movement was slight but unmistakable. He said gently: "What's wrong, Kate?" and then, his voice sardonic, "Wouldn't AD like it?"

"I don't arrange my private life to suit AD."

He didn't touch her. It would, she thought, have been easier if he had. She said: "Look, I've chucked a man I love because of the job. Why should I mess it up for someone I don't love?"

"Would it mess it up, your job or mine?"

"Oh Daniel, doesn't it always?"

He said, a little teasingly, "You did tell me I should train myself to fancy intelligent women."

"But I didn't offer to be part of the training."

His low laugh broke the tension. She liked him immensely, not least because, unlike most men, he could take rejection without rancour. But why not? Neither of them could pretend to be in love. She thought, Both of us are vulnerable, both a little lonely, but this isn't the answer.

As they turned to go back into the pub, he asked: "If it were AD here with you now, if he asked you to go home with him, would you?"

She thought for a few seconds, then decided he deserved honesty. "Probably. Yes I would."

"And would that be love or sex?"

"Neither," she said. "Call it curiosity."

45

On Monday morning Daniel telephoned the switchboard at Innocent House and asked George Copeland to call in at Wapping during his lunch break. He arrived just after half past one, bringing into the room with him a weight of apprehension and tension which seemed to encumber the very air. When Kate suggested that the room was warm and that he might like to take off his coat, he did so at once, as if the suggestion had been a command, but looked after it with anxious eyes as Daniel received it and hung it up, as if fearing that this was the first stage of some premeditated divestation. Looking at the childlike face, Daniel thought that it must have changed little since he was a boy. The round cheeks with their moons of red, definite as patches, had the smoothness of rubber, an incongruous contrast to the dry thatch of grey hair. The eyes had a look of strained hopefulness and the voice, attractive but diffident, was, he suspected, more ready to propitiate than to assert. Probably bullied at school, thought Daniel, and been kicked around since. But apparently he had found his niche at Innocent House in a job which seemed to suit him and which he obviously did satisfactorily. How long, he wondered, would that have lasted under the new dispensation?

Kate had settled him opposite her with more courtesy than she would have shown Claudia Etienne, or any of the other male suspects, but he sat facing her across the desk as rigid as a board, his hands like paws, close-fisted, in his lap.

Kate said: "Mr. Copeland, on the night of Mr. Etienne's engagement party, on the tenth of July, you were seen with Mrs. Bartrum coming down from the archives floor at Innocent House. What were you doing there?"

The question was gently put, but the effect was as devastating as if Kate had physically pinned him up against the wall and screamed in his face. He seemed literally to sink in his chair and the red moons flamed and grew, then faded, leaving him so pale that Daniel instinctively moved closer, half expecting him to faint.

Kate said: "Do you admit that you did go to the top floor?"

He found his voice: "Not to the archives room, not there. Mrs. Bartrum wanted to use the toilet. I took her to the one on the top floor and waited outside."

"Why didn't she use the lavatories in the women's cloakroom on the first floor?"

"She tried, but both cubicles were occupied and there was a queue. She was—she was in a hurry."

"So you took her upstairs. But why did she ask you, rather than one of the women staff?"

It was a question which, Daniel thought, could more reasonably have been put to Mrs. Bartrum. No doubt in time it would be.

Now Copeland was silent. Kate persisted: "Wouldn't it have been more natural for her to have asked one of the women?"

"It might have been, but she was shy. She didn't know any of them, and I was there on the desk."

"And she knew you, is that it?" He didn't answer, but he gave a little nod. Kate said: "How well does she know you?"

And now, looking full in her face, he replied: "She's my daughter."

"Mr. Sydney Bartrum is married to your daughter? So that explains it. It's all perfectly natural and understandable. She came to you because you're her father. But that isn't generally known, is it? Why the secrecy?"

"If I tell you, does it have to go any further? Do you have to say that I've told?"

"We don't have to tell anyone else except Commander Dalgliesh and it won't then go further unless it's relevant to our enquiry. We can't decide that unless you explain."

"It was Mr. Bartrum—Sydney—who wanted it kept silent. He wanted it kept a secret, at least at the beginning. He's a good husband, he loves her, they're happy together. Her first husband was a brute. She tried to make a success of the marriage but I think it was a relief when he walked out. There had always been other women and he went off with one of them. They got a divorce, but it hit her very hard. She lost all her confidence. Luckily there were no children."

"How did she meet Mr. Bartrum?"

"She came to collect me from work one day. I'm usually the last out, so no one saw her except Mr. Bartrum. His car wouldn't start, so Julie and I offered him a lift. When he got to his house he invited us in for coffee. I suppose he thought he had to. That's when it began. They started writing to each other. He went down at weekends to Basingstoke, where she lived and worked, to see her."

"But surely people at Innocent House knew that you had a daughter?"

"I'm not sure. They knew I was a widower but they never asked about my family. It wasn't as if Julie lived with me. She worked in the tax office in Basingstoke and she wasn't often at home. I think they must have known, but they didn't ask about her. That's why the secrecy was so easy when they married."

"Why shouldn't people know?"

"Mr. Bartrum—Sydney—said he wanted to keep his private life private, that his marriage was nothing to do with Peverell Press, that he didn't want the junior staff gossiping about his personal affairs. He didn't invite any of them to the wedding but he did tell the directors that he was married. Well, of course he had to because of changing his tax code. And later he told them about the baby and showed everyone her photograph. He's very proud of her. I think to begin with he didn't want people to know that he'd married—well, that he'd married the receptionist's daughter. Perhaps he was afraid that he'd lose face with the staff here. He was brought up in an orphanage, and forty years ago institutions for children were different from how they are today. He was despised at school, made to feel inferior, and I don't think he ever forgot it. He's always been a little over-concerned about his status in the firm."

"And what does your daughter think about all this, the secrecy, concealing the fact that Mr. Bartrum is your son-in-law?"

"I don't think that worries her. She's probably forgotten by now. It's not as if the firm is part of her life. She's only been in Innocent House once since they were married and that was for Mr. Gerard's engagement party. She wanted to see inside the house, see number ten and the room where he worked. She loves him. They've got the baby now, they're happy together. He's changed her life. And it's not as if I don't see them out of the office. I visit nearly every weekend. I see Rosie—the baby—whenever I like."

He looked from Daniel to Kate, imploring them to understand, then said: "I know it seems strange and I think Sydney regrets it now. He's more or less said so. But I can see how it happened. He asked us on impulse to keep it secret and the longer we did the more impossible it was to tell the truth. And no one asked. No one was interested in whom he married. No one asked me about my daughter. People are only interested in your family if you talk about them, and even then it's mostly just politeness. They don't really care. It would be very hurtful to Mr. Bartrum—to Sydney—if it came out now. And I wouldn't like him to think that I told you. Does it need to go any further?"

"No," said Kate, "I don't think it does."

He seemed reassured and Daniel helped him into his coat. When he came back from seeing him off the premises he found Kate pacing the room in a furious temper.

"Of all the bloody pompous stupid snobs! That man is worth ten of Bartrum. Oh, I can see how it happened, all right, the social insecurity I mean. He's the only one of the senior staff—isn't he?—who hasn't been to Oxbridge. These things seem to matter to your sex. God knows why. And it tells you something about Peverell Press, doesn't it? That man has worked for them for—how long?—nearly twenty years, and they've never even enquired about his daughter."

Daniel said: "If they had asked he would have replied that she was now married and very happy, thank you. But why should they enquire? AD doesn't enquire about your home life. Would you want him to? I can see how it began, the first snobbish impulse to keep it secret and then the realization that he had to go on keeping it a secret unless he wanted to look a fool. I wonder how much Bartrum would pay to prevent it being known. At least we know now why Copeland and Mrs. Bartrum were on the top floor together. Not that he needed an excuse to be there, he can go up any time. That's one small problem out of the way."

Kate said: "Not really. They were all pretty discreet at Innocent House, particularly the partners, but we've heard enough from Mrs. Demery and the junior staff to get a good idea of what was going on. With Gerard Etienne as boss, how long do you think either Bartrum or Copeland would have lasted in their jobs? Copeland loves his daughter and she loves her husband—God knows why but apparently she does. They're happy together, they've got a child. There was a lot at stake for both of them, wasn't there, Bartrum and Copeland? And don't forget one thing about George Copeland. He's the handyman. He does the repairs. He's one of the people at Innocent House who would have had no trouble in disconnecting that gas fire. And he could have done it safely at any time. The only person who regularly uses the little archives room is Gabriel Dauntsey and he never lights the gas. He takes in his own electric fire if he needs it. This isn't one small problem out of the way. It's one more bloody complication."

Book Four

EVIDENCE IN
WRITING

46

On the evening of Thursday 21 October Mandy left the office an hour later than usual. She was to meet her housemate, Maureen, at the White Horse on the Wanstead Road for a pub meal followed by a gig. The outing was a double celebration; it was Maureen's nineteenth birthday and the drummer in the band, the Devils on Horseback, was her current boyfriend. The gig was due to begin at eight but the party would meet at the pub an hour earlier for a preliminary meal. Mandy had brought a change of clothes to the office in her bike pannier and planned to go straight to the White Horse. The prospect of the evening, and in particular of meeting again the band leader, Roy, whom she had decided that she rather fancied, or was prepared to fancy if the evening went well, had cast a glow of happy anticipation over the day which not even Miss Blackett's silent and almost manic concentration on work could dim. Miss Blackett was now working for Miss Claudia, who had moved into her dead brother's office. Three days after his death Mandy had overheard Mr. de Witt encouraging her.

"It's what he would have wanted. You're chairman and managing director now, or will be when we've got round to passing the necessary resolution. We can't just leave the room empty. Gerard wouldn't have wanted it kept as a shrine."

A few of the staff had left immediately, but those who remained, either by choice or necessity, found themselves bound by an unacknowledged comradeship and shared experience. Together they waited and

wondered and, when the partners weren't present, speculated and
gossiped. Mandy's bright eyes and keen ears missed nothing. It seemed
to her now that Innocent House held her in some mysterious thrall.
She came to work each morning energized with a mixture of excitement
and anticipation spiced with fear. That small bare room in which, on
her first day, she had stood looking down at the body of Sonia Clements
possessed her imagination so powerfully that the whole top floor, still
securely locked by the police, had assumed some of the terrifying
potency of a child's fairy-tale, Bluebeard's lair, the forbidden territory
of horror. She hadn't seen Gerard Etienne's body but in imagination it
shone with the vivid imagery of a dream. Sometimes before sleep she
would picture the two bodies there together, Miss Clements lying in her
sad decrepitude; the half-naked male body sprawled on the floor beside
her, would watch terrified while the dull and lifeless eyes blinked and
brightened and the snake pulsated into slimy life, red tongue darting
to find the dead mouth, the muscles tightening to squeeze out breath.
But these imaginings, she knew, were still controllable. Secure in the
knowledge of her own innocence, never feeling herself seriously at risk,
she could enjoy the half-guilty exhilaration of simulated terror. But she
knew that Innocent House was contaminated with a fear which went
beyond her self-indulgent imaginings. She would begin to smell the
fear like a river fog as she dismounted from her bike in the mornings,
and it strengthened and engulfed her as she stepped over the portal.
She saw fear in George's anxious gaze as he greeted her, in Miss
Blackett's taut face and restless eyes, in Mr. Dauntsey's steps as, suddenly
an old man, all vigour drained, he drew himself painfully up the stairs.
She heard fear in the voices of all the partners.

On the Wednesday morning, just before ten o'clock, Miss Claudia
had summoned the staff to a meeting in the boardroom. They had all
been there, even George, his switchboard left on the answerphone, and
Fred Bowling from the launch. Chairs had been brought in to form a
half-circle and the other three partners had sat at the table, Miss Claudia
with Miss Peverell on her right and Mr. de Witt and Mr. Dauntsey on
her left. When the call to the meeting came, Miss Blackett had put
down the telephone and said, "You, too, Mandy. You're one of us now,"
and Mandy, despite herself, had felt a small surge of gratification. They
had seated themselves a little self-consciously, filling the second row
first, and Mandy had been aware of the collected weight of excitement,
anticipation and anxiety.

When the last arrival scurried red-faced to her chair in the front
row and the door was closed, Miss Claudia said: "Where is Mrs. Demery?"

It was Miss Blackett who answered. "Perhaps she thought she wasn't included."

"Everyone is included. Find her, will you please, Blackie."

Miss Blackett hurried out and, within a couple of minutes during which the meeting waited in total silence, reappeared with Mrs. Demery, still wearing her apron. She opened her mouth as if to make some derogatory comment, then, obviously thinking better of it, closed it and took the only remaining chair, in the middle of the front row.

Miss Claudia spoke: "First of all I would like to thank you all for your loyalty. My brother's death and the method of it has been a horrible shock for us all. This is a difficult time for Peverell Press, but I hope and believe that we shall come through it together. We have a responsibility to our authors and to the books which they expect us to publish to the same high standard that has characterized the Peverell Press for over two hundred years. I have now been informed of the result of the inquest. My brother died of carbon-monoxide poisoning, obviously from the gas fire in the little archives room. Precisely how that death occurred the police aren't yet able to say. I know that Commander Dalgliesh or one of his officers has already spoken to all of you. There will probably be continued interviews and I know that all of you will do what you can to help the police in their enquiries, as shall we the partners.

"A word about the future. You have probably heard rumours about plans to sell Innocent House and move down-river. All those plans are now in abeyance. Things will continue as they are, at least until the end of the financial year next April. Much will depend on the success of our autumn list and on how well we do over Christmas. The list is particularly strong this year and we are all optimistic. But I have to tell you that there is no prospect of anyone getting a rise in pay during the rest of this year and all the partners have agreed to take a 10 per-cent cut. There will be no more changes in the present staff, at least until next April, but inevitably there will have to be some reorganization: I shall be taking over as chairman and managing director, at first in an acting capacity. This means that I shall be responsible for production, accounts and the warehouse as was my brother. Miss Peverell will take over my present responsibilities as sales-and-publicity director, and Mr. de Witt with Mr. Dauntsey will add contracts and rights to their editorial responsibilities. We have recruited Virginia Scott-Headley from Herne & Illingworth to assist Maggie in publicity. She is highly competent and experienced and she will also help with the spate of press and outside enquiries about my brother's death. George has been fielding most of it magnificently but when Miss Scott-Headley arrives all those calls will be directed to publicity. I don't think there is anything else I need to say except that Peverell Press is the oldest independent publisher in the country and all we partners are determined that it shall survive and flourish. That is all. Thank you for coming. Are there any questions?"

There was an embarrassed silence in which people seemed to be steeling themselves to speak. Miss Claudia had taken advantage of it to get up from the table and had quickly led the way from the room.

Afterwards, in the kitchen, making Miss Blackett's coffee, Mrs. Demery had been more forthcoming.

"They haven't a clue what to do, any of them. That was plain enough. Mr. Gerard could be a proper bastard but at least he knew what he wanted and how to get it. They won't be selling Innocent House, Miss Peverell saw to that, I suppose, and Mr. de Witt supported her. But if they don't sell the house, how are they going to keep it up? You tell me that. If people here have any sense they'll start putting out feelers for new jobs."

And now, alone in the office, tidying her desk, Mandy thought what a difference these extra sixty minutes made. Innocent House seemed suddenly to have emptied. As she mounted the staircase to the first-floor women's cloakroom, where she would change, her feet echoed eerily on the marble as if someone unseen was walking a little behind her. Pausing on the landing to look down over the balustrade, she saw the two globes of light at the foot of the stairs glowing like floating moons over a hall grown cavernous and mysterious. She hurried over her change, stuffing her office clothes into the tote bag, pulling over her head the short, multi-layered skirt in patchwork cotton with its matching top, pulling on her high glittering boots. Perhaps it was a pity to bike in them but they were tough enough and it was easier than carrying them in the pannier.

How quiet it was! Even the flush of the lavatory roared like an avalanche. It was comforting to see George, wearing his coat and old tweed hat, still behind the reception desk and locking away the three parcels awaiting collection in his security cupboard. The malicious prankster hadn't struck since the murder but the precautions were still in force.

Mandy said: "Isn't it funny how quiet the place is when people have left? Am I the last?"

"Just me and Miss Claudia. I'm on my way now. Miss Claudia will set the alarms."

They left together, George pulling the door firmly shut behind them. It had been a day of heavy and incessant rain, dancing on the marble forecourt, streaming against the windows, almost obscuring the grey swell of the river. But now the rain had stopped and in the gleam of George's rear-lights the cobbles of Innocent Passage shone like rows of newly peeled conkers. The air held the first raw bite of winter. Mandy's nose began to run and she rummaged in her bag for a scarf and her handkerchief. She waited to mount her bike until, with maddening slowness, George began reversing his old Metro down the passage. After a second's thought she ran to signal that Innocent Walk was clear. It always was clear, but George invariably reversed out as if the manoeuvre was his daily dice with death. After he had given a valedictory grateful wave and accelerated away she told herself that at least his job was safe now, and was glad. Mrs. Demery had told her that there were rumours that Mr. Gerard had planned to get rid of him.

Mandy wove in and out of the late commuter traffic with her usual expertise and a cheerful disregard for the occasional toots of affronted motorists, and it was little more than thirty minutes later when she saw before her the mock-Tudor façade of the White Horse festooned with coloured lights. It stood back from the road on a hundred-yard stretch where the lines of suburban houses gave way to a fringe of shrubs and bushes on the edge of Epping Forest. The forecourt was already closely packed with cars, including, she saw, the band's van and Maureen's Fiesta. She rode slowly to the smaller parking space at the rear of the pub and, pulling her tote bag from the pannier, pushed her way down the passage to the women's cloakroom and joined the noisy chaos of girls hanging up coats and changing their shoes under a notice reminding them that these were left at their own risk, queuing for one of the four lavatories and spreading their make-up clobber on to the narrow shelf under the long mirror. It was when she had fought for her place and was rummaging for the plastic toilet bag which held her make-up that Mandy made the heart-lurching discovery. Her purse was missing: the black leather purse which was also a wallet, and held her money, her one credit card and bank card, prized symbols of financial status, and the Yale key to her front door. Her noisy exclamations of dismay alerted Maureen from her careful application of eye-liner.

"Tip everything out. I always do," she advised, and returned unworried to the task of outlining her eyelids with black.

"Fat lot she cares," murmured Mandy, sweeping Maureen's make-up to one side and emptying the tote bag's contents. But the purse wasn't there. And then she remembered. She must have caught it up with her scarf and handkerchief on leaving Innocent House. It was probably lying there still on the cobbles. She would have to go back. The consolation was that there was little chance that a passer-by could have found it. Innocent Walk, and Innocent Lane in particular, were always deserted after dark. It would mean missing the meal, but, with luck, not more than half an hour of the gig.

And then a thought struck her. She could telephone Mr. Dauntsey or Miss Peverell. At least that way she would know whether the purse was there. They might think she had a cheek to ask, but she was confident that neither of them would really mind. She had done very little work for Mr. Dauntsey or Miss Peverell, but when she had, both had seemed grateful and been decent to her. It would only take them a minute to look, a few yards to walk. And it wasn't as if it was still raining. It was a nuisance about the key. If the purse was there it would be too late to call for it after the gig. She would have to go home with Maureen or, if Maureen had other plans for the night, wake up Shirl or Pete. But they could hardly complain; she'd been woken up to let them in often enough.

There was a delay while she coaxed the necessary coins for a call box from Maureen, more delay while she waited for one of the two telephone booths to be free and another minute wasted when she discovered that the directory she needed was in the other booth. She rang Miss Peverell first, but got only the answerphone with its usual message, spoken in Miss Peverell's quiet, almost apologetic voice. There was very little space to manage the directory and it thudded to the floor. Outside a couple of impatient men gesticulated impatiently. Well, they would have to wait. If Mr. Dauntsey was in she wouldn't hang up until he'd been to look. She found the number and stabbed the digits. There was no reply. She let the ringing continue long after she had any real hope before replacing the receiver. And now she had no choice. She couldn't bear to spend the evening and night in suspense. She must go back to Innocent House.

She was riding now against the stream of traffic but was hardly aware of the details of the journey, her mind a muddle of anxiety, impatience and irritation. It wouldn't have hurt Maureen to have driven her to Wapping in the Fiesta, but trust Maureen not to miss the chance of a meal. She was becoming aware, too, of her own hunger but told herself that, with luck, she would have time to grab a sandwich from the bar before the gig.

Innocent Walk was, as usual, deserted. The back of Innocent House rose like a dark bastion against the night sky, then, as she looked up, her head flung back, became as insubstantial and unsteady as a cardboard cut-out, reeling against the low scudding clouds stained pink by the lights of the city. The pools in the gutter of the lane had dried now and a freshening breeze caught her at the end of Innocent Lane bringing with it the strong smell of the river. The only signs of life were the lit windows of the top flat at number 12. It looked as if Miss Peverell at least was now at home. She dismounted at the end of Innocent Lane, anxious not to disturb them with the sound of her bike, not wanting to be delayed by questions and explanations. She walked up the lane as delicately as a thief towards the shimmer of the river, to the place where she had parked the Yamaha. There was sufficient light from the lamps on the forecourt to aid her search, but no search was necessary. The purse lay exactly where she had hoped to find it. She gave a small, almost inaudible, whoop of delight and stuffed it deep into the zipped pocket of her jacket.

It was less easy to see the face of her watch, and she moved closer to the river. At each end of the forecourt the two great globes of light supported by bronze dolphins threw shining pools on the heaving surface of the water which as she watched shimmered like a great cloak of black satin, shaken, smoothed and gently billowed by an invisible hand. Mandy glanced at her watch: 8:20. It was later than she thought and suddenly she found her enthusiasm for the gig had waned. The surge of relief at finding her purse had induced a disinclination for further effort and in this mood of contented lethargy the prospect of the cosy claustrophobia of her bed-sitting-room, the kitchen to herself for once, the rest of the evening in front of the television, grew in attraction by the second. There was that video of the Scorsese *Cape Fear* which was due back tomorrow, £2 wasted if she didn't watch it tonight. Now in no hurry, she turned almost without thought to look up at the façade of Innocent House.

The bottom two storeys were faintly lit by the lights from the forecourt, the slender marble pillars gleaming softly against the dead windows, black cavernous openings into an interior which she now knew so well, but which had become mysterious and forbidding. How odd, she thought, that everything inside would be just as it was when she had left: the two word processors under their covers, Miss Blackett's neat desktop with her rack of filing trays, her diary placed precisely at her right hand, the locked cabinet of files, the noticeboard to the right of the door. All these ordinary things remained even when there was no one there to see them. And there was no one, no one at all. She thought of that small bare room at the top of the house, the room where two people had died. The chair and the table would still be in place, but there would be no bed, no woman's body, no naked man clawing at the bare boards. Suddenly she saw again Sonia Clements' body, but more real, more frightening than when she had seen it in the flesh. And then she remembered what Ken the packer had told her when she had taken a message to number 10 and had stayed gossiping, how Lady Sarah Peverell, wife of the Peverell who had built Innocent House, had thrown herself from the top balcony and smashed to death on the marble.

"You can still see the mark of the blood," Ken had said, shifting a box of books from the shelf to the trolley. "Don't let Miss Frances see you looking for it, though. That's not a story the family like to have told. But they can't clean that stain away for all that, and there'll be no luck in this house till they do. And she still walks, does Lady Sarah. You ask any waterman on the river."

Ken, of course, had been trying to frighten her, but that had been in late September, a day of mellow sunshine, and she had relished the story, only half believing it, feeling an agreeable shiver of self-induced fear. But she had asked Fred Bowling and she remembered his answer. "There are ghosts enough on this river, but none walk at Innocent House."

That was before the death of Mr. Gerard. Perhaps they walked now.

And now the fear was becoming real. She looked up at the top balcony and imaged the horror of that fall, the flailing limbs, the single cry—surely she must have cried out—the sickening crunch as the body hit the marble. Suddenly there was a wild scream and she started, but it was only a sea gull. The bird swooped above her, perched for a moment on the railings, then winged its way down-river.

She was aware that she was getting chilled. The cold was unnatural, seeping out from the marble as if she stood on ice, and the river breeze was colder now, blowing against her face with the first chill of winter. She was taking a last look at the river, glancing down to where the launch lay silent and empty, when her eyes caught a flash of something white at the top of the railings, to the right of the stone steps which led down to the Thames. It looked at first as if someone had tied a handkerchief to the rail. Curious, she walked across and saw that it was a sheet of paper rammed down onto one of the narrow spikes. And there was something else, a gleam of golden metal at the bottom of the rail. Squatting down, a little disorientated by self-induced fear, Mandy took some seconds to recognize it. It was the buckle of a narrow leather strap, the strap of a brown shoulder bag. The strap strained down to the puckered surface of the water, and beneath that surface something was just visible, something grotesque and unreal, like the domed head of a gigantic insect, its millions of hairy legs stirring gently in the tide. And then Mandy knew that what she was seeing was the top of a human head. At the end of the strap was a human body. And as she gazed down in horror the body shifted in the tide and a white hand rose slowly from the water, its wrist drooping like the stem of a dying flower.

For a few seconds disbelief fought with realization and then, half-fainting with shock and terror, she sank to her knees, clutching at the iron railings. She was aware of the cold metal rasping her hands and then the strength of it pressed against her forehead. She knelt there, powerless to move, terror squeezing at her stomach and turning her limbs to stone. In this cold nothingness only her heart was alive, a heart which had become a great ball of burning iron thudding against her ribs as if it could power her through the railings and into the river. She dared not open her eyes; to open them was to see what she could still only half believe: the double leather of the strap straining down to the abomination below.

She didn't know how long she knelt there before she was capable of sense and movement, but gradually she became aware of the strong river smell in her nostrils, the coldness of the marble against her knees, her quietening heart. Her hands were so rigid on the railings that it took painful seconds to prise the fingers away. She drew herself up and then suddenly found strength and purpose.

Running wordlessly across the courtyard, she banged on the first door, Dauntsey's, and pressed his bell. Above, the windows were dark and she wasted no time in waiting for the answer which she knew wouldn't come, but ran round the house into Innocent Walk and pressed Frances Peverell's bell, keeping her right thumb on the button while she hammered on the knocker with her left hand. The response was almost immediate. She couldn't hear the rush of feet on the stairs but the door was thrown open and she saw James de Witt with Frances Peverell at his shoulder. Incoherently she stammered, pointing towards the river, began running and was aware that they were on her heels. And now they were standing together looking down into the river. Mandy found herself thinking, I'm not mad. It wasn't a dream. It's still here.

She heard Miss Peverell say: "Oh no! Oh please God no!" Then she turned, half fainting, and was caught in James de Witt's arms, but not before Mandy had seen her make the sign of the cross.

He said: "It's all right, my darling, it's all right."

Her voice was half-muffled in his jacket. "It isn't all right. How can it be all right?" Then she broke free and said with surprising strength and calmness: "Who is it?"

De Witt didn't look again at the thing in the river. Instead, carefully, he prised the sheet of paper from the railing and peered at it. He said: "Esmé Carling. This looks like a suicide note."

Frances said: "Not again! Not another! What does it say?"

"It's not easy to see." He turned and held it so that the light from the globe at the end of the railings fell on the paper. There was almost no margin, as if the page had been trimmed to fit the words, and the sharp finial of the railing had pierced and torn the paper. He said: "It looks as if it's written in her own hand. It's addressed to all of us."

He smoothed it out and read aloud: " 'To the partners of Peverell Press. God rot you all! For thirty years you've exploited my talent, made money out of me, neglected me as a writer and as a woman, treated me as if my books aren't fit to bear your precious imprint. What do you know about creative writing? Only one of you has written a word and his talent, such as it was, died years ago. It's me, and writers like me, who have kept your house alive. And now you've thrown me over. After thirty years I'm finished, without explanation, without the right of appeal, without a chance to rewrite or revise. Finished. Dismissed, as the Peverells have casually dismissed their unwanted servants for generations. Don't you realize that this finishes me as a human being as well as a writer? Don't you know that when a writer can no longer be published she may as well be dead? But at least I can make your name stink throughout London, and believe me I shall. This is only the beginning.' "

Frances Peverell said: "Poor woman. Oh, poor woman. James, why didn't she come and see us?"

"Would that have done any good?"

"It's the same as Sonia. If it had to be done it could have been done differently, with compassion, with some kindness."

James de Witt said gently: "Frances, there's nothing we can do for her now. We'd better call the police."

"But we can't leave her like that! It's too horrible. It's obscene! We must pull her out—try artificial respiration."

He said patiently: "Frances, she's dead."

"But we can't leave her. Please, James, we must try."

It seemed to Mandy that they had forgotten she was there. Now that she was no longer alone the terrible paralysing fear had faded. The world had become, if not ordinary, at least familiar, manageable. She thought, He doesn't know what to do. He wants to please her but he doesn't want to touch the body. He can't pull it out by himself and can't bear for her to help. She said: "If you were going to try mouth-to-mouth breathing you ought to have pulled her out at once. It'll be too late now."

He said, it seemed to Mandy with a great sadness: "It was always too late. Anyway, the police won't want the body interfered with."

Interfered with? The words struck Mandy as funny. She fought an impulse to giggle, knowing that if she gave way to giggling she would end by crying. Oh God, she thought, why doesn't he bloody well do something?

She said: "If you two stay here I could ring the police. Give me the key and tell me where the phone is."

Frances said dully: "In the hall. And the door's open—at least I think it's open." She turned to de Witt, suddenly frantic: "Oh my God, James, have I locked us out?"

"No," he said patiently. "I've got the key. It was in the front door."

He was about to hand it to Mandy when their ears caught the sound of feet approaching down Innocent Lane and Gabriel Dauntsey and Sydney Bartrum appeared. They were both wearing raincoats and brought with them a sense of the reassuringly normal. Something about the three still figures, faces turned towards them, alerted them and their footsteps quickened to a run.

Dauntsey said: "We heard voices. Is something wrong?"

Mandy took the key but did not move. There was no hurry anyway; the police couldn't save Mrs. Carling. No one could help her now. And now two more faces were peering down, two more voices murmuring their horror.

De Witt said: "She's left a note. Here, on the railings. A fulmination against the whole lot of us."

Frances said again: "Please get her out."

And now it was Dauntsey who took control. Looking at him, at the skin which in the light of the globes was as sickly green as river weeds, at the lines scarring the face like black wounds, Mandy thought: He's an old, old man. This shouldn't happen to him. What can he do?

He said to de Witt, "You and Sydney could lift her using the steps. I haven't the strength."

His words galvanized James, who made no further objection but began walking carefully down the slimy steps, holding on to the railings. Mandy saw his involuntary shiver at the bite of the cold water on his legs. She thought, The best way would be for Mr. de Witt to support the body from the steps and Mr. Dauntsey and Mr. Bartrum to pull on

the strap, but they won't want to do it that way. And, indeed, the
thought of watching the drowned face rise slowly from the water while
the men pulled on the strap, as if deliberately hanging her again, was
so horrible that she wondered how the thought could have come into
her mind. Again it seemed to her that they had forgotten her presence.
Frances Peverell had moved a little apart, her hands grasping the
railings, her eyes fixed on the river. Mandy guessed a little of what she
was feeling. She wanted the body brought out of the water, the dreadful
strap removed; she needed to stay until that was done but she couldn't
bear to watch it happening. But, for Mandy, to look away was more
horrible than to watch. If she had to stay it was better to know than to
imagine. And of course she had to stay. No one had again taken up
her suggestion that she should take the key and ring the police. And
there was no hurry. What did it matter if they came later than sooner?
Nothing they brought with them, nothing they could do could revive
Mrs. Carling.

Now de Witt, descending gingerly, was in the water up to his knees.
With his right hand he grasped the bottom of the railings and, with his
left, he fumbled for the sodden clothing and began drawing the body
towards him. The surface of the river broke into ripples and the strap
slackened, then strained tight. He said: "If one of you could undo the
buckle I think I could get her onto the steps."

Dauntsey's voice was calm. He too was holding on to the railings as
if for support. "Don't let her drift away, James. And keep hold of the
railings. We don't want you in the river."

It was Bartrum who came down the first two steps and leaned over
to undo the buckle. His hands were pale in the light from the globes,
his fingers like swollen sausages. He took his time, fumbling, seeming
unaware how the buckle worked.

When at last it was released, de Witt said: "I'll need both hands.
Grasp hold of my jacket will you."

And now Dauntsey joined Bartrum on the second step. Together
they steadied and held tightly to de Witt's jacket while with both hands
he drew the body towards him and released the strap from the neck.
And now it lay sprawled face-downwards on the steps. De Witt took it
by the legs, which stuck out from the skirt like thin sticks, and Bartrum
and Dauntsey each took an arm. The sodden bundle was lifted up the
steps and laid prone on the marble. Gently de Witt turned it over.
Mandy had only one glimpse of the face, terrible in death, of the open
mouth and protruding tongue, the eye half-opened under the crêped
lids, the dreadful purple stigma round her throat, before Dauntsey,

with surprising speed, whipped off his coat and laid it over the body. From beneath the tweed a trickle of water, thin at first, then stronger, crept over the marble, as dark as blood.

Frances Peverell walked over to the body and knelt beside it. She said, "Poor woman. Oh, poor woman," and Mandy saw her lips move silently and wondered if she were praying. They waited in silence, the harsh gasps of their breath sounding unnaturally loud on the quiet air. The effort of raising the body from the water seemed to have drained de Witt and Bartrum of strength and decision, and it was Gabriel Dauntsey who took control.

He said: "Someone had better stay by the body. Sydney and I will wait here. James, you take the women inside and phone the police. And we'll all need hot coffee, or something stronger, and plenty of it."

47

The front door of number 12 opened onto a narrow, rectangular hall and Mandy followed Frances Peverell and James de Witt up a flight of steep stairs carpeted in pale green. The staircase ended in another hall, squarer and larger with a door immediately ahead. Mandy found herself in a sitting-room which ran the whole length of the front of the house. The two tall windows leading to the balcony were curtained against the night and the river. There was a pile of smokeless coal in the basket by the grate. Mr. de Witt took away the brass fireguard and settled Mandy in one of the high-backed chairs. Suddenly they were as solicitous of her as if she were a guest, perhaps, she thought, because fussing over her at least gave them something to do.

Looking down at her, Miss Peverell said: "Mandy, I'm so very sorry. Two suicides and you found them both. First Miss Clements and now this. What can we give you? Coffee? Brandy? Or there's red wine. But I don't suppose you've eaten, have you? Are you hungry?"

"I am rather."

She was, in fact, suddenly ravenous for food. The warm savoury smell pervading the flat was almost intolerable. Miss Peverell looked at Mr. de Witt. She said: "We were going to have duck à l'orange. What about you, James?"

"I'm not hungry but I'm sure Mandy is."

Mandy thought, She's only got enough for two. Probably bought it from M & S. All right for those who can afford it! Miss Peverell had planned a cosy intimate dinner. And trouble, she saw, had been taken. A round table at the far end of the room had been set with white linen, three sparkling glasses at each setting and a couple of low silver candlesticks with the candles still unlit. Moving closer, she saw the salad had already been set out in small wooden bowls, delicate leaves in a variety of green and red, small toasted nuts, slivers of cheese. There was an open bottle of red wine and one of white in a wine cooler. Mandy had no appetite for the salad. What she craved was hot and savoury food.

She could see, too, that Miss Peverell had taken trouble with more than the meal. The blue-green patterned dress with its pleated skirt and over-blouse tied with a bow at the side was real silk and it suited her colouring. Too old for her, of course, too conventional, a bit dull, and the skirt too long. It didn't do much for her figure, which could have looked spectacular if Miss Peverell knew how to dress. The pearls gleaming against the silk were probably real. Mandy hoped Mr. de Witt appreciated the efforts made for him. Mrs. Demery had told her that he had been in love with Miss Peverell for years. Now, with Mr. Gerard out of the way, it looked as if he was getting somewhere at last.

The duck came served with peas and small new potatoes. Mandy, her social insecurity swept away in a surge of hunger, fell upon it ravenously. They sat at the table with her. Neither ate but they both drank a glass of red wine. They waited on her with anxious care as if they felt somehow responsible for what had happened and were trying to make amends. Miss Peverell pressed her to a second helping of vegetables and Mr. de Witt filled her glass. From time to time they went out together into the room she guessed was the kitchen and which overlooked Innocent Passage and she could hear the subdued mutter of their voices and knew that they were saying things they didn't want to say in her presence while watching and listening for the arrival of the police.

Their temporary absence gave her an opportunity to look more closely at the room as she ate. Its elegant simplicity was too formal, too conventional for Mandy's more eccentric and iconoclastic taste, but she admitted to herself that it looked all right if this was the kind of thing you liked and had the money to afford. The colour scheme was conventional enough, soft blue-green with touches of rose red. The curtains of draped satin hung from simple poles. At each side of the fireplace was an alcove fitted with bookshelves, the spines of the books gleaming in the firelight. On each top shelf was what looked like the marble head of a girl crowned with roses and closely veiled. They were probably meant to be brides but the veils, marvellously delicate and realistic, looked more like shrouds. Morbid, thought Mandy, cramming her mouth with duck. The picture over the mantelpiece was of an eighteenth-century mother holding her two daughters and was obviously original, as was a curious picture of a woman lying in bed in a room which reminded Mandy of her schoolgirl visit to Venice. The two winged armchairs, one on each side of the fire, were covered in plain linen in a faded pink, but only one chair, with its creased seat and back, looked as if it were much used. So that was where Miss Peverell sat, thought Mandy, facing an empty chair and beyond it the river. She supposed that the picture on the right-hand wall was an icon, but couldn't imagine why anyone should want a Virgin Mary who looked so old and black, or an adult-looking baby who obviously hadn't had a decent meal for weeks.

She envied neither the room nor anything in it and thought with satisfaction of the large low attic which was her share of the rented house in Stratford East: the wall opposite the bed with her hats hung on a peg board, in a riotous flowering of ribbon, flowers and coloured felt; the single bed, just wide enough for two when a boyfriend occasionally spent the night, covered with its striped blanket; the drawing board which she used for her designs, the bean-bag cushions which littered the floor, the hi-fi and television and the deep cupboard which held her clothes. There was only one room which she longed for more.

Suddenly she paused, fork halfway to her mouth, and listened intently. Surely she could hear the grind of car-wheels on the cobbles. Seconds later James and Frances returned from the kitchen.

James de Witt said: "The police have arrived. Two cars. We couldn't see how many people they've brought." He turned to Frances Peverell, sounding for the first time uncertain, needing reassurance. "I wonder if I ought to go down."

"Oh surely not. They won't want anyone extra there. Gabriel and Sydney can give them the facts. Anyway, I expect they'll come up here when they've finished. They'll want to talk to Mandy. She is the most important witness. She was there first." She sat down again at the table and said gently: "I expect you're longing to get home, Mandy, and Mr. de Witt or I will take you later, but I think you ought to stay until the police come."

It had never occurred to Mandy to do otherwise. She said: "That's OK by me. They'll think I'm bad luck, won't they? Everywhere I go I find a suicide."

The words were only half in earnest, but to her surprise Miss Peverell cried out: "Don't say that, Mandy! You mustn't even think like that. That's just superstition. Of course no one will think you're bad luck! Look, Mandy, I don't like to think of you being on your own tonight. Would you like to telephone your parents—your mother? Wouldn't it be better to go home tonight? She could come here to collect you."

Like a bloody parcel, thought Mandy. She said: "I don't know where she is," and was tempted to add, "You could always try the Red Cow at Hayling Island."

But the words and the kindness that prompted them touched in her a previously unacknowledged need for female comfort, for the cosiness of that upstairs room off the Whitechapel Road. She wanted to smell the familiar frowst compounded of drink and Mrs. Crealey's scent, to curl up in front of the gas fire in the low chair which enclosed her like a womb, to hear outside the comforting rumble of the traffic on Whitechapel Road. She wasn't at ease in this elegant flat, and these people, for all their kindness, weren't her people. She wanted Mrs. Crealey.

She said: "I could telephone the agency. Mrs. Crealey might still be there."

Frances Peverell looked surprised, but led Mandy upstairs into her bedroom. She said, "It will be more private for you here, Mandy, and there's a bathroom next door if you need it."

The telephone was on the bedside table and above it hung a crucifix. Mandy had seen crucifixes before, usually outside churches, but this one was different. The Christ, almost beardless, looked very young and his head, instead of drooping in death, was flung back, the mouth wide as if he were crying for vengeance or pity to his God. Mandy thought it was not the kind of object she would like to find hanging beside her bed, but she knew that it had power. Religious people prayed before a crucifix and if they were lucky their prayers were answered. It was worth a try. Punching out Mrs. Crealey's office number, she made herself gaze hard at the silver figure crowned with its bush of thorns and soundlessly formed the words: "Please make her answer, please let her be there. Please make her answer, please let her be there." But the telephone continued its intermittent ring and there was no reply.

Less than five minutes later the doorbell rang. James de Witt went down and came back with Dauntsey and Bartrum.

Frances Peverell said: "What's happening, Gabriel? Is Commander Dalgliesh there?"

"No, just Inspector Miskin and Inspector Aaron. Oh, and there's that young detective sergeant and a photographer. They're waiting now for the police surgeon to arrive and certify that she's dead."

Frances cried: "But of course she's dead! They don't need a police surgeon to tell them that."

"I know, Frances, but it's normal procedure apparently. No, I won't have any wine, thank you. Sydney and I have been drinking at the Sailor's Return since half past seven."

"Coffee then. What about coffee? You too, Sydney?"

Sydney Bartrum seemed embarrassed. He said: "No thank you, Miss Peverell. I really have to go. I told my wife that I was meeting Mr. Dauntsey for a quick drink and would be a little late, but I'm always home before ten."

"Of course you must go. She'll be getting worried. Ring her from here."

"Yes, I think I'd better. Thank you." He followed her out of the room.

De Witt asked: "How are they taking it—the police I mean?"

"Professionally. How else would they take it? They aren't saying much. I got the impression they were none too pleased that we'd moved the body, or even read the note for that matter."

De Witt poured himself another glass of wine.

"What the hell did they expect us to do? And the note was addressed to us. If we hadn't read it, I wonder if they would have told us what it said? They've been keeping us pretty much in the dark about Gerard's death."

Gabriel said: "They'll be up here as soon as the van comes to take her away." He paused, and then added: "I think I may have seen her arriving. Sydney and I agreed to be at the Sailor's Return at half past seven and when I reached Wapping Way I saw a taxi turning into Innocent Walk."

"Did you see the passenger?"

"I wasn't really close enough. I probably wouldn't have noticed her anyway. But I did see the driver. He was large and black. The police think that will be helpful in tracing him. Black drivers are still in a minority."

Bartrum had made his call and now returned. He said with his usual nervous clearing of his throat: "Well, I'd better be off. Thank you, Miss Peverell, I won't stay for coffee. I want to get home. The police have said I needn't stay. I've told them all I know, that I was with Mr. Dauntsey in the pub from seven-thirty. If they want me again I'll be in the office tomorrow morning. Business as usual."

The false jauntiness of his voice disconcerted them. For a moment, looking up from her meal, Mandy thought that he was going to shake hands all round. Then he turned and left, and Frances Peverell went to show him out. It seemed to Mandy that they were all glad to be rid of him.

An uneasy silence fell; ordinary conversation, the small talk of a dinner party, chat about work, all seemed inappropriate, almost indecent. Innocent House and the horror of death were all they had in common. Mandy sensed that they would have been more at ease without her, that the bonds of shared shock and terror were loosening and that they were reminding themselves that she was only the temporary shorthand-typist, Mrs. Demery's companion in gossip, that the whole story would be round Innocent House next day and the less said by them now the better.

From time to time one of them went to telephone Claudia Etienne. From their brief subsequent conversations Mandy gathered that she wasn't at home. There was another number they could try but James de Witt said: "Better leave it. We'll get her later. There's nothing she can do here anyway."

And now Frances and Gabriel went out to make coffee and this time James stayed with Mandy. He asked where she lived and she told him. He said he didn't think she ought to go back to an empty house. Would there be anyone at home when she got there? Mandy, lying to save explanations and trouble, said that there would. After that he seemed unable to think of a further question and they sat in silence, listening to the small sounds from the kitchen. Mandy thought that it was like waiting in hospital for some dreaded news, as she had with her mum when her gran underwent her last operation. They had waited in a sparsely furnished, anonymous room in uncompanionable silence, perched on the edge of their chairs, feeling as ill at ease as if they had no right to be there, knowing that somewhere out of sight and sound the experts in life and death were going about their mysterious business while they themselves were powerless to do anything but wait. And this time the wait was not long. They had hardly finished their coffee when they heard the expected ring on the front door. Less than a minute later Inspector Miskin and Inspector Aaron were with them. They were both carrying what looked like large attaché cases. Mandy wondered if these were their murder bags.

Inspector Miskin said: "We'll talk at greater length after we've got the results of the PM. There are just a few questions now. Who found her?"

"I did," said Mandy, and wished she wasn't still sitting at the table with the smeared and empty plate in front of her. There seemed something indecent in this evidence of appetite. And why ask anyway, she thought with a spurt of resentment, you know bloody well by now who found her.

"What were you doing here? It was late to be working." It was Inspector Aaron who spoke.

"I wasn't working." Mandy was aware that her voice was sulky and took herself in hand. Briefly she described the events of her ill-fated evening.

Inspector Miskin asked: "When you found your purse where you expected, what made you go to the river?"

"How do I know? Because it was there I suppose." She added: "I wanted to look at my watch. It was lighter by the river."

"And you saw and heard no one else either then or when you arrived?"

"Look, if I had I'd have said so by now. I didn't see anyone or hear anything except the paper on the railings. So I went over to take a look, and that's when I saw the shoulder-bag lying on the ground at the foot of the railings and the straps going down into the river. When I looked down I saw what was at the end of the strap, didn't I?"

Frances Peverell broke in quietly. "It's human instinct to go to see the river, particularly at night. I always do when I'm near. Does Miss Price have to answer any more questions now? She's told you all she knows. She ought to be at home. She's had a terrible experience."

Inspector Aaron didn't look at her, but Inspector Miskin spoke, and more gently. "Do you know what time you arrived back at Innocent House?"

"Eight-twenty. I looked at my watch when I got to the river."

Inspector Aaron said: "It was a longish way to come back from the White Horse. Didn't you think of ringing Miss Peverell or Mr. Dauntsey and asking them to look for the purse?"

"I did. There was no reply from Mr. Dauntsey and Miss Peverell had the answerphone on."

Frances Peverell said: "I do that sometimes if I have a visitor. James arrived by taxi just after seven, and I suppose Mr. Dauntsey was at the Sailor's Return with Sydney Bartrum."

"So he has already told us. Did either of you see or hear anything unusual, any sound from Innocent Lane, for example?"

They looked at each other. Frances Peverell said: "I don't think we'd hear footsteps on the cobbles, not from this room. I was in the kitchen briefly at about eight to prepare the salads. I always do that at the last moment. The kitchen window overlooks Innocent Lane, and I would have heard a taxi then if it had set her down at the usual door to Innocent House. I heard nothing."

James de Witt said: "I didn't hear a taxi, and neither Miss Peverell nor I saw or heard anyone or anything in Innocent Lane after my arrival. There were the usual sounds from the river, but muted by the curtains. I think there was a certain amount of noise earlier in the evening but I can't remember when. It certainly wasn't unusual enough to cause us to go out on the balcony and see what was happening. One gets used to noises on the river."

Inspector Aaron spoke: "How did you get here tonight, sir, by car?"

"By taxi. I don't drive in London. I ought to have said earlier that I came from home. I wasn't in the office this afternoon. I had a dental checkup."

Suddenly Frances Peverell said: "What was in her bag? It looked heavy."

Inspector Miskin said: "It is heavy. This is why."

She took the plastic bag from Inspector Aaron and tipped out the shoulder-bag onto the table.

They watched while she undid the straps. The manuscript was bound in a pale-blue manila cover with the name of the novel and of the author in capitals: DEATH ON PARADISE ISLAND BY ESMÉ CARLING. And written across the cover in thick red ink were scrawled the words "REJECTED—AND AFTER THIRTY YEARS" followed by three huge exclamation marks.

Frances Peverell said: "So she brought that with her as well as the suicide note. We're all a little to blame. We should have acted with more kindness. But to kill herself . . . And to do it like that. The loneliness, and the horror. Poor woman."

She turned away, and James de Witt moved closer to her but didn't touch her. He said, turning to Inspector Miskin: "Look, do we have to talk any more tonight? We're all in shock, and it's not as if there's any doubt."

Inspector Miskin replaced the manuscript in the bag. She said quietly: "There is always doubt until we know the facts. When did Miss Carling learn that the firm had rejected her novel?"

James de Witt replied: "*Mrs.* Carling. She's a widow. She divorced some time ago and her husband died since. She knew the morning Gerard Etienne died. She came into the office to see him but we were at the board meeting and she had to leave for a book signing at Cambridge. But you know all that."

"The signing that was cancelled before she arrived?"

"Yes, that signing."

"And has she been in touch with either of you since Mr. Etienne's death or with anyone at the firm as far as you know?"

Again de Witt and Frances Peverell looked at each other. De Witt said: "Not with me. Has she been in touch with you, Frances?"

"No, not a word. It's rather odd when you come to think of it. If only we'd been able to talk, to explain, this might not have happened."

It was Inspector Aaron who suddenly broke the silence. He said: "Who was it who decided to pull her out of the river?"

"I did." Frances Peverell turned on him her mild but reproachful look.

"You surely didn't think you'd be able to resuscitate her?"

"No, I don't think I thought that, but it was so terrible to see her hanging there. So . . ." She paused and then said, "So inhuman."

De Witt said: "We're not all police officers, Inspector, some of us still have human instincts."

Inspector Aaron flushed, glanced at Inspector Miskin and with difficulty controlled his temper.

Inspector Miskin said quietly: "Let us hope you manage to retain them. I expect Miss Price would like to go home now. Inspector Aaron and I will drive her."

Mandy said with the obstinacy of a child: "I don't want to be driven. I want to go home by myself on the bike."

Frances Peverell said gently: "Your bike will be perfectly safe here, Mandy. If you like we could lock it in the garage at number ten."

"I don't want to leave it in the garage. I want to ride home on it."

In the end she had her way, but Inspector Miskin insisted on the police car driving behind her. Mandy took some pleasure in weaving in and out of the traffic and making it as difficult as possible for them to keep up with her.

When they got to her house on Stratford High Street, Inspector Miskin, looking up at the darkened windows, said: "I thought you said there would be someone at home."

"There is someone at home. They're all in the kitchen. Look, I can look after myself. I'm not a kid, OK? Just get off my back, will you?"

She dismounted and Inspector Aaron got out of the car and helped her lift the Yamaha through the front door and into the hall. Without a word she shut the door firmly after him.

48

Daniel said: "It wouldn't have hurt her to say thank you. She's a tough cookie, that one."

"She's in shock."

"Not so shocked she couldn't eat her dinner."

Wapping Police Station was quiet and they saw only one officer as they mounted the stairs to the incident room. They stood for a moment at the window before drawing the curtains. The clouds had lifted now, and the river flowed wide and calm, bearing its patterns and swirls of light under the prickling of high stars. But there was always an unnatural sense of peace and isolation in a station at night. Even when it was busy, and the calm momentarily broken by loud male voices and heavy footfalls, the air held a peculiar stillness, as if the world outside with its violence, its terrors, could lie in wait but had no power to disturb that essential tranquillity. There was, too, a deepening comradeship; colleagues talked less often but more freely. But they could expect no comradeship at Wapping. Kate knew that they were to an extent intruders. The police station was offering them hospitality, affording them all the facilities they needed, but they were still outsiders.

Dalgliesh was visiting the Durham Constabulary on some mysterious business of the Commissioner, and she didn't know whether he had yet left for London. She put through her call and was told that he was thought to be still there. They would make an attempt to find him and ask him to ring back.

While waiting, she said: "You were sure of her alibi? Esmé Carling's, I mean. She was at home the night Etienne died?"

Daniel seated himself at his desk and began playing with the computer. He said, trying to keep the irritation from his voice: "Yes, I'm sure. You've read my report. She was with the kid, Daisy Reed, from the same block of flats. They were together the whole evening and until midnight or after. The kid confirmed it. I wasn't incompetent, if that's what you're suggesting."

"I'm not. Cool it, Daniel. But she was never really a suspect, was she? The blocked flue, the frayed cord—it all needed too much advance planning. We never saw her as a possible murderess."

"So you're suggesting that I was too easily satisfied?"

"No, I'm just checking that you were satisfied."

"Look, I went with Robbins and a WPC from the Juvenile Bureau. I interviewed Esmé Carling and the kid separately. They were together that night, most nights if it comes to that. The mother would be out at her job—stripping, or night-clubbing, or a spot of prostitution, or whatever—and the kid would wait until she'd gone, then sneak off and spend the evening with Carling. Apparently it suited them both. I checked on every detail of that Thursday night and their accounts tallied. The kid didn't want to admit she'd been with Carling at first. She was a bit scared that her mother would stop the arrangement or that the Juvenile Bureau would get in touch with Social Services and she'd end in care. They did of course—get in touch with Social Services, I mean. They could hardly do anything else, given the circumstances. The kid was telling the truth. Why the doubt anyway?"

"But it's odd, isn't it? Here you have a woman whose book has been turned down after thirty years. She comes roaring in fury to Innocent House to have it out with Gerard Etienne. She's prevented from seeing him because he's in a board meeting. Then she goes off to do a signing and discovers on arrival that someone from Innocent House has cancelled it. By then I imagine she was incoherent with rage. So what would you expect her to do? Go home quietly and write a letter or storm back that evening to confront Etienne? She probably knew that he worked late on Thursdays. Nearly everyone concerned with Innocent House seems to have known that. And her behaviour since is odd too. She knew that Gerard Etienne was the one principally responsible for rejecting the manuscript. Now Gerard Etienne is dead. So why didn't she come back and make another attempt to get the book accepted?"

"She probably knew that it wouldn't be any use. The partners wouldn't like to reverse a decision of Etienne's so soon after his death. Anyway, they probably agreed with it."

Kate went on: "And there are several odd things about tonight, aren't there? Frances Peverell and de Witt would almost certainly have heard the taxi if it had come up Innocent Lane to the usual entrance. So where exactly did she ask to be dropped?"

"Probably somewhere in Innocent Walk, then she went on foot to the river. She knew that a taxi might be heard on the cobbles of Innocent Lane either by Dauntsey or Miss Peverell. Or she may have been dropped at the end of Innocent Passage. That's the access closest to where she was found."

"But the gate at the end of the passage is locked. If she got to the river that way, then who opened the gate for her and locked it again? And what about the message? Did it really read to you like a suicide note?"

"It's not typical, perhaps; but, then, what is a typical suicide note? A jury wouldn't have much difficulty in convincing themselves that it's genuine."

"And written when?"

"I suppose just before she killed herself. It's hardly the kind of thing you concoct in advance and keep handy in case you should suddenly need it."

"Then why no mention of Gerard Etienne's death? She must have known that he was chiefly responsible for rejecting her novel. Well, of course she knew. Mandy Price and Miss Blackett have both described how she burst into the office to see him. Surely his death must have made a difference to how she felt about Peverell Press. And even if it didn't—if she still felt the same bitterness—isn't it odd that the note doesn't even mention his death?"

Then the telephone rang and Dalgliesh was on the line. Kate gave her report clearly and concisely, explaining that they hadn't been able to contact Doc Wardle, who was out on a case, but hadn't tried to find a substitute since the body had been moved. It was now at the mortuary. It seemed to Daniel that she listened for a long time without speaking, except for an occasional "Yes sir."

Eventually she put down the receiver. She said: "He's flying back tonight. We're not to interview anyone at Innocent House until we get the results of the PM. They can wait. Tomorrow you're to try and trace the taxi and check whether anyone on the river that night saw anything, including any boat party who passed between seven o'clock and the time before Mandy found the body. We've got the keys to Carling's flat from her bag and apparently there's no next-of-kin, so we're going there tomorrow morning. It's in Hammersmith. Mount Eagle Mansions. He wants Mrs. Carling's agent to meet us there at eleven-thirty. First thing tomorrow he and I are going to reinterview Daisy Reed. And there's something else. Damn it, Daniel, we should have thought of it ourselves. AD wants the scene-of-crime officers here first thing tomorrow to examine the launch. The Peverell Press will have to make other arrangements to collect their staff from Charing Cross. God I feel such a bloody fool. AD must be wondering if we ever see ahead further than our own noses."

"So he thinks she used the launch to string herself up. It would certainly have been easier."

"Carling used it—or someone else."

"But the launch was tied up in its usual place on the other side of the steps."

"Exactly. So, if it was used, then someone moved it before and after she died. Prove that and we're getting closer to proving that this was murder."

49

By ten o'clock Gabriel Dauntsey had gone down to let himself into his own flat and James de Witt and Frances were alone. Both realized that they were hungry. Mandy had finished both portions of the duck but neither would have felt equal to its richness. They were in the uncomfortable state of needing food but without being able to think of anything they actually wanted to eat. In the end Frances cooked a large herb omelette and they shared it with more pleasure than either would have thought possible. As if by an unspoken agreement they said little about Esmé Carling's death.

Before Dauntsey left Frances had said: "We're all responsible, aren't we? None of us really stood up to Gerard. We ought to have insisted on a discussion about Esmé's future. Someone should have seen her, talked to her."

James had said gently: "Frances, we couldn't have published that book. I don't mean because it was a commercial book, we need popular fiction. But it was bad popular fiction. It was a bad book."

And Frances had replied: "A bad book? The ultimate crime, the sin against the Holy Ghost. Well, she's certainly paid highly for it."

The bitterness, the irony had surprised him. The comment had been so unlike her. But she had lost some of her old gentleness and passivity since the break-up with Gerard. He saw the change with a tinge of regret, but recognized that this was one more manifestation of his recurrent psychological need to search out and love the vulnerable, the innocent, the hurt and the weak, to give rather than to receive. He knew that it didn't make for an equal relationship, that a constant uncritical kindness could in its subtle condescension be as oppressive to the loved one as cruelty or neglect. Was this how he bolstered his ego, by the knowledge that he was needed, depended upon, admired for a compassion which when he looked at it with honest eyes was a particularly subtle form of emotional patronage and spiritual pride? Was he any better than Gerard, for whom sex was part of his personal power game and who got a kick out of seducing a devout virgin because he knew that, for her, surrender had been a mortal sin? He had always loved Frances, he still loved her. He wanted her in his life, in his house, in his bed, as well as in his heart. Perhaps it was possible now that they could love on equal terms.

Tonight he was reluctant to leave her but there was no choice. Rupert's buddy, Ray, had to leave by 11:30 and Rupert was too ill to be alone even for a few hours. And there was another difficulty. He felt that he could hardly suggest that he should spend the night in her spare room without presumption. She might, after all, prefer to confront her private demons alone rather than have the inconvenience of his presence. And there was something more. He wanted to make love to her but it was too important to happen because shock and grief had made her vulnerable so that she came to his bed not from an equal desire but from the need to be comforted. He thought: What a mess we're all in. How hard it is to know ourselves and, when we do, how difficult to change.

But the problem solved itself when he said: "Are you sure you'll be all right alone, Frances?"

She said firmly: "Of course I shall. Anyway Rupert needs you at home. There's Gabriel downstairs if I need company, but I shan't need company. I'm used to being alone, James."

She rang for a taxi and he took the quickest way home, paying off the cab at the Bank and taking the Central Line to Notting Hill Gate.

He saw the ambulance as soon as he turned out of Hillgate Street. His heart jolted. Breaking into a run, he saw that the paramedics were already carrying Rupert down the front steps in a chair-stretcher. Nothing could be seen of him but his face above the blanket, a face which, even now, in the extremity of weakness and stripped for death, had never for James lost its beauty. Watching the two men as they manoeuvred the stretcher with experienced hands, it seemed to him that it was his own arms that could feel the unbearable lightness of their burden.

He said: "I'll come with you."

But Rupert shook his head. "Better not. They don't want too many people in the ambulance. Ray will come."

Ray said: "That's right. I'm going with him."

They were anxious to get off. Already there were two cars waiting to pass. He climbed into the ambulance and gazed wordlessly into Rupert's face.

Rupert said: "Sorry about the mess in your sitting-room. I won't be coming back. You'll be able to tidy up and invite Frances now without either of you feeling the need to sterilize all the crockery."

James said: "Where are they taking you? The hospice?"

"No, the Middlesex."

"I'll come and see you tomorrow."

"Better not."

Ray was already sitting in the ambulance solidly and comfortably as if it were his rightful place. And it was his rightful place. And now Rupert was speaking again. James bent to hear him. He said: "That story, about Gerard Etienne. About me and Eric. You didn't believe it?"

"Yes Rupert, I did believe it."

"It wasn't true. How could it be? It was a nonsense. Surely you know about incubation periods? You believed it because you needed to. Poor James! How you must have hated him. Don't look like that. Don't look so appalled."

It seemed to James that he had no voice. And when he did speak the words horrified him by their banal futility. "You'll be all right, Rupert?"

"Yes, I shall be all right. I shall be finally all right. Don't worry and don't visit. Remember what G. K. Chesterton said. 'We must learn to love life without ever trusting it.' I never have."

He had no memory of climbing down from the ambulance but he heard the soft slam of the double doors as they were closed firmly in his face. In seconds it had turned the corner but he stood for a long time looking after it, as if it was travelling on a long straight road and he could watch it out of sight.

50

Mount Eagle Mansions, close to Hammersmith Bridge, revealed itself as a large red-brick Victorian block with the shabby uncared-for look of a building languishing between owners. The huge over-embellished Italianate porch, its stucco beginning to crumble, was at odds with the plain façade and gave the block an air of eccentric ambiguity as if the architect had been prevented by the failure of inspiration or money from completing his original design. Judging from the porch, Kate thought this was perhaps fortunate. But the inhabitants had obviously not given up hope of preserving the value of their property. The windows, at least at ground-floor level, were clean, the varied curtains hung in regular folds and a few of the window-sills had been fitted with boxes from which ivy and trailing geraniums hung against the grimy bricks. The letter-box and door-knocker in the form of an immense lion's head were polished to whiteness and there was a large rush mat, obviously new, with "Mount Eagle Mansions" woven into the bristles. To the right of the door was a row of doorbells, each with a name-card in the adjoining slot. The card for Flat 27, cut from a visiting card, read "Mrs. Esmé Carling" in an ornate script. The card for Flat 29 had the one word "Reed" in printed capitals. Kate's ring was answered after a few seconds by a female voice in which the tone of grudging resignation was clearly discerned above the crackle of the intercom.

"All right, come on up."

There was no lift, although the size of the tessellated hall suggested that one had originally been intended. Along one wall was a double row of post boxes, clearly numbered, and against the other a heavy mahogany table, its legs elaborately carved, holding a collection of circulars, re-addressed letters and a bundle of old papers tied with string. They were neatly arranged and above them swirls of dried soapy water showed that some attempt had been made to clean the paintwork, although the result had only been to emphasize the grime. The air smelled of furniture polish and disinfectant. Neither Kate nor Dalgliesh spoke, but as they mounted the stairs, past the heavy doors with their eye-holes and double security locks, Kate was aware of a rising excitement mixed with slight apprehension, and wondered whether this was shared by the quiet figure at her shoulder. This was an important interview. By the time they came down this stairway the case could be solved.

Kate was surprised that Esmé Carling couldn't afford something better than a flat in this unimpressive block. It was hardly a prestigious address at which to receive interviewers or journalists, assuming, of course, that she did receive them. But the little they knew of her didn't suggest a literary recluse and she was, after all, fairly well known. She, Kate, had heard of Esmé Carling even if she had never read her. That didn't, of course, mean that her income from writing was large; hadn't she read in some magazine article that, while a few very successful novelists were millionaires, the majority, even the well-regarded, had difficulty in living off their royalties. But her agent would be with them in an hour and there was little point in wasting time cogitating about Esmé Carling the crime writer when all the questions would so soon be answered by the person most qualified to know.

Dalgliesh had chosen to see Daisy even before he examined Mrs. Carling's flat and she thought she knew why. It was the child's information that was vital. Whatever secrets lay behind the door of number 27 could wait. The detritus of a murdered life told its own story. The evidence of the victim's pathetic leavings, letters, bills, could be misinterpreted but artefacts didn't lie, they didn't change their story, they didn't fabricate alibis. It was the living who must be interviewed while the shock of murder was still vivid in their minds. A good detective respected grief, sometimes shared it, but was never slow to exploit it, even the grief of a child.

They had reached the door, and before she could lift her hand to the bell Dalgliesh said: "You do the talking, Kate."

She replied, "Yes, sir," but her heart leapt. Two years ago she would almost have found herself praying, "Oh God, let me get this right"; now, more experienced, she was confident that she would.

She hadn't wasted time imagining what the child's mother, Shelley

Reed, looked like. In police work it was wise not to anticipate reality by premature and manufactured prejudice. But when the chain rasped back and the door was opened she had difficulty in concealing her initial look of surprise. It was hard to believe that this chubby-faced girl, staring at them with the sulky resentment of an adolescent, was the mother of a twelve-year-old. She could hardly have been more than sixteen when Daisy was born. Her face, naked of make-up, still held something of the unformed softness of childhood. The sulky mouth was very full and drooped at the corners. Her wide nose was pierced at one side with a glittering stud matching the studs in her small ears. Her hair, a bright yellow at odds with her heavy dark brows, hung in a fringe almost to her eyes and framed her face in crimped curls. Her eyes were widely spaced and set at an angle under lids so heavy that they looked swollen. Only her figure hinted at maturity. Heavy breasts swung loose under a long jersey of pristine white cotton and her long, well-shaped legs were ensconced in black tights. On her feet she wore house slippers embroidered with Lurex thread. Her hard uncompromising eyes changed as she saw Dalgliesh to a wary respect, as if she recognized a more intractable authority than that of a social worker. And when she spoke Kate detected a note of weary resignation in the ritual defiance.

"You'd better come in, although I don't know what good it'll do. Your chaps have seen Daisy once. The kid has told you all she knows. We co-operated with the police, and what do we get for it but the bloody welfare on our backs. It's not their business how I earn my living. OK, I'm a stripper. So what's wrong with that? I earn a living and I keep my kid. I'm in a job and it's legal, OK? The papers are always complaining about single mothers on social security, well I'm not on any bloody social security but I will be if I have to hang about here all day answering damn silly questions. And we don't want any WPCs from the Juvenile Bureau. That one who came last time with that Jewish chap was a proper cow."

She hadn't moved during this welcome but now, at last, reluctantly, she stepped aside and they moved into a hall so small that it could hardly hold the three of them.

Dalgliesh said: "I'm Commander Dalgliesh and this is Inspector Miskin, who isn't from the Juvenile Bureau. She's a detective, we both are. We're sorry to worry you again, Mrs. Reed, but we must talk to Daisy. Does she know that Mrs. Carling is dead?"

"Yes, she knows. We all know, don't we? It was on the local news. The next thing you'll be saying is that it wasn't suicide and we did it."

"Is Daisy distressed?"

"How do I know? She isn't laughing. I never know what that kid's feeling anyway. She'll be distressed all right by the time you lot have finished with her. She's in here—I've rung the school to say she won't be in till the afternoon. And, look, do me a favour. Make it quick, OK? I've got to get out to the shops. And the kid'll be looked after tonight. Don't you start fretting about Daisy. The cleaner here is coming in for the evening. After that you can bloody well ask the welfare to look after her if they're so worried."

The sitting-room was narrow and gave an impression of cluttered discomfort and an oddness which puzzled Kate until she saw that an artificial fireplace, the mantelshelf crowded with good-luck cards and small china ornaments, had been fitted to the external, chimney-less wall. To the right an open door showed a double bed, partly made and strewn with clothes. Mrs. Reed went over and quickly closed it. To the right of the door was fitted a curtained rail on which Kate could glimpse a row of tightly packed dresses. There was an immense television set to the left of the door with a sofa facing it and in front of the double window a square table with four chairs. The table was piled high with what looked like school textbooks. A child in a uniform of navy-blue pleated skirt and white blouse turned and faced them.

Kate thought that she had seldom seen a plainer child. She was obviously her mother's daughter but by some trick of the genes the maternal features had been superimposed incongruously on her frail thin face. The eyes behind the spectacles were small and too far apart, the nose was broad like that of the mother, the mouth as full and its downward turn more pronounced. But her skin was delicate and an extraordinary colour, a pale greeny-gold like apples seen under water. Her hair, its colour between gold and a pale auburn, hung like strands of silk framing a face which looked more mature than childlike. Kate glanced at Dalgliesh, then turned her eyes quickly away. She knew that what he was feeling was pity and tenderness. She had seen that look before, however quickly disciplined, however fleeting. She was surprised at the surge of resentment it provoked. For all his sensitivity he was no different from any other man. His first reaction on seeing a female was an aesthetic response, pleasure in beauty and a compassionate regret at ugliness. Plain women got used to that look; they had to. But surely a child could be spared that brutal revelation of a universal human unfairness. You could legislate for every kind of discrimination but not this. In everything from jobs to sex the attractive were advantaged, the very plain denigrated and rejected. And this child hadn't even the promise of that distinctive, sexually charged ugliness which, if accompanied by intelligence and imagination, could be so much more erotic than mere prettiness. Nothing could ever be done to turn up the downward droop of that too-heavy mouth, to bring the piggy eyes closer together. In the few seconds before she spoke Kate was aware of a tumble of emotions, not least self-disgust. If Dalgliesh had felt instinctive pity, almost as if the child was maimed, then so had she and she was a woman. She at least could have judged by different criteria. In reply to a wave of the mother's hand, Dalgliesh sat down on the sofa and Kate took a chair opposite Daisy. Mrs. Reed plonked herself belligerently at the other end of the sofa and lit a cigarette.

"I'm staying. You're not interviewing the kid without me."

Dalgliesh said: "We can't talk to Daisy unless you do stay, Mrs. Reed. There are special procedures for interviewing juveniles. It would be helpful if you didn't interrupt, unless you feel we're being unfair."

Kate took a chair at the table, immediately facing the child, and said gently: "We are so sorry about your friend, Daisy. Mrs. Carling was your friend, wasn't she?"

Daisy opened one of her school books and made a pretence of reading. Without looking up, she said: "She liked me."

"When people like us we usually like them in return, at least I do. You know that Mrs. Carling is dead. She may have killed herself but we can't yet be sure. We need to find out how and why she died. We want you to help us. Will you?"

Then Daisy looked up at her. The small eyes, disconcertingly intelligent, were as hard as an adult's and as judgemental as only a child's can be. She said: "I don't want to talk to you. I want to talk to the boss-man." She gazed across at Dalgliesh and said: "I want to talk to him."

Dalgliesh said: "Well, I'm here. But it's the same, Daisy, whoever you speak to."

"I won't talk except to you."

Kate, disconcerted, trying to conceal her disappointment and chagrin rose from her seat, but Dalgliesh motioned her to stay and drew up a chair beside her.

Daisy said: "You think Auntie Esmé was murdered, don't you? What will you do to him when you've caught him?"

"If the court finds him guilty then he'll go to prison. But we can't be certain that Mrs. Carling was murdered. We don't yet know how or why she died."

"Mrs. Summers at school says that putting people in prison doesn't do them any good."

Dalgliesh said: "Mrs. Summers is right. But people aren't usually sent to prison to do them good. Sometimes it's necessary to protect other people, or to deter, or because society cares deeply about what the guilty person has done and the punishment reflects that concern."

Oh God, thought Kate, are we expected to spend time discussing the case for custodial sentences and the philosophy of judicial punishment? But Dalgliesh was obviously prepared to be patient.

"Mrs. Summers says that executing people is barbaric."

"We don't execute people any longer in this country, Daisy."

"They do in America."

"Yes, in some parts of the United States, and in other countries too, but it doesn't happen any longer in Britain. I think you know that, Daisy."

The child, thought Kate, was being deliberately obstructive. She wondered what Daisy thought she was doing, apart, of course, from playing for time. Silently she cursed Mrs. Summers. She had known one or two of her kind in her old schooldays, principally Miss Crighton, who had done her best to dissuade her from joining the police on the grounds that they were the oppressive fascist agents of capitalist authority. She would have liked to have asked the child what Mrs. Summers would have done with Mrs. Carling's murderer, if murderer there was, apart of course from giving him sympathy, counselling him and sending him on a world cruise. Better still, it would have been agreeable to take Mrs. Summers to view some of the victims of murder and to face the murder scenes she, Kate, had had to face. Irritated by the resurgence of old prejudices, old resentments which she thought she had conquered, and of memories she preferred to forget, she kept her eyes on Daisy's face. Mrs. Reed said nothing but pulled on her cigarette vigorously. The air became disagreeably smoky.

Sitting close to the child, Dalgliesh said: "Daisy, we need to find out how and why Mrs. Carling died. It could have been by her own hand, and it is possible, just possible, that she was murdered. If she was, we have to find out who was responsible. That is our job. That is why we are here. We've come because we think you can help."

"I've told that Inspector and the woman police officer what I know."

Dalgliesh didn't reply. The silence and what it implied obviously disconcerted Daisy. After a short pause she said defensively: "How do I know you won't try to pin Mr. Etienne's murder on Auntie Esmé? She said you might try, she thought you might fit her up."

Dalgliesh said: "We don't think Mrs. Carling had anything to do with Mr. Etienne's death. And we won't pin the murder on anyone. What we're trying to do is to find out the truth. I think I know two things about you, Daisy: that you are intelligent and that, if you promise to tell the truth, then it will be the truth. Will you promise?"

"How do I know I can trust you?"

"I'm asking you to trust us. You have to make up your own mind whether you can. That's an important decision for you to have to make, but you can't escape it. Only, don't lie. I would rather you told us nothing than that you lied."

This is a high-risk strategy, thought Kate. She hoped that they were not now about to hear how Mrs. Summers had warned the children never to trust a policeman. Daisy's piggy eyes looked straight into Dalgliesh's. The silence seemed interminable.

Then Daisy said: "All right. I'll tell the truth."

Dalgliesh's voice didn't change. He said: "When Inspector Aaron and the WPC came to see you, you told them that you have been spending your evenings in Mrs. Carling's flat to do your homework and have supper with her. Is that true?"

"Yes. Sometimes I went to sleep in her spare room and sometimes on the couch, and then Auntie Esmé would wake me up and bring me back here before Mummy got home."

Mrs. Reed broke in: "Look, the kid was safe here. I always double-locked the door when I left and she had her own keys. And I left a phone number. What was I bloody well supposed to do? Take her with me to the club?"

Dalgliesh ignored her. His eyes were still on Daisy.

"What did you do together?"

"I did my homework and sometimes she did some writing, and then we used to watch telly. She let me read her books. She has a lot of books about murders, and she knew all about real-life murders. I used to take my supper in with me and sometimes I would have some of hers."

"It sounds as if you had happy evenings together. I expect she was glad of your company."

"She didn't like being alone at night. She said she could hear noises on the stairs and she didn't feel safe even with the door double-locked. She said that someone who had a second pair of keys could be careless with them and then a murderer could get hold of them and come creeping up the stairs and let himself into the flat. Or, she said, he could be on the roof after dark and let himself down with a rope and get in at the window. Sometimes at night she could hear him tapping against the pane. It was always worse when there was something frightening on the telly. She never liked to watch the telly by herself."

Poor kid, thought Kate. So these were the vividly imagined horrors from which Daisy, left alone night after night, had taken refuge in Mrs. Carling's flat. What, she wondered, was Esmé Carling escaping from? Boredom, loneliness, her own imagined fears? It was an unlikely friendship, but each had met the other's need for companionship, a sense of security, the small domestic comforts of a home.

Dalgliesh said: "And you told Inspector Aaron and the woman police officer from the Juvenile Bureau that you were in Mrs. Carling's flat from six o'clock on Thursday the fourteenth of October, the night Mr. Etienne died, until she took you home at about midnight. Was that true?"

Here at last was the crucial question and it seemed to Kate that they waited for it with bated breath. The child still gazed calmly at Dalgliesh. They could hear her mother pulling on her cigarette, but she didn't speak.

The seconds passed, then Daisy said: "No, it wasn't true. Auntie Esmé asked me to lie for her."

"When did she ask you to do that?"

"On Friday, the day after Mr. Etienne was killed, when she met me out of school. She was waiting at the gate. Then she came home with me by bus. We sat upstairs in the bus, where there weren't many people, and she told me that the police would be asking where she was and I was to tell them that we had spent the evening and the night together. She said they might think she had killed Mr. Etienne because she was a crime writer and knew all about murder and because she was very clever at devising plots. She said the police might try to pin it on her because she had a motive. Everyone at Peverell Press knew that she hated Mr. Etienne for turning down her book."

"But you didn't think she'd done it, did you, Daisy? Why was that?"

The sharp little eyes still looked into his. "You know why."

"Yes, and so does Inspector Miskin. But tell us."

"If she had done it she would have come here late that night before Mummy was home and asked for the alibi then. She never asked until the body was discovered. And she didn't know when it was Mr. Etienne had died. She said I was to be sure to give an alibi for the whole evening and the night. Auntie said we had to tell the same story because the police would try to catch us out. So I told that Inspector everything that had happened except for what we saw on the television, but it had all happened the night before."

Dalgliesh said: "That's the most reliable way of fabricating an alibi. Essentially you're telling the truth so you don't have to fear that the other person will say something different. Was that your idea?"

"Yes."

"We must hope, Daisy, that you don't go in for crime in a serious way. Now this is very important and I want you to think hard before you answer any of my questions. Will you do that?"

"Yes."

"Did your aunt Esmé tell you what happened at Innocent House on that Thursday night, the night that Mr. Etienne died?"

"She didn't tell me very much. She said that she'd been there and seen Mr. Etienne but that he was alive when she left. Someone had rung him to go upstairs and he'd told her he wouldn't be long. But he was long so she got tired of waiting. She said in the end she left."

"She left without seeing him again?"

"That's what she said. She said she waited and then she got frightened. It's terrible at Innocent House when all the staff have left and it's cold and silent. There was a lady who killed herself there and Mrs. Carling says that sometimes her ghost walks. So she didn't wait for Mr. Etienne to come back. I asked her if she'd seen the murderer and she said, 'No, I didn't see him. I don't know who did it, but I know who didn't do it.' "

"Did she say who?"

"No."

"Did she tell you whether it was a man or a woman, the person who didn't do it?"

"No."

"Daisy, did you gain any impression that she was speaking of a man or a woman?"

"No."

"Did she tell you anything else about that night? Try to remember her exact words."

"She did say something, but it didn't make sense, not then. She said, 'I heard the voice, but the snake was outside the door. Why was the snake outside the door? And it was a funny time to borrow a vacuum cleaner.' She said it very low, as if she was speaking to herself."

"Did you ask her what she meant?"

"I asked her what kind of snake? Was it a poisonous snake? Did the snake bite Mr. Etienne? And she said, 'No, it wasn't a real snake, but maybe it was lethal enough in its way.' "

Dalgliesh said: " 'I heard the voice, but the snake was outside the door. And it was a funny time to borrow a vacuum cleaner.' Are you sure of those words?"

"Yes."

"She didn't say his voice or her voice?"

"No. She said what I told you. I think she wanted to keep some of it secret. She liked secrets and mysteries."

"When did she next speak to you about the murder?"

"The day before yesterday, when I was here doing my homework. She said she was going to Innocent House to see somebody. She said 'They'll have to go on publishing me now. I can make sure of that, anyway.' She said she might want me to give her another alibi but she wasn't sure yet. I asked her who she was going to see and she said she wouldn't tell me for the time being, it had to be a secret. I don't think she was ever going to tell me. I think it was too important to tell anyone. I said, 'If you're going to see the murderer, he might kill you too,' and she said she wasn't that silly, she wasn't going to see any murderer. She said, 'I don't know who the murderer is, but I may do after tomorrow night.' She didn't say anything else."

Dalgliesh held out his hand across the table and the child clasped it. He said: "Thank you, Daisy. You've been very helpful. We shall have to ask you to write this down and sign it but not now."

"And I won't be put in care?"

"I don't think there's any chance of that, is there?" He looked at Mrs. Reed, who said grimly: "That kid goes into care over my dead body."

She was seeing them out when, apparently on impulse, she slipped out after them and closed the door. Ignoring Kate, she spoke directly to Dalgliesh: "Mr. Mason, he's Daisy's headmaster, says she's clever, I mean really clever."

"I think she is, Mrs. Reed. You should be proud of her."

"He thinks she could get one of them government grants to go to a different school, a boarding school."

"What does Daisy think?"

"She says she wouldn't mind. She isn't happy at the school where she is. I think she'd like to go but she doesn't like to say so."

Kate felt a spurt of mild irritation. They needed to get on. There was Mrs. Carling's flat to examine and the literary agent was expected at 11:30.

But Dalgliesh showed no sign of impatience. He said: "Why don't you and Daisy talk it over at length with Mr. Mason? Daisy has to be the one to decide."

Mrs. Reed still lingered, looking at him as if there was something else she needed to hear, some reassurance that only he could give.

He said: "You mustn't think that it's necessarily wrong for Daisy because it happens to be convenient for you. It could be the right thing for both of you."

"Thank you, thank you," she whispered and slipped back into the flat.

51

Mrs. Carling's flat was one floor down and at the front of the building. The heavy mahogany door was fitted with a keyhole and with two security locks, a Banham and an Ingersoll. The keys turned easily and Dalgliesh pushed open the door against the shifting weight of a pile of post. The hall smelled musty and was very dark. He felt for the light switch and pressed it down to reveal at a glance the simple layout of the flat, a narrow hall with two doors facing him and one at each end. He bent down to pick up the assorted envelopes and saw that they were merely circulars, with two obvious bills and an envelope which exhorted Mrs. Carling to open it immediately and win the chance of half a million. There was also a sheet of folded paper with a message in a laborious hand. "Sorry I can't come tomorrow. Have to go to clinic with Tracey on account of high blood pressure. Hope to see you next Friday. Mrs. Darlene Morgan."

Dalgliesh opened the door immediately ahead and switched on the light. They found themselves in the sitting-room. The two windows overlooking the street were close-shut, the curtains of red velvet half-drawn. At this height there was no risk of prying eyes even from the top deck of buses but the bottom halves of both windows were curtained in a patterned net. The main artificial light came from an inverted glass bowl painted with a faint design of butterflies which hung from a central rose on the ceiling, the glass spotted with the black shrivelled bodies of trapped flies. There were three table lamps with pink-fringed shades, one on a small table beside a fireside chair, one on a square table set between the two windows and the third on a huge roll-top desk against the left-hand wall. As if desperate for light and air, Kate drew back the curtains and pushed open one of the windows, then went round the room and switched on all the lights. They breathed the cool air, which gave the illusion of country freshness, and looked round at a room they could at last see clearly.

The immediate impression, emphasized by the pink glow of the lamps, was of a cushioned, old-fashioned cosiness which was the more appealing because the owner had made no concessions to popular contemporary taste. The room could have been furnished in the 1930s and left virtually undisturbed. Most of the pieces looked as if they had been inherited: the roll-top desk which held her portable typewriter, the four mahogany dining chairs of discordant shape and age, an Edwardian glass-fronted cabinet in which assorted china objects and part of a tea service had been piled and stacked rather than arranged, two faded rugs so inappropriately placed that Dalgliesh suspected they were concealing holes in the carpet. Only the sofa and two matching armchairs which surrounded the fireplace were comparatively new, furnished with plump cushions and covered in linen patterned with pale-pink and yellow roses. The fireplace itself looked original, an ornate contrivance in grey marble with a heavy overmantel, the grate surrounded by a double row of ornamental tiles, of flowers, fruits and birds. At each end of the mantelshelf two collared Staffordshire dogs with golden chains stared with bright-eyed intensity at the opposite wall. Ranged between them was a clutter of ornaments: a George VI–and–Queen Elizabeth coronation mug, a black japanned box, two diminutive brass candlesticks, a modern porcelain figure of a crinolined woman holding a lap-dog, a cut-glass vase containing a bunch of imitation primroses. Behind the ornaments were two coloured photographs. One looked as if it had been taken at a prize-giving; Esmé Carling stood pointing an imitation gun, surrounded by grinning faces. In the second she was at a book signing. The picture had obviously been carefully posed. A purchaser stood expectantly at her side, head unnaturally bent to get it in the picture, while Mrs. Carling, pen raised from the page, smiled beguilingly into the camera. Kate briefly studied it, trying to superimpose on the square marsupial features, the small mouth and slightly hooked nose, that appallingly drowned and violated face which was the first glimpse she had had of Esmé Carling.

Dalgliesh could understand the attraction this homely soft-cushioned room had held for Daisy. On this broad sofa she had read, watched television, briefly slept before being half carried back to her own room. Here was a refuge from the terror of her imaginings in simulated terror, neatly contained within the covers of books, sanitized, fictionalized, to be tasted, shared, put aside, no more real than the dancing flames of the artificial-log fire, and as easily turned off. There had been security here, companionship and, yes, love of a kind if love was the meeting of mutual need. He glanced at the books. The shelves held paperback copies of crime and detective stories, but he noticed that few of the writers were living. Mrs. Carling's taste was for women writers of the Golden Age. They all looked well read. Below them was a shelf of real-life crime: books on the Wallace case, on Jack the Ripper, on the more famous Victorian murders, Adelaide Bartlett and Constance Kent. The lower shelves held leather-bound and gold-titled copies of her own works, an extravagance, Dalgliesh thought, unlikely to have been subsidized by Peverell Press. The sight of this harmless vanity depressed him, evoking a spasm of pity. Who would inherit this accumulated record of a life lived by murder and ended by murder? On what shelf in drawing-room, bedroom or lavatory would they find an honoured or tolerated place? Or would they be bought as a job-lot by some second-hand bookseller and priced as a set, their value enhanced by the horror and appalling appropriateness of her death? Surveying the titles so reminiscent of the 1930s, of village policemen cycling to the scene of the murder, tugging their forelocks to the gentry, of autopsies undertaken by eccentric general practitioners after evening surgery and unlikely denouements in the library, he took them out and glanced at them at random. *Death by Dancing* apparently set in the world of formation ballroom competitions, *Cruising to Murder, Death by Drowning, The Mistletoe Murders*. He replaced them carefully, feeling no condescension. Why should he? He told himself that she had probably given pleasure to more people with her mysteries than he had with his poetry. And if the pleasure was different in kind, who was to say that one was inferior to the other? She had at least respected the English language and used it as well as lay in her power. In an age rapidly becoming illiterate that was something. For thirty years she had purveyed the fantasy of murder, the acceptable face of violence, the controllable terror. He hoped that when she had come at last face to face with reality the encounter had been brief and merciful.

Kate had moved into the kitchen. He joined her and together they surveyed the mess. The sink was piled with dirty crockery, the unwashed frying pan was on the stove, and the waste bin was spilling its tins and squashed cartons onto the grimy floor. Kate said: "She wouldn't have wanted us to find it looking like this. Tough on her that her Mrs. Morgan couldn't come this morning."

Glancing at her, he saw the flush rise from her throat and knew that the remark had suddenly struck her as irrational and foolish and that she wished it unspoken.

But their minds had moved in tandem. "Lord, let me know mine end, and the number of my days: that I may be certified how long I have to live." Surely few people could pray that prayer with any sincerity. The best one could hope for or want was enough time to tidy away the personal debris, consign one's secrets to the flames or the dustbin and leave the kitchen tidy.

For a couple of seconds, even as he opened the drawers and cupboards, he was back in that Norfolk graveyard hearing his father's voice, an instantaneous image powerful in its intensity and bringing with it the smell of cut hay, newly turned Norfolk earth, of the intoxication of lilies. The parishioners liked the rector's son to be present at village funerals and during the school holidays he always attended, finding a village burial more of an interest than an imposition, sharing the funeral tea afterwards, trying to contain his boyish hunger, while the mourners pressed on him the traditional cooked ham and rich fruitcake, and murmured their thanks.

"Good of you to come, Mr. Adam. Dad would have appreciated it. He was very fond of you, was Dad."

His mouth sticky with cake, murmuring the expected lie: "I was very fond of him, Mrs. Hodgkin."

He would stand there watching while old Goodfellow the sexton and the undertaker's men tilted the coffin into that neatly accommodating pit, hearing the soft thud of Norfolk earth on the lid, listening to his father's grave scholarly voice as the breeze lifted his greying hair and billowed his surplice. And he would picture the man or woman he had known, the shrouded body encased in padded imitation silk, more ostentatiously bedded than it had ever been in life, and would picture every stage of its dissolution: the rotting shroud, the slowly decaying flesh, the final falling-in of the coffin-lid on the denuded bones, and had never from childhood been able to believe that magnificent proclamation of immortality: "And though worms destroy this body, yet in my flesh shall I see God."

They moved into Mrs. Carling's bedroom but did not linger. It was large, overfurnished, untidy and not very clean. The 1930s dressing table with its triple mirror held a plastic tray patterned with violets containing a jumble of half-empty bottles of hand and body lotions, greasy jars, lipsticks and eye make-up. Without thinking, Kate unscrewed the largest jar of foundation cream and saw its single indentation where Mrs. Carling had drawn her finger across the surface. The mark, so ephemeral yet, for a moment, seeming permanent and ineradicable, brought the dead woman's image so vividly to mind that she froze, the jar in her hand, as if she had been caught out in an act of private violation. The eyes in the mirror stared back at her, guilty and a little ashamed. She made herself go over to the wardrobe and open its door. There came out with the rustle of the hanging clothes a smell that brought back other searches, other victims, other rooms, the sweet-sour musty smell of age and failure and death. She closed its door quickly but not before she had seen the three whisky bottles hidden among the row of shoes. She thought: There are moments when I hate my job. But these moments were few and they never lasted long.

The guest bedroom was a narrow, ill-proportioned cell, the one high window giving a view of a brick wall grimed with decades of London dirt and angled with heavy drainpipes. But some attempt, even if misguided, had been made to make the room inviting. The walls and ceiling were covered with a paper of twining honeysuckle, roses and ivy. The curtains, elaborately pleated, were of a matching material and the single divan, placed under the window, had a pale-pink coverlet, obviously chosen to match the pink of the roses. The attempt to prettify, to impose on bleak nothingness a feminine intensity, served only to emphasize the room's defects. The décor had obviously been designed for a female guest, but Dalgliesh couldn't imagine a woman sleeping peacefully in this claustrophobic over-patterned cell. Certainly no man could, with the ceiling's synthetic sweetness pressing down on him, the bed too narrow for comfort, the bedside table a fragile reproduction, too small to hold more than the bedside lamp.

The time looking round the flat had not been wasted. Kate remembered one of the first lessons she had been taught as a young detective constable: know the victim. Every victim dies because of who he is, what he is, where he is at one moment of time. The more you know about the victim the closer you are to his murderer. But now, as they sat down at Esmé Carling's desk, they were in search of more specific evidence.

They were rewarded as soon as they opened it. The desk was tidier and less cluttered than they had expected and lying on the top of a pile of recent unpaid bills were two sheets of paper. The first was obviously a draft of the note found on the railings at Innocent House. There were few alterations; Mrs. Carling's final version was little different from her first outpouring of pain and anger. But the writing was a scrawl compared with the firm and careful calligraphy of the final note. Here was confirmation, if it had been needed, that they were her words and written in her hand. Underneath was a draft of a letter in the same hand. It was dated Thursday 14 October.

Dear Gerard,
I have just heard the news from my agent. Yes, from my agent! You haven't even the decency or the courage to tell me direct. You could have asked me to come to talk to you at the office, or it wouldn't have hurt you to take me out to lunch or dinner to break the news. Or are you as mean as you are disloyal and cowardly? Perhaps you were afraid that I would disgrace you by howling in the soup. I'm a great deal tougher than that, as you will discover. Your rejection of *Death on Paradise Island* would still have been unfair, unjustified and ungrateful, but at least I could have said these things to your face. And now I can't even reach you by telephone. I'm not surprised. That bloody woman, Miss Blackett, is good at block-ing calls if nothing else. At least it shows that even you are capable of some shame.
    Have you any idea what I have done for Peverell Press, long before you had any power? And what a disastrous day for the firm that has proved. I have produced a book a year for thirty years, all reliable sellers, and if sales of the last were disappointing, whose fault is that? What have you ever done to promote me with the vigour and enthusiasm my reputation demands? I'm off to do a signing at Cambridge this afternoon. Who persuaded the bookshop to put that on? I did. I shall go alone as usual. Most publishers see that their top authors are properly accompanied and looked after. But the fans will be there, and they'll buy. I have devoted readers who look to me to provide what no other detective writer apparently does, a fair mystery with good writing and an absence of that sex, violence and filthy language which you apparently think people today want. Well they don't. If you have so little idea of what readers really want you'll drive Peverell Press to bankruptcy even quicker than the publishing world predicts.
    I shall, of course, have to consider how best to safeguard my interests. If I move to another publisher I shall expect to take my back-list with me. Don't think you can throw me overboard and still exploit that valuable asset. And there's

something else. These mysterious mishaps which are taking place at Peverell Press only began when you took over as Managing Director. If I were you, I'd take care. There have already been two deaths at Innocent House.

Kate said: "I wonder if this, too, was just a preliminary draft or whether she actually sent in the final version. She usually typed her letters but there's no carbon here. If she did post it, perhaps she thought it would be more forceful handwritten. This could be the copy."

"The letter wasn't among the correspondence in his office. My guess is that it wasn't sent. Instead she called at Innocent House demanding to see him. When that failed she went to do her Cambridge signing, discovered that it had been cancelled by someone at Peverell Press, returned to London in a state of high indignation and decided to call on Etienne that evening. Most people seem to have known that he worked late on Thursdays. It's possible that she telephoned and told him that she was coming. He could hardly, after all, prevent her. And if she did telephone using his private number the call wouldn't have gone through Miss Blackett."

Kate said: "It's odd, if she took the first paper with her, that she didn't take this letter and leave it with him. I suppose it's possible she did and that either Etienne tore it up or the murderer found it and destroyed it."

Dalgliesh said: "Unlikely, I think. What seems more likely is that she took with her the fulmination addressed to the partnership perhaps with the object of pinning it to the noticeboard in the reception room. That way the partners would see it and so would all members of the staff and visitors."

"They'd hardly have left it up, sir."

"Of course not. But she probably hoped that quite a number of people would see it before it was drawn to the partners' attention. At least it would cause a stir. The fulmination was probably intended as the first blow in her campaign of revenge. She must have had some very bad hours when she first heard of Gerard's death. If she did in fact leave the notice, and possibly also the manuscript of her novel, in the reception room, their presence would prove that she had called at Innocent House that night and after most of the staff had left. She must have been waiting for us to appear, knowing that the presence of the note made her one of the chief suspects. So she arranges her alibi with Daisy. And then, when the police do arrive, nothing is said about the note. So either we've missed its significance, which is unlikely, or someone has removed it. And then the person who did take it down from the noticeboard telephones to reassure her. He or she is able to reassure her because Carling is confident that she is talking to an ally, not to a murderer."

"It hangs together, sir. It's logical and it's credible."

"It's conjecture, every part of it, Kate. It can't be proved. None of it would stand up in court. It's an ingenious theory which fits all the facts as we know them so far but it's circumstantial. There's just one small piece of corroborative evidence. If she pinned the false suicide note to the noticeboard before she left Innocent House there would have been the marks of one or more drawing pins in the paper. Was that the reason why it was so neatly trimmed down before it was spiked on the railings?"

There was little else of interest in the desk. Mrs. Carling received few letters or, if she did, she destroyed them. Those she kept included a bundle of airmail forms tied with a ribbon and kept together in one of the cubby-holes. They were from a woman friend in Australia, a Mrs. Marjorie Rampton, but the correspondence had gradually grown more perfunctory and seemed to have petered out. Apart from this there were bundles of letters from fans, all with a carbon of the reply attached to the original letter. Mrs. Carling had obviously taken considerable trouble to satisfy her admirers. In the top drawer of the desk there was a file labelled "investments" with letters from her stockbroker. She had capital of just over £32,000 carefully invested between gilts and equities. In another file was a copy of her will. It was a short document in which she left a legacy of £5,000 to the Authors' Foundation and to a crime writers' club and the bulk of her estate to the friend in Australia. Another file contained papers relating to her divorce fifteen years earlier. Glancing quickly through them, Dalgliesh saw that it had been acrimonious but, from her point of view, not particularly advantageous. The payments had been small and had stopped with Raymond Carling's death five years later. And that was all. The contents of the desk confirmed what Dalgliesh had suspected. Here was a woman who lived for her work. Take that away and what had she left?

52

Velma Pitt-Cowley, Mrs. Carling's literary agent, had agreed to be at the flat at 11:30 and arrived six minutes late. She was hardly inside the door before it became apparent that she was in none too good a temper. She burst into the room when Kate opened the door with a speed that suggested that it was she who had been kept waiting, flung herself into the nearer of the two armchairs, then leaned forward to slip the gold chain of her bag from her shoulder and to deposit a bulging briefcase on the carpet beside her. Only then did she deign to bestow any attention on Kate or Dalgliesh. When she did, and her eyes met Dalgliesh's, her mood subtly changed and her first words showed that she was prepared to be gracious.

"Sorry to be late and in such a rush, but you know how it is. I had to go into the office first and I've got a luncheon guest at the Ivy at twelve-forty-five. It's pretty important as a matter of fact. The author I'm meeting flew in especially from New York this morning. And things cropped up as they always do if you show your face in the office. You can't trust people with the simplest jobs nowadays. I left as soon as I could but the taxi got snarled up in Theobald's Road. My God, this is terrible about poor Esmé. It's really terrible! What happened? She drowned herself, didn't she? Drowned or hanged herself or both. I mean, that's really sick."

Having expressed appropriate outrage, Mrs. Pitt-Cowley settled herself more elegantly in the chair and drew up the skirt of her formal

black suit almost to her crotch to reveal a pair of very long and shapely
legs enclosed in nylons so fine that they were no more than a dull sheen
on the sharp bones. She had obviously dressed with care for her 12:45
luncheon appointment, and Dalgliesh wondered what privileged client,
present or prospective, warranted a smartness which carefully combined
professional competence with sexual allure. Beneath the well-fitting
jacket with its row of brass buttons she wore a high-necked silk shirt. A
hat of black velvet, speared at the front with a golden arrow, was
crushed over light-brown hair cut in a fringe, just touching the thick,
level eyebrows and falling in well-brushed swathes almost to her shoulders. As she spoke she gesticulated; the long fingers, heavily ringed,
restlessly patterned the air as if she were communicating to the deaf,
and from time to time her shoulders hunched in sudden spasms. The
gestures seemed oddly unrelated to her words and it seemed to Dalgliesh
that the affectation was less a symptom of nervousness or insecurity
than a trick originally designed to draw attention to her remarkable
hands but which had now become an unbreakable habit. Her initial
testiness had surprised him; in his experience people involved in a
spectacular murder, provided they neither grieved for the victim nor
felt themselves at risk from the police enquiry, usually relished the
vicarious excitement of their brush with violent death and the notoriety
of being in the know. He was used to encountering eyes slightly ashamed
but avid with curiosity. Bad temper and a preoccupation with one's own
concerns at least made a change.

She gazed round the room at the open desk, at the pile of papers
on the table, and said: "God, it's too awful sitting here in her flat, you
having to rummage through her things. I know you have to do it, it's
your job, but it's sort of uncanny. She seems more present now than
when she was actually here. I keep thinking I'll hear her key in the lock
and she'll come in, find us like this, uninvited, and raise hell."

Dalgliesh said: "Violent death destroys privacy, I'm afraid. Did she
commonly raise hell?"

As if she hadn't heard him, Mrs. Pitt-Cowley said: "Do you know
what I'd really like now? What I really need is a good strong black
coffee. There's no chance of any, I suppose?"

It was Kate she looked at, and Kate who replied. "There's a jar of
coffee grains in the kitchen and a carton of milk in the fridge unopened.
Strictly speaking, I suppose we should get the bank's permission, but I
doubt whether anyone would object."

When Kate made no immediate move towards the kitchen, Velma
gave her a long speculative stare as if assessing the possible nuisance-

value of a new typist. Then, with a shrug and a flurry of fingers, she decided on prudence.

"Better not I suppose, although she won't be needing it herself now, will she? But I can't say I fancy drinking it out of one of her cups."

Dalgliesh said: "Obviously it's important for us to learn as much about Mrs. Carling as we can. That's why we're grateful to you for meeting us here this morning. Her death must have been a shock and I realize that it can't be easy for you coming here. But it is important."

Mrs. Pitt-Cowley's voice and look expressed a passionate intensity. "Oh, I do see that. I mean, I understand absolutely that you have to ask questions. Obviously I'll help all I can. What did you want to know?"

He asked: "When did you hear the news?"

"This morning, shortly after seven, before your people rang to ask me to meet you here. Claudia Etienne telephoned. Woke me up, actually. Not exactly pleasant news to start the day. She could have waited, but I suppose she didn't want me to read it in the evening paper or hear it when I got to the office. You know how fast gossip travels in this town. After all I am—I mean I was—Esmé's agent and I suppose she thought that I ought to be one of the first to know and that she ought to be the one to tell me. But suicide! It's bizarre. It's the last thing I'd have expected Esmé to do. Well of course it was the last thing she did. Oh God, I'm sorry. Nothing one says seems adequate at a time like this."

"So you were surprised at the news?"

"Isn't one always? I mean, even when people who threaten suicide actually do it, it always seems surprising, a bit unreal. But Esmé! And to kill herself like that. I mean it wasn't the most comfortable way to go. Claudia didn't seem very sure how exactly she died. She just said that Esmé had hanged herself from the railings at Innocent House and that the body was found under water. Did she drown or strangle herself or what exactly?"

Dalgliesh said: "It is possible Mrs. Carling died by drowning but we shan't know the cause of death until after the autopsy."

"But it was suicide? I mean, you're sure about that?"

"We're not sure yet of anything. Can you think of any reason why Mrs. Carling should have wanted to end her life?"

"She was upset about Peverell Press rejecting *Death on Paradise Island*. You've heard about that, I suppose. But she was more angry than distressed. Furiously angry in fact. I can imagine her seeking some kind of vengeance on the firm, but not by killing herself. Besides, that takes guts. I don't mean that Esmé was a coward, but I can't somehow see her throttling herself or throwing herself in the river. What a way to

die! If she really wanted to do away with herself there are easier ways.
Take Sonia Clements. You know about that, of course. Sonia killed
herself with drugs and booze. That would be my way. I'd have thought
it would be Esmé's."

Kate said: "But less effective as a public protest."

"Not so dramatic, I agree. But what's the good of a dramatic public
protest if you aren't there to enjoy it? No, if Esmé decided to kill herself
it would be in bed, clean sheets, flowers in the room, her best night-
dress, a dignified farewell note on the bedside cabinet. She was a great
one for appearances."

Kate, remembering the rooms of suicides she had been called to,
the vomit, the soiled bedclothes, the grotesque body stiffened in death,
reflected that suicide was seldom as dignified in practice as in imagination. She said: "When did you last see her?"

"On the evening of the day after Gerard Etienne's death. That
would be October fifteenth, the Friday."

Dalgliesh asked: "Here or in your office?"

"Here in this room. It was fortuitous really. I mean, I hadn't planned
to call. I was dining with Dicky Mulchester of Herne & Illingworth to
discuss a client and it occurred to me that his firm might be interested
in *Death on Paradise Island*. It was a long shot but they are taking on a
few crime writers. I was driving past here to the restaurant when I
noticed that there were some parking spaces free down the side road
and I thought I'd call in and borrow Esmé's copy of the manuscript.
The traffic was lighter than I expected and I had ten minutes in hand.
We hadn't spoken since Gerard's death. It's odd, isn't it, how small
things decide one's actions? I probably wouldn't have bothered if I
hadn't seen the empty space. I was interested, too, in hearing Esmé's
reaction to Gerard's death. I couldn't get much out of Claudia. I thought
Esmé might have picked up some of the details. She was a great one
for gossip. Not that I had much time to spare then. The main reason
for calling was to collect the manuscript."

Dalgliesh asked: "How did you find her?"

Mrs. Pitt-Cowley didn't immediately reply. Her face was thoughtful,
the restless hands were momentarily stilled. Dalgliesh thought that she
was evaluating the interview in the light of subsequent events, seeing it
perhaps as more significant than it seemed at the time. At last she said:
"Looking back on it, I think she behaved rather oddly. I would have
expected her to want to talk about Gerard, how he died, why he died,
whether it was murder. She just wouldn't discuss it. She said it was too
dreadful and too painful, that she'd been published by Peverell Press

for thirty years and however badly they'd treated her his death had shocked her profoundly. Well, it had shocked us all, but I didn't expect Esmé to feel much personal sorrow. She did tell me that she had an alibi for the previous evening and the night. Apparently she had a neighbour's child in here with her. I remember thinking it a little odd at the time that she bothered to tell me that. After all, no one was going to suspect Esmé of throttling Gerard with a snake, or however it was he died. Oh, and I remember she did ask whether I thought that the partners would change their minds about *Paradise Island* now that Gerard was dead. She always held him mainly responsible for its rejection. I didn't hold out much hope. I pointed out that it had probably been a decision from the whole Book Committee and that anyway the partners wouldn't like to go against Gerard's wishes now that he was dead. Then I suggested that Herne & Illingworth might be interested and asked to borrow her manuscript. She was odd then too. She said she wasn't sure where she'd put it. She'd looked for it that morning and couldn't find it. Then she said that she was too upset to think about *Paradise Island* so soon after Gerard's death. That hardly rang true. After all, she'd asked me only a couple of minutes earlier whether I thought that the partners would change their minds and take it. I don't think she had the manuscript. Either that or she didn't want me to have it. I left soon afterwards. I was only here for about ten minutes in all."

"And you have spoken to her since?"

"No, not once. That's odd too when I come to think of it. After all, Gerard Etienne was her publisher. I'd have expected her to come into the office if only for a gossip. Usually you couldn't keep her away."

"How long have you been her agent? Did you know her well?"

"Less than two years, actually. But yes, even in the short time I did get to know her quite well. She saw to that. Actually I inherited her. Her old agent was Marjorie Rampton and Marge took her on with her first book. That's thirty years ago. They were really close. There often is personal friendship between agent and author—you can't do your best for a client if you don't get on with them as well as respecting the work. But with Marge and Esmé it went deeper. Don't misunderstand me, I'm talking about friendship. I'm not hinting at anything, well— sexual. I suppose they had quite a lot in common, both being widows, both childless. They used to take holidays together and I think Esmé asked Marge to be her literary executor. That's going to be a nuisance for someone if she didn't change her will. Marge went to Australia to stay with her nieces as soon as she'd sold the agency to me, and she's still there as far as I know."

Dalgliesh said, "Tell us about Esmé Carling. What sort of woman was she?"

"Oh God, this is awful. I mean, what can I say? It seems so disloyal, indecent almost, criticizing her when she's dead, but I can't pretend she was easy. She was one of those clients who are always on the phone or calling in at the office. Nothing's ever right. They always feel you can do more, squeeze a higher advance from the publisher, sell the film rights, get them a TV serial. I think she resented losing Marge and thought I wasn't giving her the attention her genius warranted, but actually I was giving her more time than was really justified. I mean, I do have other clients and most of them a damn sight more profitable."

Kate said: "More trouble than she was worth?"

Mrs. Pitt-Cowley turned on her a speculative, then dismissive glance. "I wouldn't have put it like that myself, but, if you want the truth, I wouldn't have broken my heart if she'd decided to look for another agent. Look, I hate saying this, but anyone in the office will tell you the same. A lot of it was loneliness, missing Marge, resenting Marge for abandoning her. But Marge was an old toughie. When it came to choosing between her precious nieces and Esmé it was no contest. And I think Esmé knew that her talent was running out. We were in for big trouble. Peverell Press turning down *Death on Paradise Island* was just the beginning."

"Was that Gerard Etienne?"

"Basically, yes. What Etienne wanted went at Peverell Press. But I doubt whether anyone there really wanted her, except perhaps James de Witt, and he doesn't cut much ice at Peverells. I rang and made a fuss, of course, as soon as I got Gerard's letter. I wasn't getting anywhere. And honestly, the new book really wasn't up to standard, even her standard. Do you know her work at all?"

Dalgliesh said carefully: "I have heard of her, of course, but never read her."

"She wasn't that bad. I mean, she could write literate prose, and that's rare enough nowadays. Peverell Press wouldn't have published her otherwise. She wasn't consistent. Just when you thought: God, I can't go on with this boring drivel, she'd produce a really good passage and the book would suddenly come alive. And she had an original idea for her detective—detectives, rather. She had a retired married couple, the Mainwarings, Malcolm and Mavis. He was a retired bank manager, and she'd been a teacher. It was quite neat. Went down well with an ageing population. Reader identification and all that. Bored retired couple haring off after the clues, plenty of time to make murder their hobby, using a lifetime of experience to put one over on the police, the wisdom of old age triumphing over the crass immaturity of youth, that sort of thing. A nice change to have a detective with a touch of arthritis. But they were getting a bit tiresome—the Mainwarings I mean. Esmé had the bright idea of involving Malcolm with young female suspects and Mavis having to rescue him from his entanglements. I suppose she was aiming for light relief, but it had become a bore. I mean, geriatric sex is all right if that happens to turn you on, but people don't want it in popular fiction, and Esmé was getting more explicit with each book. Bodice-rippers with blood. That's not really her market. It wasn't in Malcolm Mainwaring's character. And, of course, she couldn't plot. God, I hate saying this, but she couldn't. You did say you wanted the truth. She used to steal ideas from other writers—only dead writers, of course—and add her own twists. It was becoming a bit obvious. That's what gave Gerard Etienne his chance to turn down *Death on Paradise Island*. He said it was a boring read and the only parts that weren't boring were too like Agatha Christie's *Murder Under the Sun*. I believe he actually uttered the dread word 'plagiarism.' Then, of course, there was Esmé's other trouble, which didn't make her any easier to deal with."

Velma sketched in the air the outline of St Paul's Cathedral complete with dome, and ended with a pantomime of raising a glass to her lips.

"Are you saying that she was an alcoholic?"

"Getting on that way. You didn't get a hell of a lot of sense out of Esmé after midday. It had got worse in the last six months."

"So she wasn't making much money?"

"Never did. Esmé was never in the big league. Still she was doing all right, until the last three years. She could live on her writing, which is more than most authors can. She had quite a faithful following of old aficionados who'd grown up with the Mainwarings, but as they died off she wasn't attracting younger readers. Last year there was a big slump in paperback sales. I was afraid we were going to lose that contract."

Kate said: "Which perhaps accounts for this flat. It isn't exactly a fashionable address."

"Well it suited her. She was a protected tenant and the rent was low, I mean really low. She'd have been crazy to leave. Actually she told me that she planned to buy a country cottage in the Cotswolds or Herefordshire and was saving her capital for that. Saw herself among the roses and wistaria, I suppose. Personally I think she'd have died of boredom. I've seen it happen before."

Dalgliesh asked: "She wrote crime novels, detective stories. Would she be likely to fancy herself as an amateur detective? Try her hand at solving a crime if one came her way?"

"You mean tangling with a real-life murderer, with whoever it was killed Etienne? She'd be crazy. Esmé wasn't a great brain, but she wasn't stupid either. I'm not saying that she lacked courage, she had plenty of guts—especially after a few whiskies—but that would have been plain stupid."

"She might not think she was tangling with a murderer. Suppose she got an idea about the murder, would she be likely to bring it to us or be tempted to do a little private investigating?"

"She might, if she thought it was safe and she could get something out of it. It would be quite a triumph, wouldn't it? Publicity-wise, I mean. 'Woman crime writer outwits Scotland Yard.' Yes, I can see her mind working like that. But you're not suggesting that she tried something like that?"

"I was interested whether you thought it was in character."

"Let's say that it wouldn't surprise me. She was fascinated by real-life crime, detection, murder trials, that sort of thing. Well, you've only got to look at her bookcase. And she had a high opinion of her own cleverness. And she might not see the danger. I don't think she had much imagination, not about real life. OK, I know that sounds odd when I'm talking about a novelist, but she'd lived with fictional murder for so long that I don't think she realized that real-life murder is different, that it isn't something you can control and write up into a plot and neatly solve in the last chapter. And she didn't see Gerard Etienne's body, did she? I don't think she ever saw a dead person in real life. She could only imagine it, and death probably seemed no more real or frightening than her other imaginings. Am I being too sophisticated? I mean, do say if I'm talking the most utter nonsense."

Performing a complicated manoeuvre with her hands, Mrs. Pitt-Cowley cast on Dalgliesh a look of histrionic sincerity which didn't quite conceal the sharper look of enquiry. Dalgliesh reminded himself not to underestimate her intelligence. He said: "You're not talking nonsense. What will happen now about her latest book?"

"Oh I doubt whether Peverell Press will take it. It would be different, of course, if Esmé had been murdered. A double-murder, publisher and writer brutally done to death within a fortnight. Still, even suicide has publicity value, particularly if it's dramatic. I ought to be able to negotiate quite a satisfactory contract with someone."

Dalgliesh was tempted to say: "It's a pity we don't still have the death penalty. You could time publication to coincide with the execution date."

Mrs. Pitt-Cowley, as if aware of his thought, looked for a moment slightly embarrassed, then shrugged and went on: "Poor Esmé, if she did have the bright idea of getting some free publicity she certainly succeeded. Pity she won't benefit. Nice for her heirs, though."

Nice for you too, thought Kate. She asked: "Who does get her money, do you know?"

"No, she never told me that. As I said, Marge was her executor, or one of them. But I'm grateful to say that she never suggested transferring that privilege when I took over the agency. Not that I would have taken it on. I did a lot for Esmé, but there are limits. Honestly, you've no idea what some authors expect. Find them commissions, get them on TV chat-shows, feed the cat when they're on holiday, hold their hand through their divorces. For 10 per cent of home sales I'm expected to be agent, nurse, confidante, friend, the lot. I do know that she had no family—at least her ex-husband has a daughter and grandchildren somewhere, in Canada I believe. I can't see Esmé leaving anything to them. But there will be some money, no doubt about that, and my guess is that Marge will get it. I may be able to negotiate a reprint of the early paperbacks."

Dalgliesh said: "A profitable client after all, in death if not in life."

"Well, it's a funny old world, isn't it?"

And with this echo of a lady with whom she had otherwise little in common, Mrs. Pitt-Cowley glanced at her watch and bent down to pick up her briefcase and bag.

But Dalgliesh wasn't yet ready to let her go. He said: "I assume Mrs. Carling told you about the cancellation of her Cambridge signing session."

"Did she not! Actually she rang me from the shop. I tried to phone Gerard Etienne but I imagine he was at lunch. I got through to him later in the afternoon. Esmé was absolutely incoherent with rage. I mean really incoherent. Perfectly justified, of course. Peverell Press have a lot of explaining to do. I was sorry for the people in the shop, she was obviously taking it out on them but it was hardly their fault. At least, I suppose you could argue that they should have rung Peverell Press as soon as the fax was received to check that it wasn't a hoax, and they probably would have done if the Press had been less secretive about the trouble they were having. The manager was out when the fax came through and the girl who first saw it naturally assumed it was genuine. Well, it was genuine in the sense that it came from Peverell

Press. To calm Esmé I told her I would take it up with Gerard myself. I would've done too but for the murder. That did rather put Esmé's grievance into perspective. I still intend to take the matter up with the firm but there is a time and place. Is it all right if I go now? I do have that luncheon appointment."

Dalgliesh said: "I've only a few more questions. What was your relationship with Gerard Etienne?"

"You mean my professional relationship?"

"Your relationship."

Velma Pitt-Cowley sat for a moment entirely in silence. They saw that she was gently smiling, a look that was lubricious, reminiscent. Then she said: "It was professional. I suppose we spoke on the phone about twice a month on average. I haven't seen him for the last four months. We did sleep together once. That was nearly a year ago. We'd both been to the same launch party. We both stayed to the bitter end. It was nearly midnight and I was rather drunk. Drink wasn't his thing, Gerard hated being out of control. He offered to drive me home and the night ended in the usual way. I suppose you'd call it a one-night stand, except that the word 'stand' isn't really appropriate. It never happened again."

Kate asked: "Did either of you want it to?"

"Not really. He sent me a spectacular bunch of flowers next day. Gerard wasn't exactly subtle, but I suppose that's some improvement on leaving fifty quid by the bedside. No, I didn't want it to go on. I've got a healthy sense of self-preservation. I don't go round inviting heartbreak. But I thought I'd better mention it. There were plenty of people at that party who might just have guessed how the evening ended. God knows how these things get out but they always do. In case you're wondering, the events of that night and particularly the next morning, which I remember more clearly, left me well disposed towards him rather than the opposite. But not so well disposed that I invited a second encounter. I suppose you want to ask me where I was on the night he died."

Dalgliesh said gravely: "That would be a help, Mrs. Pitt-Cowley."

"Oddly enough I was at that poetry reading at the Connaught Arms when Gabriel Dauntsey read. I left shortly after he'd done his stint. I was with a poet, or someone who describes himself as a poet, and he wanted to stay on, but I'd had enough of noise, uncomfortable chairs and cigarette smoke. Everyone was well tanked-up by then and the party showed no signs of breaking up. I suppose I left at about ten and drove home. So I've no alibi for the rest of the evening."

"And last night?"

"When Esmé died? But that was suicide, you said so yourself."

"However she died it is helpful to know where people were at the time."

"But I don't know when she died. I was at the office until six-thirty and then at home. I was at home all evening and I was alone. Is that what you wanted to know? Look, Commander, I really must go."

Dalgliesh said: "Just two final questions. How many copies of the manuscript of *Death on Paradise Island* were in existence, and was Mrs. Carling's copy distinctive?"

"I think there were about eight in all. I had to send five to Peverell Press, one for each of the partners. I don't see why they couldn't have copied the manuscript themselves, but that's how they liked it. I only had a couple of copies. Esmé always had her own copy bound with a pale-blue cover. A bound copy isn't much use for editing purposes. In fact it's a bloody nuisance. Publishers and readers prefer manuscripts to be submitted with the pages tagged together in chapters, or not tagged at all. But Esmé always wanted her own copy bound."

"And when you called in here to see Mrs. Carling on October fifteenth, the evening after Gerard Etienne died, did you get the impression that she was reluctant to hand over her manuscript, pretending, perhaps, that she couldn't find it, or that she didn't in fact any longer have it in her possession?"

As if recognizing the importance of the question, Mrs. Pitt-Cowley took her time in answering. Then she said: "How can I tell? But I do remember that the request disconcerted her. I think she was flustered. And it's difficult to see how she can actually have mislaid the manuscript. She wasn't careless about possessions which were important to her. And it's not as if there's a lot of space here in the flat. She didn't trouble to look for it, either. If you asked me to make a guess, I'd say that the manuscript wasn't any longer in her possession."

53

When they got back to the car Dalgliesh said: "I'll drive, Kate."
She took the left-hand seat and buckled her belt in silence. She liked to drive and knew that she did it well, but when, as now, he chose to take over, she was content to sit quietly beside him and occasionally watch the strong sensitive hands lying lightly on the wheel. Now, glancing quickly at him as they crossed Hammersmith Bridge, she saw in his face a look with which she was familiar: a stern withdrawn self-absorption as if he were stoically enduring a private pain. When she was first recruited to his team she thought that the look was one of controlled anger and feared the sudden bite of cold sarcasm which she suspected was one of his defences against lack of control and which his subordinates had come to dread. They had gathered vital evidence during the last two and a half hours and she longed to hear his reaction, but she knew better than to break the silence. He was driving with his usual quiet competence and it was difficult to believe that part of his mind was elsewhere. Was he worrying about the vulnerability of that child as well as mentally reviewing the evidence she had given? Was he grimly containing his outrage at the planned barbarity of Esmé Carling's death, a death which they now knew had been murder?

In other senior officers this look of stern withdrawal could have been anger at Daniel's incompetence. If Daniel had extracted from the child the truth about what had happened on that Thursday night Esmé Carling might be alive now. But could it really be called incompetence?

Both Carling and the child had told the same story and it was a convincing one. Children were good witnesses and they very seldom lied. If she had been sent to interview Daisy, would she have done any better? Would she have done any better this morning if Dalgliesh hadn't been there to intervene? She doubted whether Dalgliesh would say a word of blame, but that wouldn't prevent Daniel from blaming himself. She was heartily glad that she wasn't in his shoes.

They had driven over Hammersmith Bridge before he spoke.

"I think Daisy told us everything she knew, but the omissions are frustrating, aren't they? That one missing word would have made all the difference. The snake was outside the door. Which door? She heard a voice. Male or female? Someone was carrying a vacuum cleaner. Man or woman? But at least we don't have to rely on the implausibility of that suicide note to be sure now that this was murder."

In the Wapping incident room Daniel was working alone. Kate, embarrassed for him, wanted to leave him with Dalgliesh but it was difficult without the ruse appearing too obvious. Dalgliesh briefly reported the result of their morning visits. Daniel stood up. The action, reminding Kate of a prisoner under sentence, seemed instinctive. His strong face was very pale.

"I'm sorry, sir. I should have broken that alibi. It was a bad mistake."

"An unfortunate one, certainly."

"I ought to say, sir, that Sergeant Robbins wasn't convinced. He thought from the first that Daisy was lying and wanted to press her."

Dalgliesh said: "That's never easy with a child, is it? If it came to a battle of wills between Daisy and Sergeant Robbins I'm not sure I wouldn't back Daisy."

It was interesting, thought Kate, that Robbins hadn't trusted the child. He seemed to be able to combine a belief in the essential nobility of man with a reluctance to believe anything any witness said. Perhaps, being religious, he was more ready than Daniel to believe in original sin. But it was generous of Daniel to say what he had. Generous, but perhaps, if she was being cynical, and knowing AD, it had also been judicious.

He said, as if doggedly determined to make the worst of it: "But if I hadn't been satisfied, Esmé Carling would be alive today."

"Possibly. Don't over-indulge in guilt, Daniel. The person responsible for Esmé Carling's death is the person who killed her. What about the post-mortem? Anything unexpected?"

"Death by vagal inhibition, sir. She died as soon as the strap tightened round her neck. She was dead when she was put in the water."

"Well at least it was swift. What about the launch? Any news from Ferris?"

"Yes sir, good news." Daniel's face lightened. "He's found some minute fibres of cloth caught on a small splinter of wood on the cabin floor. They're pink, sir. She was wearing a pink-and-fawn tweed jacket. With luck the lab will be able to get a match."

They glanced at each other. Kate knew that each was feeling the same contained exultation. A physical clue at last, something that could be tagged, measured, scientifically examined, produced in court as evidence. They had already checked with Fred Bowling that Esmé Carling hadn't been in the launch since the previous summer. If the fibres matched, then they had proof that she had been killed in the launch. And if she had, who had subsequently moved it to the other side of the steps? Who else but her killer?

Dalgliesh said: "If the fibres match we can prove that she was in the cabin of the launch yesterday night. The obvious inference is that she died there. It would be a sensible plan on the part of the murderer to choose. He could wait with the body concealed until the river was quiet and choose his moment to string her up unobserved. But even if the fibres connect her to the launch, that doesn't mean they will connect her to the killer. We need to collect the coats and jackets of all the suspects who were on the scene and get them to the lab. Will you see to that, Daniel?"

"Including Mandy Price and Bartrum?"

"All of them."

Kate said: "All we need now is the minutest thread of pink fibre on one of the coats."

Dalgliesh said: "Not all we need. There's one depressing fact, Kate. Most of them will be able to claim that they knelt close to Esmé Carling's body, even touched her. There is more than one way in which a fibre could have got on their clothes."

Daniel added: "And what's the betting that this murderer knew damn well what he was about? He'll have taken off his coat before he got close to her, and made damn sure afterwards that he was clean."

54

Mandy had meant to get to work early next morning but to her astonishment on waking found that she had overslept and that it was already 8:45. She would probably have slept on if Maureen and Mike hadn't indulged in one of their arguments about the availability and the state of the bathroom, carried on as usual by Maureen shouting from the top of the stairs and Mike yelling back from the kitchen. A minute later there was a bang on her bedroom door followed immediately by Maureen bursting in. It was obvious that she was in one of her moods.

"Mandy, that bloody bike of yours takes up all the hall. Why can't you leave it in the front garden like anyone else?"

This was a perennial complaint. Mandy awoke to instant indignation.

"Because some arsehole would steal it, that's why. That bike's staying in the hall." She added sulkily: "I suppose it's too much to hope that the bathroom's free."

"It's free if you can put up with the state it's in. Mike's left the bath filthy as usual. If you want a bath you'll have to clean it yourself. And he's forgotten that this is his week to buy the toilet paper. I don't see why I should do all the thinking and all the work in this house."

It was obviously going to be one of those days. Neither Maureen nor Mike had been in when she had arrived home the previous evening. She had gone to bed but had tried to stay awake, listening for the door, longing to pour out her story. But it hadn't happened that way. She had fallen asleep despite herself. And now she heard them leave, two loud bangs of the door in quick succession. Maureen hadn't even bothered to enquire why she hadn't returned to the gig.

Things didn't improve when she got to Innocent House. She had looked forward to being first with the news, but there was no chance of that now. The partners had all come in early. George, busy taking a call, threw her a look of desperate appeal as she came in, as if any help would be welcome. It was apparent that the news had spread further than Innocent House.

"Yes, I'm afraid it is true. . . . Yes, it does look like suicide. . . . No, I'm afraid I haven't any details. . . . We don't yet know how she died. . . . I'm sorry. . . . Yes, the police have been here. . . . I'm sorry. . . . No, Miss Etienne isn't available at the moment. . . . No, Mr. de Witt isn't free either. Perhaps one of them could ring you back. . . . No, I'm sorry. I don't know when they'll be available."

He replaced the receiver and said: "One of Mr. de Witt's authors. I don't know how he learned the news. Perhaps he rang publicity and Maggie or Amy told him. Miss Etienne has instructed me to say as little as possible but it isn't easy. People aren't satisfied with speaking to me. They want to talk to one of the partners."

Mandy said: "I shouldn't bother with them. Just say 'Wrong number' and hang up. If you keep on doing it they'll soon get fed up."

The hall was empty. The house felt strangely different, unnaturally quiet, a house in mourning. Mandy had expected that the police would be there but there was no sign of their presence. In the office Miss Blackett was sitting at her word processor, staring at the screen as if mesmerized. Mandy had never seen her look so ill. She was very pale and her face seemed suddenly to have become the face of an old woman.

Mandy said: "Are you all right? You look awful."

Miss Blackett made an effort at dignified control. "Of course I'm not all right, Mandy. How can any of us be all right? This is the third death we've had in two months. It's dreadful. I don't know what's happening to the firm. Nothing's gone right with the Peverell Press since Mr. Peverell died. And I'm surprised you manage to look so cheerful. After all, you found her."

She looked close to tears. And there was something else. Miss Blackett was afraid. Mandy could almost smell her terror. She said uneasily: "Yes, well, I'm sorry she's dead. But it's not as if I knew her, is it? And she was old. And she did do it herself. It was her choice. She must have wanted to die. I mean, it's not like Mr. Gerard's death."

Miss Blackett, face flushed, cried out: "She wasn't old! How can you say that? And what if she was? The old have as much right to life as you."

"I never said they hadn't."

"That's what you implied. You should think before you speak, Mandy. You said that she was old and her death didn't matter."

"I didn't say that it didn't matter."

Mandy felt that she was becoming embroiled in a vortex of irrational emotion which she had no hope of understanding or controlling. And now she saw that Miss Blackett was almost crying. She was relieved when the door opened and Miss Etienne came in.

"Oh here you are, Mandy. We wondered if you were going to appear. Are you all right?"

"Yes thank you, Miss Etienne."

"It seems that next week we shall be rather thin on the ground. I suppose you'll want to leave too, once the initial excitement is over."

"No, Miss Etienne, I'd like to stay." She added with a flash of financial acumen: "If some of the staff are leaving and there's more work I think I ought to have a rise."

Miss Etienne gave her a look which Mandy interpreted as more cynically amused than disapproving. After a few seconds' pause she said: "All right. I'll speak to Mrs. Crealey. An extra £10 a week. But the rise won't be a reward for staying. We don't bribe staff to work at Peverell Press, nor do we submit to blackmail. You'll get it because your work warrants it." She turned to Miss Blackett. "The police will probably be here this afternoon. They may want to use Mr. Gerard's—I mean, my—office again. If so, I'll move upstairs with Miss Frances."

After she had left Mandy said: "Why don't you ask for a rise too? We're going to have to take on an extra load unless they recruit some replacements and that may not be too easy. It's like you said. Three deaths in two months. People may think twice about working here."

Miss Blackett had begun typing, eyes fixed on her shorthand notebook. "No thank you, Mandy. I don't take advantage of my employers in their hour of need. I have some principles."

"Oh well, you can afford them, I dare say. Seems to me that they've been taking advantage of you for the last twenty-odd years. Still, please yourself. I'll just have a word with Mrs. Crealey, then I'll make the coffee."

Mandy had tried to phone Mrs. Crealey's office before leaving home but there had been no reply. Now there was, and she gave the news succinctly, keeping to the bare facts and omitting any reference to her own emotions. With Miss Blackett listening with repressive disapproval, it was wise to be as brief and matter-of-fact as possible. The details could wait for their evening session together in the cosy.

She said: "I've asked for a rise. They're giving me another ten pounds a week. Yeah, that's what I thought. No, I said I'd stay on. I'll come into the office straight from work and we can have a talk."

She replaced the receiver. It was, she thought, a measure of Miss Blackett's odd mood that she omitted to remind her that she was not supposed to use the office telephone for her private calls.

There were more people in the kitchen than was normal before ten o'clock. Those of the staff who preferred to brew their own morning coffee rather than pay their weekly sub for Mrs. Demery's version of the drink seldom appeared before eleven. Pausing at the door, Mandy could hear the low buzz of gossiping voices. It stopped when she opened the door and they looked up guiltily, then greeted her with relief and flattering attention. Mrs. Demery was there, of course, and so was Emma Wainwright, Miss Etienne's anorexic former PA who was now working for Miss Peverell, together with Maggie FitzGerald and Amy Holden from publicity, Mr. Elton from contracts and rights and Dave from the warehouse, who had apparently come over from number 10 with the unconvincing excuse that the warehouse was out of milk. There was a strong smell of coffee and someone had been making toast. The kitchen was cosily conspiratorial but, even here, Mandy could sense fear.

Amy said: "We thought you might not come in. Poor Mandy! It must have been absolutely ghastly. I should have died. If there's a body on the premises trust you to find it. Go on, tell. Was she drowned, or hanged or what? None of the partners will tell us anything."

Mandy could have pointed out that it hadn't been she who had found Gerard Etienne's body. Instead she gave her account of the previous night but, even as she spoke, was aware that she was disappointing them. She had looked forward to this moment but now that she was the centre of their curiosity, she felt a curious reluctance to pander to it, almost as if there was something indecent in making Mrs. Carling's death the subject of gossip. The picture of that dead sodden face, the make-up washed away so that it looked stripped and defenceless in its ugliness, floated between her and their avid eyes. She couldn't understand what was happening to her, why her emotions should be so confused, so disturbing in their perplexity. What she had said to Miss Blackett had been the truth; she hadn't even known Mrs. Carling. She couldn't be feeling grief. She had no reason to feel guilty. What then was she feeling?

Mrs. Demery was unaccountably silent. She was quietly setting out cups and saucers on her trolley, but her sharp little eyes darted from face to face as if each held a secret which a moment's inattention might miss.

Maggie said: "Did you read the suicide note, Mandy?"

"No, but Mr. de Witt did. It was all about how badly the partners had behaved to her, how she was going to get her own back. 'Make their names stink,' I think that's what she wrote. I can't really remember."

Mr. Elton said: "You knew her better than most, Maggie. You did that big publicity tour with her eighteen months ago. What was she like?"

"She was no trouble. I got on all right with Esmé. She could be a bit demanding but I've been on tours with far worse. And she did care about her fans. Nothing was too much trouble. Always a word when they queued for a signing, and she would personalize every book for them, any message they wanted. Not like Gordon Holgarth. All they ever get from him is a scrawled signature, a scowl and a puff of cigar smoke in the face."

"Did you think she was the suicidal type?"

"Is there a suicidal type? I'm not sure what the words mean. But if you're asking me if I'm surprised that she's killed herself, the answer is yes. I am surprised. Very surprised."

Mrs. Demery spoke at last. "If she did."

"She must have done, Mrs. Demery. She left a note."

"A funny kind of note if what Mandy remembers is right. I'd need to have a look at that note before I was satisfied. And it's obvious the police aren't. If they were, why have they taken the launch?"

Maggie said: "Is that why we were collected from Charing Cross by taxi instead of the launch this morning? I thought the launch had broken down. Fred Bowling never said anything about the police when he met us."

"Told not to, I dare say. But they've taken it all right. Came first thing in the morning and towed it away. I thought they might have done when it wasn't here, so I asked him. It's over at Wapping Police Station."

Maggie was pouring hot water onto coffee grains. She paused, kettle poised.

"You're not saying, Mrs. D, that the police think Mrs. Carling was murdered?"

"I don't know what the police think. I know what I think. She wasn't one to commit suicide, not Esmé Carling."

Emma Wainwright was sitting at the end of the table, her skeletal fingers wrapped round a mug of coffee. She had made no attempt to drink, but was staring down at the thin swirl of foaming milk as if mesmerized with disgust.

Now she looked up and said in her harsh rather guttural voice: "This is the second body you've found, Mandy, since you arrived at Innocent House. We never had any of this trouble before. They'll be calling you the Typist of Death. If you go on like this you'll find it difficult to get another job."

Mandy, enraged, spat out her retort. "Not so difficult as you will. At least I don't look as if I've come out of a concentration camp. You should see yourself. You look disgusting."

For a few seconds there was a horrified silence. Six pairs of eyes glanced quickly at Emma, then looked away. She sat very still, then suddenly stumbled to her feet and hurled the coffee cup across the room into the sink, where it smashed spectacularly. Then she gave a high wail, burst into tears and rushed out of the room. Amy gave a little cry and wiped a splash of hot coffee from her cheek.

Maggie was shocked. "You shouldn't have said that, Mandy. That was cruel. Emma's ill. She can't help it."

"Of course she can help it. She only does it to upset other people. And she started the row. She called me the Typist of Death. I'm not bad luck. It's not my fault I found them."

Amy looked at Maggie: "D'you think I ought to go to her?"

"Better leave her alone. You know how she is. She's upset because Miss Claudia has taken over Blackie as her PA instead of her. She's already told Miss Claudia that she wants to leave at the end of the week. If you ask me I think she's plain scared. I'm not sure that I blame her."

Torn between angry self-justification and a remorse which was the more disagreeable because she suffered from it so rarely, Mandy felt that she too would enjoy the relief of hurling crockery across the room and bursting into tears. What was happening to them all, to Innocent House, to herself? Was this what violent death did to people? She had expected the day to be pleasantly exciting, filled with comfortable gossip and speculation, herself at the heart of all the interest. Instead it had been hell from the start.

The door opened and Miss Etienne appeared. She said coldly: "Maggie, Amy and Mandy, there's work to be done. If you've no intention of doing it, it would be better if you said so frankly and went home."

55

Dalgliesh had said that he wanted to see all the partners in the boardroom at three o'clock and that Miss Blackett should be with them. None of them made any objection either to the summons or to her proposed presence. They had handed over the clothes they had been wearing when Esmé Carling's body was found without argument or question. But then, thought Kate, they were all intelligent people; they hadn't needed to ask why. None of them had requested the presence of a solicitor, and she wondered whether they feared that this might look suspiciously premature, had confidence in their ability to look after their own interests, or were fortified by the knowledge of their innocence.

She and Dalgliesh sat on one side of the table with the partners and Miss Blackett facing them. At their last meeting in the boardroom, after Gerard Etienne's death, she had been aware of a mixture of emotions emanating from them: curiosity, shock, grief and apprehension. Now all she could smell was fear. It was like a contagion. It seemed that they infected each other, and even the air of the room. Only Miss Blackett showed it outwardly. Dauntsey looked very old and sat with the resignation of a geriatric patient awaiting admission. De Witt had seated himself close to Frances Peverell. His eyes were watchful under the heavy lids. Miss Blackett sat forward in her chair with the quivering intentness of a trapped animal. Her face was very white but from time to time hectic blotches spread over her cheeks and forehead like the visitation of a disease. Frances Peverell's face was taut and she ran her tongue over her lips. On her other side Claudia Etienne was outwardly the most composed. She looked as elegant as always and Kate saw that her make-up had been applied with care and wondered whether this was a gesture of defiance or a small but gallant attempt to impose normality on the psychological chaos of Innocent House.

Dalgliesh had laid on the table Esmé Carling's final message. It was now enclosed in a plastic cover. He read it through, his voice almost expressionless. No one spoke. Then, without commenting on it, he said quietly: "We now believe that Mrs. Carling came to Innocent House on the evening of Mr. Etienne's death."

Claudia's voice was sharp: "Esmé came here? Why?"

"Presumably to see your brother. Is that so improbable? She had learned only the previous day that her new novel had been rejected by Peverell Press. She had tried to see Mr. Etienne first thing that morning but had been refused access to him by Miss Blackett."

Blackie cried: "But he was in the partners' meeting! No one interrupts the partners' meeting! I was specifically told not even to put through urgent telephone calls."

Claudia's voice was impatient: "No one's blaming you, Blackie. Of course you were right not to admit the woman."

As if there had been no interruption, Dalgliesh continued: "She went straight from this office to Liverpool Street and her signing at Cambridge only to find that someone from here had sent a fax cancelling it. Was it likely that she would go quietly home and do nothing? You all knew her. Wasn't it much more likely that she would come here and make another attempt to confront Mr. Etienne with her grievances, arriving at a time when she expected to find him alone, unprotected by his secretary? It seems to have been generally known that he worked late on Thursdays."

De Witt said: "But you must surely have checked, asked her where she was that evening? If you seriously suspect that Gerard was murdered, then Esmé Carling had to be among the suspects."

"We did check. She provided a very convincing alibi, a child who claimed to have spent the hours from six-thirty to midnight with her in her flat. Her name is Daisy and she has now told us everything she knows. Mrs. Carling persuaded her to provide her alibi for that night and admitted that she had been in Innocent House."

Claudia said: "And now you're condescending to tell us. Well that makes a change, Commander. It's time we were told something positive. Gerard was my brother. You've been suggesting from the first that his death wasn't an accident and you seem no nearer to explaining how or why he died."

De Witt said quietly: "Don't be naïve, Claudia. The Commander isn't confiding in us out of consideration for your sisterly feelings. He's telling us that the child, Daisy, has been questioned and has told everything she knows so there's no point in anyone trying to trace her, suborn her, bribe her or silence her in any way."

The implication of his words was plain and was so appalling that Kate half expected a chorus of outraged protestations. None came. Claudia flushed deeply and looked as if she were about to remonstrate, then thought better of it. The rest of the partners froze into silence, apparently unwilling to meet each other's eyes. It was as if the remark had opened vistas of conjecture so unwelcome and horrifying that they were best left unexplored.

Dauntsey said, his voice a little too carefully controlled: "So you have one suspect who is known to have been here, and probably at the relevant time. If she had nothing to hide, why didn't she come forward?"

De Witt added: "And it's odd when you come to think of it that she's been so silent since. I don't suppose you were expecting a letter of condolence, Claudia, but I'd have expected some word, perhaps a fresh attempt to get us to accept the novel."

Frances said: "She probably thought it was tactful to wait a little. It would look pretty callous if she began badgering us so soon after Gerard's death."

De Witt added: "It would certainly have been the least propitious time to try to get us to change our mind."

Claudia said sharply: "We wouldn't have changed our mind. Gerard was right, it's a bad book. It wouldn't have done our reputation any good, or hers either for that matter."

Frances said: "But we could have rejected it with more kindness, seen her, tried to explain to her."

Claudia turned on her. "For God's sake, Frances, don't start reopening all that old argument. What good would it have done? Rejection is rejection. She would have resented the decision even if it had been broken to her over champagne and lobster thermidor at Claridges."

Dauntsey seemed to have been pursuing his private line of thought. He said: "I don't see how Esmé Carling could have had anything to do with Gerard's death, but I suppose it's possible she was responsible for putting the snake round his neck. That would seem rather more her style."

Claudia said: "You mean she found the body and decided to add a personal comment, as it were?"

Dauntsey went on: "But then it's hardly likely, is it? Gerard must have been alive when she arrived here. Presumably he let her in."

Claudia said: "Not necessarily. He could have left the front door open or ajar that night. It's unlike Gerard to be careless about security, but it's not impossible. She could somehow have gained access after he was dead."

De Witt said: "Even if she did, why should she go up to the little archives room?"

They seemed, for the moment, to have forgotten the presence of Dalgliesh and Kate.

Frances said: "To look for him."

Dauntsey said: "But wouldn't she be more likely to wait for him in his office? She would have known that he was somewhere in the building. His jacket was still slung over the back of his chair. Sooner or later he'd be back. And then there's the snake. Would she have known where to find it?"

Having demolished his case, Dauntsey sank again into silence. Claudia glanced from partner to partner as if inviting silent assent to what she proposed to say. Then she looked full at Dalgliesh.

"I can see that this new information that Esmé Carling was in Innocent House on the night Gerard died does put her suicide in a different light. But however she died, the partners couldn't have been concerned. All of us can account for our movements."

Kate thought: She doesn't want to use the word alibi.

Claudia went on: "I was with my fiancé, Frances and James were together, Gabriel was with Sydney Bartrum." She turned to him, her voice suddenly hard: "Brave of you, Gabriel, to walk to the Sailor's Return alone so soon after your mugging."

"I have walked alone in my capital city for over sixty years. One mugging isn't going to stop me."

"And it was convenient that you happened to be leaving just as Esmé's taxi was arriving."

De Witt said quietly: "Fortuitous, Claudia, not convenient."

But Claudia was looking at Dauntsey as if he were a stranger: "And the pub may be able to confirm when you and Sydney arrived. But it is, of course, about the busiest on the river and with the longest bar, as well as access from the river walk, and you arrived separately. I doubt whether they'll be able to be precise even if anyone remembers two particular customers. You didn't draw attention to yourselves, I suppose?"

Dauntsey said quietly: "That was not our intention in going there."

"Why did you? I didn't know you used the Sailor's Return. I shouldn't have thought it was your choice of watering hole. Altogether too raucous. And I hadn't realized that you and Sydney were drinking pals."

It was, thought Kate, as if they were suddenly conducting a private war. She heard Frances's soft anguished cry: "Oh don't, please don't!"

De Witt said: "Is your alibi any more reliable, Claudia?"

She turned on him. "Or yours, come to that. Are you saying that Frances wouldn't lie for you?"

"She might. I don't know. As it happens she isn't required to. We were together from seven o'clock."

Claudia said: "Noticing nothing, seeing nothing, hearing nothing. Totally occupied with each other." Before de Witt could reply she went on: "It's odd, isn't it, how momentous events begin with something quite small. If someone hadn't sent that fax cancelling Esmé's signing she might not have come back here that night, wouldn't have seen what she did see, may not have died."

Blackie could bear it no longer, their barely concealed antipathy, and now this horror. She leapt up and cried: "Stop it, please stop it! And it isn't true. She killed herself. Mandy found her. Mandy saw. You know she killed herself. The fax has nothing to do with it."

Claudia said sharply: "Of course she killed herself. Any other idea is wishful thinking on the part of the police. Why accept suicide when you can go for the more exciting option? And that fax may have been the last straw for Esmé. Whoever sent it bears a heavy responsibility."

She was gazing fixedly at Blackie, and the heads of the others turned as if Claudia had pulled on an invisible string.

Claudia suddenly said: "It was you! I thought so. It was you, Blackie! You sent it!"

They watched appalled as Blackie's mouth slowly and silently opened. For what seemed minutes rather than seconds she held her breath, and then she burst into uncontrollable sobbing. Claudia got up from her seat and took her by the shoulders. For a second it looked as if she were going to shake her.

"And what about the rest of the mischief? What about the altered proofs, the stolen artwork? Was that you too?"

"No! No, I swear it. Just the fax. Nothing else. Only that one. She was so unkind about Mr. Peverell. She said terrible things. It isn't true he thought I was a nuisance. He cared about me. He relied on me. Oh God, I wish I were dead like him."

She stumbled to her feet and, still howling, blundered to the door, holding out a hand before her like a blind woman feeling for her way.

Frances half rose and de Witt was already on his feet when Claudia grasped his arm.

"For God's sake leave her alone, James. We don't all welcome your shoulder to cry on. Some of us prefer to bear our own misery."

James flushed and immediately sat down.

Dalgliesh said: "I think we had better stop now. When Miss Blackett is calmer Inspector Miskin will talk to her."

De Witt said: "Congratulations, Commander. It was clever of you to get us to do your job for you. It would have been kinder to have questioned Blackie in private but that would have taken longer, wouldn't it, and might have been less successful."

Dalgliesh said: "A woman has died and it is my job to discover how and why. I'm afraid that kindness isn't my first priority."

Frances said, almost in tears, looking across at de Witt: "Poor Blackie! Oh my God, oh poor Blackie! What are they going to do with her?"

It was Claudia who replied. "Inspector Miskin will comfort her and then Dalgliesh will grill her. Or, if she's lucky, the other way round. You needn't worry about Blackie. Sending that fax isn't a hanging matter, it isn't even an indictable offence." She turned violently and spoke to Dauntsey. "Gabriel, I'm sorry. I'm so terribly sorry. I'm sorry, sorry. I don't know what came over me. My God, we've got to stand together." When he didn't reply, she said almost beseechingly: "You don't think it was murder, do you? Esmé's death, I'm saying. You don't think someone killed her?"

Dauntsey said quietly: "You've heard the Commander read that message she wrote for us. Did that really sound to you like a suicide note?"

56

Mr. Winston Johnson was large, black, amiable, apparently unworried by the ambience of a police station and philosophical about losing possible fares by the necessity to call in at Wapping. His voice was a deep attractive bass but its accent was pure cockney. When Daniel apologized for the need to encroach on his working time he said: "Don't reckon I've lost much. Picked up a fare wanting Canary Wharf on the way here. A couple of American tourists. Good tippers too. That's why I'm a bit late."

Daniel passed over a photograph of Esmé Carling. "This is the fare we're interested in. Thursday night to Innocent Walk. Recognize her?"

Mr. Johnson took the photograph in his left hand. "That's right. Hailed me at Hammersmith Bridge at about half past six. Said she wanted to be at number ten Innocent Walk by seven-thirty. No problem there. It wasn't going to take the best part of an hour, not unless the traffic was extra bad or we'd had a bomb alert and your chaps had closed down one of the roads. We made good time."

"You mean you got there before seven-thirty."

"Would've done, but she tapped the glass when we got to the Tower and said she didn't want to be early. Asked me to kill time. I asked her where she'd like to go and she said, 'Anywhere, so long as we get to Innocent Walk at seven-thirty.' So I took her as far as the Isle of Dogs and drove round a bit, then came back down The Highway. It put a few bob on the fare but I reckon that wasn't her worry. Eighteen pounds in all that cost her, and she gave a tip."

"How did you approach Innocent Walk?"

"Left off The Highway down Garnet Street, then right off Wapping Wall."

"Did you see anyone in particular?"

"Anyone in particular? There were one or two chaps around but I can't say I noticed anyone particular. Watching the road, wasn't I?"

"Did Mrs. Carling speak to you on the journey?"

"Only what I told you, that she didn't want to get to Innocent Walk until half past seven, so would I drive around, like."

"And you're sure she wanted number ten Innocent Walk, not Innocent House."

"Number ten is what she asked for and number ten is where I dropped her. By the iron gates at the end of Innocent Passage. Seemed to me she was anxious not to go further down Innocent Walk. She tapped on the window as soon as I turned into it and said that's as far as she wanted."

"Did you see whether the gate into Innocent Passage was open?"

"It wasn't standing open. That's not to say it was locked."

Daniel asked, knowing what the answer would be but needing to get it on record: "She didn't mention why she was going to Innocent Walk, whether she was meeting anyone, for example?"

"Wasn't my business, was it, guv?"

"Maybe not, but fares do chat occasionally."

"A darned sight too much, some of them. But this one didn't. Just sat there clutching her bloody great shoulder-bag."

Another photograph was passed over. "This shoulder-bag?"

"Could be. Looks like it. Mind you, I couldn't swear to it."

"Did the bag look full, as if she was carrying something heavy or bulky?"

"Can't help you there, mate. But I did notice that it was slung round her shoulder and it was large."

"And you can swear that you drove this woman from Hammersmith to Innocent Walk on Thursday and left her alive at the end of Innocent Passage at seven-thirty?"

"Well I certainly didn't leave her dead. Yes I can swear to that all right. Do you want me to make a statement?"

"You've been very helpful, Mr. Johnson. Yes, we'd like a statement. We'll take it next door."

Mr. Johnson went out accompanied by the detective constable. Almost immediately the door opened and Sergeant Robbins put his head in. He made no attempt to disguise his excitement.

"Just checking on the river traffic, sir. We've just had a telephone call from the Port of London Authority. It's in reply to that ring I gave them about an hour ago. Their launch, *Royal Nore*, was passing Innocent House last night. Their chairman had a private dinner party on board. The meal was at eight and three of his guests were anxious to see Innocent House so they were out on deck. They reckon the time was about twenty to eight. They can swear, sir, that the body wasn't suspended then and that they saw no one on the forecourt. And there's another thing, sir. They're adamant that the launch was to the left, not to the right of the steps. I mean to the left looking from the river."

Daniel said slowly: "Bloody hell! So AD's instinct was right. She was killed in the launch. The killer heard the Port of London Authority boat approaching and kept the body out of sight before he strung her up."

"But why that side of the railings? Why move the boat?"

"In the hope that we wouldn't realize that that's where she was killed. The last thing he wants is to have scene-of-crime officers crawling over that launch. And there's another thing. He met her inside the wrought-iron gates at the bottom of Innocent Passage. He had a key and was waiting for her, standing in the side doorway. It would be safer to keep to that end of the forecourt, as far as possible from Innocent House and number twelve."

Robbins had thought of an objection. "Wasn't it risky moving the launch? Miss Peverell and Mr. de Witt might have heard it from her flat. If they had, surely they'd have come down to investigate."

"They claim they couldn't even hear a taxi unless it was actually driven over the cobbles of Innocent Lane. It's something we can check, of course. If they did hear an engine they probably thought it was any passing launch on the river. They had the curtains drawn, remember. Of course there's always another possibility."

"What's that, sir?"

"That it was they who moved the launch."

57

It was only just 5:30 on Saturday, normally a busy day, but the shop was locked with the closed notice showing through the glass. Claudia rang the bell at the side and within seconds Declan's figure appeared and the door was unbolted. As soon as she was through he gave a quick look down both sides of the street, then locked the door again behind her.

She said: "Where's Mr. Simon?"

"In hospital. That's where I've been. He's very ill. He thinks it's cancer."

"What do they say, the people at the hospital?"

"They're going to do some tests. I could see that they think it's serious. I made him call in Dr. Cohen—that's his GP—this morning and he said, 'For God's sake, why didn't you see me earlier?' Simon knows he isn't going to come out of hospital, he told me. Look, come into the back room, won't you, it'll be more comfortable there."

He neither kissed her nor touched her.

She thought, He's speaking to me as if I were a customer. Something had happened to him, something more than old Simon's illness. She had never seen him like this before. He seemed to be possessed by a mixture of excitement and terror. His eyes looked almost wild and his skin glistened with sweat. She could smell him, an alien feral smell. She followed him into the conservatory. All three bars of the wall-mounted electric fire were on and the room was very warm. The familiar objects looked strange, diminished, the petty leavings of dead and unregarded lives.

She didn't sit but stood watching him. He seemed unable to keep still, pacing the few yards of free space like a caged animal. He was more formally dressed than usual and the unfamiliar tie and jacket were at odds with his almost manic restlessness, the dishevelled hair. She wondered how long he had been drinking. There was a bottle of wine, two-thirds empty, and a single stained glass among the clutter on one of the tables. Suddenly he stopped the restless pacing and turned to her, and she saw in his eyes a look of mingled pleading, shame and fear.

He said: "The police have been here. Look, Claudia, I had to tell them about Thursday, the night that Gerard died. I had to tell them that you left me at Tower Pier, that we weren't together all the time."

She said: "Had to? What do you mean, had to?"

"They forced it out of me."

"What with, thumb-screws and hot pincers? Did Dalgliesh twist your arms and slap your face? Did they take you to Notting Hill nick and punch you up, cleverly leaving no bruises? We know how good they are at that, we watch the TV."

"Dalgliesh wasn't here. It was that Jew-boy and a sergeant. Claudia, you don't know what it was like. They think that that novelist, Esmé Carling, was murdered."

"They can't know that."

"I'm telling you, that's what they think. And they know I had a motive for Gerard's murder."

"If it was murder."

"They knew that I needed cash, that you'd promised to get it for me. We could've moored the launch at Innocent House and done it together."

"Only we didn't."

"They don't believe that."

"Did they say that directly, any of it?"

"No, but they didn't need to. I could see what they were thinking."

She said patiently: "Look, if they seriously suspected you they would have had to question you under caution at a police station and tape-record the interview. Is that what they did?"

"Of course not."

"They didn't invite you to go with them to the station, tell you that you could call a lawyer?"

"Nothing like that. They did say at the end that I must call in at Wapping and make a statement."

"So what did they really do?"

"Kept on about was I really sure that we'd been together all the time, that you'd driven me back here from Innocent House. How much better it was to tell the truth. The Inspector used the words 'accessory to murder,' I'm sure he did."

"Are you? I'm not."

"Anyway, I told them."

She said quietly and through lips that no longer seemed her own: "You realize what you've done? If Esmé Carling was murdered then probably Gerard was too, and if he was, the same person was responsible for both deaths. It would be too much of a coincidence to have two murderers in one firm. All you've done is to get yourself suspected of two deaths, not one."

He was almost crying. "But we were together here when Esmé died. You came here straight from work. I let you in. We were together the whole evening. We were making love. I told them that."

"But Mr. Simon wasn't here when I arrived, was he? No one saw me but you. So what proof have we?"

"But we were together! We've got an alibi—we both have an alibi!"

"But are the police going to believe it now? You've admitted that you lied about the night of Gerard's death; why shouldn't you be lying again about the night when Esmé died? You were so anxious to save your own skin that you hadn't the sense to see that you were dropping yourself deeper in the shit."

He turned from her and poured more wine into the glass. He held out the bottle and said: "Do you want some? I'll get a glass."

"No thank you."

Again he turned away from her. "Look," he said, "I don't think we ought to see each other again. Not for quite a time anyway. I mean, we oughtn't to be seen together until all this is cleared up."

She said: "Something else has happened, hasn't it? It's not only the alibi."

It was almost laughable how his face changed. The look of shame and fear gave way to a flush of excitement, a sly satisfaction. How like a child he is, she thought, and wondered what new toy had come within his grasp. But she knew that the contempt she felt was more for herself than for him.

He said, willing her to understand: "There is something else. It's rather good really. It's Simon. He's sent for his solicitor. He's going to make a will leaving me the whole of the business and the property. Well, there's no one else to leave it to, is there? He's got no relations. He knows he'll never get to the sun now, so I might as well have it. He'd rather me than the government."

"I see," she said. And she did see. She was no longer necessary. The money she had inherited from Gerard was no longer required. She said, keeping her voice calm, "If the police seriously suspect you, and I very much doubt whether they do, not seeing each other isn't going to make any difference. If anything it will look more suspicious. That's exactly how two guilty people would behave. But you're right. We won't see each other again, not ever if I can help it. You don't need me and I certainly don't need you. You have a certain farouche charm and a mild entertainment value, but you're hardly the world's greatest lover, are you?"

She was surprised that she could walk to the door without faltering, but she had a little difficulty with the bolts. She found that he was close behind her. He said, his voice almost pleading: "But you can see how it looked. You asked me to go on the river with you. You said it was important."

"It was important. I was going to speak to Gerard after the partners' meeting, remember? I thought I might have something good to tell you."

"And then you asked me for an alibi. You asked me to say that we were together until two o'clock. You rang from the archives room as soon as you were alone with the body. You just had time. And it was the first thing you thought about. You told me what to say. You forced me to lie."

"And you've told the police that, of course."

"You could see how it looked to them, how it will look to anyone You took the launch back on your own. You were alone at Innocent House with Gerard. You've inherited his flat, his shares, his life-assurance money."

She felt the strength of the door against her back. She turned to face him and she saw the dawning of fear in his eyes as she spoke.

"So aren't you afraid to be with me? Aren't you terrified to be here alone with me? I've already killed two people, why should I worry about a third? Perhaps I'm a homicidal maniac, you can't be sure, can you? God, Declan! Do you really believe I killed Gerard, a man worth ten of you, just to buy you this place and that pathetic collection of junk which you acquire to try and convince yourself that your life has a meaning, that you're a man?"

She couldn't remember opening the door, but she heard it close firmly behind her. The night seemed to her very cold and she found that she was shivering violently. So it has ended, she thought, ended in bitterness, acrimony, cheap sexual insult, humiliation. But then, doesn't it always? She pushed her hands deep into her coat pockets and, hunching her shoulders into her collar, walked briskly to where she had parked the car.

Book Five

FINAL PROOF

58

It was early Monday evening and Daniel was working alone in the archives room. He wasn't sure what had brought him back to these close-packed, musty-smelling shelves unless it was to perform a self-imposed penance. It seemed that he couldn't even for a moment put out of his mind his blunder over Esmé Carling's alibi. It wasn't only Daisy Reed who had deceived him; Esmé Carling had too, and he could have pressed her more strongly. Dalgliesh hadn't referred again to the mistake, but it wasn't one he was likely to forget. Daniel didn't know which was worse, AD's forbearance or Kate's tact.

He worked on, taking each pile of about ten files into the little archives room. It was warm enough; he had been provided with a small electric fire. But the room wasn't comfortable. Without the fire, the cold struck with an immediate chill which was almost unnatural; with it the room soon became unpleasantly warm. He wasn't superstitious. He had no sense that the ghosts of the unquiet dead were the watchers of his solitary, methodical search. The room was bleak, soulless, commonplace, evoking only a vague unease born paradoxically not of horror's contagion but of its absence.

He had taken out the next tranche of files on a top shelf when he saw behind them a small parcel of brown paper done up with old string. Taking it to the table, he struggled with the knots and finally got it undone. It was an old leather-covered Prayer Book measuring about six inches by four with the initials F.P. engraved in gold on the cover.

The Prayer Book had obviously been well used; the initials were almost indecipherable. He opened it at the first brown stiff page and saw in crude writing the superscription: "Printed by John Baskett, Printers to the Kings most Excellent Majesty and the Assigns of Thomas Newcomb, and Henry Hills, Deceas'd. 1716. *Cum Privilegio.*" He turned the pages with some interest. There were thin red lines down each margin and the middle of the page. He knew little of the Anglican Prayer Book but noted that there was a special "Form of Prayer with Thanksgiving to be used yearly upon the Fifth of November, for the happy Deliverance of King James I and Parliament from the most Traitorous and Bloody intended Massacre by Gunpowder." He doubted whether this was still part of the Anglican liturgy.

It was then that the sheet of paper fell out of the back of the book. It was folded once, whiter than the pages of the Prayer Book but as thick. There was no superscription. The message was written in black ink, the hand uncertain, but the words were as plain as the day they were penned:

I, Francis Peverell, write this with my own hand on the Fourth of September 1850 at Innocent House, in my last agony. The disease that has laid its hold on me for the past eighteen months will soon have finished its work, and by the grace of God I shall be free. My hand has written those words, "by the grace of God," and I shall not delete them. I have neither strength nor time for rewriting. But the most that I can expect from God is the grace of extinction. I have no hope of Heaven and no fear of the pains of Hell, having suffered my Hell here on earth for the last fifteen years. I have refused all palliatives for my present agony. I have not touched the laudanum of oblivion. Her death was more merciful than mine. This, my confession, can bring no relief to mind or body since I have not sought absolution nor confessed my sin to a living soul. Nor have I made restitution. What restitution can a man make for the murder of his wife?

I write these words because justice to her memory demands that the truth be told. Yet I still cannot bring myself to make public confession, nor to lift from her memory the stain of suicide. I killed her because I needed her money to finish the work on Innocent House. I had spent what she brought as a marriage-portion but there were funds tied up and denied to me that would come to me on her death. She loved me but she would not pass them over. She saw my love of the house as an obsession and a sin. She thought that I cared more for Innocent House than for her or for our children, and she was right.

The deed could not have been more easy. She was a reserved woman whose shyness and disinclination for company meant that she had no intimate acquaintances. All her family were dead. She was known by the servants to be unhappy and, in preparation for her death, I confided to certain of my colleagues and friends that I was worried about her health and spirits. On the twenty-fourth of September on a calm autumnal night I called her up to the third floor telling her I had something to show her. We were alone in the house, except for the servants. She came out to me where I stood on the balcony. She was a slight woman and it was only a second's work to lift her bodily and cast her to her death. Then, without hurrying, I went swiftly downstairs to the library and was there, sitting quietly reading, when they brought me the terrible news. I was never suspected. Why should I be? They would not suspect a respected man of murdering his wife.

I have lived for Innocent House and killed for it but, since her death, the house has given me no joy. I leave this confession to be handed in each generation to the eldest son. I implore all who read it to keep my secret. It will come first to my son, Francis Henry, and then in time to his son, and to all my descendants. I have nothing to hope for in this world or the next, and no message to give. I write because it is necessary before I die that I tell the truth.

At the bottom he had signed his name and the date.

After reading the confession, Daniel sat still for a full two minutes, considering. He wondered why these words, speaking to him over a century and a half, should have affected him so powerfully. He felt that he had no right to read them, that the proper course was to replace the paper in the Prayer Book, rewrap the book and place it back on the shelf. But he supposed that he ought at least to let Dalgliesh know what he had found. Was this confession the reason why Henry Peverell had been so unwilling to have the archives examined? He must have known of its existence. Was he shown it when he came of age, or had it been mislaid before then and become part of family folklore, whispered about but never actually acknowledged? Had Frances Peverell been shown it when she came of age, or had the words "eldest son" always been taken literally? But it surely had no relevance to Gerard Etienne's murder. This was a Peverell tragedy, a Peverell shame, as old as the paper on which it was confessed. He could understand that the family would want it kept secret. It would be disagreeable whenever the house was admired to have to confess that it had been built with money obtained by murder. After a little thought he replaced the paper, carefully reparcelled the Prayer Book and left it on one side.

There were footsteps, light but definite, approaching through the archives room. And now, for a second, remembering that murdered wife, he was touched with a slight shiver of superstitious awe. Then sense reasserted itself. These were the footsteps of a living woman and he knew whose.

Claudia Etienne stood in the doorway. She said without preamble: "Will you be long?"

"Not very long. Perhaps an extra hour, maybe less."

"I shall be leaving at half past six. I'm turning off the lights except on the stairs. Will you turn those off when you leave and set the alarm?"

"Of course."

He opened the nearer file and appeared to be studying it. He didn't want to talk to her. It would be unwise now to be drawn into any conversation without the presence of a third party.

She said: "I'm sorry I lied about my alibi for Gerard's death. It was partly fear, mostly the wish to avoid complications. But I didn't kill him, none of us did." He didn't reply, nor did he look at her. She said, with a note of desperation: "How long is this going to go on? Can't you tell me? Haven't you any idea? The coroner hasn't even released my brother's body for cremation. Can't you understand what that's doing to me?"

Then he looked up at her. If he had been capable of pity for her, seeing her face, he would have felt it then. "I'm sorry," he said, "I can't discuss it now."

Without another word she turned abruptly and left. He waited till the footsteps had faded, then went out and locked the door of the archives room. He should have remembered that Dalgliesh wanted it kept secure at all times.

59

At 6:25 Claudia locked away the files she had been working on and went upstairs to wash and fetch her coat. The house was ablaze with light. Since Gerard's death she had hated working alone in the darkness. Now chandeliers, wall sconces, the great globes at the foot of the stairs illumined the splendour of painted ceilings, the intricacies of carved wood and the pillars of coloured marble. Inspector Aaron could turn the lights off on the way down. She wished she hadn't given way to the impulse to go to the little archives room. She had hoped that, seeing him alone, she might have extracted some information about the progress of the enquiry, some idea when it was likely to end. The thought had been folly, the result humiliation. She wasn't a person to him. He didn't see her as a human being, a woman who was alone, afraid, burdened with unexpected and onerous responsibilities. To him, to Dalgliesh, to Kate Miskin she was only one, and perhaps the chief, of their suspects. She wondered whether every murder investigation dehumanized all those caught up in it.

Most of the staff parked their cars behind the locked gate in Innocent Passage. Claudia was the only one who used the garage. She was very fond of her Porsche 911. It was now seven years old, but she wanted no replacement and disliked leaving it ungaraged. She unlocked the door of number 10, moved across the passage and opened the door into the garage. Putting up a hand to the light she pressed it down. There was no response; obviously the bulb had gone. And then, as she stood there irresolute, she was aware of the sound of gentle breathing, the knowledge, immediate and terrifying, that someone was standing there in the darkness. And at that moment the noose of leather came down over her head and tightened round her neck. She was jerked violently backwards, and felt the crack of the concrete momentarily stunning her and then its scrape against the back of her skull.

It was a long strap. She tried to reach out to struggle with whoever was holding it, but there was no strength in her arms, and every time she tried to move the noose tightened and her mind swam through an agony of pain and terror into brief unconsciousness. She thrashed feebly on its end like a hooked and dying fish, her feet scrabbling ineffectively for a hold on the rough concrete.

And then she heard his voice. "Lie still, Claudia. Lie still and listen. Nothing will happen while you lie still."

She ceased her struggles and at once the dreadful throttling eased. His voice was speaking quietly, persuasively. She heard what he said and her numbed brain at last understood. He was telling her that she had to die, and why.

She wanted to shout out that it was a terrible mistake, that it wasn't true, but her voice was throttled and she knew that only by lying totally motionless could she stay alive. He was explaining now that it would look like suicide. The strap would be tied to the fixed wheel of the car, the engine would be left running. She would be dead by then but it was necessary to him that the garage should be full of a fatal gas. He explained this to her patiently, almost kindly, as if it were important to him that she should understand. He told her that she had no alibi for either of the murders now. The police would think she had killed herself from fear of arrest or remorse.

And now he had finished. She thought: I won't die. I won't let him kill me. I won't die, not here, not like this, hauled about like an animal on this garage floor. She summoned up her will. She thought: I must pretend to be dead, fainted, half-dead. If I can get him off his guard I can twist round and seize the strap. I can overpower him if only I can get to my feet.

She summoned up her strength for this last move. But he had been waiting for just this, he was ready. As soon as she moved, the noose was jerked taut again and this time it did not slacken.

He waited until at last the body's dreadful contortions were stilled, the last gurglings silenced. Then he let go of the strap and, bending, listened for the absent breath. He got up and, taking the bulb from his pocket, stretched up and replaced it in the socket in the low ceiling.

Now, with the garage lit, he could see to take the keys from her pocket, unlock the car and tie the end of the strap round the wheel. His gloved hands worked swiftly and without fumbling. Lastly he turned on the engine. Her body lay sprawled as if she had flung herself from the open door of the car, knowing that either the noose or the fatal exhaust fumes would finish her off. And it was at that moment that he heard the footsteps coming down the passage towards the garage door.

60

It was 6:27. In Frances Peverell's flat the phone rang. As soon as James spoke her name she knew that something was wrong.

She said at once: "James, what is it?"

"Rupert Farlow is dead. He died in hospital an hour ago."

"Oh James, I'm so terribly sorry. Were you with him?"

"No. Ray was. He only wanted Ray. It's so strange, Frances. When he was living here the house was almost intolerable. Sometimes I dreaded coming home to the mess, the smells and the disruption. But now he's dead I want it to look as it did then. I hate it. It's prissy, affected, boringly conventional, just a show house for someone who's dead at heart. I want to smash it."

She said: "Would it help if I came over?"

"Would you, Frances?" She heard the note of relief in his voice with joy. "You're sure it won't be any trouble?"

"Of course it won't be a trouble. I'll come at once. It's not half past six yet, Claudia may still be here. If she is I'll get her to drop me at the Bank and take the Central Line. That'll be the quickest. If she has left, I'll call a cab."

She put down the receiver. She was sorry about Rupert but she had only met him once, years before, when he had come to Innocent House. And surely for him this long-expected death, awaited in such uncomplaining agony, must have come as a release. But James had called for her, needed her, wanted her to be with him. She was possessed with joy. Grabbing her jacket and scarf from the hall peg, she almost flung herself down the stairs and ran into Innocent Lane. But the door to Innocent House was locked and there was no light shining through the window of the reception room. Claudia had left. She ran into Innocent Walk, thinking that she might still catch her getting out the car, but could see that the garage door was closed. She was too late.

She decided to call for a cab from the wall telephone in the passage at number 10. That would be quicker than going back to her own flat. It was as she came up to the garage doors that she heard unmistakably the sound of a running engine. This surprised and disconcerted her. Claudia's Porsche, her beloved 911, was too old to have a catalytic converter. Surely she realized that it was unsafe to run her engine in a closed garage? It was unlike Claudia to be careless.

The door to number 10 was locked. That wasn't surprising; Claudia always came into the garage this way and locked the door behind her. But it was strange to find the light still on in the passage and the side door to the garage ajar. Calling Claudia's name, she dashed to it and threw it open.

The light was on, a harsh, cruel, shadowless light. She stood transfixed, every nerve and muscle paralysed by a second of instantaneous revelation and horror. He was kneeling by the body, but now he got to his feet and came quietly across to her, blocking the door. She looked into his eyes. They were the same eyes, wise, a little tired, eyes that had seen too much and for far too long.

She whispered: "Oh no! Gabriel, not you. Oh no."

She didn't scream. She was as incapable of screaming as she was of movement. When he spoke it was in the same gentle remembered voice.

"I'm sorry, Frances. You do see, don't you, that I can't possibly let you go?"

And then she swayed and felt herself falling into the merciful dark.

61

In the little archives room Daniel looked at his watch. Six o'clock. He had been here for two hours. But the time hadn't been wasted. At least he had found something. The two hours of searching had been rewarded. It might not be relevant to the investigation, but it had some interest. When he showed the confession to the team, AD might feel that his hunch had been vindicated, even if less fruitfully than he had hoped, and call off the search. There was no reason why he shouldn't stop now.

But success had revived his interest and he was nearly at the end of a row. He may as well take down and examine the last thirty or so files along the top shelf. He preferred a job to have a defined and tidy ending, and it was still early. If he left he would feel obliged to go back to Wapping. He didn't feel at the moment that he wanted to confront either Kate's understanding or her pity. He moved the stepladder further along the row.

The file, bulky but not abnormally so, was lodged tightly between two others and as he pulled at them it slipped from the shelf. A few papers, detached, fell over his head like heavy leaves. He carefully dismounted and gathered them up. The rest of the papers were tagged together, presumably in date order. Two things struck him. The file cover was of heavy manila and obviously very old, while some of the papers looked fresh and clean enough to have been filed within the last five years. The file was unnamed, but among the early papers he was scrabbling together the word "Jew" caught his eye time and time again. He took it with him to the table in the little archives room.

The papers were not numbered and he could only assume that they were in the correct order, but one, undated, caught his eye. It was a proposal for a novel, inexpertly typed and unsigned. It was headed *Submission to the Partners of the Peverell Press.* He read:

> The background and the universal and unifying theme of this novel, provisionally to be called *Original Sin*, is the co-operation of the Vichy regime in France with the deportation of Jews from France between 1940 and 1944. During these four years nearly 76,000 Jews were deported, the great majority to die in concentration camps in Poland and Germany. The book will tell the story of one family divided by war in which a young Jewish mother and her four-year-old twins are trapped in France by the invasion, are hidden by friends and are provided with false papers, but are subsequently betrayed to be deported and murdered in Auschwitz. The novel will explore the effect of this betrayal—one small family among thousands of the victims—on the woman's husband, on the betrayed and on the betrayers.

Working through the papers, he could see no response to this proposal and no communication from the Peverell Press. The file contained what were obviously working and research papers. The novel had been well researched, extraordinarily well researched for a proposed work of fiction. The writer had either visited or written to a remarkable variety of international and national organizations over the years. The Archives Nationales in Paris and Toulouse, the Centre de Documentation Juive Contemporaine in Paris, Harvard University, the Public Records Office and the Royal Institute of International Affairs in London and the West German Federal Archives in Koblenz. There were extracts, too, taken from the journals of the Resistance movement, *l'Humanité*, *Témoignage Chrétien* and *Le Franc-Tireur*, and minutes from prefects in the unoccupied zone. He let them pass in front of his eyes, letters, reports, scraps of official documents, copies of minutes, eyewitness accounts. The record was both broad-based and in places peculiarly precise; the number of deportees, the times of the trains, the part played by the policy of Pierre Laval, even changes in the German power hierarchy in France during the spring and summer of 1942. It was quickly apparent that the researcher had taken care to ensure that nowhere should his name appear. Letters from him had his signature and address cut off or blacked out, letters to him had the name and address of the sender but all other identifying marks had been obliterated. There was no evidence that any of this particular research had been used, that the book had even been started, let alone finished.

It increasingly became apparent that the researcher was particularly interested in one region and one year. The novel, if that was what it was, was becoming more focused. It was as if a cluster of searchlights had played over a wide terrain highlighting an incident, an interesting configuration, a single figure, a moving train, but had now co-ordinated their beams to illumine a single year: 1942. It was a year in which the Germans had demanded a great increase in deportations from the unoccupied zone. The Jews, after being rounded up, had been taken either to the Vel d'Hiv or to Drancy, a huge apartment complex in a suburb north-east of Paris. It was this camp which served as the staging-post to Auschwitz. There were three eyewitness reports in the file: one was from a French nurse who had worked with a paediatrician in Drancy for fourteen months until she could no longer stand the accumulated misery, and two from survivors, apparently in reply to a specific enquiry from the researcher. One woman wrote:

I was rounded up on 16 August 1942 by the Gardes Mobiles. I was reassured because they were French and were very correct at the time I was arrested. I did not know then what would happen to me but I remember that I did not feel that it would be too bad. I was told what possessions I could take with me and medically examined before I was in transit. I was sent to Drancy and it was there I met the young mother with the twins. Her name was Sophie. I cannot recall the names of the children. She had been first in Vel d'Hiv but was later transferred to Drancy. I remember her and the children well although we did not speak very often. She told me little about herself, except that she had been living under a false name near Aubière. All her concern was for her children. At the time we were in the same hut with fifty other inmates. We lived in great squalor. There was a shortage of beds and straw for mattresses, the only food was cabbage soup and we were suffering from dysentery. Many people died in Drancy, I think over 400 in the first ten months. I can remember the wails of the children and the groans of the dying. For me Drancy was as bad as Auschwitz. I went merely from one room in hell to another.

The second survivor from the same camp wrote of the same horrors, although more graphically, but had no memory of a young mother or her twins.

Daniel was turning the papers as if in a trance. He knew now where the journey was leading him and here at last was the proof: a letter written by a Marie-Louise Robert from Quebec. It was handwritten in French with a typed translation attached.

My name is Marie-Louise Robert and I am a Canadian citizen, the widow of Emile Edouard Robert, a French-Canadian. I met him and married him in Canada in 1958. He died two years ago. I was born in 1928 so was fourteen in 1942. I lived with my widowed mother and grandfather on his small farm in the Puy-de-Dôme area of France, outside Aubière, which is just southeast of Clermont-Ferrand. Sophie and the twins came to us in April 1941. It is difficult now that I am old to remember how much I knew at the time and how much I learned afterwards. I was an inquisitive girl and resented being kept out of the adults' concerns and treated as if I were a child, too immature to be trusted. I was not told at the time that Sophie and the children were Jews but I learned that later. There were many people and organizations in France at that time which helped Jews at great risk to themselves, and Sophie and the twins were sent to us by a Christian organization of this kind. I never knew its name. At the time I was told she was just a friend of the family who had come to us to be safe from bombing. My uncle Pascal worked for Monsieur Jean-Philippe Etienne at his publishing-and-printing firm in Clermont-Ferrand. I think I did know at the time that Pascal was part of the Resistance, but I'm not sure that I knew that Monsieur Etienne was head of the organization. It was in July 1942 that the police came to take Sophie and the twins away. As soon as they arrived my mother told me to get out of the house and stay in the barn till she called me. I went to the barn but I crept back and listened. I could hear screaming and the children crying. Then I heard a car and a van being driven away. When I went back into the house my mother was crying too, but wouldn't tell me what had happened.

That night Pascal came to the house and I crept down the stairs to listen. My mother was angry with him, but he said he hadn't betrayed Sophie or the twins, that he wouldn't have put my mother and grandfather in danger, that it must have been

Monsieur Etienne. I forgot to say that it was Pascal who forged the false papers for Sophie and the twins. That was his job in the Resistance, although I am not sure whether I knew this at the time. He told my mother to do nothing, to say nothing. There were reasons for these things. However, my mother did go to see Monsieur Etienne the next day, and when she came back she spoke to my grandfather. I don't think that they cared then whether I heard or not. I was sitting quietly reading in the room when they spoke. She said to my grandfather that Monsieur Etienne had admitted that he had betrayed Sophie to the authorities, but that it had been necessary. It was because he was trusted and his friendship valued that she would not be punished for harbouring Jews. It was thanks to his relationship with the Germans that Pascal had not been deported as slave labour. He had asked my mother what was more important to her: the honour of France, the safety of her family or three Jews. Afterwards no one ever spoke about Sophie and the twins. It was as if they hadn't existed. If I asked about them, my mother would just say, "It is finished. It is over." The money from the organization kept coming, although it was not very much, and my grandfather said that we should keep it. We were very poor at the time. I think someone did write to enquire about Sophie eighteen months after she and the children were taken away, but my mother wrote back that the authorities were becoming suspicious and that Sophie had left and gone to friends at Lyons and she didn't know the address. Then the money stopped.

I am the only member of my family left. My grandfather died in 1946 and my mother of cancer a year later. Pascal was killed on his motorcycle in 1954. After my marriage I never went back to Aubière. There is nothing else I can remember about Sophie and the children except that I missed the children very much when they were gone.

That paper was dated 18 June 1989. Dauntsey had taken over forty years of his part-time searching to find Marie-Louise Robert and his final proof. But he had gone even further. The last paper on the file, dated 20 July 1990, was in German, again with a translation attached. He had tracked down one of the German officers at Clermont-Ferrand. In bald sentences and official language an old man, retired and living in Bavaria, had for a few minutes relived one small incident of a half-remembered past. The truth of the betrayal was confirmed.

There was one final piece of evidence on the file and it was in an envelope. Daniel opened it and found a photograph, black and white, over fifty years old and fading, but still clear. It had obviously been taken by an amateur and it showed a smiling, dark-haired girl, gentle-eyed, with an arm round each of her children. The children, unsmiling, leaned against their mother and gazed huge-eyed at the camera as if knowing the importance of this moment, that the click of the shutter would fix for ever their frail mortality. He turned it over and read: "Sophie Dauntsey. 1920–1942. Martin and Ruth Dauntsey. 1938–1942."

He closed the file and sat for a moment so still that he might have been a statue. Then he got up and, moving into the archives room, began pacing between the racks, stopping occasionally to thump his palm against the struts. He was possessed by an emotion which he recognized as anger but which was like no anger he had ever felt before. He heard a strange inhuman noise and knew that he was groaning aloud with the pain and the horror of it. He had no thought of destroying the evidence; that he couldn't do and didn't for one moment consider. But he could warn Dauntsey, let him know that they were already close and that at last they had the missing motive. He was for a moment surprised that Dauntsey hadn't retrieved and shredded the papers. They weren't needed any more. No court of law would see them. They hadn't been collected with such patience, such thoroughness over half a century to be presented to a court of law. Dauntsey had been judge and jury, prosecutor and plaintiff. Perhaps he would have destroyed them if the room hadn't been locked, if Dalgliesh hadn't reasoned that the motive for this crime lay in the past, and that the missing evidence could be evidence in writing.

Suddenly the telephone rang, harsh and insistent as an alarm. He stopped his pacing and stood frozen, as if to answer it could shatter his intense preoccupation with the clamorous irrelevancies of the outside world. But it continued to ring. He went to the wall telephone and heard Kate's voice.

"You were a long time answering."

"I'm sorry. I was pulling out files."

"Are you all right, Daniel?"

"Yes. Yes, I'm all right."

She said: "We've heard from the lab. The fibres match. Carling was killed in the launch. But there are no fibres on any of the suspects' clothing. I suppose that was too much to hope. So we're a little further on, but not much. AD is thinking of questioning Dauntsey tomorrow—

tape-recorded and under caution. We shan't get anywhere but I suppose we have to try. He's not going to crack. None of them will."

He heard for the first time in her voice the faint questioning note of despair. She said, "Have you found anything interesting?"

"No," he said. "Nothing interesting. I'm leaving now. I'm going home."

62

He put the photograph back in the envelope and the envelope in his pocket, then he replaced all the files on the top shelf, the manila folder among them. He put out the lights and unlocked and relocked the door. Claudia Etienne had left all the lights on the stairs shining for him and as he descended he turned them off one by one. He turned on the lights on the ground floor to see his way. Each action was deliberate, portentous, as if each had a unique value. He took a final look at the great domed ceiling, plunged the hall into darkness, set the alarms and finally turned out the light in the reception room and left Innocent House, locking the door behind him. He wondered if he would ever enter it again, and smiled ironically at the thought that he, resolved on the unforgivable perfidy, the great iconoclasm, could still be meticulous about the things which didn't matter.

There was no sign of life from the small side windows of number 12. He rang Dauntsey's bell, looking up at the darkened windows. There was no reply. Perhaps he was with Frances Peverell. He hurried down the lane into Innocent Walk and it was then that, glancing to the left, he saw Dauntsey's cream Rover just moving off from in front of the garage. Instinctively he ran a few steps towards it but realized that there was no point in calling after it. Dauntsey wouldn't hear above the sound of the engine and the rumble of wheels on the cobbles.

He dashed to where his Golf GTI was parked in Innocent Lane and set off in pursuit. He had to see Dauntsey tonight. Tomorrow might be too late. Dauntsey had only half a minute's start, but that could be crucial if he had a clear turn at the top of Garnet Road and into The Highway. But he was lucky. He was in time to see the car turn right, heading east towards the Essex suburbs, not towards central London.

For the next five miles he was able to keep the Rover within sight. The homeward build-up of traffic was still heavy, a glittering, slow-moving mass of metal, and even by skilful weaving, and driving which was more selfish than orthodox, he was making slow progress. From time to time he lost Dauntsey, only to find when the traffic slightly cleared that he was still on the same road. And Daniel guessed now where he was heading. He grew more certain with every mile, and when at last they approached the A12 he no longer had any doubt. But at every light, every pause, every stretch of clear road his mind focused on the two murders which had led him to this chase, to this resolve.

He saw the whole plan now in its brilliance, its initial simplicity. Etienne's murder had been planned to look like an accident, had been devised in all its details over weeks, probably months, the ideal moment patiently awaited. The police had always known that Dauntsey was the obvious suspect. No one could more easily work undisturbed in the little archives room. He had probably locked the door while he disman-tled the fire, dislodged the rubble from the chimney lining, replaced the fire with its flue effectively blocked. The window cord had been deliberately weakened over weeks. And he had chosen the obvious night for the murder, a Thursday, when Etienne was known to work late and alone. He had timed it for half past seven, just before he left for the Connaught Arms. Had that engagement been fortuitous, arising by luck on the night he had chosen? Or had he chosen that particular night because of the poetry reading? It would have been easy enough to concoct some other appointment, but it had always seemed strange that he bothered with the poetry reading. No other well-known poet had been present and the event was hardly of major literary importance. He would have waited his moment to slip into Innocent House unob-served once everyone but Etienne had left, would have crept up quietly to the little archives room. But even if Etienne had come out of his office unexpectedly and seen him he would have made no comment. Why should he? Dauntsey had a key to the building, he was a partner, he could come and go as he chose. Etienne would have assumed he was going upstairs to fetch a necessary paper or papers from his third-floor office before leaving for the Connaught Arms.

And then what? The final preparations would have been made about an hour earlier. Daniel could picture every action and the sequence of every action. Dauntsey had carried the table and the chair and placed them in the space outside the door; it was important that Etienne should have no way of reaching the window. The room was cleaned. There must be no dust or dirt in which Etienne could smear his killer's name. His diary with the pencil attached had already been stolen in case Etienne brought it up in his jacket or trouser pocket. Next Dauntsey lit the gas fire and turned it full on before removing the tap so that the fumes would begin to build up before his victim arrived. Lastly the tape recorder was placed on the floor and plugged in. Dauntsey had wanted Etienne to know that he was about to die, that there was no chance of escape, that in this isolated and empty building no one would hear the shouting and banging on the door, exertion which would only make his end more speedy, that his death was as inevitable as if he had been thrust into the gas chamber at Auschwitz. Above all, he had needed Etienne to know why it was that he had to die.

So the scene was set for murder. Then, just before 7:30, Dauntsey had rung Etienne's office from the telephone by the door of the little archives room. What would he have said? "Come up at once, I've found something here. It's important." Etienne would, of course, have come. Why not? Mounting the stairs, he might have wondered whether Dauntsey had discovered a clue to the identity of the practical joker. It hardly mattered what he thought. The call was from a man he trusted and had no reason to fear. The voice would have been urgent, the message intriguing. Of course he would have gone up.

The killing ground had been prepared, cleaned and empty. And what then? Dauntsey would have been waiting by the door. There would have been no more than a quick exchange of words.

"What is it, Dauntsey?" Had his voice been impatient, a little arrogant?

"It's in here, in the little archives room. See for yourself. There's a message on that tape recorder. Listen to it and you'll understand."

And Etienne, puzzled but unsuspecting, had walked into the room and to his death.

The door was quickly closed, the key turned and removed. Hissing Sid had already been hidden among the files in the archives room. Dauntsey laid the snake along the bottom of the door, ensuring that even this small amount of ventilation was blocked. There was nothing more to do at present. He could leave for his poetry reading.

He had planned to be back from the Connaught Arms by about ten to do what he had to do. And he could take his time. The door would have to be opened for some minutes to disperse the fumes. Then he would replace the tap on the gas fire and restore the room to its previous appearance. The tables and chairs would be carried back, the filing trays arranged as they were on the table. Wasn't there something else he must have thought of? It would be sensible to add another file to the existing pile, papers which Etienne might reasonably have discovered, searched for, been interested in, a file which could have brought him up to the little archives room; an old contract, something relating perhaps to Esmé Carling. Dauntsey could have extracted it earlier and kept it hidden misfiled among other papers ready for use. He would then have left, making sure that the door key was on the inside of the lock, taking the snake with him.

He could have worked without hurry, probably moving through Innocent House by torchlight but knowing that he could safely put on the light once he was in the little archives room. He would have gone down to Etienne's office and brought up his jacket and keys, hanging the jacket on the back of the chair, placing the keys on the top of the table. Of course he couldn't have replaced the dust on the mantelshelf above the fire and on the floor. But would anyone really have noticed the exceptional cleanliness of the room if the death had from the start looked accidental?

And the scene would have spoken for itself. Here was Etienne studying a file which obviously interested him. He must have been prepared to work there for some time, since he had come up with his jacket and his keys and had lit the fire. He had closed the window, snapping the cord as he did so. The body would probably have been found either slumped over the table or on its face, as if crawling towards the fire. The only puzzle would have been why he hadn't realized what was happening to him and at once opened the door. But one of the earliest symptoms of carbon-monoxide poisoning was disorientation. There would have been no broken rigor of the jaw, no need to stuff the snake-head into the mouth. It would have been an almost perfect example of accidental death.

But for Dauntsey it had gone dreadfully wrong. The mugging, the hours wasted in hospital, the late return had upset all his plans. Now, home at last and with Frances waiting, he had very little time and must act with extraordinary speed, and when he was physically at his weakest. But his mind was still functioning. He turned on the bath tap very slowly so that the bath would be about filled by the time he returned. He had probably thrown off his clothes and worn only his dressing-gown; there would be an advantage in entering the little archives room naked. But he had to go back and go back that night. After the accident it would be highly suspicious if he were first in Innocent House the next morning. Most vital of all, he needed to retrieve that tape, that damning tape with its confession of murder.

Etienne had listened to the tape; Dauntsey at least had had that satisfaction. His victim had known that he was doomed but he had, brilliantly, hit on his own small revenge. Determined that the evidence should be found, he had placed the tape in his mouth. And then, disorientated, he had obviously had some idea of trying to put out the fire by smothering it with his shirt and had been crawling across the floor when unconsciousness supervened. How long had it taken Dauntsey to find the tape? Obviously not very long. But he had had to break the rigor of the jaw to get it and he knew now that there was no longer any hope that Etienne's death could be passed off as accidental. Was that why he had later co-operated so fully with the police, had drawn attention to the missing tape recorder, even to the cleanliness of the room? They were facts which the police would find out from other people; it was prudent to get in first. And there had been no time to do more than hurriedly replace the table and chair. He hadn't even noticed that the table had been replaced with the other side next to the wall so that the position of the files was altered, or that there was a small mark on the wall which showed that it had been moved. And there was no time now to find Etienne's jacket and keys.

But what to do about the forcing open of the mouth? Hissing Sid, the snake, must have been an inspiration. There it was ready to hand. He need waste no time fetching it. All he had to do was wind it round Etienne's neck and stuff its head into his mouth. He had embarked on the series of malicious pranks to confuse the investigation if Etienne's death wasn't accepted as suicide. He couldn't have guessed how vital that ploy was to prove.

But, leaving, he had noticed Esmé Carling's blue-bound manuscript on the low table in the reception room and seen her message pinned to the wall. It must have been a moment of panic, but it would quickly have subsided. Esmé Carling had almost certainly left Innocent House before he called Etienne upstairs. Perhaps he had paused for a moment wondering whether to check, and then decided that this was pointless. Obviously she had gone, leaving the manuscript and the message as a public proclamation of her outrage. Would she tell the police that she had been present or keep quiet? On the whole he thought that she would keep quiet. But he had decided to take both the manuscript and the note. Dauntsey was a murderer who thought ahead, even thought ahead as far as the necessity for her death.

63

Frances slipped in and out of full consciousness, waking to a half-fuddled comprehension, then sinking back as her mind briefly touched reality, rejected its horror and took refuge again in oblivion. When she became fully conscious she lay for a few minutes, totally still, hardly breathing, assessing her situation in small mental steps as if this gradual acceptance could make reality more bearable. She was alive. She was lying on her left side on the floor of a car covered by a rug. Her ankles were bound and her hands tied behind her back. She was gagged with something soft, she thought it must be her silk scarf. The car's progress was uneven and once it stopped and she felt the gentle jar as the brakes were applied. They must be halted at a red light. That meant they were travelling in traffic. She wondered if she could manage to dislodge the blanket by wriggling, but with her hands and feet tied found that it was too firmly tucked around her. But at least she could vigorously move her body. If they were in traffic it was possible that a passing motorist might look through the window and see the heaving blanket and wonder. Hardly had the thought come to her than the car started again and moved smoothly on.

She was alive. She must hang on to that. Gabriel might intend to kill her, but he could easily have done so while she lay unconscious in the garage. Why hadn't he? It couldn't be that he wanted to show her mercy. What mercy had he shown to Gerard, to Esmé Carling, to Claudia? She was in the hands of a murderer. The word, thudding into her mind, woke the terror which had been lying dormant ever since she had regained consciousness. It swept over her, primitive, uncontrollable, a humiliating wave, annihilating thought and will. She knew now why he hadn't killed her in the garage. Claudia's murder, like the other two, was to look like accidental death or suicide. He couldn't leave two bodies on the garage floor. He had to get rid of her, but it must be in a different way. What had he in mind? Her complete disappearance? A killing which Dalgliesh would have no hope of solving since there would be no body? She remembered reading somewhere that it wasn't necessary to produce a body to prove murder, but Gabriel might not realize that. He was mad, he had to be mad. Even now he might be planning, thinking, wondering how best to dispose of her. Whether to drive to the edge of a cliff and tumble her into the sea, to bury her in some ditch, still bound, to tip her into an old mine shaft where she would die of thirst and hunger, alone, never to be found. Image succeeded image, each more horrifying than the last. The terrifying fall through the dark air into the crashing waves, the suffocating wet leaves and earth stamped down into her eyes and mouth, the vertical tunnel of the mine shaft where she would slowly starve to death in claustrophobic agony.

The car was riding more smoothly now. They must have thrown off the last tentacles of London and be in open country. By an effort of will she calmed herself. She was alive. She must hold on to that. There was still hope, and if in the end she had to die she would try to die bravely. Gerard and Claudia, both agnostics, would have died with courage even if they hadn't been allowed to die with dignity. What was her religion worth if it couldn't help her to do the same?

She said an act of contrition, then prayed for the souls of Gerard and Claudia and, last of all, prayed for herself and for her own safety. The well-worn comforting words brought their assurance that she was not alone. Then she tried to plan. Not knowing what he had in mind for her, it was difficult to decide on alternative courses of action, but one fact was certain. She couldn't believe he was strong enough to carry her body unaided. That meant he would at least have to free her ankles. She was younger, stronger than he, and could easily out-distance him. If she had the chance she would run for her life. But whatever happened at the end she wouldn't plead for mercy.

In the mean time she must try to prevent her limbs from becoming too stiff. Her hands, wrenched behind her back, were tied with something soft, perhaps his tie or socks. He would not, after all, have come prepared for more than one victim. But he had done the job efficiently. She could not wriggle free. Her ankles were as strongly if more comfortably tied. But even bound she could tense and relax the muscles of her legs, and to make even this small preparation for escape gave her strength and courage. She told herself, too, that she mustn't lose hope of rescue. How long would James wait before he discovered she was missing? He would probably take no action for an hour, imagining she was held up in the traffic or the underground. But then he would ring number 12 and, getting no answer, would try Claudia's Barbican flat. Even then he might not be seriously worried. But surely he wouldn't wait more than an hour and a half. Perhaps he would take a taxi to number 12. Perhaps, if she were lucky, even hear the sound of the running engine in the garage. Once Claudia's body was found and Dauntsey's absence known, all police forces would be alerted to intercept the car. She must hang on to that hope.

And still he drove. Unable to see her watch, she could only guess at the time and had no idea of the direction in which they travelled. She didn't waste energy wondering why Gabriel had killed. That was fruitless; only he could tell her that, and perhaps at the end he would. Instead she thought about her own life. What had it been but a series of compromises? What had she given her father but a timid acquiescence which had only reinforced his insensitivity and contempt? Why had she come so meekly into the firm at his bidding to be trained to take over contracts and rights? She could do the work well enough; she was conscientious and methodical, punctilious about detail; but it wasn't what she had wanted to do with her life. And Gerard? In her heart she had known his sexual exploitation for what it was. He had treated her with contempt because she had made herself contemptible. Who was she? What was she? Frances Peverell, meek, obliging, gentle, uncomplaining, the appendage of her father, her lover, the firm. Now, when her life might be nearing its end, she could at least say, "I am Frances Peverell. I am myself." If she lived to marry James, she could at least be offering an equal partnership. She had found the courage to face death, but that, after all, was not so difficult. Thousands, including children, did it every day. It was time she found an equal courage to face life.

And now she felt curiously at peace. From time to time she said a prayer, mentally spoke the lines of a favourite poem, looked back on moments of joy. She even tried to doze and might have succeeded if the car hadn't suddenly jolted her mind awake. Gabriel must be driving over rough country. The Rover lurched, rolled, struck pot-holes, bounded from side to side, and she rolled with it. And then there was another stretch, but less uneven, probably, she thought, a country track. And then the car stopped and she heard him open his door.

64

In Hillgate Village James glanced at the carriage clock on the mantel-piece. It was 7:42, just over an hour since he had rung Frances. She should have arrived by now. He did again the quick calculation he had been making during the last sixty minutes. There were ten stations between the Bank and Notting Hill Gate. Allow two minutes per station, say twenty minutes for the journey, and fifteen to get to the Bank. But perhaps she had missed Claudia and had had to ring for a taxi. Even so the journey shouldn't have taken sixty minutes, not even in the rush hour and in central London, not unless there had been an unusual hold-up, roads closed or a terrorist alert. He rang Frances's flat again. As expected, there was no reply. Then once more he tried Claudia's number, again unsuccessfully. That didn't surprise him. She might have driven straight on to see Declan Cartwright, or had a theatre or a dinner engagement. There was no reason why Claudia should be at home. He switched on the radio to the local London station. Another ten minutes passed before there was the news flash. Travellers were warned of a hold-up on the Central Line. No reason was given, which usually meant an IRA alert, but four stations between Holborn and Marble Arch were closed. So that was the explanation. It could be another hour before Frances arrived. There was nothing to do but wait in patience.

He paced the sitting-room. Frances was slightly claustrophobic. He knew how much she hated using the Greenwich foot tunnel. She disliked travelling by underground. She wouldn't be trapped there now if she hadn't wanted to hurry to his side. He hoped that the lights were on in the train, that she wasn't sitting there unfriended in total darkness. And suddenly he had an extraordinarily vivid and disturbing image of Frances, abandoned, dying, in a dark enclosing tunnel somewhere far from him, unreachable and alone. He thrust it out of his mind as a morbid imagining and looked at the clock again. He would wait half an hour and try to get through to London Transport and find out if the line was open, how long the delay was likely to be. He went over to the window and, moving behind the curtains, stared down on the lighted street, willing her to appear.

65

And now at last Daniel was on the A12 and the road was clearer. He kept within the speed limit; it would be disastrous if he were caught by a police patrol. But Dauntsey would be equally careful not to attract attention, not to be held up. To that extent they were driving on equal terms, but he had the faster car. He planned how best to get ahead once his quarry was in sight. In normal circumstances Dauntsey would almost certainly know the car, would probably recognize him even at a glance, but it was unlikely that he knew he was being followed. He wouldn't be watching for a pursuer. The best plan would be to wait until the road was busy, then take his chance to overtake in a stream of traffic.

And now for the first time he remembered Claudia Etienne. It horrified him that the possibility of her danger hadn't occurred to him in his concern to get to Dauntsey and warn him. But she would be all right. He had last seen her when she proposed to go home and she must be safe now. Dauntsey was ahead of him in his Rover. The only risk was that she had decided to visit her father and might even now be on her way to Othona House. But that was one more reason for getting there first. There was no point in trying to stop Dauntsey, to overtake him, wave him down. Dauntsey wouldn't stop unless forced to. Daniel needed to speak to him, to warn him, but in calmness, not by ramming his car. The last scene of this tragedy was to be played out in peace.

And then at last he caught sight of the Rover. They were now nearing the Chelmsford by-pass and the traffic was building up. He waited his moment and then joined the stream of cars in the overtaking lane and shot past.

Esmé Carling must have had a few very bad days after the news of the discovery of the body. She would have expected the police to arrive with questions about the notice pinned to the board, the discarded manuscript. But he and Robbins had come with their harmless questions about an alibi and the alibi had been provided. She had kept her nerve admirably, he had to give her that. Never once had he suspected that there was more to learn. And after that? What thoughts had gone through her mind? Had Dauntsey telephoned her first or had she got in touch with him? Almost certainly the latter. Dauntsey would have had no need to kill her if she hadn't told him that she'd actually seen him walking downstairs carrying the vacuum cleaner. He, too, must have had some very bad moments. He, too, had kept his nerve. Esmé Carling has said nothing and he must have thought he was safe.

And then would have come the telephone call, the suggestion that they should meet, the implied threat that unless her book was published she would go to the police. The threat was, of course, baseless. She couldn't go to the police without revealing that she, too, had been in Innocent House that night. She had as strong a motive for getting rid of Etienne as anyone. But she was a woman whose mind, ingenious, scheming, devious, a little obsessional, had its limitations. She was not clear-thinking nor was she highly intelligent.

How exactly, he wondered, had Dauntsey enticed her to that meeting? Did he say that he knew or suspected who had killed Etienne and that together they could arrive at the truth and enjoy a joint triumph? Had they reached at least a provisional understanding that she would remain silent and he would return the manuscript and the paper and ensure that her book was published? She had told Daisy Reed that Peverell Press would have to publish. Who else but one of the partners could have given her that assurance? Had he presented himself in that brief conversation as her defender and saviour, or as a fellow conspirator? They would now never know unless Dauntsey chose to tell them.

One thing was certain: Esmé Carling had gone to that interview without fear. She hadn't known who the murderer had been but she was confident she knew who it couldn't have been. She had been the visitor in Etienne's office when the call came through and, at first, had waited for him to return. Then, growing impatient, she had gone up to the little archives room, glimpsing Dauntsey carrying down the vacuum cleaner as she was about to leave Miss Blackett's office. Outside the door she had seen the snake and heard the voice. Someone inside the room was speaking. The door was not substantial and she probably realized that it wasn't Etienne's voice. When the body was discovered, she could be certain that Dauntsey at least was innocent. She had seen him herself walking down the stairs while Etienne was still alive and in the little archives room talking with his killer.

How had he managed that alibi for Esmé Carling's murder? But of course; he and Bartrum had been the only two left alone with her body before the police arrived. Wasn't it Dauntsey who had suggested that the women should be taken indoors, that he and Bartrum would wait by the body? He must have arranged his alibi then. But it was surprising that Bartrum had agreed. Had Dauntsey promised to support him in keeping his job? To get him promotion? Or was there an existing obligation to be repaid? Whatever the reason, the alibi had been given. And the pub at which they had met half an hour later than they claimed had been well chosen. No one at the Sailor's Return had been able to say precisely when two particular customers had entered that large, raucous and overcrowded tavern.

The murder itself would have presented few problems, the only moment of danger the moving of the launch. But that, of course, would have been necessary. He needed the launch; only in the safety of its cabin could he kill, unseen both from the land and the river. Esmé Carling had been a thin woman and not heavy, but Dauntsey was seventy-six and it would have been easier to string her up from the launch than to manoeuvre her body, dead or alive, down the slippery tide-washed steps. And moving the launch would be safe enough if he kept the engine low. The only person living close was Frances and Dauntsey knew from experience how little could be heard from her sitting-room with the curtains drawn. And even if she had heard the noise of an engine, would she really have taken the trouble to investigate? This, after all, was a common sound of the river. But after the murder the launch had to be moved back. He couldn't be certain that there wouldn't be a trace of her, however small, in the cabin, particularly if there was a struggle. It was important that no one should associate the launch with her death.

She had come to this last fatal appointment by taxi. That must have been by Dauntsey's suggestion, and his suggestion, too, that she should be put down at the end of Innocent Passage. He would be waiting there in the shadows, standing in the doorway. What had he told her? That they could speak in greater privacy if they went on the river? He would have placed the manuscript and her message to the partners ready in the cabin. What else would have been there? A rope for the strangling, a scarf, a belt? But he must have hoped that she would be carrying her usual shoulder-bag with the strong strap. He must have seen her with it often enough.

And now, with his eyes fixed on the road ahead, his hands lightly on the wheel, Daniel pictured the scene in that narrow cabin. How long would they have talked? Perhaps not at all. She must already have told Dauntsey on the telephone that she had seen him at Innocent House coming down the stairs carrying the vacuum cleaner. That in itself was damning. There was nothing else he needed to know from her. It would have been easiest and safest to waste no time. Daniel could see Dauntsey standing a little aside, politely waiting for her to enter the cabin first, the strap of her bag over her shoulder. Then the quick flick upwards of the strap, the falling and thrashing on the cabin floor, the old hands ineffectively clutching at the leather noose as with both hands he tugged it tight. There must have been at least a second of horrified realization before merciful unconsciousness blacked out her mind for ever.

And this was the man he was driving to warn, not because there could now be any escape for him, but because even the horror of Esmé Carling's death seemed only one small and inevitable part of a greater and more universal tragedy. All her life she had fabricated mysteries, exploited coincidence, arranged facts to conform to theory, manipulated her characters, relished the self-importance of vicarious power. It was her tragedy that in the end she had confused fiction with real life.

It was after he had left Maldon and turned south by the B1018 that Daniel got lost. He had earlier stopped the car in a lay-by for a minute to consult the map, resenting every second of lost time. The shorter route to Bradwell-on-Sea was by a left-hand turn off the B1018 and through the villages of Steeple and St Lawrence. He folded the map away and drove on through the dark, desolate landscape. But the road, wider than he had expected, stretched on with two left-hand turns which he hadn't remembered from the map, and with no sign of the first village. Some instinct which he had never been able to explain told him that he was driving south, not east. He stopped at a crossroads to consult a signpost and by the lights of the car saw the name Southminster. Somehow he had got himself onto the more southerly and longer road. The darkness was intense and thick as a fog. And then the clouds moved from the moon and he saw a roadside pub, closed and derelict, two brick-built cottages with dim lights behind their curtains and a single wind-distorted tree with a fragment of a white notice nailed to the bark, fluttering like a pinioned bird. On either side of the road the desolate country lay wind-scoured and eerie in the moon's cold light.

He drove on. The road with its twists and turns seemed endless. The wind was strengthening now, gently buffeting the car. And here at last was the right-hand turn to Bradwell-on-Sea and he saw that he was passing through the outskirts of the village to the squat tower of the church and the lights of the pub. He turned once again, towards the marshlands and the sea. There was no sign of Dauntsey's car and he couldn't tell which of them would reach Othona House first. He only knew that for both of them this would be the journey's end.

66

He opened the rear door. After the enclosing darkness, the smell of petrol, of the rug, of her own fear, the fresh moonlit air touched her face like a blessing. She could hear nothing but the sighing of the wind, see nothing but his dark form leaning over her. His hands stretched towards her and he fumbled the gag. She felt the brush of his fingers momentarily against her cheek. Then he bent and untied her ankles. The knots were not difficult. If her hands had been free she could have untied them herself. He didn't need to cut them free. Did that mean that he hadn't a knife? But she was no longer worried about her own safety. Suddenly she knew that he hadn't brought her here to kill her. He had other, and for him more important, preoccupations.

He said, with a voice as ordinary, as gentle, as the voice she had known, relied upon, liked to hear: "Frances, if you turn over I can get more easily at your hands."

It could have been her rescuer speaking, not her gaoler. She turned, and it took only a few seconds to free her. She tried to ease her legs out of the car but they were stiff and he put out his hand to help.

She said: "Don't touch me."

The words were indistinct. The gag had been tighter than she had thought and her jaw was fixed in a painful rictus. But he understood. He stepped back at once and watched while she dragged herself out and stood upright, leaning against the car for support. This was the moment for which she had planned, the chance to outrun him, it hardly mattered where. But he had turned from her and she knew that there was no need to run, no point in trying to escape. He had brought her here from necessity, but she was no longer dangerous, no longer important. His thoughts were elsewhere. She could try to stumble away on her cramped legs but he wouldn't prevent her and he wouldn't follow. He was moving away from her, staring at the dark outline of a house, and she could feel the intensity of his gaze. For him this was the end of a long journey.

She said: "Where are we? What place is this?"

He said, his voice carefully controlled: "Othona House. I've come to see Jean-Philippe Etienne."

They went together to the front door. He rang the bell. She could hear its peal even through the strong oak. The wait was not long. They could hear the rasp of the bolt, the turn of the key in the lock and the door opened. The stocky figure of an old woman dressed in black stood outlined against the light of the hall.

She said: "Monsieur Etienne vous attend."

Gabriel turned to Frances. "I don't think you've met Estelle, Jean-Philippe's housekeeper. You're all right now. In a few minutes you can telephone for help. Estelle will look after you in the mean time if you go with her."

She said: "I don't need looking after. I'm not a child. You brought me here against my will. Now I'm here, I'm staying with you."

Estelle led them down a long stone-floored passage to the back of the house, then stood aside and motioned them to enter. The room, obviously a study, was dark-panelled, the air stagnant with the pungent sweetness of wood smoke. In the stone fireplace the flames leapt like tongues and the wood crackled and hissed. Jean-Philippe Etienne was seated in a high winged chair to the right of the fire. He didn't get up. Standing against the window, facing the door, was Inspector Aaron. He was wearing a sheepskin jacket, its bulkiness emphasizing the stockiness of his figure. His face was very pale, but as a log of wood crashed and flared it glowed for a moment into ruddy life. His hair was windswept, dishevelled. He must, thought Frances, have arrived just before them and parked his car out of sight.

Ignoring her, he said directly to Dauntsey, "I've been following you. I need to talk to you."

He took an envelope from his pocket and, drawing out a photograph, laid it on the table. He watched Dauntsey's face in silence. No one moved.

Dauntsey said: "I know what you've come to say, but the time for speaking is over. You are here not to talk but to listen."

And now for the first time Aaron seemed aware of Frances's presence. He said sharply, almost accusingly: "Why are you here?"

Frances's mouth still ached but her voice was strong and clear. "Because I was brought here by force. I was bound and gagged. Gabriel has killed Claudia. He strangled her in the garage. I saw her body. Aren't you going to arrest him? He's killed Claudia and he killed the other two."

Etienne had got to his feet but now he gave a curious sound, something between a groan and a sigh, and sank back into his chair. Frances ran to him. She said: "I'm sorry, I'm so sorry, I should have told you more gently." Then, looking up, she saw Inspector Aaron's horrified face.

He turned to Dauntsey and said almost in a whisper: "So you did finish the job."

"Don't blame yourself, Inspector. You couldn't have saved her. She was dead before you left Innocent House."

He spoke directly to Jean-Philippe Etienne. "Stand up, Etienne. I want you to stand."

Etienne rose slowly from his chair and reached for his cane. With its help he got to his feet. He made an obvious effort to steady himself but swayed and might have fallen if Frances hadn't moved forward and put her arms around his waist. He didn't speak, but gazed at Dauntsey.

Dauntsey said: "Stand behind your chair. You can use it for support."

"I don't need support." Firmly he removed Frances's arm. "It was only a temporary stiffness after sitting. I'm not standing behind the chair as if I were in the dock. And if you have come here as a judge, I thought it was usual to take the plea before the trial and to punish only if there is a verdict of guilty."

"There has been a trial. I've conducted the trial for over forty years. Now I'm asking you to admit that you handed over my wife and children to the Germans, that in fact you sent them to be murdered in Auschwitz."

"What were their names?"

"Sophie Dauntsey, Martin and Ruth. They were going under the name Loiret. They had forged documents. You were one of the few people who knew that, who knew that they were Jews, who knew where they were living."

Etienne said calmly: "The names mean nothing. How can I be expected to remember? They weren't the only Jews I informed on to

Vichy and the Germans. How am I expected to remember the individual names or the families? I did what was necessary at the time. A great number of French lives depended on me. It was important that the Germans continued to trust me if I were to get my allocation of paper, ink and resources for the underground press. How can I be expected to remember one woman and two children after fifty years?"

Dauntsey said: "I remember them."

"And now you have come for your revenge. Is it still sweet even after fifty years?"

"This isn't revenge, Etienne. This is justice."

"Oh don't deceive yourself, Gabriel. This is revenge. Justice doesn't require that you come finally to tell me what you have done. Call it justice if it comforts your conscience. It's a strong word, I hope you know what it means. I'm not sure that I do. Perhaps the representative of the law can help us."

Daniel said: "It means an eye for an eye and a tooth for a tooth."

Dauntsey was still gazing at Jean-Philippe. "I have taken no more than you took, Etienne. A son and a daughter for a son and a daughter. You murdered my wife but yours was already dead when I learned the truth."

"Yes, she was beyond your malice. And mine."

He said the last two words so quietly that Frances wondered if she had really heard them.

Gabriel went on: "You killed my children; I have killed yours. I have no posterity; you will have none. After Sophie's death I could never love another woman. I don't believe that our existence here has a meaning or that we have any future after death. Since there is no God there can be no divine justice. We have to make justice for ourselves and make it here on earth. It has taken me nearly fifty years but I have made my justice."

"It would have been more effective if you had acted sooner. My son had his youth, his young manhood. He had success, the love of women. You couldn't take those away from him. Your children had none of them. Justice should be speedy as well as effective. Justice doesn't wait for fifty years."

"What has time to do with justice? Time takes away our strength, our talent, our memories, our joys, even our capacity to grieve. Why should we let it take away the imperative of justice? I had to be certain, and that, too, was justice. It took me over twenty years to trace two vital witnesses. Even then I was in no hurry. I couldn't have stood ten years or more of prison and now I shan't have to. Nothing is impossible to bear at seventy-six. Then your son got engaged. There might have been a child. Justice required that only two should die."

Etienne said: "And is that why you left your publishers and came to Peverell Press in 1962? Did you suspect me then?"

"I was beginning to. The strands of my enquiry were beginning to come together. It seemed sensible to get close to you. And you were, I remember, glad enough to have me and my money."

"Of course. Henry Peverell and I thought that we were getting a major talent. You should have kept your energies for your poetry, Gabriel, not wasted them on a useless obsession born of your own guilt. It was hardly your fault that your wife and children were trapped in France. You were imprudent in leaving them at that time, of course, but no more. You left them and they died. Why try to purge that guilt by murdering the innocent? But murdering the innocent is your forte, isn't it? You took part in the bombing of Dresden. Nothing I have done can compete with the horror and magnitude of that achievement."

Daniel said, almost in a whisper: "That was different. That was the awful necessity of war."

Etienne turned on him: "And so it was for me, the necessity of war." He paused, and when he spoke again Frances could hear in his voice the barely controlled note of triumph. "If you want to act like God, Gabriel, you should first ensure that you have the wisdom and knowledge of God. I have never had a child. I caught a viral infection when I was thirteen; I am totally infertile. My wife needed a son and a daughter and to satisfy her maternal obsession I agreed to provide them. Gerard and Claudia were adopted in Canada and brought back with us to England. They are not related by blood either to each other or to me. I promised my wife that the truth would never be publicly known but Gerard and Claudia were both told when they were fourteen. The effect on Gerard was unfortunate. Both children should have been told from the start."

Frances knew that Gabriel didn't need to ask if this was the truth. She had to force herself to look at him. For a moment she saw him physically crumble, the muscles of face and body seeming to disintegrate even as she watched. He had been an old man but one with force, intelligence and will. Now everything that was alive in him drained away in front of her eyes. Quickly she moved towards him but he put out a restraining hand. Now, slowly and painfully, he forced himself to stand upright. He tried to speak but no words came. Then he turned and made for the door. No one spoke, but they followed him out through the hall and into the night and watched while he walked towards the narrow ridge of rock at the edge of the marsh.

Frances ran after him and, catching him up, seized him by his jacket. He tried to shake her off but she clung on and his strength was failing. It was Daniel, running up behind them, who clasped her in his arms and carried her bodily away. She tried to struggle free but his arms were like iron bands. She watched helplessly as Gabriel walked forward into the marsh.

Daniel said: "Let him be. Let him be."

She called back to Jean-Philippe Etienne: "Go after him! Stop him! Make him come back!"

Daniel said quietly, "Come back for what?"

"But he'll never reach the sea."

It was Etienne coming up beside them who spoke. "He doesn't need to reach it. Those pools are deep. A man can drown in a foot of water if he wants to die."

They stood watching. Frances was still held in Daniel's arms. Suddenly she was aware of the beating of his heart thudding against her own. The stumbling figure was dark against the night sky. It rose, then fell, then reared itself up and fought on. Again the clouds moved and by the light of the moon they could see him more clearly. From time to time he would fall, but then would rise to his feet again, looking immense as a giant, arms raised as if in a curse or a last beseeching gesture. Frances knew that he was fighting to reach the sea, longing to walk out into its cold immensity, further and deeper, until he could splash forward into that final blessed oblivion.

And now he was down again, and this time he didn't rise. Frances thought she could see the glitter of the moonlight on the surface of the pool. It seemed to her that almost all his body was submerged. But she could no longer see him clearly. He was just one more dark low hump amongst all the tussocks of this sodden wasteland. They waited in silence, but there was no movement. He had become part of the marshland and of the night. Now Daniel released her and she moved and stood a little apart. The silence was absolute. And at last she thought she could hear the sea, a faint susurration, less a sound than a pulse beat on the quiet air.

They were turning towards the house when the night vibrated with a harsh metallic groan which grew rapidly into a rattle. Overhead were the twin lights of a helicopter. They watched as it circled three times, then landed on the field beside Othona House. Frances thought, So they have found Claudia's body. James must have got tired of waiting for her and in the end gone back to Innocent House to search.

She stood on the edge of the field, still a little apart from the others, and saw the three figures running crouched under the great blades, then standing upright and moving towards her, over the gritty field and the wind-torn grass, Commander Dalgliesh, Inspector Miskin and James. Etienne moved forward to meet them. They stood in a group talking together. She thought, Let Etienne tell them. I shall wait.

Then Dalgliesh detached himself and came up to her. He didn't touch her but he bent from his tall height and looked intently into her face.

"Are you all right?"

"I am now."

He smiled and said: "We'll talk very soon. De Witt insisted on coming with us. It was less trouble to let him have his way."

He walked on to join Etienne and Kate and together they went towards Othona House.

Frances thought, "I am myself at last. I have something worth giving him." She didn't run towards the waiting figure. She didn't call out to him. It was slowly, but with all the intensity of her being, that she walked over the windswept grass and into his waiting arms.

Daniel heard the approach of the helicopter but he didn't move. He stood on the narrow ridge of rock still looking out over the saltings to the sea. He waited in solitary patience until he heard the approaching footsteps and Dalgliesh was at his side.

He said: "Was he under arrest?"

"No, sir. I didn't come to arrest him, I came to warn him. I didn't caution him. I did speak but they weren't the words you would have spoken. I let him go."

"You let him go deliberately? He didn't break free?"

"No, sir. He didn't break free." He added, so softly that he doubted whether Dalgliesh heard the words: "But he's free now."

Dalgliesh turned away and went back to the house. He had learned what he needed to know. No one else came near. Daniel felt isolated in a moral quarantine, standing on the edge of the marshes, on the edge of the world. He thought he saw a trembling light, bright as phosphorus, burning and darting among the humps of marram grass and the black pools of stagnant water. He couldn't see the small breaking waves but he could hear the sea, a soft eternal moaning like a universal grief. And then the clouds moved and the moon with its shaved side, so nearly full, shed its cold light on the marsh and on that distant fallen figure. He sensed a shadow at his side. Turning, he saw that it was Kate. It was with astonishment and pity that he realized her face was wet with tears.

He said: "I wasn't trying to help him escape. I knew that there could be no escape. But I couldn't bear to see him handcuffed, in the dock, in prison. I wanted to give him the chance to take his own path home."

She said: "Daniel, you fool. You bloody fool."

He turned to her and said: "What will he do?"

"AD? What do you think he'll do? Oh God, Daniel, you could have been so good, you were so good."

He said: "Etienne couldn't even remember their names. He could hardly remember what he'd done. He felt no guilt, no remorse. A mother and two small children. They didn't exist. They weren't human. He would have given more thought to putting down a dog. He didn't think of them as people. They were expendable. They didn't count. They were Jews."

She cried: "And Esmé Carling? Old, plain, childless, alone. Not a very good writer. Was she expendable? All right, she didn't have a lot. A flat, someone else's kid to spend the evenings with, a few photographs, her books. What right had he to decide that her life didn't count?"

He said bitterly: "You're so confident, aren't you, Kate. So certain you know what's right. It must be comforting, never having to face a moral dilemma. The criminal law and police regulations: they provide all you need, don't they?"

She said: "I'm certain about some things. I'm certain about murder. How could I be a police officer if I weren't?"

Dalgliesh came over to them. He said in a voice as ordinary as if they were companionably together in that Wapping incident room: "The Essex Police won't attempt to recover the body until daylight. I want you to drive Kate back to London. Do you feel able to do that?"

"Yes, sir. I'm perfectly fit to drive."

"If you aren't, Kate will take over. Mr. de Witt and Miss Peverell will come with me in the helicopter. They'll want to get back as soon as possible. I'll see you both later tonight at Wapping."

He stood with Kate at his side until the three figures had joined the pilot and entered the helicopter. The machine roared into life and the great blades slowly revolved, spun into a haze, became invisible. The helicopter lifted and lurched into the sky. Etienne and Estelle were on the edge of the field looking up at it. He thought bitterly: They look like sightseers. It's a wonder they're not waving goodbye.

He said to Kate: "There's something I've left in the house."

The front door stood open. She came with him through the hall and into the study, walking behind him so that he shouldn't feel like a prisoner under escort. The light had been turned off in the room but the flames of the fire threw dancing gules over the walls and ceilings and stained the polished surface of the table with a ruddy glow, as if it had been smeared with blood.

The photograph was still there. He was for a moment surprised that Dalgliesh hadn't taken it. But then he remembered. It didn't matter. There would be no trial now, no exhibits, no need to produce it as evidence in court. It wasn't needed any more. It was of no importance.

He left it on the table and, turning to join Kate, walked with her in silence to the car.

P. D. James is the author of thirteen books, seven of which have been filmed and broadcast on television in Britain and the United States. She spent thirty years in various sections of the British Civil Service, including the Police and Criminal Law Departments of the Home Office, and has served as a magistrate and a governor of the BBC. P. D. James is the recipient of many prizes and honors, and in 1991 was created Baroness James of Holland Park. She has two daughters and five grandchildren and lives in London and Oxford.

A NOTE ON THE TYPE

This book was set in a typeface called Baskerville, a modern recutting of a type originally designed by John Baskerville (1706–1775). Baskerville, a writing master in Birmingham, England, began experimenting in about 1750 with type design and punch cutting. His first book, published in 1757 and set throughout in his new types, was a Virgil in royal quarto. It was followed by other famous editions from his press. Baskerville's types, which are distinctive and elegant in design, were a forerunner of what we know today as the "modern" group of typefaces.

Composed by PennSet, Bloomsburg, Pennsylvania
Printed and bound by R.R. Donnelly & Sons,
Harrisonburg, Virginia
Designed by Brooke Zimmer